Pride Revisited

For my girls:
Annika, Jessica, Abigail and Megan

Pride Revisited

— — — — — —

An Anthology of Original Short Stories
Based on the novel <u>Pride and Prejudice</u> by Jane Austen

by

Tess Quinn

Additional Jane Austen-based works by this author:

Novels:

Caroline's Comeuppance (2008, LuLu Press, Inc.)
A Fitzwilliam Legacy (coming soon in 2013)
Principles of Pride (working title – available in 2013/2014)
Worst Impressions (available 2014)

Short Stories:

A Good Vintage Whine – selected and published as part of *The Road to Pemberley*, ed. Marsha Altman, Ulysses Press, July 2011 (anthology of stories based on *Pride and Prejudice*)

Table of Contents

ξ   A Dose of Sardines Is Just the Thing..9
    (For the Advancement of Affection)

ξ   Water Pump – Two Variations..21
    (A Glimpse into the Mind of a Gentleman)
    (A Variation on a Theme)

ξ   Flirting with Trouble..29

ξ   April's Fool...43
    (A Confluence of Coincidences)

ξ   Hedging...71

ξ   April Fools (A Romance)..91

ξ   A Gentleman's Gentleman...115

ξ   Darcy Takes a Walk..123

ξ   Pemberley Break - Gee's Day Out..149

ξ   Darcy Goes A-Courtin'..187

ξ   Lizzy Gets a Lesson...213

ξ   Valentine...225

ξ   Seasonal Disorder...235

ξ   Anniversary Song..247

ξ   Worst Impressions...261

ξ   Pinker Heaven...273

ξ   *Excerpt Preview: Principles of Pride (forthcoming novel)*...........295

Introduction

Welcome! I hope you will enjoy this anthology of short stories, all of which are based on and feature characters from the novel *Pride and Prejudice* by Jane Austen.

We all – those of us who read Austen's work and lose ourselves in her world of late Georgian and Regency England – have our own impressions of the characters, events and sentiments expressed therein. Novels aren't static for all they are words on a page; instead, they are a relationship between writer and reader (and many would say between the reader and the characters as well.) A reader brings a set of conditions from his or her own experience that informs interpretation of the written word; much as Miss Jane Austen took her life experiences and her understanding of human nature to inform the imaginative, delightful plots and places and people she created in her novels.

And sometimes, a book or a character so moves us that we are unwilling to let go after we turn the final page. The prevalence and popularity of Austen-based fiction evidences this.

For some, images of Elizabeth Bennet and Fitzwilliam Darcy, indeed all the Bennet family and right on down to lesser-realised characters like Colonel Fitzwilliam or Georgiana Darcy, may be suggested by whatever television or film adaptation of *Pride and Prejudice* caught a fancy. For others, these formed wholly in the imagination on reading the novel. In my case, sketches of Lizzy and Darcy et al began to form many years ago when first I read *Pride and Prejudice* at age 13.

Since then I have reread too many times to count, and with each of these indulgences, my understanding or appreciation has shifted somewhat based on my life – what I've learned about the world and human nature since the last reading; what I have learned about myself particularly; influenced a bit by film interpretations or discussion with friends, or through reading critical analysis. But largely, my sense today of Lizzy and Darcy and all the other characters was established upon introduction to them at thirteen, informed by my natural sensibilities; refined over the years since then.

The stories which follow reflect my interpretation. Possibly influenced by one of the various adaptations on occasion, yet they are book-based overall.

You will not find in these pages rewrites of Jane Austen's original chapters – there is no point; no one can improve upon them. What you will find is a number of what I consider 'interludes.' That word has several definitions, two of which are (1) an intervening episode, period, space, etc., and (2) any intermediate performance or entertainment, as between the acts of a play. My interludes are scenes that can be inserted into the larger plot of *Pride and Prejudice* at given moments without necessarily changing the original book events which preceded or follow.

There are a few offerings that imagine life after marriage for Elizabeth and Darcy – not interludes by strict definition but of similar tone – still consistent with the tenor of the original. A couple of more flagrant 'what if' offerings join these, which admittedly do meander from the book (these are identified as such in their introductory notes.) In all, however, I have tried to be consistent – to be 'true' if you will – to the spirit of the characters Miss Austen gave us, as they have been sketched in my heart these many years.

Several offer multiple perspectives, but many focus on Darcy's viewpoint and that of his sister Georgiana—a result of having been written initially as exercises to delve into their family history (back-story) and characters while working on a novel that is now nearing completion.

The final two stories are just for fun – one transfers the Darcy-Wickham relationship to a modern day scenario, the other is a pure fantasy of meeting Mr Darcy in the 'real world.' Ultimately, these sixteen pieces are *all* character studies – because I love Jane Austen's characters too much to let go of them after I finish reading (or rereading) the novel.

Love and profound respect for Jane Austen's works, and especially for *Pride and Prejudice*, has motivated me to pen these interludes. I hope this regard is reflected in my writing, and will touch your own sensibilities in some way.

Tess Quinn

28 January 2013

PRIDE REVISITED

A Dose of Sardines Is Just the Thing
(For the Advancement of Affection)

ぷぷぷ

This story began as a writing assignment from a friend – a fellow Jane Austen fan fiction author who issued a challenge to write a scenario involving Elizabeth Bennet and Fitzwilliam Darcy in a game of Sardines, a popular pastime during the Regency. The game is a variation of 'hide and seek.' In this version, one person is designated to hide and those remaining each seek him or her. When a person finds the hider, that individual then joins him or her. This continues until the last seeker finally comes upon the hiding place. Traditionally then, that last is designated as the hider for the next round. I imagine the scenes might have become quite cosy after a while, depending on the locations chosen to hide...and of course, who was playing the game!

ぷぷぷ

Darcy sat, as he had done at least a portion of every day since coming to Netherfield, writing letters at the table in the parlour. He was perfectly complacent in this attitude. By habit he spent his early hours before breakfast riding, and generally those after dinner reading in Bingley's library or drawing room with a glass of the finest brandy. He had no objection to conversing with his friends, or a contest of billiards with Bingley or Hurst, but otherwise he felt quite content to engage in solitary activity. He and Charles Bingley with his family seemed to have settled into a comfortable routine that worked well for them when they were not engaged elsewhere in the neighbourhood. The formal garden at Netherfield boasted a large central avenue well made for strolling as well as some smaller ones, and featured several notable species of flora. To walk there before dinner hour had become *de rigueur* as well during clement weather. This offered yet another pleasing activity, on those occasions when Miss Caroline Bingley's pointed attentions to Darcy did not disturb his peace and try his patience.

For the most part their easy routine had continued with little change since Miss Elizabeth Bennet's addition to their company, but that Darcy found himself seeking out that lady's notice when her sister's condition permitted her to join them in a ramble. He could not reconcile why he found Miss Elizabeth's company so desirable, as they spoke but little and much of that satiric in nature. But Darcy soon found that he looked forward to those brief periods when Miss Bennet's condition leant itself to sleep, and her sister descended to the parlour or garden.

She was present now, perched demurely on a sopha and reading a book; and though she did not speak – indeed called no peculiar attention to herself – yet her occupation of the room made it somehow more alive. He had all he could do to concentrate on his letters, and found his mind – and his eyes – drifting often to the lady.

This day, it rained again; the third such of what looked to be a lengthy drab pall, the kind that hangs for days alternating between fine mists and downpours of biblical description. Everyone showed the effects of forced confinement in the house. Miss Bingley had been quite irritable at breakfast, the Hursts squabbled incessantly—though perhaps, after all, no more than their custom—and even Bingley's usual good humour was weighted down, dampened by all the rain. Miss Bingley had been pacing like a caged animal for nearly half an hour, unable to settle; it was wearing thin on them all.

When she looked to make yet another turn about the room, Bingley stood. "I have a notion! We want a diversion to raise our spirits, do we not?" Darcy thought to himself that he needed no such thing; he was perfectly complacent. But openly he acknowledged that certainly a diversion might restore equanimity to some of them. He soon regretted the indulgence.

"Let us play Sardines!" cried Bingley.

Darcy's pen stopped in mid-stroke, and he glared at his friend. "You jest, Bingley, surely." His expression challenged Bingley to declare otherwise at his peril.

Miss Bingley looked from her brother to Mr Darcy. In general, she had no use for Charles's boyish pleasures, but her quick arts immediately saw possible advantage in this pursuit. She cared little in general that it would provide them distraction, but if properly managed, she might gain some company with Mr Darcy – a commendable distraction, particularly if it would serve to command his attention *sans* the presence of their country neighbour who seemed to draw his eye all too often. But having little art himself, it surprised Darcy when Miss Bingley enthusiastically took up Bingley's notion and pressed for the game.

Miss Elizabeth Bennet had remained silent on the subject so far, though she looked up from her book with curious expression from time to time as the issue was debated further. Louisa Hurst reviled the notion and flounced off to her bed and a compress to soothe a head afflicted from perpetual damp. Mr Hurst took the opportunity of his wife's departure to himself be excused on *pressing business*; no doubt could be admitted as to the urgency of the matter when he returned but half a second after quitting the room, only to take up a sherry glass and decanter, and depart once more.

Darcy again begged off, owing to his correspondence and asserting he had his own business to complete. But Bingley countermanded that his friend had all day to finish his letters. He petitioned Darcy to be of sporting temper.

Still Miss Elizabeth remained detached from the discourse. Miss Bingley, having now *determined* that she would have her game, appealed directly to their guest—a certain sign of her advanced *ennui* that she would petition that lady for any thing.

"Miss Elizabeth, you are not averse to the pursuit of pleasurable pastimes, are you? For we know you dearly love to laugh; surely 'Sardines' will offer more amusement than our present condition."

Miss Elizabeth regarded Miss Bingley, noted the derisive look in her eyes. She intended to excuse herself from all of it, wishing the Hursts had not beaten her to the notion; she could easily have regretted that she must check on Jane and no one could, in conscience, have objected.

But then she changed her mind. After all, she was a guest of the house – quite an unwelcome usurper in the mind of Miss Bingley, her nominal hostess; but tolerated through the generous nature of Mr Bingley. His regard for Elizabeth and especially for her elder sister had made necessary Miss Bingley's offers of hospitality. She could offer *some* conciliation to that lady for her continued sufferance of Elizabeth's temporary residence, and more for his solicitude. And the game itself gave license to Elizabeth to satisfy her curiosity about Netherfield by investigating the house quite on her own.

She placed her book to one side and replied, "If it is your desire for Sardines, for such entertainment, Miss Bingley, I am happy to comply." Her eyes sparkled.

All eyes then turned to Mr Darcy. That gentleman held steadfastly to his refusal, wished the others joy and turned back to his letter to put an end to it.

"But Darcy," said Bingley. "What pleasure can there be in only three of us engaged, and one hid from the start. You know we must have at least one more to make it sporting."

Darcy, looking in turns at the Bingleys—the hopeful anticipation in his friend's expression and Miss Bingley pleading outright with her eyes—was little moved. But then he glanced at Miss Bennet to see her smirking at him. She fully expected his demurral! Perversely, this won him over.

He capitulated to it all, but conditionally—that they must limit the number of rooms which constituted fair play so that the game could not consume the entire morning.

"Done!" said Bingley. "What shall our playing field encompass?"

After some further discussion, they agreed to limit the field to the present drawing room, the entry hall, the breakfast room, the library and dining room on the main level, as well as the two presently unoccupied chambers to either side of the stairs on the next floor.

"Will that suit your requirements for a manageable search, Darcy?" The gentleman replied that it must do.

Bingley then made one final concession to his friend. "And to assuage your reticence for the game, Darcy, we will forego the usual selection process and nominate you to hide first. You see? Then there is nothing you must do once settled in your chosen place but await the others to find you. Surely you can have no objection to that?" Darcy acquiesced; if he was resigned to participate in folly, this provided the most tolerable means of accomplishing it.

Miss Bingley had thought to put herself forward to hide, believing that, as her brother was hopelessly unobservant and Miss Bennet unfamiliar with the house, surely Mr Darcy must find her before the others could do so, particularly as she might offer some hint to him without their notice. She experienced an instant of disappointment upon hearing her brother's suggestion; but then decided that, in truth, he may have hit once more upon something useful with the offer. She was less certain that Mr Darcy would expend the requisite effort to locate her than she would do for him;

but she trusted her own power to find him quickly and earn some much-desired attention from the gentleman before the others came upon them. She seconded Bingley's idea. Soon all were agreed, and three began to mark the minutes of waiting as Darcy rose to select his hiding place.

ξ

While the others stood looking out at the windows, Darcy made to exit the room but stopped on his way to pick up the small book Miss Elizabeth had been reading. She surprised him yet again—Edward Young, *Conjectures on Original Composition*. He would not have imagined this essay would appeal to a young woman; and Young's poetry, while popular, surely was too full of 'melancholy and moonlight' to appeal to Miss Bennet.

He took it with him into the hallway nevertheless and considered where to secrete himself. He had not the will to put great effort into a choice; but then, if he made his location obvious enough to end the game quickly, he would be forced to suffer another round after, one where *he* would have to do the seeking. He would rather make this present exercise last sufficiently.

He walked across the hall to inspect the dining room. Little there to accommodate one man; and certainly no more than one, when the others began to find him. He could go through to the food warming room, but this might become grounds for forfeiture as it must in spirit be considered out of bounds. But as he stood contemplating that room within a room, the answer came to him – the perfect spot! With luck, he might peruse the whole of Mr Young's essay before being found out. Smiling to himself, he turned to leave, stopping at the sideboard to select two ripe pears from the fruit bowl. If his choice of retirement proved as remote as he hoped, he could pass some while there and grow peckish with the wait.

He checked the corridor to ensure it was empty before stepping out and hurrying along to the library. On gaining it, he leaned back against the closed door a moment to savour its aesthetics. It occurred to him now that this room may, in fact, be the first the others would expect him to inhabit, and he had little time to secure his place.

At first glance the room offered no concealment, unless he should crouch behind a sopha or stand wrapped in the draperies. Darcy would dignify neither, nor was it wanted—for there existed in the corner of this particular library an anomaly, an ingenious invention of its builder. In the far corner as one entered, where book-cases lined the walls in each direction, one section was counterfeit. The 'books' occupying it had been secured there for symmetry of design, but they were not real. They were spines only and, though in fine tooled leather, they sported false titles and authors whose names were formed by mixing up the established writers of the day. They merely gave the disguise of a book-case to what was, in fact, a door.

Some who noticed the counterfeit titles might assume it to be nothing more than a folly; with nothing behind it. But Darcy had discovered on first perusing the library, soon after his arrival at Netherfield, that there was indeed a catch hidden under a slightly protruding book spine. When activated, the door sprung open to reveal a small recessed area and a circular iron stair. The stair then led up to a narrow railed walkway across the back of the room, used only by servants on occasion to set the clock, lower the chandelier for cleaning and the like.

Darcy had no need to go out of bounds of the game to the food warming room when he could avail himself of this alternative. Nor must he brave the circular stairs there to ascend to the walk above. Immediate upon entering the closet was a window to the left, facing the back garden of the house; and set within it, a deep sill surround at just such a height to form a convenient bench. Sitting there, Darcy would be availed of ample light – even on a day of heavy rain – by which to read and so pass an hour in seclusion.

Some small part of him played at remorse for hiding himself so fully. He could not be certain if he had told Bingley of this small passageway, he rather thought not. But it was possible his friend may at one time have witnessed a servant on the walkway and learnt of it in that manner. Certainly he would be unlikely to have discovered the door in pursuit of a book, as Bingley's reading habits were sparse. They tended towards newspapers and periodicals where his short attention spans could be accommodated. Miss Bingley's reading habits were even less—had he ever known her to enter the room at all? And Miss Bennet, though she *had* entered the room and made selections, could not be well acquainted with the premises.

Perhaps, in a spirit of fair play, Darcy should leave a clue to his whereabouts. He considered it, looking down to his hands at the book and the pears; but in the end, he determined against it. Let his seekers find him or not. If they had not done before time to dress for dinner, he would emerge and find *them* to claim the day.

He thought he could discern footsteps approaching from without, and he hastened to release the catch and enter his sanctuary. Indeed as he closed the hidden door behind him, he heard the other, main one open. He waited, listening carefully, but it seemed no one had entered; perhaps they only looked in and, finding it empty, moved on again. After a moment he stuck his head out and confirmed the notion—the larger room was empty. Smiling, he withdrew to his little cell; only in the last second did his conscience persuade him to leave the false book-case open by the smallest crack. He should be forewarned if anyone approached close by. A casual observer would never notice the door's displacement; though a vigilant searcher might benefit. Content that he would be left in peace for some time, Darcy settled himself in the window seat, congratulated his arrangement as he enjoyed a pear, and opened the book.

ξ

For three-quarters of an hour, Darcy had good reason to congratulate his choice. He grew complacent, so thoroughly engrossed in reading in this quiet place, that he heard no sign of anyone's approach. His first awareness that he had been found occurred when the door creaked as it swung open on its hinges. He looked up sharply, fully expecting to see Bingley, if surprised to think that his friend had looked there so quickly as he did.

His astonishment was complete, therefore, on finding Miss Elizabeth Bennet filling the doorway. He rose in civility.

"Mr Darcy," said Lizzy. "It seems I have deduced your secret."

"Indeed. I am impressed, Miss Bennet, at your talent for detection. I had thought to see my friend in your place, with his better understanding of the house." They stood without speaking for a moment. Darcy added, "How did you come to find me with such apparent ease?"

"It took no magic, sir, I assure you; yet would you call it ease? I confess I do not. I have been searching this hour!"

"And yet," he said, taking in the small room, "you can see the others do not possess your power of deduction."

She accepted the implied compliment with a nod, and a pert smile.

"When first our wait time was expired, I thought immediately of the library. I am less acquainted with this house, as you have noted. Yet I comprehended enough of your habits of residence to surmise that you might make for here." She glanced back at the main room. "Or rather, there."

He could wonder at her knowing his habit so well after only a few days – an observant girl, did anything escape her notice?

"But then as I approached the room, I saw Miss Bingley leaving it in a state of some dissatisfaction. I presumed she had found the library unoccupied, and so turned my own step up the stairs." Miss Bennet smirked again. "I rather thought Miss Bingley would have exercised every art to secure you first; giving me to question whether, after all, you had rejected the library as too perfunctory a choice."

She shrugged. Mr Darcy said nothing, but his expression suggested his interest in her speech, so she continued. "Mr. Bingley already had searched the breakfast room – I passed him then entering the dining room when I made my way back down – and so I returned to our original starting point, wondering perhaps if you had somehow doubled back to the drawing room after we left it."

"You credit me, perhaps, Miss Bennet, with too intricate a character." He smiled.

She regarded him quizzically a moment and then, smiling enigmatically, she said simply, "I confess I had half of a mind to cry defeat and station myself in comfort on the sopha until you all should return. But it was then I noticed it."

"Noticed what?"

Her lips were pursed in such an *appealing* smirk, Darcy could forgive her the show of arrogance. "Noticed that my book – the one I had been reading previously – had gone from the table." She glanced at the very book, laying forgotten in Mr Darcy's hand, as he closed his fingers around it more tightly then. "I deduced it was a clue of sorts, for only *you* could have removed it, I think. And where else would a book reside in the usual way... but in a library? From this, I made my way here to see if Miss Bingley had not been artful enough to succeed in her pursuit of you."

Miss Bennet looked at him pointedly, a gaze rich with understanding. She was indeed observant—both regarding Miss Bingley's aspirations and, he did not doubt, of his own indifference in that quarter. But in at least one particular, she had mistaken him; perhaps did not know his character so well after all. Still, he would not correct her flawed deduction that he had taken the book with such a pointed purpose, but rather only from a curiosity in her choice of reading matter. He would not conjecture that, though she might come well in the end, her early presumptions of him were quite unfounded.

"It was a matter of moments," she concluded, "before I happened upon this corner and saw the sliver of light which escaped the crack in the door. How fitting for you that Netherfield offers such hidden depths."

"Yet it would seem that to *you*, Miss Elizabeth, I am too easy to decipher, despite all my *careful plotting*."

"I do not agree, sir. I find you exceedingly inscrutable."

Darcy considered her words, suddenly quite ill at ease under her assured gaze.

"Perhaps," he said, "in the interest of the game, of course, you should enter this closet and return the door to its original placement. We shall have likely only a few moments before the others find us; in which time I may endeavour to provide you with more clarity of my character."

Miss Elizabeth made no answer, but entered the close space and shut the door behind her, leaving it cracked just a bit more than she had first found it. She glanced hopefully towards the circular stairs.

"They are too narrow a perch for any comfort," Darcy said, anticipating her purpose as he indicated the space next to him for Elizabeth to sit. He considered, as a gentleman, giving up the seat to her wholly, but rejected the notion. There was sufficient room for them both to sit comfortably; and who could tell how long they might be required to remain there before the others found them.

She offered a spare curtsey and then sat on the end of the bench, her body pressed to the side of the casement so as to leave a good deal of space between them. The gentleman, noting her distance, smiled wryly and regained his seat. "I assure you, Miss Bennet, despite your misgivings, you are quite safe from me."

Miss Elizabeth had the wherewithal to blush at this observation, but relaxed a little, determined to make their incarceration tolerable. "You were far away when I came upon you, Mr Darcy," she said, nodding at the book. "May I ask what so fully engages you?"

"As a matter of some interest, it is the very page you were reading in the parlour, to judge by the marker you left in it. A curious book for you to select, is it not?"

Miss Elizabeth sat up straighter, bristling a little at Darcy's apparent slight. "What should you expect me to read, sir? A serial romance, with heroines of excellent character, brooding and misunderstood heroes, and happy endings all around?"

"Hardly, Miss Elizabeth. You have far too much good sense for such things. But I must confess that Edward Young is not an author I would expect to hold your interest. This does not commonly answer as reading for light entertainment, particularly for a lady who revels in laughter."

"Nor am I a common reader, Mr Darcy." Darcy took the rebuke in silence, pursing his lips in acknowledgement of his mistake. The lady continued, "But in this circumstance, do not put too much stock in my choice, for it was selected in haste from the nearest available stack of books in the library this morning."

Darcy laughed at her admission. "I commend your honesty. And remain assured, I will not rush to judgment of your character based upon accidental intelligence or wilful misunderstanding." When this remark seemed to discomfit the lady, Darcy busied himself by opening the book and reading.

"Nor are we only ignorant of the dimensions of the human mind in general, but even of our own. That a man may be scarce less ignorant of his own powers, than an oyster of its pearl, or a rock of its diamond; that he may possess dormant, unsuspected abilities, till awakened by loud calls, or stung up by striking emergencies, is evident from the sudden eruption of some men, out of perfect obscurity, into public admiration, on the strong impulse of some animating occasion; not more to the world's great surprise, than their own." [1]

Darcy looked up from the page to his companion, and smiled. "And what is your opinion on this matter, Miss Bennet? Do you believe man to be so obtuse as to prove unaware of his own attributes and powers?"

Miss Elizabeth considered Mr Darcy for a moment, saw a smug demeanour as he challenged her judgment, her very rationality of mind, and she felt compelled to respond in like temper. "Indeed I do not, Mr Darcy. In my limited experience, I rather find that *men* more often *over*estimate their attributes. What they singularly neglect to appreciate are their *failings*."

This comment, against her expectation, yielded a smile from Mr Darcy. "I see you are as severe on my sex, Miss Elizabeth, as you are on your own." He referred, of course, to a discussion they had entertained only a few evenings before concerning the conditions a woman must meet to be deemed an *accomplished lady*. He leaned towards her now, holding her gaze in his for a moment in silence; it was to be understood he judged her undeserving of the title.

Though she returned his impertinence stubbornly, quite soon his closeness disconcerted her. She began to wish she could sink farther into the wall when Mr Darcy looked down at the book finally, returned his eyes to her again, and silently held the book out to her. She took it from him, but dropped it to her lap quickly as she realized that her fingers trembled unaccountably.

Suddenly the wide window seat appeared too close for comfort, and both Miss Elizabeth and Darcy felt all the confinement of the small space they occupied. Self consciously, each looked around for something to engage their minds besides the other. At that moment, fortuitously, the hidden door creaked on opening and they were met with the smiling countenance of Charles Bingley.

ξ

"Ah! I should have known, Darcy! I cannot think why it took me so long to hit upon this little nook." He glanced about the cosy space and the window seat, oblivious to the charge in the air, and continued. "What a genius you are, my friend. I might have never found you! Ha-ha."

"Then how did you, Bingley?" Darcy asked, grateful for this idle talk to break the hovering tension.

"I entered the library, had a quick look 'round, and was about to leave when I heard voices. They were indistinct, muffled as it were, but certainly coming from this room, the library that is. As there was no other likely place to hide in the room, I recalled these stairs, and determined you must have recollected them too. And I was correct! Ah-ha."

Bingley's good humour was infectious. Both Darcy and Miss Elizabeth found themselves joining him in laughter, though if asked neither could have explained the impetus for such amusement. Only a few moments later, drawn first by the unchecked sound of conversation which now floated into the library, and then the half-opened book-case door, Miss Bingley appeared at last, to find that she was the loser in every respect. An awkward moment ensued as she learnt that Miss Bennet had usurped the place she had designed for herself, and she glared at them all with ill-concealed irritation in having lost, until sudden Bingley cried,

"Look!" They all turned at once to follow his gaze out the window, to see that the sun had emerged from behind the clouds. The rain had stopped, and a faint shimmer of rainbow could be seen in the distance hanging over a low hill.

"There," Bingley laughed, ever the optimist. "It seems our day has brightened considerably from our little diversion! Shall we take some welcome air before dinner?" The others looked around at each other and nodded in agreement; then they exited the tiny space. As they passed through the disguised doorway into the library, Darcy, the last of them, turned to look again at his window seat, then at the retreating figure of Elizabeth ahead of him. With a sigh the meaning of which he scarcely knew, he closed the door on the setting and made his way from the room, idly pocketing the marker from her book.

---

[1] *Conjectures on Original Composition*, by Edward Young, London 1759. An essay written in the form of a letter addressed to Samuel Richardson

Water Pump
(A Glimpse into the Mind of a Gentleman)

ᔭᔭᔭ

*These two complimentary scenes grew also from a Jane Austen writing challenge
devised by a friend. The parameters given for this indulgence were to ensure the inclusion of:
Elizabeth Bennet, Fitzwilliam Darcy – and a water pump.   Oh, and a max limit for each story of
2000 words in length.*

ᔭᔭᔭ

[Netherfield Park, very early in the morning]

I have taken leave of my senses completely! How else to
explain the deplorable state in which I find myself? I have forfeited
all my senses – all reason, it would seem – to the contemplation of a
single thought.

I cannot banish Miss Elizabeth Bennet from my mind.

Her image haunts me exceedingly, inserting itself unbidden
into my waking thoughts and disturbing my slumber. If I select a
book to peruse, I recollect it to be the same that she spent reading
only yesterday. I write letters to my sister, only to watch helpless as
my pen, straying of its own accord, describes remarkably fine eyes
and lively wit. (What will poor Georgiana think of me? She has had
no letter from me in days, for I have had to burn every one upon
reading them back.)   I find that Miss Bingley's arts disgust me
where once I tolerated them with amusement. Indeed, all my
attempts to comprehend this confounded restlessness and
discomposure only lead me to greater perturbation.

Since Miss Bennet's confinement at Netherfield from illness,
and the addition of Miss Elizabeth to our little resident group, I have
been oddly and sorely distracted. Yet what is she to me that all
order of mind should flounder in her wake?

She is pretty; I do not dispute the fact. But lovelier than she I
have dismissed with little regard. Something there is in her nature
that I feel compelled to comprehend. She is lively, certainly, with an
unstudied manner that is often diverting; but such diversions never
have held me in their grip before. I will concede a certain quickness

21

of mind and good understanding to match; but she so often displays a propensity to use them in satirical study. She always couches her remarks in courteous parlance – yet at the same time makes no attempt to disguise a teazing nature that makes sport of any absurdity with little mercy. She is acerbic, independent minded, witty and too observant of every thing. It is quite disconcerting. I own I am perplexed as much by her character as by my interest in learning more of it.

I arose quite early this morning, awakening as so often with the breaking of dawn. And what is the first sketch my mind must conjure, but that of Miss Elizabeth in the stable yard yesterday. Certainly a vision to ponder, with her hair only loosely bound, tendrils of it teasing her face in the breeze, a dew-kissed glow across her cheeks and brow. My courtesies, however, were met as a reproof by the lady. I am convinced she purposefully took offense where she could find any – though never was it intended – and took enjoyment in countering my every advance towards civility. Even my rescue of her when she stumbled in the yard was met as an affront I am at a loss to explain.

I tried at once, to push away the scene from yesterday. Is it not enough that this lady's physical presence distracts me? Must I remain subject also to echoed teazing in her absence as well? As if she was some sprite whose laughter is slow to fade from the ether after its owner disappears from sight?

Not willing to allow this stubborn intrusion of the lady upon my mind to continue, I decided to take out one of Bingley's mounts. Nothing clears my head so exceedingly as a long morning ride, before the world has been roused to go about its business. It was quite early and I anticipated meeting no one, and as it also was uncommonly warm, I dressed in a loose linen shirt and breeches, and a light coat, and made my way to the stables. Bingley's roan is no Parsifal, but it is an adequate animal which would, I thought, enjoy a free head to run at this early hour. And indeed such was the case. No sooner had I saddled it than it fidgeted in the morning's close air.

We set off through the estate at a moderate pace, picking our way through the orchard, then along the stream bed. The air was already quite warmed, but fresh; and I felt lulled by it into a deception of clear-headed peace at last. I was complacent; until the slight breeze stirred the wild dill growing near the banks, and once again an image of Miss Elizabeth assailed me – of another morning some days past and her startling arrival at Netherfield to visit her ailing sister.

She had walked the three miles between their estates that morning, looking quite wild on arrival. Her complexion brightened by the exercise, her skin glowed with vigour and there was a stubborn glint of determination in her fine eyes. She had walked over stiles and through meadows still damp from recent rains – her petticoat six inches deep in mud! – but with a scent wafting about her, as it so often did, of wild dill and pears; most intoxicating.

Blast the woman! Could she leave me no peace? I steered my mount full out toward open field, and rode with all speed for some while. That was infinitely better. But when finally I took stock of my surroundings, I found myself at the Bennets' Longbourn property, with their manor directly ahead. Damn and blast!

Wheeling my mount around, I pushed it yet again, sailing in the opposing direction from Miss Elizabeth's home. We eventually made a full circuit of Bingley's leased properties, though I took little notice of it with our speed of travel. To my satisfaction, I took little notice of anything else as well.

At some length, alert to the mount's growing exhaustion, we turned again for Netherfield at a slow pace. The sun was now higher and promising yet another stifling day. But I was content – I felt restored to my mind. No fates would get the better of me this day.

After dismounting, I turned the roan over to a groom, receiving a circumspect glance from the boy. I realised my appearance must have occasioned his curiosity, flushed from heat and exertion. In truth, only then did I realise quite how warm I felt as well. I strode over to the trough in the yard and worked the pump, drawing up soothing water. Thinking at first to merely splash some on my face, I altered my inclination at the cool relief it offered. No one was stirring yet, only the groom was about; so I removed my coat and stuck my head fully under the flow. Its effects were a wonder.

I could feel streams of water dripping from my hair, travelling in tickling rivulets down my face, neck and shoulders; collecting on my lashes to be blinked away in cool relief. The effect of this dousing was quite startling, doing as much for my well-being as the punishing ride had done. Feeling wholly at one with myself again, I raised my face to the sky, to dare mock the gods who would tarry with me for sport.

At once, my notice was caught by some movement at a window of the house. As I looked up, and fixed my gaze on the window, what did I see but Miss Elizabeth Bennet looking down at me! Oh, foolish man, to challenge the gods after all. I was spellbound by the vision of Miss Elizabeth. She stood with drapes parted, looking down on me as some recalcitrant angel waking from her nest – her hair falling dark around her shoulders; absently clutching her pale gown at her throat; her eyes still half-lidded with residual sleep and unaware, I was certain, of being observed.

In the instant of seeing her, all the complacency earned in my ride deserted me. I could only stare, finding her eyes through the distance and glass which lay between us. When she realised I saw her, she appeared as transfixed as I. After a moment, I looked down to the ground in some discomfort at the candour in our gaze. When I looked up again but seconds later, she had gone. The drapes lay closed and unmoving as though never disturbed.

My mind reeled from the memory of that vision. But was it memory? or was it again my reason playing me for a fool? There was no one to witness this event, save possibly the lady herself, and I could not ask her to verify our strange encounter.

But I am at pains to make any sense of it, for in truth, my senses and my sensibilities betray me much of late. Did I even see her there?

❦❦❦

Water Pump Two
(A Variation on a Theme)

I don't understand privileged people. I have leisure enough to watch them all day with their comings and goings, and to be honest, it just boggles the mind to try and understand them. Maybe it's none of my business, but what else do I have to do when I'm not working except watch what goes on around me.

Let me tell you: as a common peon on this estate who's pretty much invisible when not actively serving my master or his guests, I see a lot. We go into town for errands and the women stand around throwing hankies at my feet – well, not mine, for they wouldn't want me to touch it. No, they want their 'fancy gentlemen' and officers to gallantly return their piece of cloth to them so they can flutter their lashes and swoon. We go back and forth from country estates to town with seemingly no purpose, and from ball to ball, with the same old people in the latest versions of the same old fashion; with Sir Whatsit behind the west wall stealing kisses from any young thing he can lure out there; and trussed up matriarchs sizing up all the single men to see if their bank drafts have the right personality for their daughters; whose single thrill in life, in turn, would probably be a quick romp against the wall with the randy Sir Whatsit, bank draft or no.

Call me simple, perhaps, but to me... you see a pretty thing with a well-turned ankle that makes your blood race? You go up to her very directly, tell her she makes your knees quake just to look at, and bob's-your-uncle, you're having a very sweet tumble in very sweetly scented hay in a secluded corner of the stable a few minutes later. Completely uncomplicated!

Not these people, though, these privileged folks. They have to play their games. They pretend they're above base drives, so they posture and flirt, and deny their attractions, and make me work when they want to go out riding or visit the local, to forget their latest obsession.

Take this Darcy chap, for instance. I mean, he's okay. He's posh, but he's human. He's respectful enough for our differences in station, and usually he doesn't work us too hard. (Well, he's not our boss, that would be his friend Bingley, but his stature does give him the right to direct us and Bingley always defers to him.) And when he does demand something of us, he usually sees us right in the end.

But when it comes to the female sex? The gentleman's completely helpless for all his education and his fortune. He's had it bad for this one lady who's visiting from the next manor over, must be four or five days she's here now. So what does he do? He stands in the stable yard and gazes longingly at her with big moony eyes, while he talks to her as if she was some business acquaintance looking to borrow money! Oh, he's gallant enough. He grabs her arm when she slips in the mud, puffs out his chest to show how fit and handsome he is. And she's hardly better. Anyone with an eye can see she thinks he's the best thing since oat bread! But she employs the art of banter, wanting him to see her wit and that she's above all this tawdry concentration on fashion and funds and husband hunting. Lordy, the way they're going, they'll be sixty before they get around to a peck on the cheek!

So this morning this Darcy comes out very early. He likes to ride early in the morning to forget his troubles. Right! – more like to forget that he doesn't have a clue what to do with that woman. He can't fool me, I could hear him sighing and sputtering as he checked and adjusted the saddle and stuff. I could have told him what to do with her (a direct approach always works for me, handsome devil that I am) but we might as well speak different languages for all he'd ever listen to me. And off he rides, working up to a lather – all to convince himself that he doesn't care about her after all. An hour later, back again, all hot and bothered and thinking he's cured. Ha!

First place he makes for is the water trough, and he dunks his head under the flow of the pump. I could've used a slurp or two of that water myself at this point, but "lairds before the hired help" as my pa always said. So there he is, nice looking enough guy if you like that sort (not *my* particular fancy), tall and broad, with his shirt sticking to him in all the right places, leaning over the trough with the stream from the pump running through his locks, he basking like it's manna from heaven, and shaking his head now and then to toss off thoughts of her as much as the heat (or maybe they're the same thing, ha ha – you didn't know I was such a funny guy, did you, now?)

And I look up, and there's the lady herself in a window, Miss Elizabeth Bennet to give you her official title, she's from the next manor over. She's looking down on Darcy with what appears to me like an *'unwholesome interest.'* You can't convince me there's no passionate feeling there.

So what do they do? Do they give a wink and a head toss and make for the orchard to meet for a little nookie away from prying eyes? (Hmm, a pear would taste good about now.) Nah – that would be way too rational, not to mention satisfying. Instead, they lock eyes with one another for ages, shuffle around a bit, look at the ground, and the next thing you know, she's long gone from the window, he's swearing under his breath "Damn and blast!" and making mud in the yard with his now-forgotten drippings. And so it goes. The way he holds back, that sister of his is going to have to produce an heir for that big estate they have north of here; Mr Darcy will never progress beyond sputtering conversation!

Well, I'm certainly glad I wasn't born to the gentry. I'm a good looking guy (have I mentioned that before?) – you might even call me a stud – and I get all the action I could want. Living in the stable isn't a bad gig. They provide me with lodging within it (and the hay is pretty warm), food, drink and on occasion treats of fresh fruit; and I have enough free time to make my way with the ladies. And I'm not hampered by stilted conversation – I'm half Irish so I've got the gift of it when I need to communicate with some pretty colleen. What better could someone like me expect from life?

Oops, nice talking to you, but I've got to go. Now that the show is over between that Darcy and his woman, the groom is taking me for that drink and a brush-up. I earned it this morning, I've got to tell you. The gentleman (Mr Darcy) rode me hard! (He must've had a lot of urges to quell.) It was exhilarating, but I think I've earned a rest for a while. Then again, there is that saucy little filly in the stall across from mine...

Flirting With Trouble

❦❦❦

When Charles Bingley returned to London after the Netherfield Ball and his sisters and Mr Darcy followed him soon after to ensure he remained separated from Jane Bennet, Darcy invited Bingley to reside at his own town home in Berkeley Square rather than stay in a gentleman's hotel. This story came from the suggestions in Pride and Prejudice *that Mr Darcy might look with favour on an eventual match between his sister Georgiana and his good friend.*

❦❦❦

"I should think this a question better put to Miss Georgiana, Sir."

"Yes, and so we shall when I am better informed of my own leanings in the matter." There was a short silence then, before Mr Darcy continued. "For my own part, Mrs Annesley, I believe my sister yet unready to enter society; perhaps insertion by degrees being more palatable. She will be very young when the season begins." He stammered a bit then, stopping and starting as he abandoned and renewed approaches to say what he wished. Mrs Annesley, comprehending the source of his discomposure, relieved him of the necessity of too careful reference by owning that Miss Darcy had once related the particulars of their unfortunate dealings in Ramsgate during the summer. The proof of this surprised both Georgiana's guardians even as it allowed them less circumspect speech.

"Then you may appreciate our concern for my cousin, Madam," said Colonel Fitzwilliam. "She has not been herself these months since that... since... although we have witnessed improvements, we are of the fear that she lingers yet too much in her disappointment."

Mrs Annesley could give them no firmer opinion beyond avowing that, despite the possible good such a scheme might yield, she shared their reservations of it. Perhaps indeed it was not the right course to present Miss Darcy so soon as the coming season.

"I confess," said Mr Darcy, "I had nearly concluded to say nothing at all of it; her spirits have shown measured improvement. But there is still a melancholy in her air which too often pervades. I cannot be certain of its cause, of course. But I know of no new event which could have the power to afflict my sister as much." Mrs

Annesley quickly confirmed there had been nothing in recent weeks to draw the slightest concern.

"Yesterday, being then unresolved as to propose the season or not, I spied her playing games with our young visitor Master Robinson. One moment a lady, the very next cross-legged on the library floor like any child, engaged in spillikens. I cannot settle myself which is the right of her. I own I am at sixes and sevens." Colonel Fitzwilliam nodded in vigorous agreement of this bemused state.

Mrs Annesley laughed. "Gentlemen," she said as she apologised for her outburst; assuring she had not intended to make light of their serious concern. Then: "I dare say Miss Darcy does not know herself from one instant to another whether she is adult or child! Such are the conundrums of becoming a woman. There is no particular moment in time when one fully casts off the things of childhood to don the mantle of a lady. It is done gradually and often with great effort—greater yet confusion and discomfort. One might well liken it to the course of love." She laughed again in empathy, and the gentlemen sighed, unenlightened still.

ξ

Georgiana Darcy slipped away then and made her way to the small morning parlour to think in solitude. She had to set her mind to the possibility of what she had heard, what had been suggested.

She had gone in search of her companion before breakfast and, not finding her in any of the usual rooms, had ventured downstairs. Hearing voices in discourse as she neared the small library at the back of the house, she approached closer; the door was ajar. She had heard her cousin Richard's voice first, and her brother. She was about to interrupt to ask if they had seen Mrs Annesley, when that lady herself had spoken from within the room. What's more, she was speaking of *her*. Georgiana had stopped, her hand raised in an aborted act of knocking, curious to hear in what manner she featured in their converse. Thus she had been privy to the exchange just recounted.

Considering it now, her first instinct was a disappointing realisation that she had not, as she had believed, hid her mood as well as she should. But could her guardians truly be suggesting that she enter the season in only a few months time? It seemed they contemplated it— her brother had sought her companion's opinion as to whether doing so might contribute to Gee's recovery, or only add to her burdens.

Did she wish to come out this year? A part of her found the notion thrilling, and at this age, when she had not looked for the chance until another season, perhaps two, should pass. To be invited to balls and dinners herself – instead of relying on hearing of them with envy from her cousin Frederica, whose recountings were limited to a list of her suitors or how well her gown had been admired – this would excite Gee. New gowns, with the latest trimmings for evening entertainments; riding in the park, concerts at Spring Gardens – all the manner of events in which her brother Fitz habitually participated and sometimes enjoyed and upon whose indulgence she must beg presently for indifferent observation. Her flesh actually tingled to contemplate these scenes.

But she was only fifteen!—or at least, would pass her sixteenth year in a few months just as the season would begin. And along with dinners and balls and concerts, would follow the responsibility to exert herself as well. She would be thrust into discourse with tens or even hundreds of people all at once, expected to make conversation; to be elegant, sweetly gracious, subtly flirtatious even; and all under the keen eyes of matrons who would have about by morning any transgressions or lapses in understanding—her Aunt foremost amongst them, she was certain. The notion that she could, after fifteen years of being sheltered away with only family and a few schoolroom friends, suddenly bloom in the company of older and more experienced society – and men at that! – was unfathomable. She had no fear of the disgrace of being thought too clever; but rather of being ridiculous. Was she prepared for this?

Fitz's object, as Georgiana had comprehended the overheard conversation, was through her presentation to encourage his sister in forgetting Mr Wickham's treachery—forget Mr Wickham himself—and this object Gee also wished mightily to achieve. But how was she to know if new gentlemen she would meet would be of more honourable intention? If Mr Wickham could make love to her for the £30,000 she brought to a union, would not others do the same? She very nearly wished she had not been so well endowed; or that it should not be so well known in society. How could she believe any man's sincerity? And yet, how could she avoid offending those of earnest regard if she did not believe them?

No, she decided on the whole, she could not conceive of all this in only a few short months. This was a change of too large proportion. She was cowardly, she knew it. But she was not prepared.

ξ

In the end, neither her brother nor her cousin spoke to her of coming out, but left it to Mrs Annesley to relate briefly their discourse to a relieved Georgiana. But although she was given a reprieve for another season, they all of them resolved that she should use the time to grow more confident through gradual and limited engagements, as her brother had suggested. This course she could embrace.

Georgiana did not reveal to her companion that she knew the hopes of her guardians, that such activity might diminish thoughts of Mr Wickham. Their overheard remarks on her disturbance of mind had roused her, and she felt the necessity of appearing more like herself. She would take greater care of how she presented herself in future, striving to demonstrate only contentment.

The summer just past, spent in Ramsgate and so full of promise when they had first arrived in the seaside town, had ended badly after Georgiana and her then companion had encountered Mr Wickham. The son of the former steward at Pemberley, the ladies had conceived him from the start a stalwart family friend of old. They had allowed of a certain familiarity that quickly resolved into intimacy. Georgiana had believed herself in love with Mr Wickham; indeed, believed that love to be returned ardently. She had allowed herself to be persuaded to an elopement, the execution of which might well have succeeded had not her brother chanced to arrive some days earlier than expected. She had then thought twice of the plan and revealed it to Fitz – providentially, in the end.

For it proved that Mr Wickham was no more than a mercenary, a vile flatterer who did not scruple to take advantage of his former benefactor's daughter. Georgiana's erstwhile companion indeed had conspired with Mr Wickham for the whole to transpire – and all for money. Mr Wickham had been exposed as the worst of men, Mrs Younge ejected immediately, and Richard Fitzwilliam summoned to assist Darcy in their ward's rehabilitation. She had been returned to Town to suffer chastisement, not from her guardians who were at all times solicitous, but from herself for nearly ruining her family.

Since then, since the appointment of Mrs Annesley as her companion in these intervening months, Georgiana had recovered, if slowly. She had confessed her stupidity to the companion, who had helped Gee to find lessons in the experience rather than dwelling on the shame. From time to time, when it lay heavily on the young woman's mind or heart, speaking of it with Mrs Annesley brought a curious ease.

But for all that, there were thoughts about which she could not speak – not to her companion, nor ever to Fitz or Richard Fitzwilliam. She could not tell them that she suffered moments when a not rational part of her wished she had kept her assignation with Mr Wickham – that she thought of him, recalled compliments he had paid to her, the singular affection he had shown her, the pleasure she had found in his company; the gratifying notion of being so much a part of another person's thoughts.

It little mattered that her rational mind knew her experiences with Mr Wickham had been counterfeit, when her heart felt so incomprehensibly heavy with every attempt to evict memories of him. They had not felt counterfeit at the time! It was not reason which failed her; that had come to terms quickly enough with Mr Wickham's treachery. She understood rationally that marriage to the man would have soured very soon and brought resentment and misery. It was emotion she could not regulate; it was her sensibilities that failed her.

She was not thus afflicted constantly. She went about her days very well, and had dared until this morning to believe no one could be the wiser. But now and again she experienced a pang of disappointment – when she heard a laugh like his, or saw a man of similar form, or gazed on one of her sketches of Pegwell Bay which, however, she could not bring herself to discard any more than the painful memories they evoked. And at those low moments, she could wonder... would she ever cease to regret him? stop loving the image of the man she had installed in her affections? expel that smallest hope that remained of its all being a horrid mistake? No, of that she could not speak. She was too shamed by the unreasonable feelings. But she could – and she would – quell them with every means at her disposal so that their effects would not be discernible to her guardians. She would slowly enter society, placing all her resolve into showing well for Fitz and Richard; and in time her regrets would no longer require a concerted will to conceal.

That very same day, a wonderful notion struck Georgiana. Whilst she and Mrs Annesley sat at their work, it came to the young woman that she had a singular opportunity even now to practice social graces and earn confidence; and possibly to work some good as well. They had residing with them for an extended period a particular friend of her brother's, a gentleman who was affable, interesting, readily accessible to her – and sorely in need of cheering up himself following a disappointment over a lady in Hertfordshire. It was the perfect solution, and right under Gee's nose! She would practice by flirting with Mr Bingley!

ξ

Georgiana put her plan into motion that very evening before dinner. She and Mrs Annesley had been first down to the parlour, but only a tick after they settled, Mr Bingley arrived.

He is truly quite fine-looking in his green coat, thought Georgiana. Mr Bingley's fairness of form, however, did not extend to exciting Gee's sensibilities beyond the recognition that, coupled with the affability he always displayed, fortune had provided her a handsome subject for experiment. Even so, her own leanings towards reserve gave her pause before, gulping down trepidation, she rose from the sopha and crossed to him.

As she approached, she quickly reviewed instances where she had been privy to Miss Bingley's demeanour in the presence of Fitzwilliam Darcy. That lady formed the chief of Gee's familiarity with the art of flirtation. Cousin Frederica was too wild and silly to follow, she knew; and schoolgirl rehearsals that ended in fits of giggles were of no true assistance in the real world. But Miss Bingley was a lady of fashion, at home in society. Of course, it did not occur to Georgiana then to consider how little success that lady's efforts generally yielded from Fitz.

Assuming her brightest smile, she said, "Mr Bingley – I believe I have been remiss in expressing appropriate welcome since your coming to Berkeley Square. May I make amends to you now?"

Mr Bingley bowed in acknowledgment and returned the smile. "I assure you, Miss Darcy, I have not felt the least neglected. No amends are necessary." His ready laugh she took for reassurance, but then she realised he would say no more and it was to her to continue in some manner. She flicked a glance to her companion for moral courage, but Mrs Annesley, having no comprehension of Georgiana's plot, paid no heed to her. The lady sat reading, of all things. What good did she offer as chaperone if she could be so easily diverted?

"Um," Georgiana began without the least notion of what would follow. Mr Bingley regarded her with amiable anticipation, nothing in the world carrying now more importance than her next utterance. "Er... may I ask... how is your sister?"

She knew the absurdity of this as soon as it escaped her. Mr Bingley's sister had called only that morning and passed an hour in company, for which Mr Bingley was present the latter half. Georgiana would of course know the lady's condition as well as he – and he was well aware of it.

"You ask after Louisa, of course," offered the gallant gentleman when he noted the blush rising to Georgiana's cheeks. "Mrs Hurst does very well, though in something of a tizzy at the moment. When I called earlier, she was preparing for a journey to spend Christmastide with Hurst's relations. They leave early tomorrow and precious little had been done to satisfaction. I am afraid, although the eldest, Louisa does not possess Caroline's talents for organization. No doubt she frets even now and has driven all the servants to distraction."

"Then Miss Bingley does not accompany the Hursts?"

"No, she refused." Mr Bingley adopted a conspiratorial hush to his voice as he added, "If you must know, she cannot abide Mr Hurst's brother always putting himself in her way, making moon eyes at her. He is three years her junior, two inches shorter, carries five stone more than he should, and has about him at all times – to hear Caroline speak, of course – the odour of smoked haddock."

Georgiana giggled at this before catching herself, embarrassed at the childish display. But Mr Bingley had delighted in entertaining her. It emboldened her.

"Why, Mr Bingley, you cannot be serious!"

"Indeed I am!" Mr Bingley said, laughing. "But pray do not tell her I spoke of it. She would never forgive me."

"Never. Your secret is safe." She tried lowering her eyes and then raising them slowly to him with a coy smile, as she had seen Miss Bingley do on occasion. Mr Bingley coloured at the attention, and quickly looked over to Mrs Annesley. But the companion again offered no assistance; her eyes remained upon her book. Georgiana also was ignorant of his disquiet, having looked down once more immediately upon her act—the whole artful gesture being so foreign to her, she could not afterwards bear to witness its effects.

A pause of some duration passed now, both Georgiana and Mr Bingley inspecting the ground around them, until one of them might break the silence.

"The weather is quite mild for the seaso—"

"I wonder what is keeping your bro—"

As perfectly in unison as they had begun to speak, each stopped to cede to the other, before laughing at the concerted civilities. Fortunately, the awkwardness of the moment was carried away by the entrance of Colonel Fitzwilliam, followed immediately by his cousin.

"Pray forgive our tardiness," said Darcy with a bow; "entirely my fault for raising a matter of business near the hour." He hastened to offer a drink to everyone, but quickly on the heels of doing so, the footman announced dinner. Georgiana, as they all made their way through, lamented forgetting this duty during Fitz's absence. As much as the responsibility neglected, the procuring of drinks also would have served a ready source of converse!

ξ

Georgiana was well aware of Mr Bingley sitting next to her. Equally, she was woefully aware of her cousin Richard across the table, whose inquisitive nature would be quick to regard any word or act out of the ordinary. And yet, she debated, was it not her duty to converse with the gentleman to her side? Fitz and Richard had engaged Mrs Annesley in a discussion of interviews for a new music master. Georgiana's former, Monsieur Charbonneau, had against good advice determined to return to France. Gee liked him, she was disappointed at his leaving. But Fitz said he thought the student had surpassed the old master at any rate, and they should find another of different musical strengths if she wished to continue. While these three were occupied in this business now, however, Gee could not simply sit by with Mr Bingley. Yet, what to say?

"Do you play, Mr Bingley?" was all that came to mind.

"Not a whit," he replied. "I have no ear for music, leastways for playing it. Come to it, I cannot sing a note. And I own I have not much more patience for listening, if a piece is sombre or overlong. Give me a lively tune to which I can dance, that is the extent of my admiration."

Mr Bingley, glancing at her crestfallen expression, seemed to think he had offended. "Oh, forgive me, Miss Darcy. How stupid of me to forget your own superior skill." She assured him it was of no matter, as he went on. "Had I your talents, perhaps I should come to take more pleasure from music. Indeed, I should like to hear you play this evening, if you will."

"There is no necessity for you to punish yourself, Sir," she replied, prepared to decline before, remembering her intentions with regard to the gentleman, instead she offered, "I dare say I could muster up a lively enough reel if it came to it."

He inclined his head as he smiled. "I shall leave the selection happily to your discretion."

She glanced over at the others then, to find not her cousin Richard watching as she had feared – he was telling her companion one of his stories – but her brother with his eyes first upon Mr Bingley and then shifting to her. Fitz looked away as she caught his glance, attending with over-great interest to Richard's narrative, though it was one he had heard often. To her great surprise, Fitz had appeared neither annoyed nor concerned at what he had witnessed—a half smile had been playing about his mouth. Most curious.

Georgiana warmed to Mr Bingley's frank nature enough to keep pace with their speech for most of the meal; oddly, feeling exposed only when the servants were changing courses and conversation was suspended. They spent much effort talking of Mr Pidcock's Menagerie, an exhibition of exotic animals currently housed in the Strand. Mr Bingley had yet to take in this wonder; but was quite willing to be educated by Miss Darcy, who had attended a few days past as an indulgence of her brother's And when dinner had concluded and the ladies removed to the drawing room, she felt quite pleased with herself overall.

ξ

Mr Bingley remained the gentleman: as he accepted coffee from Georgiana, he reminded her of her promise to play. She was of mixed feeling in the matter. She knew he must ask only from a sense of obligation. And yet, she could feel much more confident, could show herself to singular advantage, when seated at the pianoforte. With her fingers gliding over the keys, calm descended upon her, a sense of freedom she seldom experienced otherwise. She was in control at such times, and it felt wonderful. She had yet to comprehend that her confidence at the instrument suited her moreover; she was never more lovely than when all her inhibitions dissolved in the notes she played. But of this she remained ignorant at present.

Her guardians looked over in surprise when the first notes of the evening proved to be a vigorous tune more suited to a country dance than a Berkeley Square parlour. More surprise followed with a reel that caught Mr Bingley and Colonel Fitzwilliam tapping their toes. Mr Bingley remained near the instrument in civility during both, and Georgiana made a point often to look up at him with a smile. When the second piece had ended, she said, "I am sorry, Sir, that we do not have a party of size to oblige you in dancing."

"Yet listening to you affords the same exhilaration, Miss Darcy."

Blushing, Georgiana began to rise; however, her brother appealed to her to play another – one of his own particular favourites of Mr Wesley's composing – which she would not refuse. But she would surely lose Mr Bingley's interest with the sonata. She wanted inspiration to retain his attentions.

A moment of riffling through the compositions on the pianoforte and she had found it. Placing the music on the stand, she called to him, "I wonder, Mr Bingley, if you will oblige me by turning pages?"

The gentleman appeared flummoxed, glancing first to Gee's companion, then to Darcy, before acquiescing. "I am happy to oblige. But, I should not be the least use to you."

She tittered. "Nonsense. I will tell you when to turn." Once again, a tilted head and demure smile appeared, which further discommoded Mr Bingley.

But he moved closer as bid, standing just to the side as Georgiana began to play. The chief of her interest, however, was not on the sheets, nor the keys; but she kept returning her glance and her smile to him, willing it to linger. She could produce the sonata with ease from memory, as often as she had delivered it. At the appropriate time, she whispered for him to turn the page. His fingers fumbled with it and once he had done, he stepped back quickly as though proximity to the parchment could burn him.

Georgiana's touch faltered then and she returned her attention to the piece immediately. She had noted Mr Bingley's unease and it fed her own. She obviously frightened the man with her unrefined overtures. Until she had done at the pianoforte, she did not look at him again except perfunctorily to direct another turn; and as soon as she later could escape the room, she wondered what he must think of her – what her brother must think if he had noticed.

ξ

Indeed, her brother had noticed. He was of two minds, but each resolved to remain silent on the matter for the moment. The first wondered at Georgiana's approaches to his friend Bingley, given her shy temperament; and especially her awkwardly overt manner of it. Even he could see she was inept in the art, yet there was something poignant, if lacking, in her ingenuous attempts. He would consult with Mrs Annesley, and direct she regard her companion with care as necessary to offer Gee guidance as she eased into society. God knew he had no wish to see his sister follow in the fashion of Miss Bingley and her ilk.

The second form of his thoughts held a peculiar sense of satisfaction in seeing the pair together. He had for some while considered the suitability of a match between his sister and his friend. It answered well. Bingley was a good man; honourable, amiable, possessed of good competence, and would respect a wife well. She was fair; would bring to the gentleman a reputable dowry, genteel temperament, education and the accomplishments of her sex in music and drawing, and connection to an old and respected family. A good match overall. True, it was one Darcy would not sanction for a time until Georgiana had been out and matured. But it was one he could support. Given that, there was little harm if the couple grew acquainted with each other, learnt to like one another with an acceptable measure of intimacy that later might be allowed to blossom into true affection. His sister was of a romantic nature, and Bingley's own sensibilities inclined towards the same. He could make her happy once his interests were engaged. And if, through Georgiana's particular interest, Bingley was able to rouse himself from lingering regrets over one Miss Bennet of Hertfordshire, all the better.

ξ

But as Darcy had noticed Georgiana's untrained efforts, so had the object of her youthful overtures done. And he was not so sanguine of his place in such matters. Darcy was his greatest friend; and Miss Darcy a well-cherished, much sheltered and protected only sister. Moreover, he was a guest in the Darcy household which carried its own responsibilities to behave with decorum. Encouraging intimacy with an unpresented young lady of the house would constitute a most contemptuous breach any guardian would find difficult to forgive. Leaving aside the notion that Bingley's affections were engaged elsewhere – for even if a union with Miss Bennet was considered an unfortunate match, his heart had not yet learnt to give her up – to allow of this course was dangerous, unconscionable. He could not contribute to its progress.

He therefore resolved at the first opportunity to address the matter—with delicacy—if Miss Darcy persisted in her attentions. And so it was that, when he came upon her alone in the breakfast room the following morning and she had acknowledged him with a timid, clumsy smile making flight impossible, he felt want of courage and diplomacy both.

"Miss Darcy," he began after the servants were out of hearing, "I wish to address... er, I mean, I feel I must... oh, dear."

Georgiana blushed violently; having all the night feared just this awkward circumstance. In a rush, she said, "Mr Bingley, forgive me, I beg you. I have trespassed sorely upon your good nature." Having begun, she blurted out her confession: that she had used him ill to practice the art of flirtation, and failed miserably.

A less amiable gentleman might have given no consideration to the lady's mortification, but fortunately Mr Bingley possessed this quality in abundance. Between his relief, his innate geniality and her innocent pliancy, each overcame discomfiture eventually to become friends over her blundering arts. Indeed, Mr Bingley agreed willingly – now comprehending her motives – to play along in her education.

And so, over the next weeks of Mr Bingley's residing in Berkeley Square, the two habitually flirted with one another with no fear on either side of harmful consequences. They came to enjoy it even, as Miss Darcy's confidence progressed – under the now understanding eye, of course, of Mrs Annesley.

But one day, having observed all this from without, Georgiana's brother approached her.

"Gee," he said, pausing to think how best to begin. "Perhaps we should sit down." He gestured to a settee in the library, and they arranged themselves there. "I wish to speak to you of Mr Bingley," he said then. Her expression adopted a wary question, but she did not otherwise respond.

"You admire the gentleman, do not you? You like him?"

"Yes, very much. He is altogether amiable."

"And would you – do you – that is to say, have you considered whether you might welcome an opportunity for him to –" this was more difficult than he had imagined, he found himself unable to say the words directly – "attach to our family?"

Her reaction confounded Darcy. Her face fell, her brow drew inward in concern. "You... you are going to marry Miss *Bingley*?"

"No! Good God! Certainly not!" His neck suffused with warm colour, and as it made its way higher, he exclaimed gracelessly. "I was conjecturing upon you marrying Mr Bingley!"

"Me! Marry Mr Bingley?" Now she competed with her brother for pride of blush.

"I have noted your attraction to him; indeed I believe you admire him more than mere attraction, is that not so?"

Georgiana sat speechless.

"You are young, my dear, and I could not sanction any understanding between you for some while yet. Certainly I have not addressed this with Bingley, nor will I do so precipitously. But I only wished to tell you, to say if a mutual attachment should transpire, that your choice would not be opposed by me, nor I think by Richard. My friend could make you a good husband one day if you wish to consider of it."

Now it was Gee's turn for ejaculation. "No! Never!"

"Wh—?"

Georgiana began to laugh now, uncontrollably. Despite every effort to bring herself under regulation, the hysterics persisted.

Completely confounded now, Darcy only stared at the young woman opposite him. "But—"

When she could speak again, Georgiana did so in gasps between regaining her breath; "I could... never marry... Mr Bingley. Why, he is... he is... like a pup... all eager affection and... loyal, but... very agreeable... but it should be like marrying my brother! Not you... but like you, do you know? Or Richard! I could never!"

Darcy shook his head. "But will you tell me I have mistaken your behaviour towards the gentleman of late? Is it possible I have done so?"

And so, painstakingly, the truth emerged. Darcy felt a small prick of disappointment at being disabused of a course he merited. Georgiana felt no small satisfaction at having played her part so well as to fool her brother, even as she regretted his misunderstanding. But in the end, she extracted a promise from him that she should never be obliged to marry where she did not wish – for whatever reasons she might object; although as her guardian he would not relinquish his right either to approve her choice or to encourage in one direction or another.

And when, some moments later, Mr Bingley himself entered the library and happened upon them together—*"My apologies, if I have interrupted intimate conversation"*— the siblings dissolved into convulsions of laughter that left their friend to question their wits.

April's Fool
(A Confluence of Coincidences)

ക്ക്ക്

I hope you may take as much enjoyment from reading this rather fanciful offering as I did in constructing it. Jane Austen gave us little of Colonel Fitzwilliam except insofar as he briefly served the plot; but it was enough to plant a very clear sketch in my own mind of a fine, affable – and amusing – gentleman. Place him with a second little-known character, his cousin Anne deBourgh, and another couple very well-known indeed, and what might happen on a day traditionally given up to... well, perhaps I've said enough.

ക്ക്ക്

"Foolish writers and readers are created for each other." -- Horace Walpole, 1717-1797

Colonel Richard Fitzwilliam sat back in his chair in a state of high anticipatory amusement. He was quite pleased with himself! *Yes, this will yield no end of pleasure, and Darcy needs a bit of lightening; his mood has been so cheerless for the last few days. When he is not scowling at some innocent remark on my part, he is instead absent in his attentions – or absent altogether, as he has taken to solitary rides and walks. What on earth has been so preoccupying my cousin and friend and leaving me to weather Aunt Dragon alone? Well, perhaps this small jest will extract the man from the gravity of his thoughts. And it may well prove my finest prank—*

Fitzwilliam looked again at the letter he had devised. It would do very well indeed. Very short, sufficiently intriguing, and he had taken great pains to write it in a hand that would be unrecognised as his own; indeed, indistinguishable as to the sex of its author as well, although he intended Darcy to believe it came from a lady. Now, he had only to ensure that it found its way to his cousin in some unremarkable manner.

Today was the first day of April and Fitzwilliam, given his easy nature, had loved since his childhood to play small pranks on his friends to mark the occasion. One had to ensure with Darcy not to give too great offence; and Fitzwilliam had learnt to his cost long ago that, though he could bring his cousin to a smile or laugh with his jests, he must take care that there be no public audience to the teazing. It had taken months for Darcy to forgive him fully on that one disastrous occasion. No, the joke must be between them alone for Darcy to mark it in good temper.

The two gentlemen at present resided at Rosings with their aunt, this being the occasion of their annual Eastertide visit to Lady Catherine deBourgh and her daughter Anne. With such property as was available to ensure privacy, Fitzwilliam had hit upon an idea to lure Darcy to a meeting point in the woods. His cousin would go there believing it to be a rendezvous with a woman – Miss Elizabeth Bennet precisely, for Fitzwilliam had noted that Darcy appeared intrigued by that young lady – but the *lady* he was to encounter would be none other than Fitzwilliam himself in disguise. He challenged himself to see how long he could engage Darcy in conversation before his cousin found him out. Fitzwilliam doubted if, given his current preoccupied state, Darcy even knew today's date, allowing this intended escapade a chance to succeed if his cousin would not anticipate the ruse. And if, on being unmasked, the colonel could bring Darcy to laugh at such nonsense, he might also manage to then elicit from his friend some explanation as to what consumed his attention.

Having congratulated himself on the form of his note, Fitzwilliam went down to breakfast, the paper secured in his waistcoat pocket. Along the way, providence smiled on him. He passed by a salver on the hall table which contained already a letter addressed to Darcy. Fitzwilliam knew it only awaited delivery to that gentleman, so he took the opportunity to slip his own smaller note underneath the original on the tray. That was the first challenge overcome. Now he had only to concern himself with how to escape the house unnoticed in his disguise later in the day. He entered the dining room at Rosings with a self-satisfied smirk and hearty appetite.

Not long after Fitzwilliam settled to his victuals, Darcy entered the breakfast room. He helped himself as well from the buffet before joining his cousin at table. After the usual morning courtesies, however, each settled to his food and his newspaper, until a footman approached to deliver some correspondence to Darcy. Fitzwilliam watched surreptitiously over his paper as his cousin took up the letters.

Darcy spent a few moments poring over the first, muttering to himself about the idiocy of solicitors at times; Fitzwilliam grew exceedingly anxious for him to put it aside for the other. At last Darcy folded the unsatisfying missive, placed it into his waistcoat pocket and turned his attention to the second, smaller letter. He regarded the front, frowning in some puzzlement before opening the missive, no doubt wondering that it did not contain his name or indeed any formal direction, only the words "In Confidence". It could be supposed meant for him only by association—of its having been delivered with the other that was distinctly addressed. He unfolded *this* note, and on reading its few interior lines, Darcy's puzzlement deepened to outright stupefaction.

Fitzwilliam took great care to maintain an impassive countenance. "Darcy, you look disturbed. Are you well? Have you had bad news?" This last he said while indicating with a nod the parchment Darcy held in his fingers. "There is no difficulty with Georgiana, surely!" *A nice touch, that*, he thought as he donned his best expression of concern.

"No, no, nothing of the kind," replied Darcy. "I am a bit distracted, that is all." Fitzwilliam shrugged indifferently to this reply and feigned, once again, a deep interest in the news of the day. He hoped Darcy would not notice this peculiarly docile behaviour – Fitzwilliam not being credited often with settling for evasive answers when his curiosity or interest was aroused. But he need not have concerned himself. Darcy had noted little of anything; he had lost all interest in his food and become quite pensive; and only a moment later, he excused himself, saying he would retire to his rooms to answer his business.

When he was certain he was alone again, Fitzwilliam sat back in contentment; his trap had been well sprung!

ξ

Darcy returned to his rooms only long enough to drop the letters carelessly onto his bed and pace the perimeter of the chamber twice, before deciding that he required greater space to think. A short walk in the air of the park would help him to order his mind and determine a prudent course to follow. Should he acquiesce to the request he had received? He removed himself to the south garden to consider it, where he paced again some while.

The letter had borne no signature, but surely it could have come only from Miss Elizabeth Bennet! It suggested – she had maintained a semblance of propriety by refraining from open invitation – that he might encounter the writer at three o'clock in the wood where they had spoken yesterday afternoon. The unsigned note intimated further that were he to venture to the little grove, he might be so fortunate as to receive intelligence to warrant and explain such a clandestine meeting.

He had met no one in the wood yesterday afternoon save Miss Elizabeth Bennet when he was out walking with Fitzwilliam—indeed it was the same grove where he had encountered this lady on several occasions since the day of their first accidental meeting there, when she had taken pains to tell Darcy it formed her customary path. He could not know Miss Bennet's hand at writing; but this bore no resemblance to Fitzwilliam's, nor would his cousin require a remote assignation to speak with Darcy in private—he would simply visit his rooms. They had encountered no one else near the hour in question.

The lady *had* appeared slightly flustered when they met the day before, though Darcy had put it down to discomfort on her part in meeting Darcy and Fitzwilliam together when she had grown accustomed to seeing him walk alone. Could it be that Miss Bennet, aware of his growing interest in her, wished to offer him encouragement? Was there more to the lady's feelings for him even than he had credited? And would a certainty of it influence the decision he had been wrestling with these days past?

Though a clandestine meeting was inappropriate – and frankly, he was astonished that she would suggest one – could he ignore it, if it would offer him a hope of reaching an understanding with Miss Elizabeth, if it offered him express permission to court her?

Surely Miss Elizabeth had meant no real impropriety with her request – he would believe her incapable of that – she merely wished to offer him the opportunity of speaking openly with her, as they had so often been thwarted from doing in company with Lady Catherine. Miss Elizabeth was not the kind of woman to trifle with a man. As such, it was probable she meant merely to ensure he knew he had her leave more openly to proffer the attentions their recent encounters had suggested. He must find out if that was the case. He would meet Miss Elizabeth in the woods this afternoon!

ξ

46

The upstairs maid, Maisie, carried a stack of clean linens down the corridor, stopping to deposit some in each of the rooms presently occupied. Once they were all distributed, she would make her way back, room by room, to make up the beds afresh. She knocked and entered Mr Darcy's chamber, and confirmed him to be out. She placed a clean set of linens on his bed. Then, as she was walking out, she stopped and set the remaining ones down also. She knew she took a chance at being discovered – and if that happened she could be dismissed summarily – but she could not help stopping a moment to look about for a sense of the gentleman in the room. His cousin, Colonel Fitzwilliam, who usually accompanied him to Rosings, was very jovial and approachable and she liked it when the Colonel visited as well. But Mr Darcy! He was so handsome – tall and dark – and so impressive in his bearing and formality! And Mrs Burleigh always spoke as how generous and condescending Mr Darcy was whenever he visited. A real gentleman, that one was...

She walked idly about the room; running her fingers, as she contemplated him, over his writing desk, picking up first his quill, then a blotter. But when she heard a noise coming from the hall, Maisie quickly grabbed the remaining linens from the bed where she had placed them, and left Mr Darcy's chamber. She scurried to the next set of rooms and left linens for Colonel Fitzwilliam, then entered the last in that hallway, that of Mistress Anne. Placing the clean linens on the lady's Davenport desk temporarily, Maisie stripped the bed of its old ones, and made it up anew. As she took the last of the sheets from the desk, a paper which had temporarily affixed itself to the bottom of the cloth, fluttered to the surface of the desk. Maisie noted it, but would not trouble to look closely at the address, as she had never learnt to read. She finished making up the room, and departed, just as Mistress Anne made her way down the hall to her chambers after breakfast.

Anne entered her chamber with the intent of retrieving a book and then making her way to the library for a morning of reading. As she approached her opened desk and took up her book, she noted a letter sitting on the edge of the desk's surface, marked "In Confidence" on the front. It must have been delivered by the maid while Anne was at her morning meal – she had seen Maisie leaving just then after straightening the room.

She took up the letter and opened it. There was little substance to it, and yet it filled Anne with unease. The note *had* to be from her cousin Darcy, for it referred to a meeting in the wood yesterday, and he was the only person whom Anne and Mrs Jenkinson had encountered there – though, curiously, the note stated yesterday 'after noon', and her meeting with him had occurred before breakfast. But her cousin had been quite distracted these days past, the time of their conversation could easily have gone unnoticed by him. Indeed, their entire conversation yesterday was characterised by a preoccupied inattentiveness on his part.

As Anne stood considering the note, a sense of foreboding overtook her. If her cousin was asking for an audience, and owing to his distractions of late, it could only mean that he had succumbed finally to her mother's harassment, and meant to offer marriage at last. Anne had long believed that, like herself, Darcy was not in favour of the match Lady Catherine had promoted since their youth; but she must have been mistaken. What other purpose could Darcy have for this private meeting at three o'clock, in so secluded a setting?

She would have to meet him – she could not offend her cousin by rejecting his advances outright, nor would her mother ever allow a refusal if she knew the overture to have been made. At least if they met in privacy this afternoon, with her mother having no advance knowledge of it (surely that was the case given the nature of invitation,) Anne might find the courage to reason with Darcy and come to some mutual agreement of release. She must *attempt* it. She would find a way to elude Mrs Jenkinson this afternoon and make her way to the designated spot just near the wood at three o'clock.

Thus decided, Anne tucked the letter into her book and made her way to the library. She found her companion there already, along with the vicar's wife. It seemed that Mrs Collins had come that morning to practice the pianoforte in the quiet part of the house and, having encountered Mrs Jenkinson as she departed, asked whether she might retrieve for her husband a book that Lady Catherine had recommended he consult in preparing his next sermon. The two ladies were perusing the library shelves for the book in question when Anne entered.

Anne returned a curtsey to Mrs Collins in greeting and in doing so, a paper fell unnoticed to the floor from the book she carried. Following a moment of clumsy discourse – for Anne never knew what to say to Mrs Collins – she asked the vicar's wife to convey her particular regards to Miss Bennet (for she had noted that Darcy took some interest in that lady, which could be useful) and then removed to a corner of the room to sit near a window and read.

While Mrs Collins resumed her search for the sermons on the shelf, Mrs Jenkinson noticed a letter on the carpet. She retrieved it and, presuming it to have fallen from the bundle of music Mrs Collins had placed on the table nearby when she entered, Mrs Jenkinson tucked the note back in among the music sheets. A few moments more, and Mrs Collins found the requisite book of sermons, took up her music, and departed for the parsonage.

ξ

Elizabeth Bennet was enjoying her weeks spent with Charlotte, but nonetheless she was happy for the solitary interlude she enjoyed this morning while her friend was at Rosings. Lizzy had much on her mind, though she kept telling herself it would come to nothing. Her visit to Hunsford had turned out quite differently, so far, from what she had imagined; owing in large part to the addition to the Rosings party of Mr Darcy and Colonel Fitzwilliam. Mr Darcy she found still an enigma and, quite often, an unpleasant one. But she had enjoyed her conversations with the Colonel, excepting that he was so often accompanied by Mr Darcy, it seemed. She had even noted that the Colonel seemed to find her handsome, and she did not revile the idea.

She realised that nothing could come of it, for Colonel Fitzwilliam, though son of an Earl, was a younger son and, as such, he must marry to advantage. But she was enjoying the flirtation with the good Colonel; she liked as well that she could flaunt before Mr Darcy the notion that at least someone in his family line appreciated her as more than barely 'tolerable.'

Lizzy heard the back parlour door open and close and knew that Charlotte must have returned. She moved to the mirror to straighten her kerchief, and went to find her friend.

Charlotte had indeed arrived home, and proceeded to put away her pianoforte music in a small storage chest. As she did, a small letter which had been tucked unknown to her between the music pages slid face down onto a chair. Charlotte saw it laying there a moment later and picked it up. Believing that she herself, in passing the chair-side table a moment ago, must have knocked it off of Lizzy's fan which lay there as well, Charlotte replaced the note, tucking it under the edge of the fan to anchor it. She was curious of its content given the strange address it contained, but heard someone approaching and, with great will, turned her back on it. A moment later, Lizzy entered the room and the two embraced in greeting.

"And how did you find the *inmates* of Rosings this morning?" Lizzy asked archly.

"Those few I saw are well enough," Charlotte replied. "I would have seen no one at all in that part of the house where Mrs Jenkinson's rooms lay, but I went to the library afterwards on an errand for Mr Collins." She held up the book of sermons. "I am most fortunate, Lizzy, that Lady Catherine allows us to practice at Rosings, even if *you* laugh at her condescension. For even the pianoforte in Mrs Jenkinson's rooms is superior to any I have ever been honoured to play before. Oh, and I am commended particularly to give you a message from *one* of the inmates there, indeed from—"

Charlotte's attention was arrested in mid-sentence by a frantic call from her husband outside in the garden. He sounded in great distress. "Oh, dear," she said, "I had best go and find out what Mr Collins is on about!" With that, Charlotte forgot all about her charge to convey Miss deBourgh's regard, and went out into the garden to see what new crisis her husband had manufactured. Truly, he could be so annoying, turning every little insect or mold spore he found into a full-scale pestilence for his peonies.

ξ

Lizzy chuckled at yet another domestic crisis that Charlotte would smooth over with her good sense, and went to retrieve the fan she had left earlier in the morning. Tucked under it, she found a letter which, on overturning it, she found marked "In Confidence." Ah. This must be the message Charlotte had alluded to before Mr Collins interrupted their discourse. But how very oddly it was addressed! She retreated to her bedroom to read in privacy.

She had to sit down on the bed in wonder when she finished the short missive. What could this mean? She felt relieved she had not opened the note in the parlour where Charlotte or Mr Collins might have entered at any time.

The note was unsigned; but Lizzy could attribute it only to one person. It had to be from Colonel Fitzwilliam! The few lines mentioned having met in the wood yesterday afternoon, and it was true that while out walking, Lizzy did come upon Colonel Fitzwilliam and Mr Darcy in a pretty clearing there.

Mr Darcy would never deign to request a meeting with Lizzy; indeed, by his speech, his whole manner of watching her, he had made it clear that he found her company barely tolerable in all respects. There was a conversation after dinner at Rosings she recalled particularly a few nights before, which had left Lizzy curious about the man – and possibly the smallest bit guilty for having bested him with her wit, for he had seemed taken aback and curiously pained by her words. But no matter; he had deserved them then, and no doubt any injury had been quite short-lived, given his overall opinion of her, or rather his high opinion of himself. Surely he would not demand an interview between them, and in private, to seek satisfaction. She enjoyed a laugh merely at the idea of it.

There had also been that peculiar call he made upon her one morning at the parsonage. For one brief moment, Lizzy had thought that perhaps he had come to apologize to her for his arrogant behaviour directed towards her; this was the only reason she could account for his not being able to converse fluently, when his own cousin had once confirmed that it must be attributed generally to his being unwilling to give himself the trouble.

She laughed again at the memory of that visit. Words of apology naturally would come hard to a man like Darcy, she thought, and so it had proved. That part of him that was a gentleman and understood his continual offences against Lizzy warred apparently with the proud man who believed her undeserving of contrition on his part. She half believed that the gloves he had sat wringing so assiduously were, in his mind, a substitute for her own neck. In the end, with Charlotte's arrival, his haughty reserve had won the battle and he had departed unshriven.

No, Mr Darcy would not willingly seek a meeting with Lizzy. Even on those occasions when she had met him in these very woods he now directed her to, when he would turn and walk with her, she could only believe it had been from a sense of obligation, so silent did he prove for much of it.

Therefore, the request to meet this afternoon must come from the good Colonel. Lizzy knew the Colonel to be of good character and, as such, could not believe that he would request such a private audience with her unless it be with one object in mind – to seek her hand! And yet, as much as she enjoyed their flirtations, she had difficulty believing that the affections of either had moved beyond such a stage. Given the gentleman's reduced financial means and Lizzy's lack of dowry, it would not be an advantageous match for either, but especially for him. She did not love him; indeed, she liked him very much, too much so to accept him solely on that basis when the marriage could do little good for them. She would have to meet him this afternoon, if only to refuse gently what each knew rationally to be an ill-devised match. Still, she felt flattered at drawing the attentions of such a man.

As she thought this, she reflected back with some little regret on Mr Collins's proposal to her at Longbourn some months ago, and the needless embarrassment he had suffered at her refusal being witnessed by her entire family. She could not, of course, regret that she had rejected Mr Collins then, or now; only the mode of it. She would spare Colonel Fitzwilliam a similar fate by meeting him privately in the wood. Surely no one could judge her harshly for wishing to treat the man's sensibilities kindly.

ξ

At two o'clock, Fitzwilliam and Darcy sat on the terrace at Rosings, enjoying a respite from Lady Catherine. She had accosted both men that morning and asked them to attend her in the drawing room, as she wished to ask their advice on some small estate matter. The small matter, as they knew it would, took hours to discuss... or rather, took hours of forbearance on the part of the gentlemen as Lady Catherine discussed it with herself. For she allowed no opinions on the subject other than her own and having, after an interminable length of time, convinced herself that her initial decision was the right one, she had finally gone off to wreak havoc with her steward, no doubt, until dinner.

The two men shared the contents of a brandy decanter, well-earned in their opinion, as they absorbed the peaceful air of a warm spring day; only an occasional birdsong dispelled the quiet. Darcy glanced often at his pocket watch and began to wonder how he could extricate himself from Fitzwilliam's company within the next half hour or so, in order to make his way to the wood for his appointment with Miss Bennet. He was therefore surprised, but gratified, when Fitzwilliam professed to suffering a headache and asked Darcy's leave. With a perfunctory show of concern for his cousin's well-being, Darcy sent the man on his way. He continued his leisure on the terrace until he could stand the suspense no longer. At half past the hour, Darcy began to make his way through the woodland paths to the clearing where he had last met Miss Bennet in the west end of the park.

Fitzwilliam, when he quit the terrace, had made his way to his chambers and, with the assistance of the footman, Crawley, on loan to him as valet during his tenure at Rosings, he began his transformation into a woman. He received a careful shave, even though he had already done the same this morning – he did not wish a trace of shadow to give away his true identity too soon – and then began the process of donning his attire. Through stealth, he and Crawley previously had procured items to make up a full ensemble from the dressing rooms of Lady Catherine, Mrs Jenkinson, his cousin Anne, and a storage closet in the housekeeper's wing. There had been no opportunity to perfect his impersonation in advance, but Fitzwilliam thought he could do quite nicely – how difficult could it be? He favoured his mother in looks, did he not? And he had heard her proclaimed a handsome woman.

Thinking in this manner that it should be a simple process to dress, they soon learnt otherwise. They began with a corset. After several minutes of cursing, tangling, more cursing, untangling, and yanking (at one point during which, Crawley had his foot leveraged on Fitzwilliam's posterior), the two men finally had the monstrous device in place with some efficacy of purpose, and stuffed with rolled neck cloths to fill out the bosom. Fitzwilliam had a likeness for good food and drink – his would never be the form of a stylish young lady; yet the corset held in enough to give the impression of something between a coquette and a childbirth-weary matron.

The process, however, took such a time that Fitzwilliam knew he would be late arriving in the grove. He could dawdle no longer, for Darcy would not have the tolerance to wait long alone there. He hurried then to don the remaining articles – petticoats, gown, tucker, stockings. He paused long enough to wonder how women ever arrived anywhere on time with all these foolish fashion necessities to attend to first. Thankfully, Mrs Jenkinson had rather large feet and he had found in her dressing closet a pair of slippers into which he could just squeeze his feet.

Doubting he ever would make his way to the wood (and at this point, wondering why he had committed himself to this folly) when he could hardly breathe for the corset, and the pointed toes of the slippers pinched his feet miserably, Fitzwilliam nevertheless started towards the door to quit his chambers when Crawley called out, "Sir!"

Turning to the footman, Fitzwilliam beheld the woman's wig in Crawley's hand, and he reached up to touch his own head as he laughed. He would not get far in his deception if he should forget that! It would all of it be for nothing. Crawley settled the wig on Fitzwilliam's head, and the two poked and prodded to ensure all of the gentleman's locks were obscured by the hairpiece. Having completed the job to satisfaction, they then regarded Fitzwilliam's appearance in the mirror. Not an attractive woman by any means, Fitzwilliam thought to himself, but perhaps with a well-positioned fan to obscure his face, he could fool his cousin for a few moments. He completed his attire by donning a bonnet and light cloak.

At signal from Crawley, who had surveyed the corridor to ensure no one was about, Fitzwilliam followed the footman down the back stairs and through the servant quarters to depart the house unnoticed. He began to make his way to the clearing in the west grove, to where he and Darcy had come upon Miss Bennet the afternoon before. He should be only a few moments late for the rendezvous.

ξ

Anne deBourgh and Mrs Jenkinson had passed the hours after noon in Anne's private parlour over some letters. Every few minutes, when she knew Mrs Jenkinson's attention to be engaged in writing, Anne glanced at the regulator clock on her mantel to gauge her time. Just before half past two, she sighed. Drawing no reaction from her companion, she sighed again, louder this time.

"Miss Anne?" said Mrs Jenkinson, and looked at the young woman with concern.

"Oh, it is nothing, truly," responded Anne, "only a slight indisposition. Perhaps it is a strain on my eyes from writing so long, after reading earlier? I shall recover in a moment, I am certain—it is only a passing faint."

"Nonsense!" cried Mrs Jenkinson, jumping up. "We can finish our letters tomorrow, you must not overtire yourself, my dear." As she spoke, Mrs Jenkinson turned down the coverlet on Anne's bed, and motioned her charge to come over and rest. "Why, whatever will your mother say if you are too unwell to dine this evening, what with Mr Darcy being here and all? I am sure she will have my head on a platter for it!"

Anne got into bed and allowed herself to be tucked in snugly, while Mrs Jenkinson continued. "Now, you rest there while I go and prepare a tisane for your ailment."

"No!" Mrs Jenkinson fair jumped at the vehemence of Anne's demurral, and Anne hastened to calm down. "I am sorry, Mrs Jenkinson, for startling you. I only meant that I do not require a tisane." As her companion began to shake her head in disagreement, Anne precluded her commenting. "I feel more myself already, truly. I am certain that if we draw the drapes, and I lie quietly just for a while – and *undisturbed* – I will be quite fit for dinner this evening with Mr Darcy and Colonel Fitzwilliam."

With reservation, Mrs Jenkinson agreed. She drew Anne's drapes before leaving. "You rest, my dear. I will ensure that no one disturbs your peace," she said as she exited the room.

Anne regretted deceiving Mrs Jenkinson in this way, for she was an excellent companion and a good friend to Anne. But, in the end, she also was a servant of Lady Catherine, and would have felt honour-bound to report to her employer any private appointment between Anne and Darcy. Anne resolved to make it up to her in some way later, despite that the lady could not realise she was being assuaged for an offence.

Anne took up a cloak and quietly made her way out of her room, reflecting that, although she hated her sickly constitution generally, there were times such as these when it could be used to advantage, for no one suspected her of deceit when she claimed an indisposition.

Fortunately, she met no one as she left the house, and she skirted its walls as cover until reaching the garden path that would take her towards the south wood. She sighed in relief on nearing it, at her continued good fortune in meeting no one. She only hoped her interview with Darcy would go as smoothly.

ξ

Elizabeth Bennet and Charlotte Collins had spent the after noon in the fresh air, embroidering cushion covers for the parlour at Hunsford. It was such an unusually warm spring day that Mr Collins had suggested they have their chairs moved into the garden, and this they had readily agreed upon. While the women tended to their stitching, Mr Collins trimmed plants, removed some rose hips which had escaped his attentions last autumn, and practiced his Sunday sermon on the voles and rabbits that scurried now and again through the border hedges.

Lizzy had positioned her chair such that she could look in through the parlour window and, if she craned her neck just a bit, she could see the long-case clock in the corner of the room. This she did with regularity until she noted that the time had gone half past the hour of two. She stretched her limbs a bit so that Charlotte would notice and, indeed, upon her friend's glancing her way, Lizzy said, "Charlotte, my dear, you know I have limited patience for sitting long with a needle. Would you mind awfully if I were to walk a while?"

Charlotte agreed, as Lizzy had known she would do. Of course Eliza was welcome to her walk! An offer was on Charlotte's tongue to join her friend for a turn in the park, but she observed that Lizzy bit her lower lip slightly as though forming an excuse for just such a suggestion. Instead, Charlotte asked Lizzy if she would mind going on her own, as she herself was quite settled in her chair in the sunshine; and she noted with some amusement that her friend took palpable relief in this, as she made her way from the garden.

Charlotte did wonder at Eliza's real purpose; but hoped that this might have something to do with the gentlemen now residing some weeks at Rosings. On several previous walks, Eliza had *accidentally* met with one or the other of Mr Darcy and Colonel Fitzwilliam and the gentlemen had turned to accompany her back to Hunsford parsonage. Charlotte had no wish to stand in the way of the natural order if something might transpire in that quarter; she often hoped a more intimate association would result for her friend from one of these gentlemen.

ξ

Darcy had arrived well before the appointed hour, his anxiety over the coming meeting driving his pace. Once there, he walked the perimeter of a grassy opening in the grove, turned and retraced his steps, rehearsing in his mind what he might possibly say to Miss Bennet, wondering what she intended saying to him. He found it difficult to concentrate, for recalling his fool's performance a few mornings before at the parsonage; and also because, as Miss Elizabeth had requested this conference, he must follow her turn in it. This was certainly not a position in which he was accustomed to find himself. He did, for a brief moment, smile to reflect that since this morning's meeting was out of doors, he still wore his gloves - at least they would be safe on this day from additional mutilation. But the humour he found in this was short-lived as he quaked at the possibility of a similar conversational performance today. Why did this woman so get under his skin as to make of him either a blathering fool or a mute!

ξ

Colonel Fitzwilliam meandered on the path through the west wood, stopping every few steps to wince at the pain in his arches. This small hoax of his had seemed a perfect jest in the planning of it, but the thing itself was of another sort; he had not adequately accounted for the discomfort of women's fashion. If he remained much longer in the blasted corset, his breathing would be constricted for life, and he was certain that he had already formed bunions on both feet. Never again would he complain about his boots after a long day!

Fitzwilliam was still some yards from the small opening in the grove when he caught the first glimpse of Darcy, pacing back and forth and muttering to himself. At least his cousin was still there waiting – the colonel, since Darcy had not given up and left when no one appeared on time, had not suffered the discomfort of his disguise only to find no audience to appreciate it. He readjusted his corset as best he could, and cleared his throat so as to enable him to raise the register of his voice in anticipated discourse; and he took a step towards entering the little clearing. Before he could complete that first step, however, he stopped in his tracks; for on the far side of the clearing, he espied Miss Elizabeth Bennet walk into view. He watched as Miss Bennet approached his preoccupied cousin.

ξ

"Mr Darcy!" the lady exclaimed. "I expected... that is, I thought..." She stopped her speech entirely, apparently uncertain how to continue.

"Miss Elizabeth." Darcy bowed to the lady, who curtsied in return automatically. A profound silence then ensued, with each party awaiting the initiation of discourse by the other.

Oh, bother, mused Lizzy, *not another awkward encounter as seems to have become our habit.* Lizzy sighed, and shifted her position. *At least today, he cannot mangle a blameless pair of gloves! Although he is doing creditably with the long edge of his coat...*

Colonel Fitzwilliam, seeing that his prank had suffered a setback, stood transfixed, debating whether to join the couple and reap his humiliation from them both, or wait to see if Miss Bennet would withdraw after common pleasantries. Darcy *may* have presupposed he would meet *her* there, but the lady could have no inclination other than this was a chance encounter. *Perhaps I should have anticipated that Miss Bennet might take it upon herself to walk to-day in the same direction as yesterday. How do I always manage to bungle the best-laid deceptions? If only I had not been delayed by this blasted corset!*

Miss Elizabeth glanced around the clearing as if in expectation of finding something – or someone – else. Finally, her countenance puzzled, she turned her gaze upon Darcy. "The Colonel... he does not accompany you today?"

"No. No, he does not." Darcy frowned with incomprehension; little knowing that Colonel Fitzwilliam from his hiding place among the trees, beamed at being thus remembered.

Miss Elizabeth has requested this confluence, posited Darcy; *surely she did not presume that I myself should secure another party to act as chaperone. Does she play with me for sport?* He felt need to expound on his denial. "Indeed, Madam, you seem surprised to see me here." *Had she believed I would not respond to her letter; would fail to come to the grove?*

"Yes, I am somewhat," Lizzy replied. *For I was expecting someone else entirely!*

A hundred thoughts raced across Lizzy's mind at that moment as she struggled to settle on one. The first to establish itself, quite resolutely, was that she had made a horrid mistake. It was not Colonel Fitzwilliam who had written her the letter, but Mr Darcy after all. But in that instance, what could it possibly mean?

Meanwhile, Colonel Fitzwilliam again cursed the folly of this ill-founded venture. He considered that he would do well to divorce himself from any blame Darcy might apportion to him in bringing about this meeting. In addition, he fast became discomfited at being privy to the clear tension existing between his cousin and Miss Bennet. Why had he never noted this before?

As such, the good colonel decided to make his way quietly back to Rosings and leave Darcy to whatever might transpire in his chance encounter with the lady. With luck, he would reach his rooms, change back into the affable Richard Fitzwilliam, and none would be the wiser but Crawley, whose silence the Colonel was sure he could find ample incentive to secure.

For an instant, he had nearly made himself known to the couple for the sake of Miss Bennet – he had not previously considered her reputation in the matter, either in her actual appearance now by an unhappy accident, or even in Darcy's supposing her to have written him. He should have to atone to the lady somehow.

Carefully retracing his steps until sufficiently distanced from the others, Fitzwilliam then hobbled back towards the house, exclaiming in pain with each step and with the hope that the worst this day would bring might be sore feet and a greater appreciation for the grace and beauty that women managed to convey with such apparent ease.

ξ

Fitzwilliam's departure was so timed that he missed Elizabeth's next attempt to draw out Darcy's purpose. "An unsigned letter is perhaps an unusual method to gain one's attention, Sir..." she ventured.

"I cannot disagree, Miss Bennet. One must acknowledge, however, that it has served its purpose." With these words, he took some steps towards Miss Bennet, closing the gap between them to but a few paces so that they could speak in more modulated tones. But it seemed silence was still to be the order of day. It settled over them once again as a blanket, punctuated only by the occasional chirp of a wood thrush or a rustling of the spring breeze through linden branches.

Darcy flicked his glance to the left towards the wood from whence Miss Elizabeth had come. In his discomfort, the rueful question came to him as to whether the same cat claimed her tongue now as had captured his own so many times. Perhaps the lady regretted her rash behaviour in having issued an invitation for private assignation, even as he now certainly regretted accepting it.

At long last, the lady could bear the ludicrous silence no more. If the gentleman had some business with her, let him get to it; for with every moment they prolonged this farcical exchange, the unseemliness of their private encounter grew in severity. For someone quick to disdain impropriety in the conduct of others, Mr Darcy seemed to hold himself accountable to a lesser standard; but Lizzy determined she would compromise herself no further.

"Mr Darcy," she began, and the gentleman returned his attention to her. "You have something you wish to say to me?"

Darcy was taken aback at the Miss Bennet. *Good heavens*, he thought, *but she is quite forward, is she not? How ever am I to answer such impertinence, and not being cognisant of her intentions?*

"Have I something I wish to say to you?" he replied. Miss Bennet noted the distracted repetition of her question, and the ungenerous thought came to her that she could have had the same or similar converse with one of Lady Catherine's parrots, and at far less risk to her reputation. But Darcy realised it was incumbent upon him to do more than repeat Miss Elizabeth's own words, and he continued.

"I trust you are well, Miss Bennet?" Darcy picked at his coattail yet again as he asked this. He knew it to be a laughable question as soon as the words escaped him, yet he was so puzzled by Miss Elizabeth's presumptuous manner that platitudes seemed the extent of his talents of discourse at the moment.

"Yes, quite well." She answered him, but her countenance took on an expression of annoyance. *Really, the man is insufferable. He lured me into this wood with a cryptic note* (for she was far less forgiving of the method of communication now that she realised it had not been from the Colonel) *and then expects me, apparently, to carry the burden of conversation!* Lizzy's mind drifted to their history – and particularly to a disastrous dinner party some nights before at Rosings. Was that what this is about? She knew he had been offended when she turned his aunt's very phrase against him to exhort him to the trouble of practicing the art of conversation. But – had he taken her remark to heart? Was this his attempt at such? And could their nonsensical meeting at the parsonage a few days before have been another such attempt?

While Miss Bennet was thus turned inward, Darcy watched her for some sign that she might come to her purpose at last. So far, this had been a highly unsatisfactory exchange, and certainly unworthy of the clandestine nature of the invitation. As he thought on this, he became more and more annoyed as well at the imposition on his time and his repute. Cognisant that he had thought little enough of it these past days when he would meet her in the wood and turn to walk back with her to Hunsford—they had indeed been alone then as well with no cause for censure; but the mere fact of their both knowing this one to have been solicited purposely (if that purpose should ever come to light) made it unseemly in the extreme.

In a final attempt to move things along, Darcy asked, "And are you having a pleasant visit at the parsonage, and in Kent generally?"

"I have enjoyed it very much *to date*, Sir." Darcy wondered at the lady's emphasis on 'to date' and noted the edge of exasperation in her tone. Whatever had he said or done now to warrant her displeasure, except to accede to her wishes in being here? Before he could form a reply, however, Miss Bennet continued.

"I have known Mrs Collins for many years, since we were children; and her remove from Hertfordshire after her marriage has been strongly felt by her many friends. As such, I have welcomed this opportunity to restore our intimacy." Elizabeth could not help but redirect this discourse to her own purposes, since the gentleman refused to come to his point. Thinking not of Charlotte, but of her dear sister Jane and Mr Bingley, she went on. "My sister's being in Town since the new year also diminished my source of amusements at home; as such, the opportunity to call upon my relations in Kent was fortuitous."

She paused for an instant, and watched Mr Darcy closely as she then said, "Do not you agree, Mr Darcy, that it is a sad condition when two people who care for one another are separated by distances, real or imagined, and denied the opportunity to further their amiable feelings?" Elizabeth was uncertain still of the particular role Mr Darcy may have played in separating Jane Bennet from her heart's desire; she hoped by this subject to elicit corroboration of his complicity, if such was to be had.

"I do indeed, Miss Bennet." Darcy dared not hope that he was interpreting her correctly. Was this, in fact, the confirmation he had anticipated—that she welcomed his advances? "There is no question but that earnest affection should be given the opportunity to flourish."

"Indeed," echoed the lady. "And is it not also true, Sir, that 'earnest affection' as you call it, is further desecrated when a want of fortune in one party prohibits its natural progress?"

"It is." Darcy tried not display on his part how astounded he was at Miss Bennet's forthright manner. That he had also wrestled with this issue over the past months was undeniable, yet to have the lady herself raise it so openly to him was a surprise, especially when she, in fact, held the inferior position in their circumstance. Surely, this was an acknowledgement of the disparity between their own stations; but was she conveying to him her persuasion that they could neither of them acknowledge any affection on the basis of it, or lamenting that his superiority in such things made it impossible for her to confess openly any warmth of feeling for him?

Elizabeth watched Mr Darcy closely as he considered her question. His reply had been simple enough—too taciturn by far— and gave nothing away. Yet his demeanour was unsettled, and suggested to Elizabeth that he might, indeed, have been the primary party to have spirited Mr Bingley away from Netherfield last autumn. It was just as she had always surmised. Small wonder if he now lacked the courage to admit of it openly.

Darcy wanted time to consider Miss Bennet's words and their import. He must not act rashly, must carefully weigh her opinions in relation to his own. But he was heartened by the suggestion that she might harbour some esteem of him. Still, he was confused by her cold manner which was decidedly at odds with her words. He decided finally to address the lady more directly.

"Miss Bennet, in your letter, you..." he began.

"In my letter!" The astonishment in Miss Bennet's voice stopped Darcy in mid sentence.

He began again, "Yes, in your letter wherein you suggested this appointment..." Again, he was interrupted.

"Sir!" Her eyes flared with indignation. "I dispatched no letter, indeed I am instead in receipt of one! I have it here. Can you deny that you had it delivered to me?" So saying, she produced a note from the pocket in her skirt and held it out.

Darcy took a step forward where, at a nod of permission from the lady, he took the parchment from her. He glanced down at it quickly, then back to her. "Miss Bennet, I do not comprehend. I do *indeed* deny having proffered this invitation; however, this letter is quite similar to one delivered to *me* but this morning. It sits now in my room at the house."

Miss Bennet was stunned, yet some small part of her could not help but wonder if Mr Darcy prevaricated, since his 'letter' conveniently was not on his person. Perhaps this was just a ploy to deny culpability in organising what had become another great muddle. *But then*, she relented, *he does appear truly astonished, and for all my dislike of the man, I cannot imagine him so little a gentleman as to compromise my honour, or his, in such a way.*

Mr Darcy continued to study the letter, noting that it was not only similar, but precisely the same as that he had received, even down to the torn corner on the bottom left of the parchment. This was curious indeed. Could someone have spirited the letter from his own rooms and delivered it to another party? Namely, to Miss Bennet? How? And moreover, who would have done so? Even as he wondered this, a glimmer of possible explanation came to him. *Fitzwilliam*, he mumbled under his breath.

"Mr Darcy? Do you speak to me? I could not distinguish it."

Darcy looked up again at Miss Bennet. "Forgive me. I believe perhaps my cousin Fitzwilliam has something to answer for here."

"The colonel! But what purpose could he have? Why?"

Darcy explained that, if neither of them had in fact written the note, Fitzwilliam must have done. "Who else would know that we met in the wood yesterday in this very spot?" His brow moved into a frown then. "But as to why, I cannot fathom it."

It seemed they were both at a loss—first to understand and then what to do next. They fidgeted and glanced about some moments, until a notion came to Darcy.

"Miss Bennet, I beg you will indulge me a moment more." She looked at him, curious. "What is today's date?"

"The date?" Elizabeth wondered if the gentleman had lost his senses now. "Er… let me see… today is Tuesday… the first of April."

The information, once spoken aloud, informed both parties at once. Elizabeth closed her eyes even as Mr Darcy said, "Madam, I believe we are unwitting victims of an April Fools' jest."

Elizabeth winced and nodded in agreement; then opened her eyes once again to Mr Darcy. "But why would your cousin choose such a form of prank; what amusement can he gain from it?"

"Why I cannot hazard to say, nor what pleasure could be gained from it. But as to whom…I am convinced." Darcy saw the same in Miss Bennet's eyes even without want of confirmation. For who, indeed, but Colonel Fitzwilliam knew that they had met in this glade the day before. Darcy said, "I am afraid my cousin has always had a penchant for this date and its inherent license to make fools of his friends. Since childhood, it has been characteristic also that he *bungle* the job miserably. I suspect this is another such poorly executed endeavour. No doubt he meant to be here to engineer some further mortification, but was prevented doing so."

"Well, Mr Darcy," replied Elizabeth, "it appears we *were* made the fools, you and I – does it not?" Darcy detected a note of amusement in Miss Bennet's statement, and yet underneath it, some deeper meaning he could not like. She continued, "There could be no two people, I believe, with less to say to each other in such an assignation. But perhaps Colonel Fitzwilliam, being as he must unaware of our history, had some innocent purpose." When the gentleman remained silent but reddened considerably, she concluded, "Now that we have unearthed this plot, then, I will bid you good day, Sir, and return to my friends with no harm done."

"Indeed. Good day, Miss Bennet." Darcy longed to say more – longed to tell her that their meeting, though arranged under false pretence, might yet take a serious turn if she would consider his advances; for surely the interest she had conveyed to him before discovering the counterfeit purpose of their meeting had been sincere. Certainly she had been content enough to come to the grove, to engage him in converse when their paths crossed, and for those few moments that she believed the letter to have come from him. But he spoke none of this. He bowed in farewell and watched as she began to walk away. He was just rousing himself to return in the opposite direction to Rosings when, at the edge of the clearing,

Miss Elizabeth turned around and the two held each other's gaze for a moment before proceeding along their separate paths.

ξ

As Fitzwilliam approached Rosings from the wood, he once again stopped short and emitted a groan. Lady Catherine was established on the west terrace, and, what was more, she apparently entertained two ladies unknown to the Colonel. There was no way for him to regain the house from this direction without being seen, and Fitzwilliam would suffer a corset for weeks on end rather than be caught in his present state by his aunt. She would never forgive him (and would remind him of such at every turn) if he were to humiliate her in front of her acquaintances.

Wisely, he determined that he would walk the longer path through the wood, and approach the house from the south side in hope that he could evade detection. After several minutes, he passed again out of the wood into another opening that led to the garden. He knew that if he turned towards the east at this point, he would gain the house in short order. So intent was he on this goal that he did not notice he had company in the clearing. He was nearly at the end of it and ready to enter the garden yet again when he spied his cousin Anne sitting very still to one side on a flat rock. Her companion did not accompany her. Most curious.

She had obviously seen him, he could tell by her puzzled expression. He could not continue on without stopping to acknowledge her. Taking a deep breath, he limped over to Miss Anne and, adopting his most lady-like voice, said, "Good day to you, Miss deBourgh."

"Good day... er... Madam." Anne hesitated another instant before continuing, a hint of amusement in her tone. "Are we acquainted, Madam?"

Fitzwilliam spent some moments devising a plausible story of being a relative newcomer to the village of Hunsford. He introduced himself as one Mrs Ambrose, a widow lately arrived from Wiltshire. Lady Catherine had offered to counsel her new neighbour as to settling in to the area and its society, and Mrs Ambrose had been on her way to consult that good lady on a recommendation for a local dress maker. 'She' acknowledged then that she had recognized Miss Anne from having seen her pass with her mother in their carriage on occasion.

Anne, as this strange person related 'her' tale, wondered at just what Richard Fitzwilliam was about. As she had sat waiting for Darcy to arrive, she had become increasingly concerned that she would end this day engaged to the gentleman for being unable to convince him not to make an offer. As the minutes had passed and Darcy did not appear, Anne was uncertain whether to be relieved that he might have changed his mind, or alarmed that he must be making his appeal directly to Lady Catherine while Anne fretted in the wood. She began to feel a proper *fool* indeed. And with that notion had come the realisation that today was the first of April.

Anne deBourgh may have suffered her six and twenty years with a weak constitution, but there was nothing wrong with her mind. In fact, her forced lifestyle of inactivity gave her intellectual powers great opportunity for exercise. She began to wonder if her solitary tenure in this spot was some sort of silly jest, although she could not see how anyone could glean satisfaction from a joke he could not witness. She had been considering this point when she noticed someone enter at the near side of the wood. It appeared to be a woman at first glance, and yet there was nothing womanly about the form.

As the person had drawn closer, as yet unaware of Anne's presence, she could see that the *'woman'* was in fact her cousin Richard Fitzwilliam. Of course! Fitzwilliam had been attempting ruses on the first of April since they were all children together, and usually failed miserably at them. Although still she could ascertain no purpose in this one, Anne knew it quite clearly for another in a long line of her cousin's botched pranks. With great effort, she adopted an impassive expression and decided to use this encounter to her own ends.

'Mrs Ambrose,' or rather Fitzwilliam, stopped talking as he noted that Anne's countenance had taken on a decidedly morose aspect. Again using his best female voice (deplorable if he had only known it), he asked, "My dear, are you ill?"

Anne smiled inwardly while maintaining her sad expression. "No, Mrs Ambrose, not ill. But I am sorely distressed and want desperately for someone to speak to of my miserable circumstance. May I confide in you?"

Fitzwilliam spluttered in his attempt to dissuade Anne from this course, but she would have none of it. She insisted that she recognized a figure of sensibility and compassion in Mrs Ambrose and, before he could pull himself out from the situation, Fitzwilliam found himself seated next to his cousin on the rock, listening to her story unfold.

"You see, Mrs Ambrose, my mother would have me marry my cousin, Mr Darcy. It is something she has devoutly wished since we were children, without any regard for the feelings of me or of the gentleman." Fitzwilliam was profoundly uncomfortable with the direction this dialogue was moving, but Anne continued so quickly that he could do nothing to extricate himself from it. "This morning, I received a letter from Mr Darcy, requesting that I meet him here regarding a matter of some import…"

"A letter!" demanded Fitzwilliam. Anne needed all her strength to maintain her composure and not laugh outright at the fact that 'Mrs Ambrose's' voice had suddenly deepened considerably. Fitzwilliam recovered his higher register, and followed with, "You received a letter from the gentleman? To-day?"

"Indeed I did, Mrs Ambrose. It was marked 'In Confidence' and directed me to meet him in the wood where we had some converse yesterday. This very wood and this clearing, Mrs Ambrose, is where I saw him yesterday morning. Given our family's expectations, I can only conclude that he meant to propose. Except the gentleman has not appeared and it is well past the hour appointed."

'Mrs Ambrose' fidgeted for a moment, wondering all the while at how his letter could have fallen into *Anne's* hands as well. Could Darcy not be trusted to discretion? But he must address the issue to hand. "Perhaps the gentleman was afraid that you would refuse him?"

"You see, that is the problem. I *would* refuse him, and he would be glad of it, for I am certain he would ask only from obligation. He does not care for me, not in that way; nor do I for him. But he has not come today, for me to encourage our release."

Fitzwilliam knew he should say something, but he could think of nothing the least useful. He knew, of course, that Darcy was disinclined to accede to Aunt Catherine's match, but he had never considered whether Anne shared the feeling. Some part of him was pleased with this intelligence, though he could little explain why it should matter to him. As he considered how to answer Anne, she continued.

"But there is, Mrs Ambrose, another complication which arises in the circumstance." Fitzwilliam could not conceive what further complication could exist. He was inclined to *wish* to know nothing of it in the least, but his cousin, now leaning closer to him, had other ideas. "May I confide to you the deepest secrets of my heart? For I have no one else at my disposal, you see, who is not concerned in the affair – and I should so like to relieve my bosom of this burdensome anguish." She waited not at all for her friend to offer consolatory approval or to demur, but immediately said, "You see, as it happens, I am in *love* with my cousin. Very deeply, irreconcilably in love with him."

Fitzwilliam nearly choked. How could he possibly respond to that? He began, "But Miss deBourgh, you have only just said that you do not care for him in that way! I do not understand…"

Anne smiled ingenuously. "Oh, you are correct. I do not care for Mr Darcy in that way. You see, it is my *other* cousin whom I love desperately. Colonel Fitzwilliam." She blushed and smiled sweetly. "Dear Richard. I have been in love with him these many years, since we were children."

'Mrs Ambrose' nearly fell off the rock.

While her cousin sat, astounded into immobility, Anne rose gracefully, sighing deeply as she did so. "Mrs Ambrose, thank you so much. I cannot tell you how much better I feel for having spoken the truth aloud. Just saying the words to another living soul has lightened me considerably, even if my predicament is not resolved. I believe I will return to the house now; I grow fatigued from the air. May I accompany you and show the way to my mother?"

Fitzwilliam still sat, trying to absorb what he had just heard. Anne repeated her invitation to escort 'Mrs Ambrose' to Rosings, and finally, with great effort, Fitzwilliam replied that he thought he would come back another day after all. The hour was advancing now and 'she' could not wish to call at such an unwelcome one. She would remain instead a few moments to rest there in the sun before making her way back to her own house in the village.

Anne smiled, thanked the 'lady' once more for listening so well, and walked home serenely. Cousin Richard would certainly remember *this* first day in April for a long time to come. For that matter, so would Anne.

She also could not help but acknowledge something else. She truly had felt better for having such a perfect opportunity to speak the truth about the direction her affections took. Now it remained only to be seen what her cousin might do with the information.

Hedging

ઠૐૐ

The English language is wonderful – so often a dozen words may be used to designate the same thing; and at other times one word may have multiples meanings, and even more levels of nuance.

hedge (n.): originally any fence, living or artificial; figurative sense of "boundary, barrier;" a row of bushes or small trees planted close together; hedgerow; an act or means of preventing complete loss of a bet, an argument, an investment, or the like, with a partially counterbalancing or qualifying one. (v.): "make a hedge," also "surround with a barricade or palisade;" "dodge, evade;" "insure oneself against loss," by playing something on the other side. To prevent or hinder free movement; obstruct. To protect with qualifications that allow for unstated contingencies or for withdrawal from commitment

ઠૐૐ

It was a glorious morning! Much too glorious to remain indoors when Providence had arranged for the benefit of the former Charlotte Lucas (now Collins by a lesser Providence) to combine a day of unmitigated sun with an all-too-brief few hours of leisure. She had not an obligation in the world until her husband should return from his visit to the next parish. Then they would all dress for an engagement of dinner at the great house. But not wishing at present to dwell on the evening to come and diminish the sunny mood she enjoyed, Charlotte applied herself instead to determining how she might best pass this brief respite from the responsibilities of Hunsford parsonage and its vicar.

She could not, as she had already resolved, remain indoors— not with the boon of an unnaturally warm spring day. She considered whether to apply herself to her gardening – this activity being mostly the domain of her husband by her own encouragement, but for the small kitchen garden which had been relegated to her care as part of her domestic management. But that very fact resolved her against such a course. This gift of time would *not* be given over to duty. She had had very few such gifts since removing to Kent upon her marriage four months before. No, she would exercise the gratifying abandonment of duty which her husband always sermonised against. These precious hours begged true leisure!

And with that thought, she knew *just* where she would go.

Lady Catherine, with society thin at present, had offered the grounds and gardens of Rosings to the vicar's family and guests with nearly unfettered access. And Charlotte sketched now quite clearly in her mind a pretty little bench at the farthest end of the extensive garden there. Situated near a corner and tucked almost *within* a large hedge, one might repose upon it without being seen by any body in the shrubbery who did not approach it with purpose. Standing even two feet on either side would only suggest a slight recession in the hedging with no inkling that an intimate rest might be found on an oak seat a mere step away.

Charlotte had discovered this little inlet of calm soon after her establishment in Kent. Not yet accustomed to the dictates of her husband and, more particularly, of his esteemed patroness, Charlotte had braved winter one day to get away from them both; and seeking the farthest distance she could affect, had chanced upon this haven in her hour of need. Its existence appeared to be her little secret: she had once early on ventured to mention its delights to Lady Catherine, who only stared haughtily at Charlotte before declaring the younger woman to be mistaken, there being of course no structure of such rudimentary description within the garden of Rosings.

A quick flicker in the eye of Anne deBourgh at the time had suggested that she might have some knowledge of Charlotte's little find; but she neither stepped in to correct her mother on the occasion nor appeared inclined to admit of any information to corroborate or dismiss the fact. Charlotte had noted the reproving glance of her husband then that she might gainsay their hostess and she had dropped the matter; content to own that small secluded piece of property to herself—or to herself and one other likely. Never in her rambles there, however, had she actually encountered Miss deBourgh.

As the memory of its discovery waned, Charlotte realised she wasted precious actual moments of refuge in that very sanctuary – not to add that every moment spent in debate at home risked an interruption which might place other demands upon her – and she ran to her room to procure a shawl and a book, changed her slippers for half-boots, and went on her way.

ξ

She leaned back into the weathered oak and let its sun-baked warmth seep into her, recalling in more particulars as she did so the first time she had discovered this retreat, now that she had leisure for the indulgence without fear of interruption.

The discovery had occurred one afternoon in January mere weeks after her marriage to William Collins. Her husband's patroness and owner of this significant property of Rosings (the palings of which gave off at the little village of Hunsford wherein lay Charlotte's new home), Lady Catherine deBourgh had graced the young couple with her third visit in half as many weeks, ostensibly to inquire (yet again) that the improvements she had caused to the parsonage met the approval of its new mistress. Lady Catherine had then proceeded to criticise the strength of the tea she drank; cluck at the size of Charlotte's joint on inspection of the kitchen; rebuke Charlotte for her familiar address of her housemaid; and then culminated with a too-minute instruction on the arrangement of the linen closet upstairs—and all to echoing strains of agreement from Charlotte's new husband.

Charlotte had gritted her teeth through the ordeal and more and, as soon as the arrogant woman had gone, escaped for some much needed air. Despite the frigid clime she had trod the lane and crossed the stile into Rosings' park, quite by accident in her meandering to find this spot which proved sanctuary from both the bracing winter wind and overbearing meddlers. She had sat miserable for a few moments—wondering what she had done to herself, how she could have been so nonsensical as to remove herself far from family and friends to set up here with this fatuous man and his imperious sponsor—before her pragmatism once again was restored through reflection.

After all, she fully believed that, while Mr Collins must lack several desirable qualities, he was by no means the worst of men. There resided in him no real evil beyond want of reason. He was altogether respectable and sometimes nearly likable, a far cry from the horrors some women must endure. She would learn to admire him by schooling herself to overlook his defects, putting to practical application her philosophical leanings on the married state. Lady Catherine was certain to give up her profound interest in the young couple's lives before long—it was only a novelty to her in those early weeks surely. Charlotte would learn to admire *her* as well, in her own interest.

And this she had done; or at least, had made a fair start. She had learnt to offer Lady Catherine the deference she demanded in the interest of the peace.

The new Mrs Collins was an observant woman. It had taken her no time during the *first* of Lady Catherine's officious visits to understand that her real purpose in making them was to receive the gratitude of the younger woman for her condescension and largesse—and Charlotte Collins was nothing if not adept at adjusting to circumstance to give herself the best possible advantage in life. She had already taken the largest step in furtherance of this goal, by marrying a gentleman few could envy her for catching. Oh, many of course would envy the future her alliance purchased: becoming chatelaine of Longbourn one day, though the estate could not equal Rosings in grandeur, was no mean fate. But some there were who, behind parlour doors or openly, considered living as the wife of a ridiculous man as too high a price for security.

Eliza Bennet fell among these.

In fact, it was only Lizzy's refusal to become the wife of her cousin Mr Collins that had allowed Charlotte's procuring this title. *She* had not been his first choice. Plain in looks, at seven and twenty having very little dowry to speak of, and never before any serious attachment, Charlotte Lucas had looked to a future promising loneliness and dependence upon her family. But then Elizabeth Bennet without pause (and with some of her renowned liveliness apparently) had rejected Mr Collins outright; even in the knowledge that to accept him would have secured her own future and that of her sisters by retaining their home – and all deriving from the grounds that she could not *love* the man!

William Collins, it was true, was a man few would love for himself—at once a pompous and snivelling exhibit, a toady given to effusive instruction and even grander enthusiasms for his benefactress, Lady Catherine, to whose attention he had been presented nearly a year prior and who, following several lengthy interviews, had offered him the respectable living of Hunsford. He had few personal attributes to commend him to any other eligible lady; he was not a sensible man and the deficiency of nature had been but little assisted by education or society. He was conceited, narrow-minded and silly – possessed of a humility of manner counteracted by the self-conceit of a weak head. The best summary, as it were, that might be spoken of his character must include 'tedious' and 'unctuous'.

But he possessed one great over-riding quality: he offered surety! Mr Collins was the only male relation, the heir to whom Longbourn must pass in entail upon the demise of Mr Bennet. And until that event—the upheaval of her friends in the act Charlotte's only source of misgiving—he held a good benefice with a comfortable home – Charlotte's own home to manage now, nearly – free of material want.

Charlotte was no romantic, her temperament well-suited to overlooking—or at least tolerating—a character that her younger and prettier friend Eliza could not reconcile. And so, when Lizzy refused Mr Collins in her frank manner, Charlotte had taken fate into her own hands. In the guise of offering help to Lizzy, she had befriended the vicar—a man the freshness of whose injury at the tongue of Elizabeth Bennet might yield a willingness to reduce his previous standards for a wife. Could he be moved instead to offer to a woman otherwise firmly on the shelf?

Charlotte had succeeded all too well in her object: within two days having reached an understanding and received her delighted papa's consent; and within a month being wed, her future secured and on her way to Kent.

Her intimacy with Elizabeth Bennet had suffered in consequence; this was Charlotte's biggest regret in the transaction. Lizzy could not understand—or *would* not—how a woman of sense could find life even barely tolerable with such a man. It had set her to questioning the whole of Charlotte's nature, to evaluating anew a character she had previously thought she understood and admired in a companion of so many years. Their long friendship had been stretched near to breaking—Lizzy too prideful to accept that her decidedly poor opinion of the man would not be adopted by everyone; and Charlotte accusing Lizzy (if only in thought) of resenting that she could have stepped out from behind the livelier girl's shadow. They had reconciled before Charlotte's wedding; but their intimacy never would be quite as easy as once before, with the memory of this disagreement of principle between them.

ξ

Thoughts of Lizzy now brought Charlotte from her reverie to feel again the sun on her face and bask in spring's renewing warmth. She pondered idly to which part of the park her friend might have wandered—for their friendship had so far recovered that Elizabeth Bennet had travelled with Charlotte's father and sister to visit Hunsford. She had arrived a few weeks before to spend Eastertide in Kent, remaining along with Maria even after Sir William Lucas returned home to Hertfordshire.

How happy had Charlotte been to welcome her father, Maria and Eliza into her home! The mere remembrance of it now sent a wave of satisfaction through her. "My own home!" she said to the hawthorn bush, a 'peep' from somewhere within the only reply — but how she delighted again and again at the sound of those words. Sir William had remained only a week, his aims in coming safely to deliver his daughter next in age for a visit, and to ensure that his eldest was settled well. Having achieved these, and spent some hours walking the area with his new son, he felt quite satisfied to quit Kent; returning to Lucas Lodge in Hertfordshire with much of which to boast satisfaction, and not the least claim being the footing he now shared, after no less than three evenings as her guest, with Lady Catherine deBourgh of Rosings Park, who could count among her own triumphs that she had danced at the Court of St James.

Maria Lucas, a timid girl of fifteen, was much in awe of every thing she witnessed and every one she encountered—most particularly, of Lady Catherine. Charlotte had hoped Maria might benefit from a lengthy stay at the parsonage, by emerging somewhat from her reticent nature. And she had made some progress. But Lady Catherine could frighten the poor girl with a mere glance of recognition; Maria so concerned of saying or doing the wrong thing as to acquit herself poorly and draw down the judgment of the high lady.

As such, when a summons had arrived during breakfast from Lady Catherine, not for Charlotte as might be expected but for Maria alone, the girl hastened to dress and report not an instant past the designated hour, all with encouraging reminders from Mr Collins as to proper decorum. Maria was wanted to pass the morning entertaining Miss deBourgh—an odd request certainly, to Charlotte's mind, given the disparity in age between the two, as well as that they had never in the weeks of Maria's stay at Hunsford exchanged more than greetings and leave-takings as civility dictated.

But theirs was not to question the will of the ladies of the great house, as Mr Collins reminded them; theirs was to rejoice and be grateful of the notice of such high members of society. With such admonitions echoing in her head, Maria duly set out on foot, in good time, with a promise that she would be returned some few hours hence to make herself presentable for the dinner engagement to follow that same evening.

Eliza, too, had taken advantage of the clement weather to set out walking, accompanying Maria a short way before turning off for her own destination. Charlotte never quite knew what area of the country Elizabeth had staked for her own particular path; but whatever part of the park she had chosen, she returned often for exercise. The year had brought an unusually warm and dry spring, just the sort to encourage ambling; and Elizabeth had always been a great walker in all but the worst weather. She was likely to be out for some hours as well; for which, in light also of her sister's being called to the great house and her husband to the neighbouring village of Thenglehurst four miles distant, Charlotte could now credit some leisure time of her own.

She glanced down at the book in her lap, chuckling to realise that so bound in memories had she been, she had sat for three quarters of an hour without once opening the cover to find her place. She did so now but almost immediately shut it again. To read would require attention to the page. But the day was too lovely to ignore. She would instead continue to allow her thoughts to ramble as they would, whereby she could look about her at fresh blossoms on wild cherry trees in the distance, and the yellow catkins of Hazel, and creamy white flowers of Blackthorn, in the hedges all around; listen to birdsong from the nests in the latter and now and again spy a bird working its way in to carry food to its babies. The call of nature's wonders on a spring morning was too insistent, even for a woman without romantic inclination; or perhaps especially so.

Her friend's visit had certainly enlivened proceedings at the Hunsford parsonage. If you are thinking perhaps of ill feeling between the cousins on account of their history, dear reader, I must protest you are mistaken. The liveliness was of a much pleasanter kind—in the persons of Colonel Fitzwilliam and Mr Darcy both of Derbyshire. But more of them in a moment.

Eliza and Mr Collins had agreed tacitly, it seemed, to put their history behind them during Eliza's visit, although Charlotte could not help but note her husband's pointed references to his good fortune in house, garden and patronage – and occasionally in his wife – as often as chance allowed; as if to demonstrate the gross error in judgment his headstrong cousin had committed when she had refused him. Elizabeth in her turn tolerated his remarks, and answered with civility in his hearing those she could do without either causing her host injury or encouraging him to visit dissatisfaction upon his wife. This accord they all achieved when added to the fact of Charlotte's foresight in having chosen for her own particular use a small parlour at the back of the house. She, Maria and Elizabeth passed happy hours together there, secure in the understanding that Mr Collins much preferred his own study which looked out upon the lane and Rosings Park, and was thus unlikely often to grace the ladies with his company.

But company they did get in the persons of the aforementioned Colonel Fitzwilliam and Mr Darcy, nephews to Lady Catherine making an annual visit to their aunt for Eastertide as well. They had arrived on the Monday before Easter to be precise, and had quickly established a pattern of calling upon the inmates of Hunsford parsonage of a morning. Or rather Colonel Fitzwilliam established a pattern from the beginning, the more reserved Mr Darcy warming to the notion as they passed into their second week there.

This was the very same Mr Darcy who, some months before, had frequently been seen by the ladies after he accompanied his friend Mr Bingley into Hertfordshire when Charles Bingley had leased Netherfield Park for an indefinite period. Somewhat conceited, even haughty one might say—and *many* had said (though on further acquaintance perhaps diffident was a more apt descriptor)—Mr Darcy nevertheless appeared at the parsonage now several times each week, often with his cousin the colonel, sometimes alone, to call upon Mrs Collins and her party.

Colonel Fitzwilliam was as amiable a gentleman as one could wish— passing what felt mere moments in genial discourse of every subject only to find an hour had passed as they were thus engaged; while his companion Mr Darcy frequently sat there ten minutes together without opening his lips; and when he did speak, it seemed the effect of necessity rather than of choice – a sacrifice to propriety, not a pleasure to himself. Charlotte knew not what to make of him. Certainly he was not always so taciturn, for his cousin occasionally laughed at his stupidity, proving that he was generally different, which her own knowledge of him could not have told her.

She knew she had Lizzy to thank for the gentlemen's interest, both of them. They never would have ventured so often to the parsonage just to see Charlotte. But she did not mind it; still she benefited in pleasure from their calls. She would have liked to believe Mr Darcy's reticence to be the effect of love, and the object of that love, her friend Eliza, and she set herself seriously to work to find it out. She watched him whenever they were at Rosings, and whenever he came to Hunsford; but without much success. He certainly looked at her friend a great deal, but the expression of that look was disputable. It was an earnest, steadfast gaze, but she often doubted whether there were much admiration in it, and sometimes it seemed nothing but absence of mind.

She had once or twice suggested to Elizabeth the possibility of his being partial to her, but Elizabeth always laughed at the idea; and Charlotte did not think it right to press the subject, from the danger of raising expectations which might only end in disappointment; for in her opinion it admitted not of a doubt, that all her friend's dislike would vanish, if she could suppose him to be in her power. Elizabeth's pride had been hurt at their first meeting, though she had spoken of the incident mockingly at the time, when Mr Darcy disdained to dance with her, pronouncing within Eliza's hearing that she was only tolerable. But had not he then made some amends by dancing with her at the Netherfield Ball some weeks later when no other Hertfordshire ladies were afforded such distinction?

And had not Charlotte come upon the gentleman only a fortnight before now, hastily rising in embarrassment as she entered her parlour to find him alone in conversation with her friend? He had demonstrated, to Charlotte's mind at least, that he was capable of a change in opinion—he no longer found Eliza only tolerable, if it was a large step yet from making any declarations of affection. Charlotte sighed in consternation. No, she simply could not make out Mr Darcy's interest.

In her kind schemes for Elizabeth, she sometimes planned her marrying Colonel Fitzwilliam. He was beyond comparison the pleasantest man; he certainly admired Lizzy, and his situation in life was most eligible; but, to counterbalance these advantages, Mr. Darcy had considerable patronage in the church, and his cousin could have none at all.

Charlotte had closed her eyes as she had been contemplating these things, neatly easing into a doze in her comfortable bower, when she was brought back to alertness by the sound of voices. They grew louder as she listened. She knew that behind the hedgerow lay part of a path linking an open grove with the Hunsford lane; but these voices did not suggest the muted tones of passing through several feet of hedge to reach her. These sounded very clear to her, they must originate somewhere in the garden itself.

"...expect your assistance! I demand it."

Charlotte recognized the voice as belonging to Lady Catherine, and felt a rush of panic. She could have no knowledge whether the speech came from the left or right of her or from how far away, nor to whom Lady Catherine spoke. Instinctively, she pressed herself back against the oak settle, even as she debated whether she should make her presence known. In the end, curiosity won out. She opened her book so that, if caught there, she might pretend to have been absorbed in its pages, but remained otherwise as she had been.

"Your Ladyship, I will do what I am able. But I have heard your daughter's mind in this matter. She does not—"

"*My daughter's mind in this matter bears no consequence!*" Charlotte had jumped a little at the vehemence of Lady Catherine's avowal, as she registered that the other speaker was Mrs Jenkinson, Miss deBourgh's companion. From what she had heard, obviously Miss deBourgh must not accompany them in their walk.

"Mr Darcy and my daughter have been promised to one another from their infancy," Lady Catherine said, returning to a conversational, if determined, tone. "It was an agreement between my sister and myself; and the moment has come for them to marry. This is an obligation past time to fulfil!"

"Yes, Madam. But perhaps—"

"Do you question my judgment of what is best for my daughter? Question my dear *dead* sister's wishes for her son? Can not you comprehend the prudence of marrying two great properties into one?" Her voice lowered instinctively. "Do you wish to see my daughter whispered over among society like any common spinster on the shelf?"

"No, Madam. Of course I do not."

"Well then."

There was silence for a moment. As the ladies had been speaking, their voices stopped growing, an indication that the pair also had stopped moving towards her, and Charlotte hoped very much this was the case. Given what little she had heard, she assuredly would not wish to be found out now.

"Well? I can see you have something to say. Speak, woman."

"Lady Catherine, with great respect, I must register protest on behalf of Anne. She does not wish to marry Mr Darcy; indeed she does not wish to marry at all. And she feels that she need not do so if it is not to her liking. She will stand to inherit Rosings upon—"

Mrs Jenkinson stopped abruptly, and a silence hung in the air for an instant, even the birds having stopped their chatter to learn the fate of the companion for her ill-judged utterance. Charlotte wished she could see Lady Catherine's expression in the pall which had descended. However, when no reproach was immediately forthcoming, Mrs Jenkinson changed direction. "And Mr Darcy has expressed no peculiar leanings for Anne's company. Neither of us can credit that *he* wishes this match to occur."

Lady Catherine, whether in forbearance or by way of recognising a weightier concern than the foretelling of her own demise, answered the latter with only passing reference to the other. "And who would inherit Rosings when Anne is gone? Marrying is their duty. Perhaps such a concept is beyond your ken; but I assure you that my daughter and my nephew certainly understand—and they will *do their duty* as it was agreed upon long ago, to preserve the family." After a slight pause, she added, "It only falls to us—to you and to me—to encourage *Anne* to act now, when Darcy has indicated his inclination to consummate the business. Do you refuse to assist me?"

"No, Madam. I cannot."

"Very well."

To Charlotte's ear the speakers had begun to move closer yet again, sending a chill through her.

"Then you must ensure that Anne looks at her best tonight. Direct the maid to press her finest gown – the blue sateen, it best sets off Anne's complexion – and while she is at the work, *you* must convince my daughter to put herself forward this evening, make herself agreeable to Mr Darcy. She has spoken barely three sentences to him since he arrived."

"Yes, Madam." Mrs Jenkinson spoke so softly, Charlotte very nearly did not hear; but yet her resigned air spoke volumes.

"Darcy has delayed his departure; my nephews have stayed a week longer than planned. Obviously, it gives him pain to think of leaving this, his Kent home. This is his way of working up to speak with Anne, I know him—I judge him right. *He* at last has embraced my appeals to his duty, he is resolved. We have only to ensure that they are given the opportunity—and that Anne will behave properly when he proposes!"

"Yes, Ma—"

"Oh, do let us turn back, I have never liked this part of the garden. I only brought you out here to say my piece in privacy."

Charlotte breathed deeply with relief, as her fear had mounted considerably while the voices had approached her position. Now as they receded quickly, the speakers' backs to her, she only heard one last remark before losing the conversation entirely.

"Now return to Anne and talk sense into her, while I order a cart to send that stupid girl back..."

ξ

She might have taken umbrage on her sister's behalf had Charlotte not been more disappointed over what she had heard. Given her own musings before overhearing Lady Catherine, she sighed now to confirm she must have been wrong about Mr Darcy. He had no especial feelings for Eliza; or none so strong that he felt inclined to act upon them.

Perhaps that explained why she had been unable to determine his partiality: the gentleman was attracted to her friend, but precluded from feeling more because of his obligation to Anne deBourgh. Although Charlotte had been told previously of Mr Darcy's attachment to his sickly cousin, she had looked at him on occasion to see how cordially he deferred to Miss deBourgh, but during none of those moments could she discern any symptom of love; and she must suppose that as he was to marry her it was in consequence of being his relation. A sensible course certainly, she could acknowledge; if it yet was not to her liking when her preference lay with Eliza.

She looked down at her book now, and began to laugh. How very fortunate, indeed, that Lady Catherine had not discovered her hiding within the hedge as she would have had no adequate explication as to how she could study her tracts upside down!

ξ

Even righted, the tracts on obedience – these having been a wedding gift from her husband that she had never to now found opportunity to complete – held no interest for Charlotte. She pondered still the anticipated marriage of Mr Darcy and Anne deBourgh. And tonight, apparently, was to be the night it should be secured at last. She could only wonder if perhaps Lady Catherine had schemed for this after having witnessed for herself an attraction forming between Mr Darcy and Elizabeth Bennet.

But still, if Charlotte had been mistaken in Mr Darcy's attentions to her friend, Colonel Fitzwilliam was not encumbered in the same manner as his cousin. And if his prospects were not as grand as Mr Darcy of Pemberley, he had amiability and an obvious affinity for Lizzy. Charlotte could yet see her friend married and happy.

She pulled a watch from her pocket to check the time – happy to note that she could enjoy her respite yet awhile. Setting the book aside, she stood to stretch and considered making a turn about the garden when for the second time that day, voices could be heard approaching. In all the occasions she had been coming to this place, never had another human being crossed her path—but for today. She might have continued on her stroll had not she recognized the speakers as Lizzy and Colonel Fitzwilliam, the very subjects of her late conjecture. They approached her position along the path from the grove apparently, behind the hedge.

Their voices dulled by the shrubbery between, yet she heard them well enough and, once more, curiosity held her quietly in her place.

"...he has at least great pleasure in the power of choice. I do not know any body who seems more to enjoy the power of doing what he likes than Mr Darcy," said Lizzy.

Or perhaps not so much, thought Charlotte, fresh from the discourse she had just overheard.

"He likes to have his own way very well," replied Colonel Fitzwilliam. "But so we all do. It is only that he has better means of having it than many others, because he is rich, and many others are poor. I speak feelingly. A younger son, you know, must be inured to self-denial and dependence."

As it happened, the pair had just reached the curve of the path that coincided with Charlotte's position, and to her advantage, the colonel's remark had stopped Eliza in her tracks. Her voice came clearly when she replied with her customary frankness:

"In my opinion, the younger son of an Earl can know very little of either. Now, seriously, what have you ever known of self-denial and dependence? When have you been prevented by want of money from going wherever you chose, or procuring any thing you had a fancy for?"

"These are home questions—and perhaps I cannot say that I have experienced many hardships of that nature. But in matters of greater weight, I may suffer from the want of money. Younger sons cannot marry where they like."

"Unless where they like women of fortune, which I think they very often do."

Just like Lizzy to offer a satirical retort. But the colonel's voice offered some hint of disappointment as he answered with intention.

"Our habits of expense make us too dependent, and there are not many in my rank of life who can afford to marry without some attention to money."

Charlotte's heart sank. Had she just been privy to the colonel delicately offering Eliza friendship and no more? Was her friend destined to captivate only unattainable gentlemen? Mr Wickham, too, had been drawn to Eliza for some time, causing more than idle speculation some months before—until Miss King was known to have won an inheritance of some size and he had transferred his attentions.

"—and pray, what is the usual price of an Earl's younger son? Unless the elder brother is very sickly, I suppose you would not ask above fifty thousand pounds."

As was so often the case, Lizzy's glib response could signal her indifference or hide her distress. Sometimes Charlotte wondered if even Lizzy understood the distinction.

The colonel answered her in the same style, from which followed a silence to give Charlotte to wonder how much either were affected by what had passed. Soon after, Lizzy spoke again, changing the tone of their converse.

"I imagine your cousin brought you down with him chiefly for the sake of having somebody at his disposal. I wonder he does not marry, to secure a lasting convenience of that kind. But, perhaps his sister does as well for the present, and, as she is under his sole care, he may do what he likes with her."

This last became less clear as the couple had moved on again, walking in the direction of the lane to Hunsford; and soon after Charlotte lost all notice of them.

She immediately sat down on the bench, but all the warmth seemed to have seeped out from the wood. Yet why should *she* feel so disappointed when her friend could make light of the colonel's revelation?

She knew the answer without having to search one out. Without conscious desire, she had hoped that Elizabeth Bennet would make a match with one or the other of Colonel Fitzwilliam and Mr Darcy, not solely for *Lizzy's* benefit, but for Charlotte's—and with dual purpose. First, if her friend were to marry one of Lady Catherine's nephews, they should be certain to visit Kent regularly and, while they would be staying of course at Rosings rather than at the parsonage, Charlotte could be assured of regular meetings with her long-time friend; able to maintain a connection in that manner with her former life in Hertfordshire, and to maintain an intimacy she longed for in her present circumstance and doubted to find in this country otherwise.

And with equal importance, she wished simply to see Lizzy settled. She could not deny that when she thought of one day leaving Hunsford to take up residence at Longbourn—back in Hertfordshire near her family again and with a house of some consequence to manage free of interference—it gave her fortitude. She used the thought to console herself that the parsonage was only temporary; that although she could not *wish* for Mr Bennet's demise, nonetheless it was inevitable one day and when that sad day came, she would truly have her own home.

But it was the home also of her friends *now*. Whether Charlotte had married Mr Collins or not, Longbourn could not remain with the Bennet ladies, it must pass to their cousin. She supposed Mr Collins might have been prevailed upon to marry one of the other sisters after Lizzy's refusal if Charlotte had not courted him when he was vulnerable; though the measure of his bruised pride at the time suggested otherwise. In any event, Charlotte would assume her proper place one day at Longbourn in much greater contentment if she knew that Eliza and Jane, at least, were not to be thrown out summarily; that they would have homes of their own before their father expired, and one or either of them able to take in those who remained unattached.

It was her own conscience wanted relief, which heightened her disappointment now. But she was to be thwarted twice. First Mr Darcy – and now Colonel Fitzwilliam, as much as she knew he liked Lizzy, would wait for a woman of greater substance, or at least greater income.

Ah, well. She must leave Elizabeth Bennet's life up to her friend to make in whatever manner she could, just as Charlotte had done. Lizzy knew her own mind and heart. She had declined the chance to save herself several months ago on principle; Charlotte would have to trust in that same principle to secure Lizzy a future of tolerable comfort. If only Mr Darcy were not destined for Anne deBourgh!

ξ

Charlotte scooped up her tracts preparatory to walking home, thinking her leisure had not produced quite the serenity of spirit she had anticipated, when for a third time that day, voices in conversation stopped her. These again came from the other side of the hedge—two men, it would seem, arguing with one another. The deep tones of one gentleman clearly identified Mr Darcy. The other... was it not impossible?—so like the first—so much that it must indeed *be* the same...was also Mr Darcy! The words grew and diminished in volume with something of a regular pattern, confusing Charlotte momentarily as to their owners, until she realised that Mr Darcy was alone and talking to himself, pacing back and forth in such a manner that when he approached the hedge, Charlotte could distinguish him clearly; but when he turned and walked back away from her position, he sounded a muffled echo of himself. Embarrassed lest she should leave now for home and startle the man – who obviously believed himself solitary in the grove – Charlotte sat down on the oak bench yet again. And though she knew it was wrong, she would not stop herself listening.

"...could I?"

That was tantalizing, particularly since Charlotte thought she had heard in the jumble before these words the names of Anne deBourgh and *Elizabeth Bennet*. What could those two have in common to be spoken in the same breath?

"But only think on it, man! Consider her family! Her mother, blast it all! Can you reconcile yourself to... to *that* for a relation?"

Well, that could as easily apply to Anne deBourgh as to Eliza Bennet, Charlotte thought, still unclear as to the man's purpose and forgetting that Lady Catherine already claimed right of relation to him.

"Everything speaks against it! Society—reason, for God's sake!..."

Charlotte wished Mr Darcy would not allow his speech to drop to a mumble when he had his back to her. How would she ever decipher his meaning when she must miss half his monologue? But the disturbance of his mind could be heard in each word that she did comprehend.

As if in answer to her wish, the gentleman stopped pacing (she knew from the sudden cessation of boot-steps along the path) and stood what must be mere feet from her position which was yet protected by its dense curtain of branches and leaves.

"It would be a degradation to marry her; there is no other way to see it. It is impossible."

Charlotte gasped for breath, grateful for the denseness of the hedge which prevented Mr Darcy's discovering her behind it. He *was* speaking of Eliza, then! And with great feeling!

"The family obstacles are too much. So inferior are they all; they will not be tolerated in society, nor should they. But Elizabeth! She does not deserve the same censure, nor does her elder sister." A long groan now escaped him. "Bingley! Could I be kinder to myself than I have been to him?"

Bingley! Mr Bingley, lately of Netherfield Park? What could he have to do with the matter, unless Charlotte was mistaken as to what matter Mr Darcy debated.

"I cannot. At every turn I see objection of import."

You can, Mr Darcy!, she wanted to shout to him. *And moreover, you should!*

"But can I ignore the shades of Pemberley? My duty to it? To my own family? To Georgiana?"

You can, Mr Darcy! she shouted again in her mind.

His voice adopted a tone of gentleness now, carrying almost an audible smile. "In truth, Georgiana would like Miss Bennet—she needs a woman's confidence, especially now; and Elizabeth Bennet is just such a woman of understanding, well capable of influencing my sister for good."

Indeed she is—and might I add that Eliza can influence you *for the good as well?*

"And what of me? Can I continue to deny that Miss Elizabeth is exactly the woman who, in disposition and talents, would most suit me? Her understanding and temper, though unlike my own, would answer all my wishes. It could, indeed, prove an union to the advantage of both; by her ease and liveliness, my cares might be softened, and from my judgment, information, and knowledge of the world, she must receive benefit of greater importance."

He swings closer to a happy outcome. Charlotte was struck now with the full conviction that one of them at least knew what it was to love. Of her friend Eliza's sensations she remained a little in doubt; but that the gentleman was overflowing with admiration was evident enough. In that instant, Charlotte envied him that realisation even though it presented him with larger considerations over which to ruminate.

"I can struggle no longer. I must tell her how ardently I love and admire her."

Charlotte heard the confession with incredulity, but elation for her friend. Mr Darcy had resolved for Eliza, Charlotte was certain of it. He had only to say them, those final words that would give her the greatest joy! *Say it, Mr Darcy – do!*

"I will do it, I will! I shall marry Miss Elizabeth Bennet of Hertfordshire, and society be damned if they do not like it! I will like it, very much, that is what matters! I shall settle it with her this very night, after dinner."

Yes! There was a God in the heavens and he had smiled down upon the former Charlotte Lucas, now Collins by result of a previous smile from the firmament. All her wishes for Elizabeth Bennet – and perhaps for herself – were within reach! It required only that same small word—yes—from Lizzy when the gentleman offered for her. And Charlotte was certain that her friend, though she had rejected Mr Collins with no hesitation, could never decline to become the wife of so prominent a man as Fitzwilliam Darcy, nor mistress of Pemberley and half of Derbyshire.

Charlotte waited impatiently for a moment to ascertain that Mr Darcy, having reached his resolve, had left the little grove. When she was certain of it, she slipped around the hedge—that glorious, wondrous hedge—and ambled home with a lighter heart than she had felt in months, quite anxious now for the day to progress to the hour appointed for presenting themselves at Rosings house.

Her own desire was to be met, even exceeded; her wishes for her friend granted, and – with only the briefest notion of sympathy for Anne deBourgh's transitory discomfort – to make Charlotte's joy complete, Lady Catherine's design was to be thwarted as well!

Oh, how very much she looked forward to dinner in company this evening!

April Fools (A Romance)

ØØØ

One thing upon which most of us who love <u>Pride and Prejudice</u> agree is the requirement that there must occur two proposal scenes between Elizabeth Bennet and Mr Darcy; and far be it from me to dispute such sagacity. That acknowledged, however, what if one day in a fit of foolishness I took up my pen and ink in order to rearrange things a bit – create a bit of havoc? What if I were to alter just a little the sequence and timing of events for our two beloved characters, and perhaps a select few phrases of Miss Austen's making as well? What if …

ØØØ

"In vain I have struggled. It will not do. My feelings will not be repressed. You must allow me to tell you how ardently I admire and love you."

Elizabeth's astonishment was beyond expression. She stared, coloured, doubted, and was silent; even as Mr Darcy, receiving no rebuff from the lady, proceeded to enumerate in detail every deficiency of her suitability. Indeed, she had never known him to be as loquacious on any subject as he now proved. Had the same energy of words, the same warmth of feeling, been applied only to a recitation of the merits of her person – her beauty, her satirical mind, her kindness of heart, any of the myriad reasons he might offer for his ardour – perhaps she might be persuaded to consider now this proposal of marriage with some purpose. Perhaps in such a case that smooth purr of his voice uttering her name would send her into a swoon; though she never had yet succumbed to fainting – such a useless exercise.

But Elizabeth risked no embarrassment of it now. Mr Darcy, it seemed, preferred to expend his newfound eloquence on the degradation to him and his family of inviting her to join with him in marriage. He sprinkled an admiring titbit here and there but far too few to mitigate the rising tide of ire in her breast; in its best aspects, his speech did nothing to recommend his suit.

At first sensible of the pain he should suffer when she rejected him, quickly she lost all compassion in anger and resentment as he continued. Mute initially from disbelief, now the condition was fed by a cold determination to answer him, when he should have done, with a display of patience and reason that would shame his poor opinion of her family's manners. Unfortunately, she could not feel so tolerably composed when finally he concluded with representing to her the strength of that attachment which, in spite of all his endeavours, he had found impossible to conquer. She had felt her indignation increase with each new utterance. His last provoked her pride.

When finally he expressed his hope that the detestable weakness of character which compelled him to love her would now be rewarded by the acceptance of his hand, Elizabeth's lips twitched in perverse satisfaction at becoming the agent of disappointment to Mr Darcy – a man so little accustomed to suffering that affliction which he nevertheless so excelled at meting out to others. A host of responses vied for the honour of removing from his offending expression the assurance of favourable answer she detected there. A simple *"no"* in this instance could not suffice; no, not even a *"Never!"* Something less to the point perhaps to offer more satisfaction: *"I must decline, Sir, as I cannot return the affection you bestow upon me so unwillingly"* – or *"You have insulted me in every possible manner and I can now have nothing further to say to you"* – or *"You could not make me happy, and I am convinced that I am the last woman in the world who would make you so."*

As quickly as these entered her mind, however, she dismissed them again. They were all too civil, delivered the blow too quickly and mercifully. Her affronted vanity demanded he squirm in his abasement. She smiled to herself as she composed a reply in her mind, and smiled again to see that Mr Darcy interpreted this as prelude to a mere formality of acceptance.

You chose to tell me, with so evident a design of offending and insulting me, that you like me against your will, against your reason, and even against your character! And add to the injury by standing expectantly with the supposition of my gratitude, overlooking all your past provocations of me and of my family. Had not my own feelings decided against you, had they been indifferent even, do you think that any consideration would tempt me to accept the man, who has been the means of ruining, perhaps for ever, the happiness of a most beloved sister? I have every reason in the world to think ill of you. But it is not merely this affair on which my dislike is founded. Long before it had taken place, my opinion of you was decided, and confirmed many months ago in a recital from Mr Wickham.

Oh, no, Mr Darcy, your faults are heavy indeed! But yet you flatter yourself that any offer on your part – even one such as you have now made, filled with contempt for my station and my family, will have me swooning at your feet.

You are mistaken, Sir, if you believe that your proposal should affect me in any other way than to secure my everlasting derision for the name of Darcy. You could not have made me the offer of your hand in any possible way that would have tempted me to accept it. But I suppose I should thank you that the mode of your declaration, has spared me the concern which I might have felt in refusing you, had you behaved in a more gentleman-like manner. In short, Mr Darcy, you must now console yourself that the feelings which, you tell me, have long prevented the acknowledgment of your regard, can have little difficulty in overcoming it after this explanation. (Elizabeth especially favoured this turn of phrase.)

All this, of course, came to her in an instant whilst Mr Darcy awaited her reply in a haughty stance, secure for the moment of her answer. Once again, indignation flared within her. The rehearsed words queued in her throat as soldiers in formation, eager at last to join a fight too long in the planning – having begun with the circumstance of their first introduction in Meryton so many months before. Taking some anticipatory pleasure in his downfall now, Elizabeth at last entered the fray.

"Mr Darcy, I cannot be insensible to the compliment of such a man's affection," she began, preparatory to then turning it all around on its head; "Yet aware as I am of the great honour you do me... I can offer no other reply to you but this—"

ξ

When Mrs Collins entered her guest's chamber, Elizabeth was perched on the edge of her bed, still in her night clothes and idly picking at the nap on a coverlet she had pulled around her despite a suffocating closeness in the room.

"Lizzy?" Charlotte said, leaving the door ajar for the illumination the hallway offered. No reply came. She crossed to Elizabeth, repeating her friend's name as she stood in front of her.

"What have I done?"

Charlotte could not catch the words Elizabeth mumbled, but became alarmed at her distracted air. "Eliza, shall I summon a doctor?"

Elizabeth looked at her then, coming to herself at last if not *entirely* herself. "Oh! Charlotte." She glanced in confusion from her friend's day dress to the dark room and drapery-covered windows. "What is the hour?"

"It is nearly half past eleven."

"Only so late?" Even as she studied Charlotte's gown again, bewildered, Mrs Collins crossed to the windows and opened the drapes, thus flooding the room with sunlight. Elizabeth winced but did not complain; she understood now the change in her friend's attire. "It is *morning*," she said. She took note then of the oppressiveness of the room, shaking off the coverlet and drawing in a deep breath when Charlotte opened the casement window to the air.

"You had retired before we returned home last evening, and when you did not come down for breakfast this morning, I grew concerned for you." She studied Elizabeth's face as she spoke.

"I regret alarming you needlessly, Charlotte. What a poor house guest I am."

"Nonsense. But if you are yet ill, Lizzy, if you require a doctor –"

"No! I assure you, I do not. Only give me a few hours to shed the effects of a poor night's sleep and I shall be well enough again."

Her friend was not convinced and, to distract her from too close an examination of the cause of Elizabeth's present ills, she asked Charlotte for an account of the previous evening at Rosings.

"Much as usual at the first." She chuckled. "They are all much the same in my experience. Lady Catherine reigns, Mr Collins fawns"—she blushed slightly at this disloyalty of speech –"Mrs Jenkinson panders to Miss deBourgh who coughs and sighs; and I bite my tongue when I cannot divert myself with other guests. At the most one may be assured of good tea and victuals."

"I am sorry, Charlotte, that I did not attend for your diversion." Her friend could not possibly comprehend just how much Elizabeth regretted her eventful evening spent at home.

"Never mind it; an aching head should not be subjected to such occasions as Lady Catherine offers. I made do well enough with the amiable Colonel Fitzwilliam. Oh! but you *would* have been as amazed as I at the close of the evening. Such a kerfuffle!"

"Over what?"

"I cannot say for certain. It was very odd. Perhaps you might make sense of it where I can not."

"Miss deBourgh uttered a complete sentence, I suppose."

Charlotte chuckled again. "No. But I am encouraged at seeing you have *some* wit about you this morning. No, this was even more amazing, if you can believe it. It was Mr *Darcy* who provided the disturbance!"

Lizzy felt herself begin to turn green. "Mr Darcy!"

"Mmm. He appeared distracted all throughout dinner, left the gentlemen early apparently and disappeared for upwards of an hour, claiming business which must not wait."

Elizabeth knew his business all too well, but forced herself to reply in a disaffected manner. "Not so strange. Mr Darcy is accustomed to doing as he chooses, and when, without concern for those at his disposal."

Charlotte regarded Elizabeth curiously, causing that lady to fear what was to follow. "But that was not the oddest bit. When he returned, we could see he had not been to his rooms to write a letter as we had all supposed; but had instead been out of doors – his collar was dampened from the rain, his hair windblown, for all he took notice of it, and—"

Elizabeth dreaded the worst now. Had she been undone? Had he, by revealing to all the party their own converse last night, made it impossible for her either to remain here another day or to return home with her secret and her dignity? She closed her eyes to await the fearsome words.

"...and he was *happy*! Giddy with joy. It was most strange and *unnatural*, I am sure you would agree could you have seen him! He grinned from ear to ear nearly, can you imagine? Going on about what a fine evening it was even as he brushed the droplets from his sleeves. And not Lady Catherine's imperious demands or Colonel Fitzwilliam's teasing could make Mr Darcy confess the source of his altered manner. He would say only that he had been released from an affliction of long standing and owned himself once more. Most extraordinary!"

Elizabeth closed her eyes again, incredulous at the entire turn of events. The world was turned upside down – it was the only explanation for this madness; how else could Mr Darcy be in a joyous state whilst *she* now suffered such an unaccountable confusion of feeling?

"Lady Catherine was none too pleased, I can tell you. She berated her nephew still when the carriage was brought round for us and we departed. Oh, I *am* sorry you missed that, Lizzy. Poor Mr Collins dithered all way home at Mr Darcy's disregard of his noble Aunt."

What? Lady Catherine angry? Had Elizabeth missed some part of the recitation of events in her near stupor? She soon learnt, however, that his Aunt's annoyance grew from Mr Darcy's refusal to satisfy her curiosity as to his jocular condition.

As she listened with half an ear now to Charlotte saying she would send up a tray, Elizabeth realised that if she would resolve the matter of her own confused feelings, she must, against *all* her wishes, speak with Mr Darcy one final time – alone and with some haste. Although he and the Colonel had been anticipated to reside at Rosings until Saturday, she knew now he would not remain so long. He would depart before nightfall by her own doing.

She *must* see him – must place this bizarre circumstance behind her once for all. She could never marry Mr Darcy; it was unthinkable – and so, how was it then possible that her emotions could not settle the matter? Mr Darcy could not be allowed to depart Kent before she spoke with him to resolve the tormenting images which had kept her awake all night.

Recalling that the gentleman had often met her when she strolled in the grove at mid-day, she wondered if, as a person of peculiar habit, he would do so today as well. There was no time to waste in finding out if she was to discover him there – and it would be her last opportunity, of that she was certain. She declined any victuals and announced her intention to take a walk to shake off her lassitude, to shed her headache once and for all.

ξ

Elizabeth knew that Charlotte watched her from the study window as she turned up the lane from the parsonage – it had been the devil's time of it to persuade that she wished to be solitary some while when her friend would have accompanied her out of concern – and so she walked down the little lane that led her farther away from the turnpike road; the opposite direction from the grove. The park paling was still the boundary on one side. At the earliest opportunity, she slipped over one of the stiles into the ground and wended back, all the while bent on conjecturing how this present state of affairs had come about. A night's frantic questioning had proved fruitless. It had only left her dull and stupid. Even now she could hear over and again in her mind the answer she had given him. *I can have no other reply to offer you but this – I accept.*

What madness could have elicited so material a reversal in her that, when the moment for answer had arrived, her tongue had so easily betrayed her intentions? Brevity, she dared think, may be the soul of wit, but her own wits had entirely fled her! She might not even have been aware of the words formed of her speech had not Mr Darcy's response confounded her. He expressed no surprise at being refused, no mortification, no flicker of pain or regret; contrarily, almost instantly, his smile broadened and in seconds only he had crossed the room to her and taken her hand up in his. His touch was so warm as to cause her to shiver, and indeed, so overwhelmed was she to realise then what she had said, that she nearly *did* swoon but that he supported her to a nearby chair. She scarcely knew what form their converse had taken afterward – truly she could recall nothing at all of it – only his leave-taking after.

Of that she had miserably perfect recollection. She raised her fingertips now to her cheek to think on it, lightly testing the hollow just under the bone where his lips had brushed her before moving down towards the corner of her mouth. There she had felt the caress of his breath as he murmured a final endearment and then took his leave with some abruptness. In all, a very chaste response to their engagement – and yet, why then did she recall it with awful clarity? How detect still in the air the faint whiff of claret he had been drinking at dinner – and feel the imprint of his lips? The caress had left no visible mark upon her cheek; she had reassured herself of that several times in the looking glass before leaving the parsonage – and yet, still she could sense its feathery weight upon her skin much as she could the light muslin shawl now lying across her forearm.

Could this account for her impossible declaration – a (dare she think the word) passion for his physical person? No one would disagree that the gentleman from Derbyshire was handsome in form, she must acknowledge it to be true. Uncommonly tall, broad across the shoulder allowing of a well-turned figure – he was well proportioned and with no lack of symmetry or of grace in his movement and stature (particularly, for some unaccountable reason that made her blush to think on it, when espied from behind in his greatcoat.) His eyes suited, a most unsettling shade of blue that darkened or lightened intriguingly with his mood. They were really very fine looking and carried an air of intelligent discretion when not bent on judging her inferior in close study. And when not scowling, in those unguarded instances, it now struck her, when he smiled at *her*, Mr Darcy was indeed one of the handsomest men of her acquaintance.

But – ridiculous! Elizabeth did not credit people for their outward beauty when their characters were so thoroughly objectionable!— And could hardly have found him *so* handsome last night, whilst he stood enumerating all the unfortunate attributes that confirmed her a poor match, as to cause her to lose her wits and accept the man! She *could not* suppose herself capable of such folly consequent on attraction alone.

Perhaps she could lay blame at Charlotte's feet for her present misery? Before Charlotte Lucas (as she was) obliged Mr Collins some months past, she and Elizabeth had nearly fallen out over the former's estimation of marriage. Elizabeth could not credit that Charlotte would sacrifice every better feeling to worldly advantage, should marry an odious toad of a man – indeed one that Elizabeth herself had refused only three days before her friend accepted him – and then try to persuade that happiness might be found even in such an arrangement through the material comforts of a home of one's own. Elizabeth had strenuously opposed such judgment; could not conceive of marrying without affection – deep affection – even over Charlotte's insistence that warmth of feeling might just as easily grow after marriage as before. Elizabeth still recalled in the main her friend's words. *Happiness in marriage is entirely a matter of chance. If the dispositions of the parties are ever so well known to each other, or ever so similar beforehand, it does not advance their felicity in the least. They always continue to grow sufficiently unlike afterwards to have their share of vexation; and it is better to know as little as possible of the defects of the person with whom you are to pass your life. I am convinced that my chance of happiness with Mr Collins is as fair, as most people can boast on entering the marriage state.*

While Elizabeth had been little persuaded to these opinions at the time, she had to admit that seeing her friend now, the married condition did appear to advance Charlotte's happiness. She obviously revelled in her comfortable home, and her piglets. How much more might she find fulfilment one day at Longbourn, without Lady Catherine's domestic interferences? She seemed even to have settled to a liking of sorts for Mr Collins, had found ways in which to manage the man as efficiently as their home.

Had this picture of domestic felicity influenced Elizabeth more than she supposed? Was she – in spite of herself – coming round to accepting that Charlotte may not have been so entirely wrong?— particularly as their circumstances were not unlike? Elizabeth's future *would* be secured in marrying Mr Darcy, just as Charlotte's had been on taking the Collins name. Indeed, for Elizabeth, the gains would be far greater – *and* her entire family would benefit, would be saved, by such a marriage – especially beneficial now that poor Jane's prospects with Mr Bingley had vanished.

But the very same Mr Darcy had been *responsible* for Jane's disappointed hopes! How was Elizabeth ever to grow into a feeling of affection for such a man as could ruin, for a while, happiness for the most affectionate, generous heart in the world; and no one could say how lasting an evil he might have inflicted. Not even to think of his own friend's felicity as well, involving Jane and Mr Bingley *both* in misery of the acutest kind for his own purpose!

And what of his treatment of Mr Wickham? Any one who knew what *his* misfortunes had been, and all of Mr Darcy's infliction, could not help feeling an interest in him. He had been reduced to a state of poverty; had advantages withheld which had been designed for him; had the best years of his life deprived of an independence which was no less his due than his dessert. Yet, was Elizabeth to grow to love a man capable of such despicable acts against his boyhood friend, his father's favourite? Impossible! She *knew* it to be impossible!

Had she been goaded, then, into her hasty acceptance by the impertinences of Lady Catherine? That woman had been insufferable since the moment Elizabeth had met her – no, even long before simply through hearsay. For Charlotte's sake, Elizabeth refrained from the worst of her retorts to the high lady, and had mastered over the past weeks the art of a well-placed fan across her countenance to mask her emotion. But the woman galled her with her haughty disdain. It was no secret that she intended Mr Darcy to marry her daughter, the sickly Miss deBourgh – and quite honestly, Elizabeth felt the two deserving of one another.

But for all that, if *she* were to accept Mr Darcy, Lady Catherine would be beside herself with rage. The woman had not been in the habit of brooking disappointment, particularly one of such consequence attributable to a young woman lacking any consequence at all. Lady Catherine held that her daughter and her nephew had been formed for each other, destined for each other by the voice of every member of their respective houses. She would view Elizabeth, surely, as a pretentious upstart, without family, connections or fortune. Were the shades of Pemberley to be thus polluted? Elizabeth smiled to imagine the retribution she might exact for all of Lady Catherine's insolence these weeks.

But again, that was no adequate explanation for Elizabeth's rash act last night. What joy could be found in gaining this hollow triumph over a woman who, in the end, was so wholly unconnected to Elizabeth; when the cost of a moment's gloating satisfaction was to pass her entire adult life with a man she could not admire? She would never concede herself capable of such a self abasing act.

As she approached the little grove now, Elizabeth gave up all attempts to explain her actions on the previous evening, acknowledging the exercise to be futile. She may as well blame it on the full moon for all it mattered now. Instead, she must concentrate her powers of reason on *extracting* herself from this engagement, this capricious promise. It was *not* too late! It *must* not be, if only Mr Darcy would be walking in the grove. She could rectify this terrible, this awful, mistake. She only had to find him and withdraw her disastrous pledge before he dispatched to her father a request for audience and rode for Hertfordshire. He would despise her hereafter for the reversal – but what was that to her? No doubt she would never see him again after this morning.

ξ

Elizabeth stopped upon gaining the break in the trees that led into a little clearing in the grove. This was where, time after time without desiring it, she had come upon Mr Darcy during her walks in recent weeks, little comprehending the meetings to be any thing but accidental. This was where she *hoped desperately* to come upon him now. A fear of finding the place unoccupied momentarily robbed her of the will to enter it, even as she knew her only hope lay in taking those last steps. Deliberately shrugging off futile anxiety, she took a bracing breath and moved through the opening in the thicket; and then stopped until another shiver of unintended origin passed.

He was there!—seated on a fallen tree trunk with his back to her, apparently deep in thought, with a letter residing on the makeshift bench beside him.

Mr Darcy was deep into his own distractions – he had not heard nor turned at her approach. Elizabeth stood a moment watching, he quite still but for the indistinct rise and fall of his shoulders as he breathed. Part of her yet tried to find some rational explanation for last night's events, even as she ordered her mind – now that she would achieve her desired interview – for what she must say to him.

Frankness was best, she resolved. Though still she resented his offenses the previous evening, the present circumstance called for unimpassioned speech, much to the point for clarity, and settling the matter quickly and decisively with no cause for rancour on the side of either party. Mr Darcy surely conducted his business affairs in such a manner – indeed this must serve as a matter of business – he could comprehend well the advancement and respond in kind. She had only to make known her presence and then, quickly, her reconsideration.

As she groped for the right turns of phrase to begin, her attention rapt on the quiet scene before her all the while, she became aware that Mr Darcy was not alone on his perch. A small rabbit rested on its hindquarters, looking up in wonder, nose twitching, at this oddity occupying the log – was it predator or friend? Mr Darcy could not be aware of his woodland companion; its colouring so nearly matched the bark upon which it sat as to render it invisible. Elizabeth would not have noted it, save for its movement as it ventured warily closer to the gentleman. She pressed her hand across her mouth to prevent a giggle escaping.

It was a young one, a leveret possessing of both the natural reserve and natural curiosity of the breed, uncertain in this instance of the level of danger poised in front of it, and yet enraptured. Elizabeth could just glimpse a tuft of white on the underside of its tail. As it took a cautious glance away from the towering obstruction, the sun lit upon the delicate pink skin inside its ears, bathing it in translucency. In her mind, Elizabeth found herself calling the creature *Pinker*. She could not but feel some fondness for the innocent animal, so very tiny in juxtaposition to its wholly ignorant companion.

After a moment—when Mr Darcy continued unmoving – the rabbit lost interest and looked about it, espying the letter which lay so close by. It sniffed the air around the paper, tested it gingerly with an advanced paw, and then – when the article remained dormant – it bent its head and began to nibble at one corner.

"Mr Darcy! Your letter!" cried Elizabeth, before she knew what she was about; causing the gentleman to leap up and turn to her in wonder, having distinguished her alarmed voice, her presence, but not her words. The effect of his sudden movement, as might be imagined, was to cause an equally startled *Pinker* to flee, an event of no consequence but for the letter still in its maw which fled with it.

Mr Darcy's attentions were wholly caught by Elizabeth's arrival. He had no comprehension of the fate of his missive. Elizabeth, acting on instinct, ran forward to try and catch the rabbit before it disappeared into the labyrinthine thicket with the letter – repeating as she went her warning to Mr Darcy about the imminent loss of his correspondence even as she wondered whether it were addressed to her father and contained an appeal for an interview.

Curiously, the leveret did not complete its escape into the tangle of wood when it could have done. At the edge of the clearing, it turned and sat, laying the letter on the grass in front of it. It looked on Elizabeth, who had slowed so as not to frighten the animal further, and then to Mr Darcy, who at last had obtained a grasp of the predicament.

Elizabeth took a step towards the creature now, and it acted immediately – it took up the letter in its mouth once more and hopped to the side to regain its advantageous distance. Elizabeth stopped before again attempted to approach the rabbit, moving cautiously. Again, the creature took up his prize and moved away, yet made no attempt to gain the safer wood nearby. It might have been playing a game of catch-me-if-you-can with Elizabeth, so deliberate were its movements.

When a third attempt brought the same result, Elizabeth stopped and regarded Mr Darcy in wonder, her urgency for their meeting entirely forgotten in the moment. The expression of incredulity she found to match her own made her laugh; and this brought the gentleman to his senses.

"Most extraordinary!" he whispered. *Pinker* turned its head to him at the sound but made no further retreat.

Matching his low tone, she replied. "Indeed. I have never seen its like! Tell me, Mr Darcy, will your cost be great if the letter is lost to the woods?"

He smiled at her. "To my pride perhaps. I spent a sleepless night composing, discarding and refining what I can not seem to find proper words to convey in speech." Elizabeth wondered if perhaps, rather than her father, this difficult missive was meant to inform his aunt of last night's understanding, when he finished with, "It is a letter to *you*! I have been sitting this three-quarter hour in hope you would come."

"To me?" A hopeful thought now was allowed to form. Perhaps Elizabeth was not the only party to last night's event to reconsider their rash engagement. A man of any honour would indeed find difficulty in admitting of such a mistake, composing careful words on paper to retract his offer. But were it so, a withdrawal of the promise would so fulfil Elizabeth's wishes that she might pardon him the egregious offense of it. She could perhaps read it from time to time and take some private amusement in having been jilted creditably. At once, she resolved to retrieve the correspondence intact.

"Perhaps, Sir, if I were to engage *Pink*... er, this creature's, attentions, you might make your way round opposite me without its notice, placing the leveret between us. Then we can attempt one or the other to save your letter by stealth. The rascal can not look in two directions at once."

Agreeable to this notion, Mr Darcy sidled cautiously to a point several yards behind the rabbit while Elizabeth cooed to it to maintain its interest in her. Having positioned himself out of the animal's vision, Mr Darcy then began with the greatest care to advance, stopping every step or so to ensure he was not detected. But the leveret's attention remained wholly fixed on Elizabeth's soft words, one ear or the other now and again flopping over as it cocked its head this way or that. In this manner, Mr Darcy came within an arm's reach and a half of the square of parchment on the grass.

Stopping, he took an instant to set his purpose, then made a lunge for the article.

Pinker was not to be outwitted so easily. At the last possible second, it took the letter up and bolted towards the centre of the clearing, disappearing into a burrow under the fallen tree trunk. As it had begun to move, alas, so had Elizabeth; and the small distance between the lady and Mr Darcy – and the momentum carrying him forward – brought about their unfortunate collision at just the spot the rabbit had vacated. The impact sent Elizabeth spilling; and when he tried to save her, sent Mr Darcy spilling right after. A raucous call followed – birds flew up out of the trees at the disturbance, circling the clearing a few times before then settling back down onto their perches to watch what might now transpire.

Elizabeth found herself stretched full on the ground, her shoulder pinned there by the weight of Mr Darcy who was prone partially across her. She stared up at the only thing available to her vision – a pair of enlarged blue eyes mere inches from hers. The shock of impact in their expression quickly gave way to concern for her and then, seeing some thing particular in her countenance and before he could act to remove himself from her person, gave way again to amusement. His ensuing smile turned to a chuckle; and that followed to a laugh – a deep, full-throated laugh that began quietly but grew rapidly. Elizabeth was caught up in it. She began to laugh as well. And there the two lay, sensible of the absurdity of their having been made fools of by a mere leveret, and giggling like school children after a particularly exhausting summer time game of tag.

ξ

It is a truth universally acknowledged in such circumstances as these, that the release of one pent up emotion can in consequence produce the liberation of a chain of others that have been too long held within. The physical proximity of these two – man and woman – suddenly impressed upon them. As quickly as they had begun to laugh, they stopped, turning very serious indeed. Elizabeth could feel the gentleman's heart beating in time with hers, could note that his breathing accelerated at just the same rate as she now experienced. For what might have been an eternity, they remained in this attitude, each intent on the other, unable to lower their gaze. As the tension grew weightier, Mr Darcy's face seemed to drift minutely ever closer to Elizabeth's – an inevitable meeting of two opposing forces – until it stopped but a hair's breadth away.

She raised hers to meet it and closed her eyes.

It was the gentlest kiss, yet Elizabeth could sense power closely held in check behind it; it frightened her, not for mistrust of Mr Darcy's regulation but for *her* instigation and then fervent wish for the feeling of excitement to last. She closed her eyes tighter to summon self will. But Mr Darcy, it seemed, was made of sterner stuff. After only an instant he pulled away and quickly righted himself into a sitting position; then extended a hand to assist Elizabeth.

"Forgive me," was all he said. He was very grave, his humour all but spent.

He helped her to sit up, and the two rested there a moment in the grass without words, trying with little success to regain their former distance.

"Miss Elizabeth," finally he began. He glanced about him as if searching some thing, drawing her eyes to follow, but nothing out of the ordinary met their quest. She realised he was looking for their little friend, or perhaps simply for his letter, but neither was any where in evidence. "Miss Elizabeth," again, "it appears I have need of my power of speech after all, for there are words I would say to you. One might conjecture I would recall my lines with perfect clarity, having composed them half the night and then again. Yet I find I have forgotten them all. But I must tell you – must beg your indulgence and your generous nature, for forgiveness—"

"Mr Darcy, if you would withdraw your offer—"

"No!" He composed himself then. "No. You mistake me. I would not do you such a grave dishonour. Last evening, the happiness which your reply gave to me was such as I have never felt before – that is, until I retired for the night and had leisure to think on the proceedings."

Ah, thought Lizzy. *He is too much the well brought up gentleman after all to breach the engagement, yet he would by rational argument persuade* me *to do so.*

This was luck; he was providing to her the very circumstance she had come to bring about. So why did she suddenly feel a knot growing in her chest of something like regret? Should she interject her own change of intention now, to save them both the discomposure of his unconfident discourse? She knew she ought – it was the kindest thing to do, perhaps for them both – but perversely, she very much desired to hear how he might begin. She held her own words in check and in their stead asked, "What could have intruded upon your leisure with such force as to rob you of a night's rest?"

"My proposal to you." He fumbled about, and then finally blurted out, "It was *wrong*! *I* was wrong to address you as I did."

Elizabeth's grim smile conveyed her surmises.

"You look conscious. Young ladies have great penetration in such matters as these."

"There is little to credit in that. I must confess I have been half expecting the alteration."

"But I think I may defy even your sagacity, to discover the name of the person who forced me to think on it. It was my aunt. Lady Catherine," he added unnecessarily.

"Lady Catherine!" Oh, this was an unwelcome twist indeed. So Darcy had not held his tongue after all. He had felt bound to apprise his aunt of the understanding between them, rendering it impossible now to sever it quietly and without disgrace.

"Yes, my aunt. When I returned to the house yester eve, she noted the change in me; indeed all the party remarked it. I am ill equipped for disguise, never desiring the talent before last night. My aunt and my cousin Fitzwilliam both began as soon as they noted my peculiar demeanour to quiz me for its source; *he* with better humour but both relentless in their way. Colonel Fitzwilliam eventually gave up the sport and retired, but Lady Catherine only grew more determined at my discretion."

He hesitated now, looked around him at the little grove before turning back to Elizabeth. "I regret that I must cause you pain; but I must repeat hurtful words in order to explain myself in full." Unable to trust her tongue if it once started, she only gave him a faltering nod to go on. After all, she was about to receive what she had ventured out to obtain; she could curb her natural bent for a few moments until he had said his piece; which he began to do in an equally faltering manner.

"My Aunt... took to a review; of the evening, you see... no doubt to loosen my tongue before coming back to the matter of her interest. At length, she happened upon your name. I am afraid her remarks were not complimentary."

"I will not feign surprise at this intelligence," said Elizabeth, "nor hold you to account for *her* disparagement."

"I am grateful for as much. But I took her insults only too well to heart. I took *offence* at them on your behalf."

"Whatever could she say injurious to me?"

Mr Darcy simply shook his head. Then, "she began by denouncing your failure to attend her evening, into which I put no credence for censure; but soon had moved on to your general character and that of your family, much of her information no doubt supplied by her ungenerous clergyman, your own disloyal cousin. My aunt spoke thus for some minutes under some protest from me, until I could no longer bear to hear it."

Lady Catherine's opinions, then, thought Elizabeth, had goaded her nephew into revealing their engagement in spite; and succeeded, it would seem, eventually in bringing him around to her will. Here was some thing for which Elizabeth might think less of him.

"I retired as soon as I might rather than further engage in a debate from which neither side, I was certain, could be moved. As I prepared for my bed, my bitterness towards my aunt escalated both for destroying my joy of the evening, and for insults rendered unfeelingly to you. How arrogant my relation was, how insolent and disdainful – so proud as to be able only to think meanly of one who did not share her exalted class, but certainly deserved better—"

Elizabeth had never been more at a loss to make her feelings appear what they were not. It was necessary to her purpose to maintain her calm when she would rather have laughed riotously – but for the words which tumbled quickly after from Mr Darcy.

"It was then impressed upon me in an instant of clarity, as I defended you in my mind, that these very opinions, indeed some of the very phrases my aunt had conjured, had but an hour before passed my own lips. Mine caused the greater injury, perhaps, for speaking them *to you*. Such unfit discourse for professions of love! I stood incredulous looking into my shaving glass, mortified to comprehend what I had done after I had recognised it exampled so boldly in my aunt."

What was this he was saying? Elizabeth had been secretly forming a desperate resolution, believing perhaps he might be doing the same; now she could not reconcile this reversal. She must set aside her carelessly constructed presumptions until she was certain of his direction; she must attend him with complete attention.

"My behaviour to you last night, seen in this light, had merited the severest reproof. It was unpardonable. I cannot think of it without abhorrence."

For the second time in as many days, Elizabeth was astonished by Mr Darcy's revelations.

"There was one part especially, at the middle of it, which I should dread your having the power of recollecting. I can only believe you thought me devoid of every proper feeling. I am sure you did. I can remember some expressions which might justly make you hate me."

"The conduct of neither if strictly examined, will be irreproachable; indeed, I confess, Mr Darcy, that when you surprised me with your offer, I had every intention of rejecting you outright and with great vigour."

Now it was his turn to be taken by surprise – clearly, despite his present enlightened condition, he had never expected any reply from Elizabeth but the positive one he had received at the time. "But—you did not..."

"No, no I did not. And I cannot explain my actions to you, as I hardly know myself what compelled me! I had felt certain that you could not address me in any possible way that would induce me to accept you. My acquiescence astounded me in a manner it could not have done for you – for I believe *you* had then felt persuaded that I should oblige you."

"Indeed I had." Mr Darcy's brow furrowed as he reconsidered all that had transpired before. "What will you think of my vanity? I believed you to be wishing, expecting my addresses."

"My manners must have been in fault, but not intentionally I assure you. I never meant to deceive you, but my spirits might often lead me wrong. How you must hate me for this admission."

That he was moved by her honesty was immediately apparent. The painful enlightenment he had achieved on his own the night before now suffered an increased blow under this new intelligence. The silence lengthened as he tried to make sense of the altered situation; and Elizabeth, who experienced some remorse at further humbling him after his unsolicited admission, tried to mitigate her feelings of self-reproach.

"Mr Darcy, I regret my caprice, even as I cannot explain its impulse. Indeed, I also passed a sleepless night in reflection, but came away with far less understanding of my sensibilities than you appear to have achieved."

The gentleman acknowledged her, and the awkward silence descended again. At last, he said, "Miss Elizabeth, it seems we are both of us culpable of rushing headlong into where we had little business." The dejection in his voice gave her pause. "While we are on this rocky ground of speaking openly, I would know—" He stumbled and stopped; then drew upon some reserve of determination to continue. "—I would know your feelings of me, your inventory of my faults of character which have given way to the unfavourable estimation in which you hold me."

"I did not get on at all in my reflection, I hardly know. I am met with such different accounts of you as puzzle me exceedingly."

"I can readily believe," answered he gravely, "that report may vary greatly with respect to me; but I could wish, Miss Bennet, that you would sketch my character as it informed your inclination to reject my suit."

Elizabeth saw that Mr Darcy's request lacked any bitterness of spirit; and she felt her former fixed opinion begin to crack in light of it. She resolved to answer his courage with equal candour, and cited first in doing so his interference in her sister's relationship with his friend at Netherfield. To this, he mounted a defence, citing his opinion that, upon close observation, he believed Jane indifferent to Mr Bingley. Elizabeth nearly regained her old dislike of him when he continued to hold firm that he had done no wrong by acting in service to a friend; but she must admit that *if* one could truly believe as he did, his actions might be interpreted to fall in with reason. She reserved too great an opinion in either camp for the moment.

When they began to feel the damp of the ground, by agreement they moved to sit upon the tree trunk where Elizabeth had first spied Mr Darcy, and he asked her again about her ill feelings towards him, disbelieving his actions against her sister to be all that stood him in poor stead. After some pause to consider, she broached the subject of Mr Wickham and the evils that had befallen him.

"Ah," said Mr Darcy in a low tone and with heightened colour, "I had noted you take an eager interest in that gentleman's concerns."

He listened nevertheless as she related what she had learnt from Mr Wickham, his silence causing her no little surprise for his forbearance. When she had done, he looked long at the ground, marshalling his thoughts before speaking.

"With respect to this other, more weighty accusation, of having injured Mr Wickham, I can only refute it by laying before you the whole of his connection with my family. You will, I hope, pardon the freedom with which I demand your attention – your feelings, I know, will suffer undeservedly; but my honour demands it of justice. The offences laid to my charge concerning Mr Wickham, taken all together, would be a depravity, in defiance of honour and humanity. I shall hope to be in future secured, when an account of my actions and their motives has been given. If, in the explanation of them which is due to myself, I am under the necessity of relating feelings which may give pain to yours, I can only say that I am sorry.—The necessity must be obeyed."

He began to speak of his history with Mr Wickham and at last came to a portion that assuredly caused him great pain to relate – his young sister's near destruction by Wickham, the inducement of which Mr Darcy laid jointly to her fortune and to Wickham's hope of revenging himself on his former friend.

As Elizabeth heard his account unfold, she began by rejecting every detail in her mind based on her former feeling for Mr Wickham. She wished to discredit it completely; but then must allow that the story had a ring of truth to it. Surely Mr Darcy would not conjure such a story – so injurious to his own sister – in service to false vanity! She began to recall the former behaviour of Mr Wickham, the inconsistencies between his words and his actions whilst they all resided in Hertfordshire; and could not long sustain her disbelief – particularly when Mr Darcy recommended she appeal to Colonel Fitzwilliam to uphold the facts. It now seemed certain that all the truth lay on one side, the appearance of it on the other – and Elizabeth wholly mistaken in attribution of it. Mr Darcy's conduct made him entirely blameless throughout the whole of his relations with Mr Wickham.

Mr Darcy had stopped speaking to allow her to consider all that had passed. How very differently did every thing now appear in which he was concerned. Every lingering struggle against his favour grew fainter and fainter. Elizabeth grew absolutely ashamed of herself; her quickness of mind now piecing together her own large part in distorting truth. Of neither Darcy nor Wickham could she think, without feeling that she had been blind, partial, prejudiced, absurd.

Till this moment, she never knew herself. From herself to Jane – from Jane to Bingley, her thoughts were in a line which soon brought to her recollection that Mr Darcy's explanation *there*, had appeared insufficient. But her bias could not stand on a second consideration. How could she deny that credit to his assertions, in one instance, which she had been obliged to give in the other? He declared himself to have been totally unsuspicious of her sister's attachment; and Lizzy could not deny the justice of his description of Jane, whose feelings, though fervent, were little displayed; and that there was a constant complacency in her air and manner, not often united with great sensibility.

"Mr Darcy, it appears," she said after a great interval, "that we are alike in having much to learn about ourselves. I have wilfully misunderstood— and misjudged you exceedingly."

"And I have little acted the gentleman; judging you unfairly from the start—"

They were quiet again, aware of a shift in their relations but as yet unable to reconcile it with their sensibilities. The grove was so still – not the rustle of a branch in the breeze or the caw of a bird to upset the delicate air between them. After some time, Mr Darcy spoke again.

"Miss Bennet, we entered into a promise last night, both of us, on poor understanding." Elizabeth was too much embarrassed to say a word. After a short pause, her companion added, "You are too generous to trifle with me. If your feelings are still what they were last night, tell me so at once. *My* affections and wishes are unchanged, but one word from you will silence me on this subject forever."

Elizabeth feeling all the more than common awkwardness and anxiety of the situation, now forced herself to speak, and immediately, though not very fluently, gave him to understand, that her sentiments had undergone so material a change since the twelve hours past, as to make her receive with gratitude and pleasure his present renewal of assurances.

Mr Darcy smiled in a manner wholly lacking the overly confident air he had worn on the prior evening. "I know enough of your disposition to be certain that, were you absolutely, irrevocably decided against me, you would acknowledge it to me, frankly and openly." When Elizabeth made to answer, he silenced her and, sliding from his seat beside her, knelt on one knee facing her and took her hand in his. "I must tell you, you have bewitched me utterly. My hand, my fortune, all I own and am – my heart and my very soul – are yours if you will have them. I can imagine no greater contentment than to never be parted from you." His expression became even more grave. "But I would not enter a marriage absent mutual affection, deeply formed regard. I have no doubt that we could be the happiest couple in the world. But are you quite certain enough of *your* feelings, dearest, loveliest Elizabeth?"

Elizabeth felt her colour rise under the deserved perusal. But her reply was immediate and confident. "My dear Mr Darcy," and she smiled as her fingers reached out to his cheek; "I am convinced now my *feelings* were never in question. It was my *reason* that found fault where none should stand, my *reason* which failed me. My opinions, my accusations, were ill-founded, formed on mistaken premises. Last night, my better feelings, comprehending somehow that reason erred, overruled the objections I sought rationally – but today the two speak in concert. I both *know* and *feel* myself to be happy."

The happiness which this reply produced, was such as to exceed his on the previous night for its being shared between them; and Mr Darcy expressed himself on the occasion as sensibly and as warmly as a man violently in love can be supposed to do. Had Elizabeth been able to encounter his eye, she might have seen how well the expression of heartfelt delight, diffused over his face, became him; but, though she could not look, she could listen, and he told her of feelings, which, in proving what importance she was to him, made his affection every moment more valuable.

When at last Mr Darcy rose from his kneeling situation and joined his betrothed on the log, he began to laugh. Perplexed, Elizabeth followed his gaze. There in the grass at their feet sat the

young rabbit, nose and whiskers twitching in approbation, and Mr
Darcy's letter laying next to it with Elizabeth's name writ clearly
across the outside. It was little the worse for its travels with *Pinker*.
They had, in the hour past, completely forgotten it.

This time, when Mr Darcy bent down to the leveret, it made no
attempt to flee, but allowed him to scoop it up in his large hand. He
held the creature while Elizabeth caressed its ears, and she thanked
it for its perseverance in bringing them together. Mr Darcy then
retrieved the letter and would have placed it in his pocket, but
Elizabeth begged to read it.

"Oh, no! Better now that it be burnt! We have said what
mattered, our little friend here has seen to that." Elizabeth
acquiesced with some disappointment, wishing to pore over his
writing on her return to Hunsford; until her gentleman promised to
write her another forthwith which would speak not of apology for
regrettable words, but of the magnitude of his love for her and all
without a single line of poetry.

At length, they parted – the one for Hunsford, the other for
Rosings – under the same agreement that they had made the
previous evening; but with far greater understanding, confidence and
anticipation of their future together. Mr Darcy followed Elizabeth's
receding form until he could no longer espy her through the trees –
and then glanced down at the young rabbit still in his hand and,
smiling at his new friend, on a whim gently placed it within his
greatcoat pocket. As the gentleman himself left the clearing a
moment later, *Pinker* stretched its head up out of the cavernous
retreat, glanced quickly around at its former home, and seemed for
all the world to smile as well.

ξ

And so, dear reader, you have come to the end of my tale. It
has been my express wish that you find it to your liking. Indeed, I
toiled to make it so. If I have succeeded, I am content. If I have
not, if my words have no power to delight, then I beg you forgive me
for taking up so much of your time. And you, in your turn, if in the
reading of my little lark, you gave it any degree of credence that the
courtship of Miss Elizabeth Bennet and Mr Fitzwilliam Darcy truly
transpired in this manner, then I feel compelled to leave you with an
approximation of some words Charlotte Lucas once spoke to
Elizabeth. "We are *all* fools in love... and in April."

A Gentleman's Gentleman

ひひひ

As her fans know, Jane Austen never presumed to apply her pen to recording conversations solely between gentlemen, or indeed scenes in which only men are involved. For me, it has served only to pique my curiosity about characters such as Mr Darcy. (Well, whose curiosity is not piqued by that gentleman?) With apologies to Miss Austen, the following 'outtake' imagines the relationship between Mr Darcy and his valet, at a time when the gentleman has something on his mind.

ひひひ

"Grayson…"

The valet, stopped in the act of reaching for his employer's boots, turned to face him.

"What sort of man do you see before you?"

"A most excellent sort, Sir."

"No. No, that will not do!"

Grayson, taken aback as much by the countenance he remarked as by the words – a disturbance of mind visible in every feature – maintained his customary calm with only the greatest will. Clearly, something of great import troubled the man before him— something having originated during their recent sojourn, assuredly. Never given to effusions, the master had become even more withdrawn since then; indeed had become quite uncommunicative even before they made their return to Town.

If anyone may be privy to the vagaries of mood of a gentleman, it is his man who rouses him in the mornings, attends to his every activity and sees to his retirement each night. Few wives can lay claim to as comprehensive knowledge of a husband as is afforded an attentive valet. And Grayson was attentive.

He had been with his present employer ten years, the fourth he had maintained since his elevation nearly twenty years gone. The first, a kindly baronet, had suffered an untimely passing mere months after promoting Grayson from a footman. The young servant might have been relegated again had not a potential suitor to the baronet's daughter been calling at the time. This visit proved auspicious for Grayson: Sir Humphrey Riverton had, only lately, found himself doubly deprived of accustomed personal attentions when his valet had run off with his prettiest maid.

When Sir Humphrey abruptly departed the bereaved household, he left behind a disappointed lover – having decided against waiting until the lady's mourning period should be observed to acquire what, after all, could be counted only a modest fortune – but he had gained a grateful manservant. Grayson served him for three years.

Indeed, Sir Humphrey proved quite willing to train his new man in every detail. For his new employer was what one might call a 'dandy'—fastidious to a fault, so much so as to discard complete sets of garments with every new dictate of fashion, the preponderance of which fell to Grayson to rework into habitable attire for his own use. In addition to thus augmenting his wardrobe by these whims, Grayson learnt to be a valet of the first quality. He was tutored in every facet of care: the proper starching of neck cloths; Sir Humphrey's own secret to making incomparable boot blacking (the secret being in the amounts of tallow and wax added to the mixture); foolproof remedies for the after-effects of a night of carousing— suffice it to say, with such an employer, no detail was allowed to pass unexamined.

Sir Humphrey did not entertain marriage after his first abortive dalliance. Indeed, his interest in the female sex had always been lacklustre, being confined to their fortunes or favours. Then his aunt, who had provided for his lifestyle for years, commanded that he settle to his responsibilities and marry her ward. When, in a rare show of defiance, he declined to consider his homely 'cousin,' he found himself summarily cut off. Unconcerned at first, he believed his formerly indulgent aunt could not long punish his independence, and would soon relent. She could, and did not. When some months following he fled to France to avoid the duns at his door, it was Grayson who was left behind, without benefit of severance or character.

Despite this disadvantage, Grayson had not been long without employment before coming to the notice of one Abednego Fletcher, a man of considerable property, a large wife and larger family in Ireland, and smaller properties with oft-resident smaller mistresses in England. He was a person of considerable and varied appetites. Though Grayson experienced some misgivings, his circumstance was too precariously felt to pass up work, and he took on the duty.

Mr Fletcher made two visits to Ireland in the years Grayson saw to him, each of short duration. The first was an obligatory journey to hire a new steward, a task he would trust to no one else, since he was so often from home for exceedingly long periods. The second, nine months after the first, to bury his wife who had surrendered finally to either extended neglect or the birthing of her tenth child. As the weak infant had also expired during this laborious effort, Mr Fletcher left the remaining nine dependents to the care of a distant relation and departed once more.

Two years further on he fell in thrall to an actress who aspired to be a lady. The untameable rake turned meek as a mouse! — wholly subservient to his new wife's will. Her first order of business had been to curb her husband's appetites—all of Mr Fletcher's past associations were severed with as little courtesy or cost as necessary. This comprised not only his various mistresses, but also long-time retainers who were all too aware of Mrs Fletcher's inauspicious history.

The valet and four other servants had been given one month's half-pay and set adrift. On this occasion, Grayson did succeed, however, in securing an excellent recommendation.

(Though we here leave the character of Mr Fletcher, it may interest the reader to know that he remained subservient to his lady far longer than anyone had wagered—nearly a six-month—until he could tolerate his subjugation no further. He quietly secured his solicitor, who then secured his not inconsiderable fortune, selling outright what he could not otherwise invest in protected assets for his client; and following which, Mr Fletcher achieved a moonlit escape to Portsmouth with a trunk full of coin, and boarded ship for a dawn departure to the Americas. He was never heard from again by any of his various relations. When the new owner of the property and all its servants and furnishings – down to the chamber pots – came to evict an astonished Mrs Fletcher, that particular lady had no recourse but hastily to gather what clothing she could carry and return to the boards. She subsequently became celebrated by theatre critics for her extraordinary ability to portray disappointed hopes and harpies.)

Grayson's own summary dismissal at length brought him to his next situation: a young man just turned eighteen and preparing to embark on the grand tour. The temperaments of former masters and the one newly acquired could not have been further removed.

Where Sir Humphrey had gloried in ostentation of manner and dress, the new master preferred understated elegance; though he proved no less attentive generally to his person. Mr Fletcher had indulged in every kind of gaming and debauchery; the new master preferred quieter pursuits—the improvement of his person through fencing, riding, and industry; and of his mind through reading. He was particular concerning his fencing gear, riding tack and his extensive library. More to the point, where the former employers each were accustomed to hold forth upon waking (which occurred no earlier than mid-day) and stop nattering only upon retiring late at night, the new master proved an early riser and far more taciturn. Beyond daily orders, there was little of discourse with Grayson during the first several months of his service. The valet, however, was secured finally of stable employment; his initial apprehension of the youth's likely wild habits had proved unfounded.

With this dramatic change in situation, Grayson—himself a serious sort by nature— took very well to his new place. Over time the pair settled into a routine of mutual respect and satisfaction. The valet grew to comprehend his master's likes and dislikes, to distinguish his contented silences from distracted ponderings or perturbed temper—his turns of mind and heart. As time passed, they increasingly engaged in general discourse whilst dressing or retiring. They could not be said to be intimate—despite the intimacies of service provided—but they achieved a comfortable understanding of just the right distance to suit. And Grayson learnt much of the character of his master by observation, particularly following the untimely passing of his father when the young man assumed fully his duties to his estates and remaining family, his young sister.

Ten years now having passed in this service, no man garnered greater respect from Grayson; indeed, he wished for nothing more than to serve his master until he grew too old to serve at all. His one remaining curiosity concerned when his employer might come to marry, being now nine and twenty.

"Grayson?"

Called from these stirring memories, Grayson begged excuse for his mind's wanderings. It was waved off haphazardly, further proof if needed, of his employer's own distraction. "But," his employer pressed—"I should like your thoughts." He asked again. "In your estimation, what sort of man am I?"

Again, anguished expectancy was to be found in the drawn brow, the tightness around eyes, an absolute stillness of expression but for the slow rise and fall of the man's chest as he breathed.

Grayson hedged a bit. "Might I inquire, Sir, as to what these questions tend? They are so broad as to cause consternation to one in my place."

"Merely to the illustration of my character—I am trying to make out how it is perceived by others."

Grayson's equanimity had been pricked with the initial question; now it suffered greater disturbance.

"I am the last man to qualify for such an assessment, being so placed as to perceive you in a manner materially different from what others may do," he replied at last, hoping by vagueness to skirt the issue.

"Yes," came the reply. "But you must have an opinion." When the servant remained silent: "I wish you would oblige me. I have of late been given to review my character. You may speak without prejudice; your opinion as an intelligent servant being most valuable."

"Might I also ask, then Sir, the impetus for such study?"

"You might wonder, I suppose." There was a lengthy silence before his master sighed with resignation and he confessed, "It is a woman."

"Your cousin?"

"Good heavens, no! Whatever could make you think it?"

"You embarked upon this... study... since quitting the country lately, Sir." Even as he recalled their visit, he realised who must be the lady in question.

"Ah, you see? You cannot say you do not notice, man."

"I notice much, Sir. But I make habit not to divulge what I see or to judge closely of it."

"Wise, perhaps, but little help in this instance." He breathed in, and expelled it slowly. "Very well. I met a woman – a most intriguing woman – who is not the least inclined to like me. In fact, she finds me abhorrent."

"Surely you mistake her, Sir. There is not a lady of your acquaintance who could—"

This animated the other's expression. "Oh, no! There is no mistake to be made! She has expressed quite plainly her opinion of me, if you will not! It does not bear contemplating."

"Yet you contemplate it, Sir?"

"Indeed I do." He sighed again. "Indeed I do. She accuses me of incivilities, behaviours most unbecoming, some dishonourable even."

"Then she cannot know you, Sir."

A sad smile overtook his features. "So I persuaded myself when first I...er, we had discourse. But afterward—some time afterward—my genuine regard for the lady could not allow me to disregard her assessment summarily. I had desired her good opinion, and she denied me with great energy. My faults, according to her calculation, are heavy indeed: arrogance, conceit, a selfish disdain for the feelings of others; shameful boasts of what misery I am able to inflict upon others. This is her opinion of me! This is the estimation in which she holds me."

"Sir, I can know nothing of these. My observation always has shown a fair and rational master, diligent in your charge for the furtherance of all whose happiness lies within your influence. There is not one of your tenants or servants but what will give you a good name; of that I am certain."

This point was considered but briefly. "Perhaps. But what of those not dependent upon me?"

"Of that, Sir, I am not well placed to judge. But I can hardly believe you to be two so very different men at once."

His employer's eyebrows raised in contemplation. "And yet, Grayson, this lady's words, received most unwillingly, have forced such scrutiny as to make me believe it possible."

Grayson understood his employer now required not reassurances, but an audience in his examination.

"I was given good principles, Grayson, but left to follow them in pride and conceit—to be a selfish being all my life in practice; perfectly overbearing; and to care for none beyond my own family circle..."

Grayson felt his master's distress, even as he believed the flaws he enumerated to be less egregious than the lady had alleged. Wisely, however, he forbore to interrupt.

"...think meanly of all the rest of the world, to wish at least, to think meanly of their sense and worth compared with my own."

Grayson could remain silent no longer. "Perhaps your manner, Sir, suggests more of reserve than other men of privilege. But that hardly—"

"No." He smiled involuntarily, despite the negation. "No, she has quite properly humbled me, Grayson. When I consider my addresses to the lady I must concede there is force in her accusation. Had I *behaved in a more gentlemanlike manner*... how the impeachment preys upon me." He squirmed somewhat in his seat then. "Too well do I remember now some of my expressions which might justly make her hate me. She has every reason in the world to think ill of me."

This woman's disapprobation truly afflicts him, thought the valet. His employer's speech, its duration and especially its rare intimate nature, furthered Grayson's understanding of the penetrating depth to which the lady's poor opinion was felt; it was quite obvious the man was not merely intrigued by her—he loved her; and judging from the extent of his present anguish, he loved ardently.

"I cannot escape the severity of that blame which was so liberally bestowed. She shewed me how insufficient are all my pretensions, Grayson." He grimaced. "I was angry when first we spoke, but these last days, my anger has taken a proper direction. These retrospections of reproach, these painful recollections ought not, indeed will not, be repelled. I must attend to her reproofs." He looked directly at Grayson then; their eyes met for an instant of raw understanding.

Profound silence now ensued, the small room seeming to bounce their thoughts off the walls and back to them in dead quiet echo. Nothing like such intimacy had ever passed between these two and the comprehension of the vulnerability this had produced in each now quickly made them as strangers one to the other. They looked away, glancing everywhere about the small dressing room—eyes trying to settle anywhere but upon one another. Finally they could ignore their circumstance no longer: "Thank you, Grayson, for your steadfastness."

"Sir." A nod of acknowledgment, and then Grayson found much-needed relief in action. Picking up his master's boots at long last, he said, "I will just take these down." He was answered with a distracted nod of dismissal.

He walked to the door but, before passing out of it, he thought better and turned to the man who was once more deep in his own disturbed thoughts.

"Ahem," he coughed and, drawing the other's notice, he said, "Sir, might I after all address your first request and then never speak of it again?"

He was met with a slow, bemused smile that he took for assent.

"I comprehend nothing, nor wish to, of the particulars of your lady's accusations, Sir. But I know this. It has been the work of my life to serve four employers, vastly different in character. Beyond these, my service has put me in the way of observing closely men of all sorts, as well as overhearing intimate details of them from their man-servants. I do not participate myself in such tongue wagging."

The mere idea of it placed upon his visage an expression of such disgust, that his employer hastened to concur that no assurances of the sort were necessary. Grayson cleared his throat and continued. "I own of great pride for my personal standing amongst these men." He hesitated. "Are you aware, Sir, that on three separate occasions I have been approached and made offers to change my situation, to leave your service for greater gain?"

Clearly from the surprise he evinced, his employer had not been aware. "I declined them," said Grayson unnecessarily, "with neither serious consideration nor regret. I say no more now than the truth, and what everybody will say that knows you. I can imagine no one I could better...that is—I would not now continue to serve a man who is not worthy of my attentions. A good man; the very best of them." This once, he allowed his governed demeanour to slip, to offer a rare smile of encouragement to one who as rarely sought it.

"A gentleman, Mr Darcy," he affirmed, as he closed the door on his departure.

Darcy Takes a Walk

♌♌♌

I love to imagine the relationship between Mr Darcy and his sister Georgiana as she grows into womanhood, as well as the back stories – the family history – that defined his character. And coupled with this, I like to contemplate the life of Fitzwilliam Darcy in the intervals between his interactions with one Miss Elizabeth Bennet. This story that follows encompasses a week in early summer between Darcy's disastrous first proposal to Lizzy and his later accidental meeting with her at Pemberley. It stands alone as a character study; but also combines well with the story which follows in this collection, Pemberley Break-Gee's Day Out, as the events described in each story dovetail.

♌♌♌

[Excerpt of a Letter to Georgiana Darcy]

...Your letter of yesterday brought me particular enjoyment. The house here has seemed peculiarly empty since your removal to Derbyshire. How delighted I was by your recounting of meeting our new foal, and how it nearly knocked you over in its zeal to introduce itself. Given the exuberant character you ascribe to it, I heartily approve of the name you suggest: 'Comus' it shall be. I assure you the "god of mirth" certainly brought a smile to me as I read of you making fast friends.

Richard and I have discussed some revision to your activities and are in accord. You have attained levels of accomplishment in your studies beyond reproach. But given your presentation next year, it has been suggested that you give some additional attention to preparing for society. Yes, my dear, I have had a letter from our aunt. But notwithstanding the source, we are in agreement with Lady Catherine's counsel on this occasion (but if you ever were to tell her this, we shall deny it vigorously). I would have you feel confident to converse on any manner of subject with ease. And so we will introduce some new activities – reading and such – to this purpose, and Richard and I both will undertake to assist you. And certainly during your residence at Pemberley, the park and wood will allow of instruction in the natural sciences as well as providing ample subjects for your drawings. I believe you will take pleasure from these additions at least equal to the good they will provide. At any rate, I shall discuss this with you and Mrs Annesley when next I see you both.

Indeed, that day will be sooner than you may have had cause to anticipate. My affairs here in town are in good order, and I have no wish to lumber about the house with no occupation when Pemberley offers diversion during this season. My time will be much better employed on the estate; and I have been away from it too long. I confess I have been longing for our hills and woods, for our home. As well, of course, for your companionship, for I find that I miss our recent habit of evening conversation. I am

123

resolved, therefore–I depart tomorrow for Cambridge, where I will call upon my old tutor there whom I have learnt, sadly, is very ill. I will rest there only the one night, however, so you may expect my arrival at Pemberley on Thursday in time for dinner. I trust you will have Comus behaving under good regulation by such time for a formal introduction to me.

Until we are once again together at home, I remain,
your loving and devoted brother, Fitz

ξ

[Pemberley, Friday]

The buffet contained a modest assortment of selections as per the habit of the master of Pemberley. This gentleman had filled his plate in moderation, leaving his appetite for the addition he knew would be delivered to him at any moment. Indeed, no sooner had he laid his dish at his place and seated himself than Lennox entered in his smart uniform, a silver platter bearing two perfectly poached eggs, freshly hot from the Dutch skillet that cook preferred. Darcy marvelled at the footman's timing, and cook's for that matter. Indeed, he took a moment to marvel at his staff in general. How well run was his entire house, as exampled in this morning ritual. Through some prescience servants always seemed to place food on the buffet just before Darcy entered the room, and the revered poached eggs arrived to take their rightful place on his dish the moment he sat. His entire household was managed in this way: never so much as a book out of place, every surface with a polished sheen; and yet almost never did he actually witness the servants at their work. It was as if bedclothes righted themselves, the detritus of meals cleared themselves, wilting flowers replaced themselves with fresh blooms, or fireplace grates whisked their own ashes and reset themselves for the next blaze – though Darcy well knew otherwise. He was fully cognizant of the efforts made behind the green baize doors to provide this ease of life to him, and to Georgiana. Not for the first time did he thank providence for the excellent management of Mrs Reynolds, her senior staff, and their recommendations for employing the best workers in the area. That lady had been relied upon heavily when Darcy's mother had passed, and for many years since; and she had excelled. And even now, willingly did she pass on her expertise, along with the assistance of Mrs Anneseley, to Georgiana – to ease her into managing first

Pemberley for her brother, and eventually her own home upon her marriage.

This distinction in service extended beyond the household, for the entire estate was managed admirably from the lowest stable boy to his steward, Thomas Gordon, in whom he had the utmost confidence.

Darcy rarely indulged in this particular repast of poached egg excepting when he was in residence at Pemberley, somewhat owing to conditioning himself to lighter breakfasts, but more so because no one could produce this particular fare as well as Cook. For years, cook had been repeating the same to Darcy whenever he complimented the dish – adding just a hint of vinegar to the boil, then simmering the eggs perfectly in water barely covering them brought that rare combination of flavour and texture that was unparalleled with other preparations. Even the celebrated kitchen at his club in town could not reproduce it for quality. Since his being introduced to them some thirteen years past, poached eggs had become a particular favourite for Darcy, just as it had for his father before him. Looking at his dish now, this memory of his father came unbidden to him. His mind slipped into the past, to those mornings he had shared with Edward Darcy.

ξ

Mrs Reynolds stood quiet and still in the doorway and watched Mr Darcy. She felt content today, for she liked it when Mr Darcy came home, and he had been away so much in recent months. If only he would marry, she thought with a grim smile, perhaps we should see him more settled here. But he had shown little inclination for it – just as his father had done before him; she hoped Mr Fitzwilliam would not wait as long as Mr Edward had done but might choose as well in the end, a woman of substance. For now, just to have both her master and Miss Georgiana in residence even for a short while raised a smile of complacency to their housekeeper and friend.

She smiled further to see the dish Lennox had just delivered, the sight taking her back several years to the contemplation of Edward and Fitzwilliam Darcy, father and son. Soon after Edward had goaded Fitzwilliam into tasting his first poached egg, the favoured breakfast had become a ritual shared between the two men, one moving out of his middle years, the other barely entered manhood, yet so alike in many ways.

Young Fitzwilliam Darcy had inherited more from his father than a love of simmered eggs. The physical resemblance as he grew into himself was uncanny. Fitzwilliam shared his father's stature and bearing, though as might be expected given the years that separated them, the son was broader of shoulder and slightly less thick in the midsection than his sire. The youth also had a size advantage by some two inches even at sixteen, and long legs that gave the illusion of even greater height. That much his parentage had given him—his propensity for riding, and for climbing the edges on their estate, had added strength to his form, a sureness of foot and excellent general dexterity, as well as the colour of health in his cheeks. He excelled at sword play, and riding; and was a natural at choosing horse flesh.

These things, Mrs Reynolds knew, his father had delighted in – that Fitzwilliam enjoyed activity and pursuits out of door in equal measure to his studies and his library. Edward felt it boded well for his son's stewardship of the estate some day, the combination of well-exercised body and mind.

Edward Darcy had also loved his son's handsome countenance, much like his own but for the boy's incredible eyes. Those had been the gift of Fitzwilliam's mother, so like were they to hers. Of changeable shape and hue given the youth's moods, it seemed, and yet always a blue of intensity, whether the icy pale of anger, the reflection of bright skies when his interest was excited, or the depths of a storm-tossed sea when sorely troubled. Edward Darcy had confessed to Mrs Reynolds one day in reflection that, when he met his son's eyes over their morning meal, it disconcerted him to see those that he had fallen in love with fully six years before the boy's birth: the beautiful Lady Anne Fitzwilliam's. Such a bittersweet memory, since he had lost his wife ten months before to a severe case of influenza. Of course, Fitzwilliam the son's did look different married to his dark mop of hair and strong features than they had in Lady Anne's fair gentility. But Edward Darcy met in his son the perfect blending of his own and his wife's better attributes, a nearly perfect youth sure to become the finest of men. At the time, his little daughter Georgiana more nearly resembled Lady Anne in her colouring and willowy form; yet it was she who had inherited Edward

Darcy's rounded grey eyes. It remained to be seen in the toddler which parent she might more favour as she grew.

Mrs Reynolds laughed to herself – imagine standing about indulging in memories when there was work to be done – and retreated from the doorway to leave Mr Darcy to his breakfast. She could not know that the gentleman's mind inhabited similar reminiscences.

ξ

Darcy tried to shake himself from recollections of his father and those mornings half a lifetime past, and he applied his attention to his eggs before they could grow cold and congeal. But once again memory intruded to slip him back to an earlier time. Those shared breakfasts had been a singular source of pleasure to father and son. Georgiana still inhabited the nursery, too young to take meals with the family. George Wickham often would be found with his godfather and his friend at other points of the day, but not at the breakfast hour. That hour belonged only to father and son. And after Lady Anne's passing, the two revered this time alone with one another.

Fitzwilliam Darcy would talk of his studies or his latest discovery of some new wonder on the estate, or relate with some delight the latest activities in the stables where he spent so much of his leisure time. And Edward Darcy loved to hear of his son's exploits; he would question him for details, drawing his son out of his quiet demeanour over some event that had excited his interest. In his turn, he would regale Will with stories of their family or his aspirations for his son. This was the setting where Darcy learned much about his grandfather, George Darcy, who had died long before his own birth but for whom both his sister and his friend Wickham were named. It had been George Darcy who had significantly increased the Darcy holdings by marrying the only daughter – indeed the only child – of an adjacent landowner, merging families and estates into one. Though there existed little true affection between George and Isabel Darcy, yet they had settled to a life of learnt mutual respect and gain.

Edward Darcy would speak also of his own courtship and marriage to Lady Anne, and of his good fortune that the girl he loved so deeply – for indeed she had been only a girl of sixteen when they met; he had waited fully four years to marry her – she had, by providence, also been considered a match of advantage for him.

Looking back now, Darcy could recall feeling ill at ease to hear his father speak so warmly and openly of his mother; but the strength of his parents' regard for each other was not lost on him. Even so, Edward Darcy counselled his son to someday take a wife equal to his character to secure long lasting happiness.

His father also impressed upon Darcy the charge that went with being custodian of their properties, fortune and assets; and the proud heritage of the family Darcy that traced back to William the Conqueror's expansion of his reign into Derbyshire. Young Fitzwilliam had absorbed all his father's histories with zeal, though he had heard them a hundred times or more since he was a small boy. It gave him satisfaction to know that he was part of something so long established – he was proud of his birthright and determined to be worthy of his legacy.

Darcy shook his head to yet again dispel this reverie. What was it that kept drawing him back to such memories? Certainly an egg, no matter how extraordinary the taste, could not wield power to evoke such associations. Though he felt the loss still of his father these six years – and indeed of his mother so long before that – he had learnt of necessity to compartmentalise his life into orderly fashion for greater regulation; and such memories as these ones resided behind a door Darcy seldom allowed himself to unlock. Why, now, did it seem to open so easily of its own accord to draw him within?

Perhaps it was down to no more than being at Pemberley? He had not passed much time there in the year preceding and there was no denying that, as much as he owned and inhabited the estate, it also resided within him – in his very soul. More than their other properties, Pemberley had always represented perfection to Darcy: the broad landscapes; extensive and beautiful woods; its ridges of high hills; the meandering streams that swelled from time to time into greater rivulets; and the house itself, glorious in stone and placed well on rising ground framed by hills and streams in a manner by which nature and man's devises were in full complement. Yet now he realised fully how much more it was than stone and wood. It represented family, permanence, a purpose in life and a legacy to pass on. It represented home in every distinction of that word.

For the first time since acceding to his father's position, Darcy felt he truly understood his responsibility in its fullest sense –

stewardship of all this, not just for his own lifetime, but for future generations; of their smaller properties, of Pemberley and their financial assets, certainly – but more importantly of the furtherance of the Darcy *family*. The long lines that connected the Darcys (and for that matter, the Fitzwilliams) back through time must be preserved. They were real, as factual as Darcy himself or Georgiana. Darcy's obligations to this maintenance had never felt so weighty as on this sunny Derbyshire morning in the breakfast parlour.

ξ

His relief when Georgiana entered, looking rested and fresh with life, was palpable. If anyone could lighten his mood and banish these weighty considerations, it was his sister. She was not the family merely of memory, but of youth and the present. It was true, her slender frame and natural grace of movement uncannily matched their mother's, as did her features in the main. And her grey eyes were those of Edward Darcy, in a softer form. But Georgiana was without question her own person in temper; and if somewhat aloof and unfathomable to others in general, she had become known intimately, especially in the two years past, to her brother and to Richard Fitzwilliam, their cousin and her guardian along with Darcy.

In their company, there was less reticence in Georgiana; only a loving nature and an openness of heart that Darcy envied a little even as he welcomed its balm to his soul. He knew that Georgiana was both excited by and dreading her presentation in society the following year, for the responsibilities it would occasion and the loss of childhood's indulgences it would signal. Darcy himself rather leaned toward the latter feeling himself, dreading the inevitable alterations that Georgiana's womanhood would evince in their own relationship.

He had noted some alteration already just in this year past, though for the most part these early ones were welcome; he had gained a confidante in some measure. But for now, she was still his sweet 'Gee'; and she always could produce a smile in her brother's heart.

When she entered, Georgiana started first toward the buffet, but halfway there she turned direction to the table. She threw her arms around her brother's neck impetuously, interrupting him in the act of knifing the last bit of egg into his mouth. As he looked up to meet her greeting, she placed a quick kiss on his cheek and said, "It is so good to be at home with you, Fitz. I have missed you dreadfully."

Darcy smiled – he felt lighter already. As Georgiana, not awaiting reply, fairly skipped to the buffet to fill a plate, her brother said, "Good morning, my dear. I have missed you as well. I hope to make up for our recent separations by remaining here some days. I have no pressing business in town, and in truth I am weary of uprooting myself so often of late."

Georgiana grinned with delight. She knew that the normal cycles of life would continue. She would still spend hours in her practice or studies each day, and Darcy would spend much of his time about the estate. Yet the idea of renewing their recently-begun habit of passing time with her brother in conversation of an evening was most acceptable to her; and even simply that he remained within her sphere, though not beside her all the day, was sufficient to gladden her heart. For so it is with people one loves -- sometimes just knowing them to be close by is enough.

Georgiana returned to the table with a filled dish. Darcy wondered not for the first time at how slender his sister was, given the volume of food she consumed. She applied herself diligently now to it, glancing up now and again to smile at her brother as he watched her with amusement. His own last bit of egg sat forgotten on his plate.

"I do not know how you can eat those vile things," said Georgiana, motioning toward the offending morsel.

Darcy laughed. It had been a running discourse of theirs for as long as Georgiana had been joining him for meals. Darcy had introduced his sister to the taste six years before, shortly after their father's death. Perhaps he had hoped to transfer the shared ritual element of it to his sister, but the young girl would have none of it. She had taken one bite of his poached egg, wrinkled her nose in some distaste, and pronounced it most disgusting. Her ten-year-old candour had provoked her to add that it was rather like consuming eyeballs, and having said so and set the image into her mind, it was some months before she could even bear to be in the room when her brother was served the dish.

When Georgiana had consumed most of her breakfast, she sat back and studied her brother for a moment while he pretended to be riveted to his newspaper. In truth, his mind had strayed to a breakfast some months earlier, at Netherfield Hall in Hertfordshire: a day when, carrying the freshness of morning in with her, Miss Elizabeth Bennet had appeared in another dining room in search of her ailing sister. He was reliving his sense of wonder at Miss Elizabeth's otherworldly form when he realized that his sister addressed him. He returned once again to Pemberley, and asked Georgiana to repeat herself. "I asked, what are you thinking of, to take you so far from here?"

Darcy smiled, and tried to cover himself. "I was thinking of our mother, and how like to her you are."

Georgiana's gaze did not waiver from her brother's eyes. He tried to hold the look, but found himself unable to do so, and glanced down again at the newspaper. Georgiana knew her brother prevaricated, and thought she knew the true source of his thoughts. She recalled too well their discourse only a few weeks before in Town, when Darcy had admitted to his feelings for Elizabeth Bennet and, worse, to having been rejected summarily by that lady. The expression Georgiana noted in her brother's countenance now was not of a kind she would normally associate with thoughts of their mother. But she decided to offer him kindness in his discomposure.

"Am I so like her in truth?" she offered, to allow him a graceful exit from the moment.

Still hovering between two worlds, Darcy looked disconcerted. "So like her? Who?"

"Like our mother, Fitz. Am I truly so like her? For I confess I cannot remember her well; and I have difficulty in seeing any resemblance when I look on our aunt, Lady Catherine." A trace of sadness appeared on Georgiana's usually serene countenance, and this brought Darcy fully to the present.

"My dear sister, yes, you are very like her. You have father's eyes, but in all else you reflect Lady Anne. You have seen her portrait in the hall, surely that would tell you the same. Lady Catherine cannot show you as much; she and Mama shared few physical traits, themselves favouring differing parents."

Georgiana smiled and screwed her face in concentration as if to try to recall the woman in question directly.

"But the resemblance is due to more than just your features," said Darcy. "You have her natural grace as well, and her sweetness of temperament, and her always ready smile, though you bestow it in your own inimitable way. You inherited from her your skill at drawing and painting as well, and have exceeded her at the pianoforte. I have to speak truth and say that Mama could speak with ease in French or Italian, whereas you..." This last comment as it trailed off now earned one of Georgiana's sheepish smiles, and it brightened Darcy's heart to see it. She wrinkled her nose at him in mock censure, and he imitated the gesture, blinking as he did so. This was unusual enough for him – it had been long since he had been openly playful with her – that it sent both of them into a moment of unchecked laughter.

Not wishing to break the lightness of mood and become entangled again in memories, Darcy changed the direction of their converse.

"Gee," he began. "I am going to take a walk this morning about the estate."

The statement, innocuous as it sounded, somewhat startled Georgiana. "Did not you ride this morning with Parsifal?" It was her brother's custom to do so when at Pemberley.

"No, I had some business to attend with Mr Gordon. I will walk instead when I have done here."

"A walk?" she questioned again. She began to wonder if the mount was ailing when her brother surprised her further. "Mmmm. I have been contemplating the benefits of such exercise of late. And it is good now and again to see the world from a different perspective. I wonder if you would be interested in foregoing your studies today, to join me in this venture? We can ask cook to supply us a bit of refreshment and stay out through the afternoon if you like, the day is sufficient for it."

Georgiana was all astonishment. She stared at Darcy for a long moment in wonder, not knowing what to say. Then, afraid of a reversal in fortune if she should delay in answering, Georgiana got up and rounded the table, hugged her brother's neck with enthusiasm while she whispered that she would go inform Mrs Annesley, and left the room in haste before the offer could be rescinded. Darcy himself settled back into his chair for a moment in a state of contentment he had not felt in some weeks.

When Georgiana came down to the entry hall a while later, having fixed their plan with Mrs Annesley and changed into a gown and boots more suitable for traipsing the out of doors, Darcy had already arranged for refreshments to carry with them and stood ready near the door. He suggested they begin their excursion with a trip to the stables. Georgiana wondered that he may have changed his mind about walking and determined to ride after all, but before she could question him, Darcy added, "After all, I am anxious to make the acquaintance of your Comus."

"Of course!" exclaimed Georgiana, well content to show off her foal, as though she herself might have produced it. She had forgotten that Darcy had not met their latest stable resident yet. Her brother had arrived yesterday only just before dinner, and they had spent the evening quietly with Georgiana playing her latest mastered pieces for him. They set off at once now with high expectations for a rewarding day.

As they walked toward the stable, Darcy regarded his sister and could not help but think of Miss Elizabeth Bennet yet again – certainly not from any physical resemblance between the young women. But Georgiana had worn an old gown for her lengthy walk, a muslin the colour of hornwort, knowing her brother's propensity for straying off of established paths. Its simple construction and mossy shade brought to Darcy's eye a sketch of Miss Elizabeth Bennet at the Meryton Assembly on that evening which ended his indifference to the charms of the female sex and to his peace of mind—had he but known it at the time. *Confound it*, he thought to himself, *am I consigned to find something of this lady in everything I look upon, even my own sister? Shall I never find respite from her haunting image and words?*

Georgiana, too, glanced up sidelong at her brother and noted that his thoughts were far away again. She smiled ruefully to herself. She really must try to draw her brother out, for she could see that what occupied his thoughts so – and she knew their source – was gnawing at him. She had reached sufficient age and maturity that it was time for her to repay him the protection and encouragement he had shown her all her life; and this she determined to do. She must persuade her brother to speak of Miss Elizabeth, for his own good. And if she could not, she could at least try to distract his contemplations of the lady.

They reached the stable yard and found Bryce, one of their grooms, with Scheherazade and her foal in the outer enclosure.

Darcy fed the mare a treat and then stroked its forelock when the horse nuzzled him for more notice. Georgiana had immediately claimed the attentions of Comus, they had obviously formed a bond in their long week's acquaintance. Georgiana made formal presentation of it to her brother, and the antics of the foal lived up to his namesake. He neighed and nickered his approval of having an audience, then gambolled and pranced about. When Georgiana was diverted to speak with the groom, Comus butted her arms ineffectually for attention, moving quickly around one side of her to the other to try his luck there. The lady's eventual notice sent Comus off yet again, and giving them all—including her brother to her delight—to chuckling.

Scheherazade looked on as if embarrassed by its offspring's behaviour, though pride could also be detected in its maternal eye. The two humans spent some minutes in play with the foal beneath the protective eye of the mare. At last, they left the horses to their care with Bryce, and turned to leave. Before quitting the stable yard entirely, Darcy went in to greet Parsifal. He stroked his favoured stallion for a moment, making promise for a good airing the next day, and left instructions with Evan to give the mount its exercise.

ξ

Darcy and Georgiana then began by making their way across the field behind the stable, walking though wild oat that had been cropped by the park's deer; then entered the long wood which would take them to the beginnings of a ridge that eventually rose up behind the house. The day was uncommonly warm under a cloudless sky. The wood offered shade from a strong sun that filtered its rays liberally through the sparser trees in the outer reaches, then narrowed to bright spears haphazardly thrown from time to time, it seemed, in the denser centre of the wood. As they made their way along a well-worn path, the siblings stopped here and there to challenge each other in identifying the trees and plants they encountered: the carpets of small wood daisies, dog rose, bluebells and meadow vetch around their feet; the massive oak trees interspersed with Wych Elm and Ash, and further into the depths of the wood, liberally threaded with Yew. Darcy, for his greater experience of the land, always knew the answers to Georgiana's challenges. She, for her turn, did well but stumbled on a few lesser-known varieties; her brother corrected her gently and with good humour. Thus they passed through the wood congenially, genuinely enjoying each other's companionship. When they emerged from the wood onto the upland slope of the ridge, their challenges moved to the purple loosestrife growing along the stream bank, the willow herb's delicate pink flowers swaying in the breeze, hawthorn and pussy willow hedgerows, and the Rowan Mountain Ash growing among the limestone outcroppings. It was too early in the season for the Rowans' trademark profusion of red berries, but they were full of new growth. Darcy stopped and removed a small, thick branch end that had been partially broken away and hung from its limb. He did not throw it away, but held onto it and fingered it absently as they continued on their way.

They climbed the edge some way, Darcy assisting Georgiana in her footing when they met with rocks and steep slopes. Finally, they reached a natural plateau where a large flat boulder jutted out over the park land below. They agreed it a perfect stopping place – they would rest there a while, and eventually proceed back to the house using a different, less arduous route than they had used for their ascent. Georgiana marvelled at how well her brother knew every bit they had traversed, indeed every inch of the entire estate, for as they sat together on the flat-topped rock, he pointed out to her in the distance stream sources, stands of Durmast Oak, and the beginnings of the moorland to the east. There was no square of this land that Darcy had not explored over the years—on foot as a youth, on horseback these recent years, growing to know it intimately such that it now could hold few secrets from its master.

He opened the satchel and removed some cheese, two rolls from breakfast – the kitchen had provisioned them well – and a surprise from cook as well of strawberries, ripe red and juicy sweet, a real treat. The siblings shared their bounty, as well as lemonade contained in an old leather flask. Their faces were flushed from the exertion of their climb, but they were content in the welcome respite the outcropping provided. While they sat there, Darcy removed a small knife from its wrappings, and began to pare the bark from the rowan wood he'd purloined during their progress.

When they had been resting in companionable silence some while, Georgiana noted again a faraway glazed expression settling in to Darcy's countenance. She considered that if she was to persuade her brother to talk to her, this setting provided an opportune moment. But how to begin? Screwing up her courage, she asked in a solemn voice, "Will you tell me about her, Fitz?"

Darcy turned his eyes to his sister, his expression inscrutable. "Hmm? Do you mean Mama?" He believed his sister to have reverted to their earlier breakfast discourse.

"No." This was offered so softly, and accompanied by such earnest concern, that there could be no doubt of whom she spoke. Yet Darcy tried to stall her with a question. She cut him off before the first word of it was released.

"Dearest brother, I do not wish to cause you distress. Quite the opposite – I cannot bear to see you so unhappy. But any one can see your thoughts move in unguarded moments away from Pemberley, and I know where they travel – or at the least to whom they go. I wish you would tell me more of this lady who can so overtake your thoughts."

Georgiana's sincerity was plain to see as well as her kind intent, but an awkward moment ensued. Her own aborted love affair the year before had taught Georgiana the import of facing one's feelings, the painful consequences of ignoring overpowering emotion such that it could not seethe and fester. Her brother had saved her from George Wickham twice – first nearly a year past when Wickham's plot to marry her for her fortune was uncovered; and again only weeks before, when his own afflicted heart made her realise that she had never really loved Wickham. The comprehension had lifted a burden of long standing. She would do anything now to repay her brother and relieve his heavy heart. Seeking with a little lightness to ease the tension around them, she said, "Unless of course you are thinking of proposing to Lady Honoria Parkhurst. If that is the case then please spare me that intelligence, as I have no wish to know she will become my sister sooner than is necessary."

Both siblings laughed, and Darcy continued to look on his sister in silence, but it gained in comfort. "I *should* marry Lady Honoria, if only to punish you for such impertinence, my dear," he said with a chuckle finally, "but that I would find the worst of the punishment directed at myself." They laughed again.

For several minutes more the only sound to be heard was the occasional rush of a breeze through the wood below them. Finally, Darcy began. "Miss Bennet. Miss *Elizabeth* Bennet, that is. She is most difficult to describe, Georgiana, for I find her altogether changeable, a conundrum." Georgiana feared at first that this would be the end of her brother's resolve. She noted that he seemed to war inside himself between his innate wish for privacy and his need to speak of things his mind would not allow him to ignore.

"Begin with her features. Surely those do not change!" Georgiana suggested.

"Oh, but they do, sister, truly they do. But I will attempt what you ask, if I can see no point to be served." He appraised his sister from her head to her feet, now dangling over the edge. "Miss Elizabeth is nearly your height, and similar in form. Her features are delicate enough, though perhaps her mouth is a bit wide to consider her beautiful by convention. She has an elder sister, Miss Bennet combines all the elements of exceptional beauty; by comparison I would judge Miss Elizabeth to be very pretty only.

"But she loves to laugh and, when she does so, her mouth curves up playfully, surpassing most of the painted lips of the ladies in Grosvenor Square and transforming her into a true beauty. Her most arresting feature by far, however, is her eyes. They are the shade of chestnuts, and they meet you with such directness some time as to be disconcerting. They shine with intelligence and with the lively wit that resides within. That is what makes them truly arresting."

"But I thought men do not like a lady of wit; we are counselled against possessing any surely. Fordyce, Gregory, Gilroy – all of the courtesies teach that a lady should not... that it is a danger to the social order for a lady to laugh at others or speak her mind too freely."

Darcy regarded his sister closely; she was truly perplexed. Well, and no more so than he. "Fordyce and the others, to this mind, are wrong, Gee. Or at least too cautious. I might have agreed with them in the main once; but I have since learnt that a woman who combines a lively wit with a kindly heart is an altogether attractive prospect—far more stimulating for requiring greater exercise of my own wits, and less tedious by far, than any dozen fawning girls who only smile and nod." He shook his head in a bewildered smile. "You would do well," he added, "to use your own good foundation to selectively take counsel from Fordyce, from them all. Perhaps we all need from time to time to reflect on what truly marks one out a lady – or a gentleman."

Georgiana could not reconcile her brother's words. She was astonished into silence, until her brother roused his mood, and said "What were we speaking of before?"

"Miss Bennet's fine eyes—that sparkle with wit," said Georgiana with a smile.

"Ah. Of course." Darcy looked as though he was sorry he had asked; his expression changed, grew more thoughtful. "Yet they can be cold, and piercing, when the woman is provoked; and it seemed no matter of my intent, I provoked her sorely during our acquaintance—more so than I realised."

As she wanted her brother to continue, Georgiana steered him from the course his last statement turned toward, and asked innocently, "And her hair? Is it dark, with her eyes?"

"Her hair matches her eyes, the colour of chestnuts in autumn, and draws one's attention to those fine features. I thought her handsome enough when first we met."

Georgiana opened her mouth in surprise. "Handsome enough!" she cried. "How can you say only that, when you have just described her as the most enchanting creature!"

"Because I know what you do, sister. You are not quite so adept in your feminine arts to fool me. I have had matches thrust upon me by every busybody in London, the best of them in their trade. You think to make me lose my head in describing Miss Elizabeth, and determine to meet her again." Georgiana tried to stifle an embarrassed smile, but her brother caught her at it. "You see?" Despite his teazing words, there were pain and resignation in the tone.

"But, Fitz, do not you hear yourself? You do love her; it is in every word you speak and in the very air around you. Surely you can make her see that for herself; you can win her again."

"You're being fanciful, Georgiana. I do not deny I loved Miss Bennet, or that I could wish she had returned my sentiments, or that I find her intelligence engaging. But it is not to be. It is folly to pursue further; there are too many impediments, you know there are – on her side and on mine. Things I tried to set aside; but my intractable nature nonetheless offended the lady in raising them. I fear my own character cannot change. I told you of all this in the last weeks in town; a change of location has not altered them—nor will any passage of time."

Darcy's expression took on a closed aspect that warned Georgiana she would get little else from her brother, especially when he added, "I can see you have not learnt to temper your romantic nature."

Perhaps it was the sting she felt from this last rebuke that gave her courage to risk one last question to him. "Are you certain, brother, that you do not use those impediments to your advantage, to justify avoiding a course of action that terrifies you?"

Darcy turned sharply to look at his sister, and in so doing, the knife he had been working into the rowan wood slipped out of his control, nicking and drawing blood from his left thumb. He dropped the knife and brought his hand to his mouth, to stem the bleeding. Georgiana, with a look of alarum, rummaged in the satchel to find the cloth the bread had been wrapped in, shook it free of any crumbs and, taking her brother's hand she bound his thumb in the cloth, tying the corners in a tidy knot. This she had done while enduring a terrible silence. When she finished, she turned her eyes to him, tears brimming over in a countenance of repentance, and whispered, "Fitz, I am sorry."

Darcy took in her tears and her concern, and his heart could not hold any anger or resentment towards his sister. In tacit agreement to close the subject of Elizabeth Bennet, he drew his sister to him, held her against his shoulder, and they comforted each other in stillness. While tears slowly slid down Georgiana's cheeks, she could not know that her brother fought to control his own as he looked out on their beloved landscape that was his to preserve.

After some while Darcy released his sister, and wiped her last tears with the back of the cloth bound around his hand. They laughed shyly at the bulbous shape of his thumb from so much cloth; and then gathered their belongings into the satchel to begin the walk home. Their mood was constrained at first, but then they renewed their challenge game, and in so doing the easy companionship they had shared most of the day returned to them. They descended in late afternoon, when the sun had lost its ability to sting, and the breeze took on a coolness that gave a chill to Georgiana. Darcy removed his coat to wrap around her, and they continued through the recently landscaped parkland behind the house. They did not renew their intimate converse, yet each knew it had not retreated from the other's thoughts.

ξ

When they entered the house, Georgiana moved to go upstairs and rest before dinner. Darcy would head for his library and a much needed brandy before retiring to his own chambers. But Georgiana turned back from the first step and went to her brother to return his coat, helping him on with it in the absence of Grayson. Then she hugged him with great depth of feeling, and said, "Thank you, Fitz. For to-day. For our outing. It meant a great deal to me."

Darcy returned her affectionate gesture and smiled, saying "And to me as well, my dear. This will not be the last of them." As he spoke, he took her hand and pressed something into it. It was the rowan wood, carved now into a rudimentary shape of a horse's head and *Comus* crudely scratched into its base. Georgiana was so moved as to bestow another hug on her brother before, released at last from the prolonged embrace, she began again to mount the stairs.

From several steps up, as Darcy was beginning to walk toward the library, Georgiana said, "Do you know, brother?" Darcy stopped and turned back toward her. "You can no more choose *not* to love someone than you could choose to marry Lady Honoria." Delivered in all sincerity, her pronouncement hit Darcy with violence. But immediately after the words escaped her, an impish smile and a twinkle in her eyes appeared, and Georgiana Darcy ran trippingly up the remaining stairs and out of sight.

Darcy was left standing with a dropped jaw, a throbbing thumb, and a sense of wonder that his sister – this beautiful sprite – could be imbued with all the wisdom of women through the ages in one moment, and all the innocent guile of childhood in the next.

When he recovered himself, Darcy strode purposefully to the library with some haste. It would take more than one brandy, he determined, to settle his spirits this afternoon.

ξ

[Five Days Later]

As Darcy flicked back the drapes in his bedchamber, there was no appreciable change in the level of light within the room. Darkness pervaded it still, with only shadowy outlines of the room's furnishings visible. Eventually, this fact reached into Darcy's consciousness. It drew him from that stumbling haze of groggy half-awareness that always characterized his waking after a night of unsettled sleep. He considered the window – he knew that it should be morning, it was well past dawn. Though his chambers faced the south, still the room should have been bathed in light after parting the thick brocaded drapes.

Darcy's own plot of Derbyshire had enjoyed a particularly good spell of weather during the sennight he had been in residence here. It had seemed that the sun shared Darcy's preference for Pemberley, as it had visited consistently these last several days, embracing it in lengthy and warm caresses. Late spring and early summer in the country could bring myriad delights, and Darcy had been fortunate in the timing of this latest visit. He had come to expect a bright greeting every morning, casual afternoon walks through sweet-scented grasses with Georgiana, evenings on the terrace until the sun had sunk below the horizon, and nights that allowed him to exercise a preference for sleeping with windows thrown wide. Particularly in recent nights he appreciated this last, since his slumber had been erratic and undependable. He found strange companionship during sleepless hours in the sounds of night – the distant whispering of willow trees, the haunting calls of bard owls, the rustlings of badgers and shrews. He fashioned that he could recognize now the individual calls of these denizens of the wood who shared his nocturnal wakefulness.

During the day, with Helios' countenance to brighten his sensibilities, Darcy could feel at peace, or persuade himself of it. He could focus his attentions on Georgiana and her new selections from the library, which they had begun reading together in the garden of an afternoon. He could lose himself in matters of account ledgers and crop yields, and all other manner of records for the estate which Thomas Gordon yielded to Darcy amiably enough, pretending not to notice the master's intrusion into the daily details of the steward's domain. He could saddle Parsifal and survey his lands, galloping in perfect partnership as they traversed Pemberley's grounds. And he could, in all manner of these activities, hold at bay with some success thoughts of Hertfordshire where she must be now – of fields of wild dill and pear orchards, dark hair adorned with pearls, fine chestnut eyes, the residual tingle from the touch of a delicate hand in his while dancing; or the spiralling tension between two people that developed beyond the manoeuvres of a dance when their tempers were challenged. He could forget Eastertide at Rosings and walks through the grove there, and the misunderstandings that had resulted in his disastrous proposal. He could forget that the one person of his acquaintance whose opinion of his character most mattered, thought little of it; had in fact despised him.

But at night, in the solitude of his chambers, these sketches fought for prominence in his mind's eye, denying him sleep in the furore of their competition. Georgiana had recommended all sorts of remedies to bring sleep to her brother, some simple ones which he tried – tea with honey; closing his eyes and meditating his body into a relaxed state; a vase of lavender near his head. But many of her suggestions he refused to consider. He could not reconcile himself to drinking warmed milk laced with valerian, so bitter was its taste; and he certainly had no inclination to hang himself over the side of his bed with his head resting on the floor. He could not see how sleep would *ever* come in such discomfort or in such a humiliating arrangement. And so he welcomed the sounds of those nocturnal friends without his window for distracting him, however briefly, from his inner disquiet.

Involuntarily, Darcy had taken to eluding sleep until the hours before dawn's onset, and yet still he always rose just before or after dawn. He determined to remain active throughout each day in the hope that extreme fatigue would overcome his nightly watch, but such had not been the case. And so he had arisen this morning, conditioned to expect another bright day, only to be met with unexpected darkness.

He looked again out the window, believing at first that he must be mistaken in the hour and it must be night still; but that there was a different quality to the inky sky. Ah! There it was, finally -- the summer storm that had been hinting at its approach for the last days. Even as the local populace made much of their good fortune in the recent clime, nature had been preparing itself for an onslaught. Small animals could be seen foraging the gardens for food, dragging what they found to their burrows to pile stock for an extended siege. Caterpillars inched their ways into thick grassy tufts and curled themselves tight, joining the snails which inched their way down onto low, thick leaves and stems to weather coming winds. For near two days, the forests had taken on a muted colouring overall, as the trees turned over their leaves to call for rain. Deer stayed close to the protective wood's edge in their grazing; sheep gathered into close huddles, and the cattle on the farms lowered their thick bodies to the ground to settle themselves in for the duration.

And now it had come. Darcy looked towards the far ridgeline beyond the landscaped garden, his eyes now adjusting and alert to the low light. He could discern clouds, black and swirling, with dark fingers reaching down to the hilltops, already pummelling the summits with driving rain, no doubt. Though it would move slowly, still it moved inexorably toward Pemberley; it would arrive, most likely, within the hour.

Darcy lit a candle and noticed it was nearly seven o'clock. Quickly he donned some clothes and made his way purposefully out of the house to the stables to see if he could help secure everything there. He knew his farm staff, local cottagers and household staff would be busy at work doing the same in their domains. And as he would expect as he neared the stables, he found Evan and Bryce closing the lofts, pitching hay from the paddock into the storage shelter to bolster stores, and taking great care to secure the horses in their stalls. Darcy joined them in their labours for a short while and, when all looked to be completed, he stopped to visit Parsifal. The sensitive horse showed some uneasiness, reacting to the pressure in the atmosphere, as the first muted rumblings of thunder reached the estate. Darcy spent a few moments calming the high-strung mount before making his way home to dress properly for the day. The first sporadic drops of rain fell around him as he reached the entrance.

ξ

By the time Darcy came down to his morning meal, the storm had moved in fully. Thunder resonated around the house, rain lashed at windows, and there was a charge in the air inside and out. But fires had been laid in all the grates, and lit in the study, the library and the private quarters, where the warming blazes brought a semblance of sanctuary. Georgiana had come downstairs directly behind Darcy, and the two had a quick meal together before separating to their respective activities: Georgiana to her studies with Mrs Annesley, Darcy to his study to respond to correspondence.

The first letter he picked up was one from Charles Bingley that had arrived the day before. For the most part the letter was typical of Bingley, genial chatter concerning the latest news from town. But there was an undercurrent to his friend's writing, a melancholy air that one would not generally associate with the usually affable gentleman. Bingley's malaise had begun when he, along with his sisters and Darcy, had left Netherfield Park in Hertfordshire months ago to return to town. Time and distance obviously had not lessened Bingley's affections for Miss Bennet. He was a young man with many friends and in great demand with them, and most of the time acted his old self. But on occasion, as now, his emotion got the better of him. He remembered a fair beauty, and regretted the loss of her.

Darcy had not regretted his part in convincing Charles to quit Hertfordshire at the time. He believed that if his friend had continued to pursue Miss Bennet, he would have been accepted, but for all the wrong reasons. Miss Bennet seemed to like Bingley well enough, but her regard had not appeared to extend beyond a general fondness, she displayed little evidence of any peculiar partiality for the man over any other. If she were to accept Bingley, Darcy had thought, it would be for the security he would provide – the young woman's mother had made that clear in all her prattling. Darcy had not been able to stand by and see Bingley so used. And so, he had done what he thought best.

And worse, Darcy now knew differently – or at least must believe that he was likely mistaken. Miss Bennet *had* returned Bingley's love, it would seem. If Miss Elizabeth Bennet was to be credited, as she must be, with an understanding of her sister's sensibilities, then Jane Bennet was guilty of no more than too careful a display of her preference. Darcy hated to see his jovial friend in distress, more so now that he too suffered the pain of separation forever from a woman he loved. He should confess to his friend the knowledge he now had gained – should admit he may have been wrong to separate them so quickly – but must determine how best to approach such a thing. He rather thought he should not do the thing thus, in a letter. It was a discourse better conducted in person. But how then should he answer his friend's missive now?

He put Bingley's letter aside to reply later, when his own head and spirit could better address his friend's disquiet. In its place, he picked up a report from Alastair Ransom detailing a new investment opportunity. This he responded to, as well as several other letters of business. He passed some hours in this fashion, glancing up from his writings now and then to note that the storm outside showed no sign of abatement.

Some time after noon, Darcy moved to the library. He took down the book he had begun a few days before and poured a brandy to sip at his leisure. Before finding his seat by the fire, he went to the windows. Steady rain cascaded down the panes, the angry black clouds of the morning having given way to an overall pall of grey that showed no sign of waning soon – a good afternoon to pass some time reading; there was little else to be done. His mind flickered back momentarily to his desk in the study, saw Bingley's letter still vying for his attention and he hesitated. But in the end, the reading won out. After all, what succour might he offer to Bingley when his own composure was in such turmoil? He settled himself in his chair and opened *Introduction to the Principles of Morals and Legislation*. Jeremy Bentham's moral philosophy based on Helvetius' "greatest happiness for the greatest number principle" interested Darcy, though he had yet to be persuaded that only consequences mattered, that actions should be judged strictly on the basis of how their outcomes affected general utility.

Turning to his marked page, Darcy began to read, but he soon realized that he had perused several paragraphs without retaining a single phrase. Some part of his mind kept reverting to Bingley's letter, and that in turn, led his thoughts to Miss Elizabeth Bennet yet again. He imagined her standing in his park, the ridge behind her some ways with those black clouds trailing their tendrils down onto the hills, the wind blowing her sodden gown and her loose hair wildly about her. She looked like Eris, goddess of chaos and discord. When the clouds began to approach her with swiftness, threatening to engulf her as she danced in the swirling storm, Darcy tried to call out to her, but his words were lost in the wind. As the tempest engulfed Miss Elizabeth, he tried yet again to call a warning. His voice brought him awake sharply, and he realized he had fallen asleep in his chair. He had been dreaming. He took a gulp of brandy to clear his head, and stood to stretch his legs, feeling slightly better for it.

Darcy recalled the sketch from his dream and laughed to himself. Chaos, indeed. That lady stubbornly continued to cause discord within him, eroding his equanimity.

He went back to his book; but philosophy could not hold his attention this afternoon. He perused the extensive shelves for an alternative, selecting finally a volume of Blake. Perhaps poetry would sooth his overworked sensibilities. Before returning to his chair, Darcy yet again stood at the window. Dark clouds continued to hover over Pemberley, though the morning's biblical deluge had subsided to rain falling in a regulated rhythm. The earth had absorbed its fill, such that water now collected in pools, and formed shallow channels to run down the sloping lawn to the lake.

Darcy spent a moment constructing by instinct a list in his head of what would be required to restore the property when the storm moved on, and tucked this list into a compartment of his well-ordered mind. He would retrieve it for implementation the next day, the rain should have dissipated finally then. The ground would be sodden for some time. Darcy blinked to expel yet another image forming in his mind: Miss Elizabeth, her skirts sodden, the hem coated in mud at least six inches, but her face flush with health, her hair which had loosened during a walk drifting down across her shoulder. It had been nine months since that morning at Netherfield. She had been breathtaking in such attitude. Eris, indeed.

He fingered the small leather-bound volume of Blake, and returned to his chair, stoking up the fire before settling back into the cushions. He had no sooner established himself thus than there came a knock on the door from the adjoining drawing room. The door opened to reveal Georgiana on the threshold. "Would you mind some company, brother?"

Darcy's smile confirmed her welcome. Georgiana stood off to one side a moment, opening the door to its full extent so that Lennox could wheel in a tea cart. The server held tea on top, as well as dishes on a lower shelf with an array of foods. There were small pies, cheese, slices of gammon, apricots, and – best of all – currant buns freshly warm from their baking. Georgiana smiled at Darcy. "I knew you would neglect dinner, brother, so I have brought it to you, or a fair substitute. You would bury yourself in your books or your work all day and never think to eat, but I must have sustenance or I shall perish." This last was offered quite dramatically while Georgiana feigned an expiring attitude, drawing a chuckle from Darcy.

It was true that he had not once reflected on food during the day, but the manifestation of this unusual feast before them now evoked an appetite in him. He thanked his sister for her thoughtful gesture; she in her turn protesting she did not deserve his approbation. She readily boasted that her primary motivation had been the rather audible rumbling she had been experiencing this last hour or more from her own stomach. Darcy could not help but laugh again as she continued to liken her riotous stomach to nature's thunderous threats that morning.

Lennox had positioned the tea table between the two fireside chairs, and then departed. When he had gone, Georgiana flopped unceremoniously into the vacant chair. Darcy offered his sister a look of arch reproach at her lack of decorum; but she only shrugged her boredom in reply. Her brother laughed and shook his head as if to deny any responsibility for his sister's common manners. He was smiling, however, all the while.

"Has your day been so tedious, my dear?" he asked.

"No, not tedious. Simply long, and sorely lacking in nourishment." A pointed glance at the serving tray and then at her grinning brother followed this irreverent pronouncement. "And also I have grown accustomed now to our walks and activities out of doors, that it seems a disappointment not to be able to continue. But I suppose we have been fortunate in the weather before today. I know that I should not mind it so. *You*, dear brother, have probably been so buried in books all day that you would not even notice the rain."

Darcy did not answer his sister. How could he explain with any sense of rationality the fantastic images his mind had conjured today amidst the gloom? Instead, he leaned forward to serve himself some food, and Georgiana followed suit. She held up a cup and, after he nodded in assent, made tea for both of them. When each was served, they sat back to enjoy their unusual repast – dinner, tea and supper all in one. The room fell silent for several minutes but for the clink of flatware on china.

When they had eaten to their satisfaction, Georgiana refilled both their cups, and they sat back to enjoy their tea in leisure. Darcy asked his sister how she had spent her day, and she began to recite a list of her studies. In the beginning, Darcy interrupted occasionally to ask questions, either for clarification or to test her knowledge. But when she began to tell him about her day journey to Buxton a few days before with Mrs Annesley, Darcy sat back just to listen, enjoying the soft tones of his sister's voice.

Georgiana had enjoyed her day out with Mrs Annesley. She stared into the fire as she told Darcy about it, creating images out of the flames – sketches of shop windows, smartly dressed matrons, and wide tree-lined streets. She stopped to ask her brother his own impression of the town, but cut off the question unfinished as she turned to him. Darcy was slumped in his chair, teacup balanced precariously on his knee. His eyes were closed, his head lolled to one side and his hair spilled across his brow. His chest rose and fell evenly as he took long, deep breaths.

Darcy was sound asleep. Georgiana laughed to think that, apparently, they had found the remedy for his insomnia – he had only to ask his sister to tell him a story.

She looked on her brother and thought how young he looked when relieved of the care he wore in his waking countenance. He was so handsome; and with all the other loving qualities she knew him to possess, she could not imagine a woman who would not welcome his attentions. She rose slowly so as not to disturb him, and carefully retrieved the teacup from his knee to replace it on the serving cart. She crossed to the other side of the library, returning with a travelling robe, and lightly covered her brother with it. She looked for another moment on this man she had loved all her life— who was brother, and father, and teacher; yes, and friend to her. Before she made to leave him to his peaceful slumber, she leaned down and placed a kiss of gratitude on his brow. As she stood again, she heard him murmur, "Lizzy."

Some day, she was determined to meet this Elizabeth Bennet who had so thoroughly taken up lodging in her brother's resisting heart.

Pemberley Break –
Gee's Day Out
ऌऌऌ

As with the story immediately preceding this one, the relationship that develops between Fitzwilliam Darcy and his sister Georgiana as she grows into womanhood is explored during the interval between Darcy's first proposal to Miss Elizabeth Bennet and his later summertime accidental meeting with her and the Gardiners at Pemberley. It stands alone; but also combines well with Darcy Takes A Walk, *the events of which precede and dovetail with those in this story. Author's note: I have taken some license in this narrative with timing: the caves in Castleton actually did not open to the public for several years after the events described herein.*

ऌऌऌ

Georgiana Darcy awoke and stretched her limbs slowly. She was feeling rather lazy this morning and contemplated for a moment the idea of staying abed for a while. Alyce had entered the room after knocking, and was pushing open the drapes. It looked to be a glorious day. Indeed, after a violent storm that had assailed them for fully two days and a half, the sun once again had claimed Pemberley for its own, banishing all the clouds and rain to the south. Its bright rays now lay crossways on the bed and warmed the coverlet, in turn increasing Georgiana's drowsy complacency.

Alyce had gone into the dressing room, but returned immediately with a tray bearing chocolate and some buns. She marvelled at Georgiana's natural lithe figure given her mistress's fondness for eating. "What do you wish to put on today, Miss Darcy?"

Georgiana gave it idle thought. Her mind was still fixed on the idea of enjoying her repose a while longer. "The green, I suppose," she replied with a sigh. Alyce regarded her curiously.

"Oh, but Miss Darcy! Do not you wish to wear something newer, perhaps brighter, for your day out?"

Her day out? Oh! Of course!

ξ

The storm had begun to taper off in mid-morning the day before, and by noon the rain had stopped altogether. Immediately, restoration of the grounds had begun. The household staff and gardener began to clear debris from around the house and landscaped grounds, and to check the drainage around the foundations. Georgiana and Mrs Annesley had donned work aprons and joined in, though they were only allowed light sweeping on the terraces. Still, the activity felt good after being housebound for three days. Georgiana's brother had coordinated with Mr Gordon the reparation of the remaining grounds. The storm had downed several old trees, and had blown varied other natural debris all around. Every man who could be spared his customary duties was called to join in the restoration.

Darcy himself had followed on Parsifal as Bryce and Evan drove a wagon along the woods' edge, stopping where trees had fallen to chop them, load the logs onto the wagon, and cart them back for storing. The work was tedious, and there was much of it to be accomplished. Though several farm workers had joined the grooms for this labour, Darcy also took his turn at chopping wood. He enjoyed the occasional justification to engage in such effort. At any time, it provided him a tangible connection to his land and to his tenants and workers – and the latter respected him for it. But particularly now, it offered him also an occasion where all his effort was required for the physical task at hand, which left little possibility to engage in distracting thoughts.

By the end of day's light, a significant restoration had been effected, and Darcy met with Mr Gordon to review a plan for its completion. During their converse, Mr Gordon recollected that he had been supposed to travel to Castleton on the following day to complete the purchase of some Leicester Longwool sheep being introduced on the farms. He would send word to postpone the meeting so that he could personally oversee remaining efforts to offset the storm's aftermath. Darcy, however, offered to go in Mr Gordon's stead and complete the negotiations himself; Mr Gordon could then send drovers for the sheep when Pemberley was back to its unspoiled state. The two men agreed readily on this plan.

At dinner, Darcy had told Georgiana of his errand, and asked if she would like to accompany him to Castleton. He could dispatch his business, he had said, in under an hour; and following, they could spend the remainder of the day visiting the village. They might call, in particular, on his friend Henry Wentworth, who owned a most agreeable and comfortable inn. Georgiana was delighted at the prospect.

ξ

But in her leisurely awakening to-day, she had not remembered they were to go to Castleton.

"Alyce, I had quite forgotten!" she cried, and immediately her lethargy fled, replaced with enthusiastic vigour. She sat up in bed straight away and swung her legs around over the side. She smiled in anticipation. "You are quite right, thank you! I think I would like to wear my new cream gown today."

Alyce smiled, approving of Georgiana's choice. Though one was maid to the other's mistress, the two girls were only months apart in age. They might have been friends but for the draw of their births. Still, Alyce liked Miss Georgiana and bore no resentment for serving her. It was simply the way of things. "Yes, Miss," she said with a curtsey, and went into the closet to pull together Miss Georgiana's *ensemble* for the day.

For her part, while Alyce collected her attire, Georgiana fair attacked her chocolate and buns, anxious now to meet the day's activity. "What time is it, Alyce?" Georgiana called unceremoniously into the closet.

"Near on eight o'clock, Miss; and Mr Darcy said as he had planned to leave at half past the hour. Plenty of time for you, Miss, to make yourself ready." Alyce chuckled at the ill-concealed excitement in Georgiana's tone. She herself would love a day out, away from her daily routine – her half-day this week had been forestalled by the storm. But even more, she could wish to walk about on the arm of the Master. *That Mr Darcy in't half a looker, and could buy and sell half of England*, she thought. And to add to it, he was always nice to her, even knew her name, not like some toffs; and he was ever so fair to his servants as long as they were good workers. *Why, just the May past, he allowed old Mrs Donnell the right to stay in her cottage until the end of her days, just because her husband Patrick had been a loyal servant for years before his Whitsuntide passing.* There were employers, Alyce knew, who would have had the old widow turned out of house and home as soon as her allotted forty days' quarantine for grieving was expired, with no thought as to where she might go. *Yeh, Mr Darcy was everything a girl could dream about – handsome, rich, ever so proper...*

While Alyce's thoughts were thus occupied, she collected everything required for Georgiana and returned to her mistress, who had now finished washing in the basin. Alyce helped her young lady into her clothes for the day – an ikat muslin petticoat, overlaid with a visiting gown of cream-hued tissue with its three-quarter sleeves and hem embroidered both in a shell design. A delicate lacy tucker at the neckline befitted her youthful state; and a rose-coloured sash tied in back into a bow. To finish off her attire, Georgiana donned fine linen stockings, and slid her feet into rose-colored slippers—fashionable as these were, their buttery leather nonetheless encased a sole sufficient for town walking. Alyce left her mistress's fair hair loose, but swept the sides up into a chignon.

When they had finished, Alyce stepped back to admire her handiwork. The effect was quite stunning, a veritable lady of refinement but with still a suggestion of her youth. "Oh, Miss!" she exclaimed, "You look lovely!" Georgiana smiled with gratitude. "Why," said the maid, "you are altogether lovely enough to walk on the arm of that handsome brother of yours!"

They both knew that Alyce had spoken too freely with this last, and Georgiana duly cautioned the maid. But the admonition was half-hearted; and Georgiana found herself as impertinent in her own answer. "I am well aware of my brother's appeal to our sex, Alyce. Indeed, I have seen fully *half* of London nearly swoon at his feet for attention." A mischievous gleam appeared in her eyes as she concluded: "And the other half which does not... is *men*!"

The two young women giggled together, until the impropriety on both their parts was felt, and they sobered with some effort. Georgiana instantly regretted her over-familiar exchange with Alyce. She knew she must learn that no good could come from making an intimate friend of a servant. Lady Catherine deBourgh had counselled Georgiana over and over as to how it was not only improper, but led to eventual indolence on the servant's part. But Georgiana had few friends of her own age, and Alyce was far from her home in the mountains of Gwynedd. They were of an age together and sometimes it was very difficult to maintain the decorum required between maid and mistress.

Georgiana ventured one last comment on the topic of her brother. "I wish Mr Darcy would find a wife to equal his qualities, and I gain a sister in the match, Alyce; but I despair of it ever coming to pass! He is not such a fool as to fall for every pretty girl who looks up at him artfully. Yet he was fool enough to refuse to see what was in front of him! and for reasons of such trifling import. I am learning, Alyce, that men can be very nonsensical indeed, even my brother." Georgiana grimaced; Alyce gathered she must be thinking of a particular lady of her brother's acquaintance. Then the maid drifted into a dreamy expression as she imagined Mr Darcy being "nonsensical" over her.

A sharp knocking brought both to their senses, as the deep tones of the very gentleman they had been contemplating came through from the corridor door. "Georgiana, are you quite ready? It is nearly three-quarters past the hour!"

The girls flinched, and Georgiana called to her brother that she was coming directly. She smoothed her skirt and her hair, and started towards the door. Alyce, reaching it first, opened it wide, gave a quick curtsey to Darcy with eyes cast down and a blush on her cheeks to rival Miss Georgiana's rosy sash. She fair ran down the hall to the back stairs.

Darcy regarded the fleeing maid for a moment then, with a slight shrug of puzzlement at her unaccustomed scurrying, he turned towards Georgiana and moved into her room. The sight of her arrested his progress, however, and he stopped abruptly in mid-step, staring drop-jawed. Georgiana faced him, expecting his admonishment on her lateness. When he stood and said nothing, his sister finally asked, "Fitz?"

A tentative smile broke on Darcy's face, an element of the bittersweet to it. After another slight pause, he exclaimed, "Gee, my dear, you look beautiful!"

Georgiana rose up self-consciously on her toes and shrugged her shoulders, but her shy smile deepened to one of immense gratification as she took in her brother's compliment. That it had been offered in such an unstudied manner was not lost on her and only added to her pleasure. She stepped lightly up to Darcy, raised herself in her rose-coloured slippers to proffer a soft kiss on his cheek, and said, "Thank, you, Fitz!"

Georgiana had not anticipated such a reaction from her brother, and she took some great satisfaction in the effect she had produced with her appearance. While she beamed with pride, however, Darcy's expression had settled into one of uncertain consternation. Once again, Georgiana had to prod him into attentiveness. "Fitz?" she repeated.

Darcy sighed, relieving his paralysis, and offered a smile and his arm to Georgiana, saying playfully, "Shall we be on our way at last, then, my lady?" Georgiana giggled, slapped lightly at his proffered arm, and marched out the door towards the stairs, leaving her brother in her wake. With a shake of his head and a murmured "woman and girl all at once," he followed.

Though Darcy's natural stride outpaced his sister's, she had purposely made haste in her exit; by the time Darcy was halfway down the staircase, Georgiana stood at the bottom tapping her foot lightly as if, for all the world, it had been Darcy who had held up their departure at the appointed hour. She offered him a feigned look of grudging patience and an audible sigh, as her toes measured the beat of his footfall on the steps with their own rise and fall. Upon reaching the entry hall, Darcy stood in front of Georgiana, looked at her with an eyebrow raised and lips pressed into a line of reproach. He held up a curled fist in her general direction, reprimand inherent in the straightened attitude of his pointer finger, but in the end he could not sustain the ruse of annoyance. They both laughed together and exited the house to their awaiting carriage arm in arm.

ξ

Georgiana sat back in the coach and looked at her brother as he settled himself opposite her. "How long will it take us to get to Castleton, Fitz?" she asked, anticipation written in her expression.

"Near two hours, I expect," Darcy replied, and saw her smile begin to recede a bit at the thought. "For the roads have been improved much of late. But if we encounter little other traffic upon them, we might arrive more quickly." He could see this hope enter her expression, and he added, "There is, however, beautiful country to appreciate on the journey, some of the loveliest in all Derbyshire." He looked pointedly out at the landscape as he said this, to direct Georgiana by his example. "We should make something of our good fortune in such fine weather."

"Oh, I know, Fitz," she countered. "But I have seen it so many times, at least for some few miles beyond Bakewell; it will be far more of interest to me nearer to Castleton where I have not visited before." She looked at her brotherly warily. "To pass the time, we could... talk?"

Darcy took his eyes from his land and gazed instead at his sister. Her tone disconcerted him for some reason, yet even as he wondered what plot she was devising, he responded. "I am happy to oblige you, Gee. Shall we spend our time constructively and review your studies?" He looked without guile directly at his sister.

"Ugh! No!" she cried, with a pronounced look of disgust that brought a smile to Darcy. She continued, "A day's release from my studies should be just that! – a day's release! I want to talk of... other things..." Her voice trailed off a bit, and she bit her lower lip.

Oh, dear, thought Darcy, *I can too well imagine what she wants to speak of*; and he prepared himself to fend her off. He was surprised, then, when he heard her say –

"Tell me about Castleton, and your friend, Mr Wentworth. Have I ever seen him?"

"I daresay you have, my dear, though I do not expect you will recall it, for you were very young. Wentworth and I were at university together, and he accompanied me to Pemberley from Cambridge several times before travelling on to his own home in Castleton. You could hardly have been more than six or seven."

Georgiana, he could see, dismissed her earlier introduction as irrelevant given the circumstances, but then a puzzled expression formed to preface her next question. "He was with you in Cambridge?" Darcy confirmed that to be the case, that they had shared apartments there. "But, then," she followed, "he is an innkeeper now?"

"Indeed," came Darcy's reply; he intentionally withheld additional explanation, chuckling at the curiosity he saw mounting on her face.

"Well?" she asked.

Darcy raised his eyebrows to convey ignorance of her purpose. He was in good humour today and enjoyed playing a bit with his sister now, in retaliation for her coyness before their departure. At her 'tsk' of frustration, however, he smiled and answered finally.

"I will explain the history to you fully, Gee, but I must caution you that this is not to be discussed when we meet Mr Wentworth today." After an eager nod from his sister, he went on.

"Well then; I must go back to Mr Wentworth's father, Mr Josiah Wentworth. That gentleman was the third and youngest son of a baronet residing near Bolton in Yorkshire. With two elder brothers, each of whom had already heirs of their own, Josiah Wentworth had little expectation of inheritance himself beyond a token – and so he must make his way through some profession. His father encouraged him to take orders, but this he refused to do, being in no way suited to the church. Similarly he could not like the law; and could little imagine himself in purchase of a commission. And so, to his family's horror, he chose contrarily to go into business.

"He began by taking on management of an inn that was owned by a friend's relation. This was located in Cornwall – as far as he might achieve from his home country in respect of his family. Still it caused quite an uproar at the time, but he would not be dissuaded from this chosen course. His father disowned Josiah, and in Cornwall the son remained for some years." Darcy paused, looking at his sister to gauge her interest in the narrative. Gee was quite attentive, indeed, leaning forward towards him in her seat with bright, curious expression. Darcy was relieved, thinking that if he could prolong this story, it might preclude other, more intimate, topics of discussion being introduced.

"When his father died, Josiah Wentworth's brothers chose to re-establish a connection with their erstwhile relation. After some time, the eldest brother convinced the middle one that, as a rightful inheritance from his estranged father, an inn should be purchased for Josiah. They believed to be an *owner* of an inn at least preferable in society than managing someone else's property. At length, when an inn in Castleton came open for sale, it was procured. The property fitted all their requirements admirably, as well as bringing Mr Josiah Wentworth back to no greater a distance than fifty miles of his family.

"If they hoped by such proximity to persuade him to give up the inn over time, they mistook again his resolve. Eventually, the family became reconciled to Josiah's insistence on remaining in trade. And Josiah, in recognition of his family's grudging reclamation of him, relieved in great measure their embarrassment, by turning the Castleton Inn into no ordinary way-station."

"How? What did he do?" asked Georgiana, interest clearly heightened.

"Using well a generous stipend from his eldest brother, he secured additional loans, and then refurbished the large inn completely. He had converted several small upper lodging rooms into fewer but opulent suites and chambers, each with its own personal servant. He hired the best cooks, housekeepers, ostler and grooms – as if for a fine estate. He catered only to wealthy travellers who could afford his tariff; and the inn fast became exclusive to the ton. Accommodation there became increasingly sought after and his trade thrived. Josiah went on eventually to purchase five additional inns between London and the Lake country. And this made everyone in the family quite content; for not only did his brothers recover their investment with interest, but it brought a fortune to Josiah Wentworth and greatly enhanced his standing. Indeed, his personal fortune then exceeded that of either brother's estate."

"Oh, my!" began Georgiana, and then she stopped, unable quite to determine how to proceed. Darcy smiled, anticipating the question she might have.

"Mr Josiah Wentworth married somewhat late in life after acquiring this fortune. He had two children: my friend Mr Henry Wentworth, the eldest; and a daughter two years Henry's junior. Henry was given every opportunity – to include education at Cambridge -- as befits a gentleman. Indeed, he and I read classics together there under the same tutor, which is where our friendship formed. Father never pressed for son to succeed him in the business of inn keeping, but rather encouraged Henry to choose his own course; remembering, no doubt, the strife which resulted from his own sire's lack of tolerance. With a substantial endowment, Henry Wentworth could have purchased a property with ease.

"But in the end, he chose to return and follow his father. He is a very affable fellow and takes pleasure in seeing personally to the comforts he can render his acquaintances in their travels. Upon the death of Mr Wentworth senior some years ago – in fact, shortly after our good father's passing – Henry Wentworth inherited the fortune *and* the inns and assumed proprietorship. And *that* should suffice to answer all your questions on the subject. Does it not?"

Georgiana absorbed this information, and said, "I have only one more."

"What is that?"

"Is he handsome?"

This caused Darcy to start. He looked at his sister a moment, then said with a touch of incredulity in his voice, "Is he...? How should I come to know if he is handsome? And *furthermore*, Miss Darcy, why do *you* wish to know?"

"I am only curious," she said, but her ingenuous smile did not fool her brother.

"Gee, Mr Wentworth is a good and loyal gentleman, and better friend to me. I like him exceedingly; but he is too old for you to consider. It is unthinkable! Do not romanticise him."

"Fitz! I was thinking no such thing. I was simply asking!" She pouted a bit. "But if I was so inclined, he is *only* of an age with you, is not he? You are not so very old *quite* yet."

Darcy laughed, wishing she had not added the 'quite yet' qualifier onto her observation.

"That is as may be, but he is still not for you. Being wife to an innkeeper, however rich, is not a life to aspire to, nor what Fitzwilliam or I could wish for you."

"What of Mr Wentworth's sister?" Georgiana countered. "Does she work in the Inn with the gentleman? Will we meet her to-day? Is she yet unmarried?"

Relieved at the change in the direction of their converse, Darcy laughed at Georgiana's lack of subtlety. "No, not in Castleton. And before you get any ideas, although Miss Eleanor, as she was, has many charms, she has been married some years – she is now Mrs Huxley, and lives with her husband and small children in Hawes, managing Wentworth's inn in that town."

"Oh." Georgiana looked slightly deflated for an instant, but quickly recovered, to her brother's dismay. "Is Mrs Huxley with her many charms as charming as Miss Elizabeth Bennet?"

ξ

Darcy sighed, wondering at how he came so easily to fall into the trap of raising Miss Bennet's shade. *Truly*, he thought, *is it some natural, God-given, talent in women to so often divert converse to those subjects that will most discomfit men?* He should never have taken Gee into his confidence; should have realised she would not let the matter go after witnessing the depth of disappointment he suffered when Miss Bennet rejected him. She would have him pursue the lady further; believed Miss Bennet could not long oppose grand romantic gestures – how little she knew of that lady – and he could make it all well in the end.

Now he must reply somehow – but he was too near full of feeling and unrelenting thoughts of Miss Bennet to trust himself. "Georgiana, your impertinence is great, and your question wholly immaterial! And before you protest, let me assure you that I will *not* discuss that lady further. Any continued mention of her will serve only to ensure that the rest of our journey will transpire in silence on my part." He glowered at his sister to press his point.

Georgiana shrugged as if to suggest it was of no import to her; inwardly she realised with irritation that she had mistimed an introduction of Miss Bennet into conversation. She would have to be patient and, perhaps if her brother's mood were lighter some time later in the day, she would attempt again to broach the subject of that lady. There was something he hid, she was sure of it—but she was equally certain that his disappointment in Miss Bennet's rejection preyed upon him still.

"Very well," she said, and sat fully back into her seat. She looked out at the scenery then to elude Darcy's persuasive glare. She longed to tell him she was sorry but could not trust herself not to cry, even while her pride rejected such inclination. After a few moments, they settled into an easier silence and watched as they passed through increasingly steeper land.

When Darcy returned his gaze to his sister some time later, he noted that Georgiana had, in fact, fallen asleep, her head leaning back against the high rest of the seat. She was missing the very scenery she had expressed a desire to see, but he chose not to wake his sister, in order to avoid any further discussion (or evasion of such) concerning Miss Bennet. He had never explained fully to Gee the disdain with which Miss Elizabeth had answered his offer, the evils she believed him capable of; her complete lack of any regard for him as a gentleman, must less her suitor. Perhaps he should have done, so that she would let the matter rest. But no, she could never comprehend it all, that he could not make another approach to Miss Bennet. His pride forbid it, but even more, he could not withstand another such rejection – to see reflected in her eyes the despicable man she believed him to be. No, the subject was a closed one. For the remainder of their journey to Castleton, however, he had stubbornly to work to banish that lady from his mind, after she had been invited there yet again by his sister's well meant suggestion.

In one attempt to redirect his thoughts, Darcy looked back on the morning and his astonishment at beholding Georgiana in her rooms. For many months now, he had been forced to acknowledge changes in his sister, alterations serving notice of her metamorphosis from a girl to a woman. Yet with each moment of *womanhood* he had witnessed, it had always quickly followed with a giggle or a pout – or a sudden change in conversation to something fully childlike – that deluded Darcy into believing he had time still to reconcile himself to her being fully grown.

As she was now, asleep on the coach seat, her head tilted and face warmed to a soft glow by the sun, he might deceive himself she could stay a child forever. But the sight of her this morning in her new frock had struck him forcibly. He had beheld a beautiful young *woman* and been at a loss how to respond. He had frowned, he knew – bemused – but almost instantly, this had yielded to a smile. She was truly a lovely sight, and his heart swelled with family pride. Was this what all parents experienced to see their chicks grow independent?—this mixture of pride and dread? Or was it he alone felt it, given the special nature of his relationship with his sister?

They had stood for a moment that morning, he lost in appreciation of his sister's delicate beauty, and she clearly embarrassed yet gratified at her brother's silent compliment, before well-deserved words of praise passed his lips. More than at any other time before, Darcy had seen the woman overtake the girl. It was more than her burgeoning figure or the stylish fashions she wore – there was something in her air that spoke of a milestone having been passed irretrievably.

He had called her "Gee" with regularity of late, a childhood nickname from the nursery. He realised now, looking at her peaceful countenance, that it was a futile attempt to call back the child in her. But that was impossible! *She is sixteen*, he thought. *She will be presented after another winter and you will not have her for long after that.*

Had he given it conscious thought in that instant, he would have admitted that his relationship with her had changed already – had he not been confiding in her these months about his own feelings, and had she not in those moments shown real wisdom and compassion in their conversations? And yet he reflected on how she could find humour or excitement still in the most nonsensical things; still make him laugh; teaze him in those rare times when her awe of him was momentarily forgotten, as she had done earlier that morning; still cry to see an animal suffer pain (or her brother's of late) – how was he to reconcile that childlike innocence with this new vision of elegance?

Unbidden, the image of Miss Bennet surfaced again. Though young, *she* was a woman – no doubt of that! – but yet she retained childlike characteristics that enhanced, rather than counteracted her womanly appeal. Darcy groaned inwardly to recognise both that his sister had now passed into that realm, and that once again Miss Bennet overtook his senses. Heaving a sigh to expel her uninvited shade, Darcy turned his mind deliberately to his upcoming negotiations in Castleton. No more thoughts of women or girls – men and sheep were far less complicated!

ξ

"Gee…" Darcy called his sister's name softly and touched her sleeve to wake her. After a repetition of this, she opened her eyes slowly and sighed. She looked at her brother as though unaware of her situation, but then the movement of the coach entered her consciousness, and she was roused fully. "We approach Castleton, my dear."

At once, Georgiana became alert and looked around her. Up in the distance she could see grey buildings scattered on both sides of the road, becoming more plentiful as she looked further ahead. Eventually as they drew closer, the stone cottages and shops became quite dense, placed higgledy-piggledy up the hillside, as small bridges in the same native stone criss-crossed the stream that meandered through the village.

Up on the hill to the left, Georgiana could see the remains of Peveril Castle that her brother had described to her the night before; once a stronghold of William the Conqueror's son, William Peveril, and where King Henry II had accepted the fealty of Malcolm of Scotland some six hundred years before. And further up, about a mile distant and rising above everything, was Mam Tor, called the 'shivering mountain' for the loose shale that often slid down the grit stone, giving the impression that the mountain moved.

All these were very impressive indeed, but as the carriage entered the town proper, Georgiana noted shops and inns in close succession, and enthusiasm brightened her eyes. She smiled at her brother, who returned it with real joy to see Georgiana happy. Bunting, their driver, came to a stop some short way ahead outside the farm agent's office.

Darcy allowed that his business would not take long, and Georgiana was happy to accompany her brother into the agent's establishment. Bunting was dismissed with directions to attend them again at the Castleton Inn at half past four for their return journey. The carriage and driver dispatched until such time, brother and sister entered into a cramped, dark office. Two clerks, both doddering old men, worked at tables near the window. When Darcy asked for Mr Pettigrew, one of the men ushered him into a room at the back, then settled Georgiana in a comfortable chair nearby and made offer of his services should she require any thing.

Georgiana passed this time of waiting by trying to imagine what Mr Henry Wentworth was like. She had barely settled in to her imagination, it seemed, before the door to the back room opened and Darcy emerged with another man, presumably Mr Pettigrew. They shook hands, confirmed that drovers would be engaged to call for the agreed-upon Leicester Longwools in three days' time, and then Darcy was ready to depart.

As they stepped from the dark office into a radiant morning sun, Georgiana felt a shiver of anticipation. Somehow, she just *knew* that something exciting would transpire in Castleton to-day!

ξ

"Now, what shall we do to occupy ourselves?" asked Darcy when they reached the pavement, deferring as promised to Georgiana's desire to make this a special day for her.

Georgiana looked about her; Castleton was not a large town but yet it was a hive of activity, people bustling around them. "I want to do everything!" she beamed, and then added, "but do not fear, brother, I will settle on a reasonable number of activities. What time is your Mr Wentworth expecting us to call?"

"I wrote to expect us at three. It is half past eleven presently, so ..."

"How do you know that?" asked Georgiana. She had not seen Darcy consult a pocket watch, nor did she see any clock tower in evidence. "Have you some talent as a seer that is unknown to me?"

Laughing at the presumption that he might foretell *anything* in his present life, Darcy replied, "No, Gee. But I noted the clock in Mr Pettigrew's office as I made to go and it was twenty minutes past the hour. Accounting for our subsequent farewell and sorting you out to leave, it must be near half past now. So, my dear... you have three hours and a half to command me."

Georgiana smiled as she studiously calculated what could be accomplished in such time. "Well, then..." she started, "may we visit the castle?" She looked up the hill where the imposing fortress ruins stood guard over the town it had named. She saw a look of doubt cross her brother's face and gazed up at him beseechingly, eyes wide and a tentative smile.

"Gee, your feminine wiles will not move me, nor are they necessary," he chuckled. "My *only* concern in venturing the castle, my dear, is *you*. For you are very finely attired in your fetching new gown to be making a climb of such nature, with only a few narrow paths to take us there. And are your slippers sufficiently adequate for this?"

He could see the truth of his concern hit the mark, as his two Georgianas – the inquisitive girl and the refined young woman – battled for supremacy. "Oh," she said with something of a pout, and wavered. Darcy stood watching her internal struggle, wondering which would win out. She looked again wistfully up the hill, clearly gauging the effects of a climb, and he saw the wonder and romance in her eyes. Perhaps he did have his 'Gee' yet for a while? But then she looked down at her gown and slippers and he could see her swaying to the side of decorum.

"Errm... beggin' yer pard'n, Sir?"

Darcy turned to face the owner of this address, and he and Georgiana beheld a man standing off to the side. He was wiry and small, smaller than Georgiana, of indeterminate age – he may have been in his middle years, or perhaps a young man who simply wore heavily the harsh winters and harsher living this region must exact. He was dressed in the manner of a small freehold farmer. He had narrow, twinkling eyes and a bulbous ruddy nose above a grizzled ruddy beard. His skin had that thickness about it that attested to a living out of doors.

The man remembered himself and doffed his cap to Darcy, then removed it completely and fidgeted with it in his hands as he spoke again. "Sir, if yer please, Ah heard yer talkin'. If yer young lady wants as to see the castle, Sir, Ah kin take yers there, leastways part there." He looked up to gauge the gentleman's reaction to his impertinent address and, seeing no reproach, continued. "Ah has a cart, Sir – nuthin' fancy, mind, but clean, me wife, she do take on so if it ain't clean – an' ther's a track what goes most way up yon hill, tho' not all way to top."

Darcy did not reply immediately, but looked to his sister, raising his brow in question. This new intelligence decided for her immediately and she said, "Oh, yes... please?" Darcy laughed – so, he did still have "Gee" for just a while longer, it seemed.

"Very well, then, Mr..." Darcy began.

"Archer, Sir, if yer please. Just Archer," the man finished, and bowed awkwardly, cap still rotating in his hands in a nervous gesture.

"... Archer then. Thank you. Have you your cart close by, then?" Darcy glanced around but saw no likely conveyance in the area.

"Nossir, it's at me cottage not half mile from here." He pointed towards Mam Tor. "But Ah kin have it here within the hour for you?"

Once again, Darcy looked to Georgiana, and she treated him to unbridled enthusiasm. "Very well, then, Archer, we shall have your escort. We will meet with you here in, say, three quarters of an hour?" The little man nodded to seal the bargain. "And what do you require for such use of your cart and your time?" Darcy added.

"Oh, no Sir, ... Ah cudn' accep' no paym'n, oh no, oh no... it's m' pleasure, Sir, to oblige the young lady." He flicked a glance at Georgiana with a fawning smile, then returned his gaze to Darcy, bowed hurriedly and rushed off down the street.

"While we await our coach and four, Madame, would you care to visit some shops?"

"Oh, yes!" cried Georgiana, eyes sparkling. Together they set off to canvass the ones on their side of the street. "It was awfully nice of Mr Archer, was not it," Georgiana continued, "to offer his services for no cost?"

Darcy chuckled at his sister's *naiveté* before explaining to her that the man had no intention of such a thing. "He merely says it in order to garner him a few extra coins of gratitude from me of greater value than the sum he could otherwise reasonably name." Darcy paused a moment. "And so he *will* get it, if he makes 'my lady' happy today."

With that, Darcy doffed his own hat to his sister and offered her his arm. She in her turn answered with a quick curtsey and accepted it with a giggle. Together they walked the length of the village, pausing at shop windows to admire wares that particularly caught their eye.

When they stopped outside a milliner's, Georgiana admired a bonnet in the far corner of the display window. It was of flax with a moderately-sized brim, and trimmed in flowers and wide ribbon that appeared the exact rose shade Georgiana now wore in her sash and slippers. Darcy offered to purchase it for her, but she demurred, saying that she had too many bonnets at home already. But noticing again the wistful look of admiration in her eye, he insisted – saying that it would give him great pleasure to indulge her. The persuasion had barely escaped his lips before Georgiana was in the shop, asking to have the hat removed from its form. With good humour, he followed her into the shop to complete the purchase.

The bonnet now in its proper place atop Georgiana's head, her old one toted in a hatbox by Darcy, brother and sister moved on. There were a great many people about the village on this beautiful day, and Darcy noted that those who passed them always gave a second glance at the couple. He also noted that many of those glances were directed at Georgiana. This was something he would assuredly have to learn to accept without suffering the tightening knot he felt in his stomach now.

They stopped in to several more shops, crossing the road and making their way back down the establishments on that side. They came to a curious shop, a long and narrow room, lit up by the sun in its front windows and another at the far end, but somewhat dark in the centre. On close inspection, they found the shop filled with blue john, the local stone that had been discovered in the hills of this particular area. Mined for its beauty and unique colouring, artisans were beginning to form it into all manner of things – vases and other small decorative household items, but mostly jewellery.

Darcy and Georgiana entered the shop to look, Darcy engaging the proprietor in conversation about the working of the stone while Georgiana perused the displays with a very attentive young clerk. Some time later, the Darcys emerged, having made some purchases; Georgiana was certain Mrs Annesley would enjoy the pendant selected, and her cousin Anne would receive a brooch in the stone with silver filigree edges when next they met. Georgiana too had made one additional purchase while her brother was in converse with the shop owner, a surprise for him.

At length, they made their way back to the centre of the village. True to his word, Archer had returned and stood next to a simple farm cart, ready to escort his passengers to the castle. It was large enough to accommodate them in the back of it – but narrow and sturdy enough to manoeuvre the hill it must traverse. There was nothing for it but for Darcy and Georgiana to sit in the back of the cart, there being no room at the front for any but the driver; but the farmer (or more likely his wife) had lined the cart with clean linen. It might not offer much by way of comfort, but they had done their best. Georgiana looked on it as an adventure as Darcy easily lifted her onto the back of the cart, and then joined her there. She drew her knees up under her to keep her skirts free of dirt the moving cart might throw up, and it seemed Archer had given much thought to his guests' comfort, for he immediately offered her a light lap robe for propriety and to keep clean as well. She gratified him with a smile as she tucked it around her.

The cart started on the smooth main road through the village, but soon veered off and began its ascent to the castle. On more than one occasion, the strain on the horse with the steep incline was evident, but it never faltered—good farm stock. Georgiana smiled as she looked all around her at the vistas that opened up as they climbed. Mam Tor in the distance some half-mile, the dark Kinder peaks beyond it, and to the east the Hope Valley. What a beautiful situation Castleton had, she thought, so rugged and solid looking with its faces of grey stone, yet surrounded by land as green as any she had seen. She was quite taken with the tranquillity that emanated from the village. It put her in mind of Pemberley, for though the landscape here was rougher, yet that same sense of peace always filled her when she looked on her brother's estate.

Finally, the cart pulled into a natural lay-by and stopped. "As far as she kin go, Sir," said Archer. "Bu' the castle is jes' up on that rise there, if yer care to walk it." He did not need to add that he would await their return and safeguard their parcels.

Darcy thanked the farmer and helped Georgiana down. Together they made their way to the top using a narrow path that had been formed by the footsteps of visitors to the site over the years. From this height, the views of the surrounding countryside were truly breathtaking. They walked through the ruins for a few moments before Georgiana said, "Fitz, you need not escort me if you do not wish it – I am perfectly happy to explore by myself."

Taking this as dismissal, Darcy left her to her amiable wandering. He spied a large flat-topped stone, probably a foundation stone at one time, and sat down, pulling from his coat pocket a small volume. He always carried a book with him when he travelled – for just such rare opportunities as these – and it was a perfect day and glorious location to lose himself in his reading. After a quick wave to Georgiana in the distance, he got as comfortable as might be. In moments, he was wholly absorbed in his book.

ξ

Georgiana wandered with no set direction through the ruins, finally ending up on the far side from where she and Darcy had parted company. She could just picture the whole of it as a lively medieval fortress, gallant knights on the ramparts protecting their ladies and children within the keep. She had constructed a lovely tale in her mind of a handsome knight rescuing her from being carried off by an attacker. The image was so clear in her imagination that she did not notice an obstacle on the path until she collided with it.

Stopping in surprise, she gasped along with the person who had formed the obstacle. Regaining all her senses, she glanced up to find herself confronted with a young man.

"Oh!" each cried, and then stood awkwardly looking at the other. Georgiana's face coloured, quite becomingly had she but known it, and her eyes grew nearly as large and round as the 'O' her mouth had formed in her exclamation of surprise. The young man blushed as well, before both cast their eyes down to the ground. In an instant he said, "Forgive me, Miss! Entirely my fault... I am afraid I was not paying attention to my path. Please, do excuse..."

"Oh, no, Sir," Georgiana cut off his apology. "I also am at fault. I was not watching my way at all." Again, she blushed, even more so at the young man's ensuing smile. "I confess I was lost in a daydream, picturing this castle in its heyday," she blurted out. She looked at the young man. "It is breathtaking, is it not?"

"Yes! Breathtaking! My very thought!" The young man seemed then to realise that he had been staring overlong at

Georgiana, and hoped she had not taken offence that he referred to more than the ruins and general prospect. His entire countenance turned crimson from the top of his head down to his neck, and he began to shuffle his feet in the dust.

Georgiana's followed his eyes to the ground, and she played with the bow of her bonnet in her nerves. She looked up again first and took, as the opportunity arose, just a moment to assess the youth who stood before her. He looked to be not much older than she, perhaps eighteen at the most. He was above the norm in height; not so tall as her brother but a good hand's length above Georgiana herself; just enough that to look into his eyes, she would have to raise hers such that they presented an innocent, bright aspect that she could not know only added to her looks.

But for now the young man's eyes were still fixed firmly on a low gorse bush just off the path to the side of Georgiana. He had an unruly mop of light brown hair to which sunlight added reddish glints here and there. It was straight; he wore it to a length just below the collar and tucked behind each ear on the sides. He had a thin, aquiline nose, perhaps just a bit too long for convention, which anchored a longish, narrow face. *A very handsome face*, thought Georgiana, *those small indentations to each side of his lips give one the impression that he is always on the verge of breaking into a smile.*

When he finally looked up again, Georgiana was called upon, with difficulty, to stifle any notable reaction. His eyes were common enough in their almond shape, and well balanced to his face. But their colouring was extraordinary. They were hazel, with the reddish-brown base customary in such, but they contained flecks of colour that altered one's impression as his eyes moved to catch the light. One moment they appeared the colour of the ripe fruit of their namesake, the next the faded green of speckled pears.

He regained his voice. "Well, Miss, again my apologies." He began to step off the path. "I will not detail your progress further."

Georgiana was reticent to end the encounter, but could not with any propriety prolong it in the circumstance, so she curtseyed to the young man and took a step to move around him. As it happened, however, at that precise moment the breeze caught the brim of Georgiana's bonnet and, with its ribbons loosened from her absent fingering of them, the bonnet flew off her head before she could catch it. It fell to the earth and rolled down the hill several steps away even as she cried out at its loss.

The young man immediately took off down the hill, causing a ruckus from several jackdaws which flew up from their nests to complain. He picked up the bonnet, waved it in the air to remove any dirt it may have acquired in its tumble, and strode back up the hill, presenting it to Georgiana with a bow and flourish.

She smiled with delight; her eyes glinting with something more than gratitude. "Thank you, Sir! But you should not have gone after it. As much as I should hate to lose my bonnet, this hill does not look safe – you could have been hurt."

"Nonsense!" he replied. "I have been exploring this castle for several days now and wandered all up and down the hill. Indeed, did you know that just down there..." he turned to point almost directly below them, and Georgiana reluctantly moved her gaze in the same direction to the spot he indicated some yards away, "... there is a cave where, long before Peveril Castle was built, men used to spend their days making rope!" Georgiana looked at him again with wonder, bringing an affirmation from the youth. "Truly!—You can still see the blackened marks in the cave floor from their fires."

"How extraordinary," said the young lady. She found herself tongue-tied, and could not manage anything else.

This was a subject of obvious enthusiasm to the youth, however, and he had found his own tongue. He began to expound on the activities this hill had seen from the time before recorded history, until he noticed that he was overwhelming his audience and drew up short. "Oh, forgive me, Miss. I fear I lose myself when I contemplate such things."

Georgiana's smile assured the young man he had caused no offence, and she hastened to excuse him with words as well. She even acknowledged that she understood the habit, as her cousin had a similar one of lecturing with exuberance on topics that excited his interest. Following this, however, there seemed no other conversation they could broach given the circumstances of their unusual meeting. Georgiana thanked him again for recovering her bonnet and, with genuine reluctance, took her leave of the youth.

The gentleman, for his part, stood for long minutes watching Georgiana's path as it took her away from him – first as she remained in view, then for some time after she was gone. With a wistful sigh, he eventually turned and made his way down the hill towards the rope-makers' cave.

Georgiana walked about the ruins some minutes more after leaving his company, afraid that if she returned to Darcy too soon he would notice the change in her attitude – indeed, she was feeling quite flustered and was certain that it must show to anyone who saw her. When finally she had calmed herself, she looked back with mild regret towards the spot where her encounter had taken place, and returned to where she had left her brother. Unsurprising to her, she found Darcy sitting on a large stone, reading and oblivious to her approach.

"Ahem," she said, and Darcy looked up, smiling as he met her gaze. *Does he look strangely at me*, Georgiana wondered, *does he detect some alteration in me?* But he greeted her as always, asking if she had seen her fill and was ready to return to the village. His smile held a hint of mirth, yet surely that was unconnected to her current feelings; indeed, perhaps she imagined it in her discomfiture. She said nothing of it, merely replied that she had enjoyed it very, very much. Darcy put away his book, and they made their way carefully down the path to the waiting Archer, with his cart.

"Reddy ter go back, Sir?" he asked.

Darcy affirmed it, and settled Georgiana once again in the back of the cart. *Is it my imagination*, Georgiana thought, *or does my brother study me overlong? That hint of a smirk still resides in his expression. But no, it is my own unsettled feelings alone that give meaning where none warrants.* She put the thought out of her mind as they began their slow and careful descent of the hill.

ξ

While Darcy and Georgiana endured the bumps and dips of the cart's wheels as they made their way back down Castle Hill to the village, the young man Georgiana had encountered had entered the rope-makers' cave. He had come to search for other traces of ancient habitation, but after only moments he gave up his task, and sat at the cave's entrance to look out across the valley. It was useless to try to concentrate on ancient history anymore when his recent history – as recent as only moments before – was forefront in his mind.

He conjured up the vision of the young lady as she had looked when he recovered her bonnet – she was beautiful! He thought she must be near his own age, perhaps a bit younger. He could have lost himself in those large, ingenuous grey eyes; could not be entirely certain he had not! –indeed, would have done with no regret. When her bonnet flew off, her golden hair had framed a face of the sweetest features, proportioned for refinement; her timid smiles made him blush with delight. And though he had not dared to study her overmuch, it had required only a quick glance to see that she was coming into a most attractive form. His senses had never before been assailed to such a degree. It was not an unpleasant sensation, but disconcerted him just the same.

He wondered who she could be, for he knew he had not seen her in Castleton before. She must be a day visitor or perhaps – staying at one of the market town's many inns? But what was she doing there, all on her own? He had not seen anyone else in his wandering about the castle grounds. And how did she make her way to the top of the hill in her fine attire?

As he sat looking out, a movement caught his eye to the left and he noted a local farmer, Archer, making his way down an old track in his cart. Though it had made progress already, he spied his young lady riding in the back – along with another person: a gentleman by his dress, though appearing very much older than his companion from this distance. He wondered at their relationship. Though it little concerned him, he hoped that she was not some sacrificial family offering to a lecherous old squire in barter for land or influence.

Oh, stop, he thought to himself; *her companion does not look so old, nor did the lady seem in distress when we met. For all I know, she is quite in love with the gentleman* he espied now. With green dismay, he acknowledged that he would never see her again, and wished that he had found some way of prolonging their encounter even as he knew he could not have done so with any propriety.

Finally, heaving a large sigh of reluctant acceptance, he stood again and began to make his way back to Castleton on a steep, well-worn path. There was no point staying there any longer, for he would not see anything of interest but a sketch of gentle grey eyes and a bashful smile. He might as well return to the village and try to fill the hollowness he felt in his stomach with food and drink at his customary pub.

ξ

When they had traversed about two-thirds of the way, Archer slowed the horse to turn in his seat and inquire, "Erm, Sir, wud there be anywhere else yer and yer lady wish ter go?" Darcy, who had consulted the time just after they left the ruin, suggested that they ride up towards Mam Tor and stop at one of the caves there. Mr Pettigrew had mentioned one which was very soon to open to the public as an attraction. They should just have time for a quick look at it before they would be expected at their friend's inn. Georgiana readily agreed to this plan, though she showed less enthusiasm than she might have done earlier in the day; for in truth, she was somewhat distracted with the lingering image of a certain young man. Darcy duly asked Archer to take them to the cavern and, on reaching the main thoroughfare at last, the farmer turned his cart west, pointing out his own modest farm along the way.

They were in luck—they arrived at the location in conjunction with the owner of the property. Archer brought him to Darcy's notice. Mr Lincoln the proprietor, upon introduction, immediately offered an escorted tour. He also offered to return the gentleman and his sister to Castleton in the greater style and comfort of his own carriage after their visit. Darcy accepted, and returned to where the farmer sat waiting.

"Thank you, Archer," said Darcy, as he pressed something into the farmer's hand. "You have been most obliging. We shall return with Mr Lincoln at his invitation. You may return to your own business." Archer doffed his cap deferentially, adding an enthusiastic "Thank yer, Sir, very kindly indeed" before clucking to his horse to move off. He had no need to look into his palm; the very feel of the coins in his hand told him he had done a very profitable service. As his cart passed the young lady, standing next to Mr Lincoln, Archer dipped his head to her and, just as he was to pass by, he gave her a crooked smile and a wink. Georgiana, recognising no harm in his intentions, repaid him with a happy smile.

ξ

Mr Lincoln proved a most amiable guide, delighting in showing Darcy and Georgiana the cavern in its present state. He confirmed that the caves were not yet open to public viewing, but would be soon. He was commissioning final accommodations made for the comfort of the public – lamps installed at proper intervals, boats to navigate the underground waterway through parts of the cave; and he had installed a small room at the front of the cavern with a supply of wraps and robes to offer visitors – for the temperature of this underground world was appreciably cooler than out of doors.

Darcy and Georgiana walked with him to an opening that broadened out into a large, high-ceilinged bowl of a room. Georgiana, whose thoughts had little strayed from her young man on Castle Hill since their descent, came to herself again with a gasp as she entered this part of the cavern. Darcy uttered an exclamation as well. Several lamps were lit round the perimeter, casting wavering lines of light and shadow through the space, which seemed to glow throughout. There was a smooth path of sorts laid out upon which people might soon walk about, but the centre portion was filled with stalactites and stalagmites – limestone formations derived from hundreds of years of mineral deposit as water seeped into the cavern through the porous stone above. The effect of these columns of cone-shaped limestone with the lamplight was magical, creating a wonderland. Georgiana was entranced once again.

Mr Lincoln pointed out to his visitors the near walls of the cave, which were filled with the fossils of marine animals and shellfish from thousands of years before. Georgiana noted some lines of darker material threading through the walls as well, and asked Mr Lincoln about them. The owner explained that this was what made their caverns special – blue john, a form of fluorspar found only, so far, in this area of the peaks. He went on to describe how workers had been mining these hills for several years now to reap a harvest of blue john – so called for its blue and yellow banded colour patterns – for the making of decorative items. She thought of the small polished and cut pieces lying in her reticule, and liked them all the more to see how they began their existence.

At length, Darcy indicated that they could claim no more of Mr Lincoln's generously-proffered time, and they retreated to the entry. While Mr Lincoln had some words with his foreman to one side, Darcy led Georgiana to the waiting carriage and handed her into it. He joined her and, as they awaited their host, he asked his sister again if she enjoyed her day.

"Oh, yes!" exclaimed Georgiana with much feeling. "It is wonderful, Fitz!" She leaned in impetuously to give her brother a kiss on his cheek, then embraced him for good measure to make her point well and good. He laughed and returned the embrace, releasing her as he saw Mr Lincoln approach.

For the short ride back to the village, Darcy and Mr Lincoln conversed about the business aspects of his venture to open the caverns to the public, which left Georgiana to her own musings. She could not help but recall the stalactites she had seen in flickering lamplight, and how their changeable colour very much mirrored that of a pair of eyes she had met on this day. She smiled idly at the thought, a smile that her brother noticed if she did not. If he wondered at it, however, he gave no indication, but continued to converse with Mr Lincoln.

Their new acquaintance deposited Darcy and his sister at the Castleton Inn some quarter hour before three, with an invitation from Mr Lincoln for Mr Darcy to seek him out again at any time his travels brought him to Castleton. And then the mine owner went on his way; and the Darcys entered the Inn, asking after Mr Wentworth of a clerk in the entry.

Now that they had arrived at the Inn, Georgiana recalled her curiosity about her brother's friend on the ride to Castleton that morning. But though she still wished to meet the gentleman, the degree of her interest had waned after the day's activities. Instead her mind kept returning to a young man on a hillside. *Oh, what is the point*, she thought to herself, *for I will never see him again.*

ξ

Henry Wentworth came from a door behind the entry bearing a wide smile and outstretched arms. He and Darcy clasped each other in greeting, before Wentworth clapped his friend on the back, catching Darcy off guard and nearly knocking him into a case clock for all his size. Wentworth apologised with laughter, only to profess the fault lay in his intense delight at seeing his friend once more. "It has been too long, Darcy. What has kept you away for such periods?"

The question required no answer and Darcy offered none, but instead introduced his friend to Georgiana. She curtseyed to the gentleman as he exclaimed, "Why, I am dazzled, surely! Can it be so long since I visited Pemberley, Darcy? For surely this elegant lady is not the same pretty child I met not so long ago..."

Georgiana blushed and replied that, indeed, she was the same. Wentworth's manner was quite avuncular, it made Georgiana feel at ease immediately; and Darcy did not seem affronted by it in the least. His sister wondered for a moment at the friends Darcy seemed to accumulate; they were often so different on the surface than her reserved and meditative sibling. Henry Wentworth was a full head shorter than her brother, but with an open face that seemed never without some degree of smile. His jet hair he wore cropped close, most likely to contain its tendency to curl haphazardly. He had narrow, dark eyes that gave a first impression of laziness, and they nearly disappeared, swallowed by his cheeks, when his smile deepened. Not the handsomest man, yet his exuberant nature gave him an attractiveness that overruled nature's decree. But the greatest difference with her brother was his temperament – for he talked with great ease, and more than anyone Georgiana had ever met before.

In due course, Wentworth escorted his friends into his private chambers in the back portion of the inn. They entered a beautifully appointed parlour which was filled with afternoon sun from a bank of glass-paned doors that opened onto a garden terrace. Wentworth sent for lemonade to be brought, and then sat with his guests to catch up on their news. Georgiana decided that her surmise was correct as to the appeal to her brother in having Mr Wentworth for a friend – the gentleman was so unreserved as to make it unnecessary for Fitz to contribute much himself to their discourse. But she liked Mr Wentworth for this easy manner. She knew him to be of the same age as her brother, yet he looked somewhat younger, perhaps owing to the fact that he did not seem to take anything at all seriously. She could see where this affability would suit him well as proprietor of an inn.

At Darcy's asking, Wentworth spoke for some minutes about his sister Eleanor and her family. As he came to a close on their various states of health, refreshment was served and the three enjoyed cakes and lemonade while they conversed. An hour slipped by in this manner, Georgiana was happy to see. She was not eager to leave; Mr Wentworth was such delightful company that time did not drag as it could with less amiable associates. From the bracket clock on the mantel, Georgiana noted that Bunting would arrive with their carriage in only half an hour, and she found she was sorry to think of ending their visit so quickly.

Her reverie was broken by the slam of a door outside coming from the direction of reception, and they all looked to the noise. "Ah," said Wentworth, "that is only Nathaniel, I expect." He turned to Darcy: "You know Hewitt, of course, from school?" Darcy nodded as Mr Wentworth explained to Georgiana that Mr Hewitt was the eldest son of the Earl of Cranford, and they had all been intimate friends in their years at Cambridge and passed a portion of their grand tour in company.

"This is his brother, young Nathaniel. He is staying with me for some weeks – has an inordinate interest in antiquities and goes exploring all day long. He is off to follow in his brother's wake at the start of next term to study natural history."

As he spoke, Wentworth crossed the room and opened the parlour door. His guests heard him say, "Nathaniel, my boy, join me a moment, will you? I would like you to meet yet another Cambridge crony of Edmund's and mine." He swung the door open more widely, and stepped aside to allow the new person entry. In walked a young man, and Georgiana's heart nearly stopped. She drew breath sharply, unsure how to navigate this turn of events. She sank back into the cushions of her chair trying to make herself invisible.

The young man breezed into the room and approached Darcy. "The Honourable Nathaniel Hewitt, meet my excellent friend, Mr Darcy of Pemberley," said Wentworth. The two gentlemen bowed to each other cordially, and Wentworth continued. "And this," turning to the other side of the room, "is Mr Darcy's excellent sister."

ξ

Nathaniel Hewitt turned towards her as Georgiana wished herself to be anywhere but in that parlour. *Will he give our acquaintance away?* she wondered. *I did not mention our encounter to Fitz; will he be angry with me if it comes to light?*

The young man appeared sensible of her discomfiture. He took a few steps towards Georgiana, addressing her with a pregnant expression, and bowed deeply. "I am delighted to make your acquaintance, Miss Darcy. How do you find your visit to Castleton?"

Georgiana presented a rather over-wide smile to the gentleman in her relief, and replied that she took great pleasure in it indeed. Mr Hewitt then smiled mischievously and asked if she had chanced to visit Peveril Castle, as its grounds had much to commend it. He teazed thus, knowing that his back was to Darcy and

Wentworth and only Georgiana could see his expression. Before she could panic at formulating a reply, she was aided unwittingly by Mr Wentworth, who laughed and said, "Oh, Nathaniel, please, you will bore us all to the death with your lectures!" He good-naturedly slapped his young visitor on the back, apparently a gesture common to the inn-keeper, and directed him to sit and join them in their refreshment. This the young man did, selecting a seat to Darcy's left that allowed him a line of vision to Georgiana across the room.

While Darcy spoke with young Hewitt, asking after the young man's brother and family, and his plans while at Cambridge, Georgiana made an attempt to compose herself. She could not help but slide her gaze every moment or so to the young man, then would blush and look away as she found his eyes so often on her. She was in such a state of flutters that she was scarcely aware of the conversation around her. Once or twice, she saw that her brother looked at her with some curiosity, and it took all her effort not to avert her eyes from his questioning glances. She smiled at Fitz and hoped neither her nerves nor her occasional glances at Nathaniel were peculiarly notable.

It was with some mixture of relief and regret on Georgiana's part that a knock on the door was followed by the announcement that the Darcy carriage had arrived. She found the charged air in the room with both Mr Hewitt and Fitz in attendance unbearable—was she the only one who felt it?—and yet she wished she could have more time to visit with the young man now that they had been formally introduced. She rose with the others, and they made their way out of the room.

When they reached the entryway of the inn, and made to walk outside to the waiting carriage, Wentworth stopped and said, "Ah! Darcy! One moment more, will you? I clear forgot some business I need to discuss with you!" So saying, he pulled his friend into the public parlour, unoccupied at that hour, and leaving Georgiana and Mr Hewitt to wait upon them. After a few timid glances one to the other, the young couple moved together towards the main door to put distance between themselves and the clerk, and began to talk quietly.

In the drawing room, Wentworth began by asking Darcy about his business in Castleton this morning. Darcy replied, describing his quick and easy negotiations with Mr Pettigrew, at which Wentworth expounded upon that agent's good character and honesty. Darcy glared at his friend, wondering at the importance of intelligence such that Wentworth had to secure their privacy to discuss it. After a few more of Wentworth's forays into idle converse, Darcy challenged his friend directly. "Wentworth, what *are* you going on about? Do you have anything of importance to relate or do you not? If you have, get to it, man!" His impatience was clear.

Wentworth looked a bit uncomfortable then, hemmed and hawed a bit, and finally confessed: "Oh, for mercy sake, Darcy, I just wanted to give our young friends a moment to talk! Can not you see that they are taken with each other?"

Darcy, having suspected as much, spluttered, "You what? Wentworth, my sister is barely out of childhood!"

"Oh, blast!" said his friend with a chuckle. "That is fiddlesticks, and you well know it, Darcy." Wentworth was accustomed in their long acquaintance to ignoring his friend's darkening countenance. "Miss Darcy is a young woman, and a beautiful one. You said yourself she will be presented next year. You cannot mean to keep her a child forever!"

"How I 'keep her' is my own affair, Wentworth!... you have no idea..."

"Yes, of course it is. I only mean that some day and soon, Miss Darcy is going to come fully into her own, and there is nothing *you* can do to stop it. I see your protective nature, and I comprehend it, I do! I felt much the same about Eleanor and she was near my own age. You... you have been both brother and father to Georgiana these many years. It is an imposing responsibility to bear, I warrant. Nathaniel Hewitt is an excellent young man; you could do a lot worse than encourage his attentions. He is honourable, bright, comes of a good family – his father is an Earl, for mercy sake!" Wentworth bit his lip as Darcy said,

"Yes, and he is a third child, and second son."

"True, but no pauper for all that. Nathaniel stands to inherit a fairly extensive manor in his own right from his mother. Really, Darcy," he repeated, "he is a fine young man and I think you would find he shares a lot of your own interests as well."

Despite his annoyance with his friend, Darcy laughed ruefully. "To whom do you seek to commend the young man, Wentworth, my sister or me?"

"You, I daresay, for I believe the young man has already done the job with your sister without my assistance!"

"Yes, that is my fear..." Darcy's comment trailed off as he looked into the adjoining room at his sister and once again faced the prospect of eventually losing Georgiana to marriage – to anyone.

Wentworth took this opportunity, since his friend had not yet torn him limb from limb, to venture another comment, and he said quite softly, "Darcy. You cannot hold on to Georgiana for your own ends. She cannot be made to account for your happiness and companionship. It would be easier for you to let her grow up if you, yourself, were to make a good match—."

At this, Darcy did look about to pummel Wentworth. With great effort of will, he clenched his hands at his waist and said coldly, "Sir, this is none of your business – you overstep yourself."

"Yes, I do, for someone has to! And you know I only mean for you to secure your own welfare. We have been friends far too long for me to stand by idly and see you go along in the world so much on your own."

Darcy retorted, "What of you, my friend? I have yet to meet your wife!"

"Ah." Wentworth looked somewhat wistful. "That is true. But that result is not for lack of trying on my part. I have been unlucky in love. You, however, are pursued by every eligible woman between here and the Cinque Ports. It has ever been so. Surely there is one among that throng worthy of your affections."

Darcy remained silent, glowering at his friend, jaw line pulsing as he ground his teeth in annoyance. Something in his countenance must have changed, however, for his friend became quite animated.

"There is!" Wentworth cried. "Darcy, what are you concealing from your long-time friend? Who is this exalted lady?!?"

"There is no one, and I will thank you to mind your inn-keeping and stop making matches for me—or for my sister."

Wentworth and Darcy glowered at each other for a moment; Darcy with as much menace as he could muster towards his friend, and that gentleman assuming a hurt expression that lasted but a moment before he broke into an easy smile.

"Very well, Darcy, I will leave you your secrets. But I know there is someone. She must be quite extraordinary indeed; yet I sense some impediment. I will say no more, other than to exhort you to do all you can to win your lady. For I have never known you to be this angry with me, for all my outrageous affronts to you. It bespeaks strong feeling indeed on your part."

After a moment, Darcy redirected the conversation. "So, my interfering *friend*, has your young protégé had enough time to win her heart, or may I now reclaim my sister?" The inn-keeper smiled, knowing that this was tantamount to Darcy's forgiveness for his meddling. No matter how offended his friend had been, Darcy would not hold a grudge against Wentworth for this; they had been through too much together during the last ten years for a disagreement of this nature to do lasting damage. Extending a hand in a gesture of capitulation, Wentworth was happy to see that after a moment's struggle with his emotions, Darcy clasped it, though his countenance still held a scowl. Without further word, they returned to the reception room.

ξ

"Miss Darcy, I must say I am very glad to have met your brother!"

Georgiana looked at Mr Hewitt with some surprise. After an awkward moment of silence following Fitz's departure with Mr Wentworth, this was certainly not the conversation she had imagined taking place – she had rather hoped that the young gentleman would express his joy at having met *her.*

"Why, I am certain he is glad to have made your acquaintance as well, Mr Hewitt." She did not know what else to say.

"What I mean is, I am glad the gentleman *is* your brother." Georgiana still could not quite take Nathaniel's meaning. "That is to say, that he is not...erm... someone... *else* to you!" Georgiana continued to look at him with a puzzled expression, until it occurred to her what the young man might be suggesting, and she blushed deeply.

"Mr Hewitt! Of course he is my brother; else I would not be travelling in his company alone."

"Oh, Miss Darcy, I beg your pardon, please. I meant no disrespect, I..." The young man floundered for a moment, trying to find the right words. "It is just – well, I thought perhaps you might be married."

His expression of alarum was so earnest as to make Georgiana feel warm of a sudden. Her eyes roamed the room, falling briefly on the clerk who made occasional glances in their direction but seemed to pay no special attention to the two young people. She turned her gaze to the drawing room, where she could see Fitz, apparently arguing with Mr Wentworth. Turning back finally to Nathaniel, she said, "No, Mr Hewitt, I am not married. I will not be presented before next spring." As she said this, she cast her eyes downward modestly.

"Oh, I see," said Nathaniel with an ingenuous smile. "I wonder then, Miss Darcy, if, when you are presented, you will consider obliging me with a dance?" He looked quite eager, as if such event was imminent rather than months away.

"But, Mr Hewitt, you are attending Cambridge soon, are you not, where you will encounter all manner of new...people, new experiences? I am certain that by next year, you will have forgotten all about your request." Georgiana hazarded a look up at the youth. His countenance was quite serious.

"Miss Darcy, indeed I hope to encounter new experiences; but I assure you, I will not forget our meeting. Just the anticipation of a dance at your coming out, will sustain me through all manner of trials at school!" His tone was serious, but his lips formed into a wide smile full of question and hope.

"Very well, then, Mr Hewitt. If you find yourself present for my coming out, you shall have the first set. After all, I owe you a debt of gratitude for preserving my bonnet this afternoon."

"Yes, Miss, so you do; and I would ask you to recall the dangers of the steep incline and thorny gorse I braved in accomplishing the deed." Nathaniel tried to maintain a sober countenance, but it would not hold. Both the young people suddenly laughed, drawing Darcy's notice from the other room.

A moment later Darcy and Wentworth joined the others, and they all made their way out to the carriage. Darcy stepped forward quickly to assist Georgiana into the coach, not ready to encourage presumptions on the part of Nathaniel Hewitt. If pressed, he would grudgingly admit the youth was of good family and Darcy could find no defects in his behaviour to this point. Yet though he could not fault the student's interest in Georgiana, neither would he lightly offer opportunities to advance it. Darcy stepped into the carriage with his sister, and gave the nod to his driver. Before it was put into motion, however, Wentworth stepped forward again.

"Darcy, I will be accompanying young Mr Hewitt to Cambridge in some days' time. I wonder if we might call upon you at Pemberley as a way-stop. I should like the opportunity to meet you again. It truly has been too long, my friend."

Darcy threw an irritated glance at Wentworth before recovering his manners. "Of course you must stop with us." Warming again to his old friend, he determined to make an effort at civility with their schoolmate's brother, and he directed his comments to the youth. "Are you a fisherman, Mr Hewitt? For Mr Wentworth and I are long-standing rivals, and we are currently even in our trophies. A deciding match is in order, I believe."

Young Hewitt's attention turned from his casual study of the carriage (or more accurately, an occupant of the same) to Darcy. "I would be honoured, Sir, to witness your deciding match; though I do not claim any particular talent at fishing, I enjoy the activity."

Darcy nodded his satisfaction, and managed even to smile at the young man as the carriage pulled away; though perhaps he was smiling as much at the prospect of detaining young Hewitt out of doors for some hours at Pemberley and thus precluding encounters between the student and Georgiana.

ξ

The carriage was on the outskirts of town before either occupant spoke. Georgiana's gaze had lingered in the direction of the Castleton Inn, Darcy noticed, yet she said nothing. "Are you fatigued, my dear?"

"No, not at all. I found the day quite stimulating, brother." She blushed as she considered how he might interpret her words, and added, "...and educational. Thank you for the indulgence."

Darcy shook his head to wave off thanks. Then, his eyes took on a mischievous look, a quality that unnerved her for some reason. But when he spoke, all he said was, "Tell me, what did you find of most interest on the day?" He looked at his sister quite pointedly, as if her answer held him in suspense.

"Oh, Fitz, I cannot say, there were so many things to excite my interest, each appealing to a different nature." Darcy smiled at her indulgently. He noticed her shiver slightly and asked if she was cold. The sun was still out, but it hung lower in the sky and it did not hold the same warmth as it had earlier in the day. When Georgiana indicated that she felt a bit of a chill, Darcy moved across to join her on her bench, securing her light shawl around her shoulders and drawing her close in to his side for additional warmth. Georgiana removed her bonnet; she could see her brother better in this manner. She held it by its ribbons in her lap.

"Your bonnet suits you well," said Darcy. "I hope its use will bring you happy memories of this day in future."

Georgiana smiled, but then the smile faded a bit. She seemed to ponder some matter of importance. Darcy sat quietly and waited to hear if she would share her thoughts with him.

"Fitz," she began. She hesitated for an instant before plunging on. "Fitz, I must tell you that I almost lost my bonnet today at the castle."

"Did you?" replied her brother with utmost care to display no especial curiosity.

"Yes," said Georgiana, and then proceeded to tell Darcy of her encounter with Mr Hewitt—though she did not comprehend that to be his name at the time, of course they had not introduced themselves—and of the young man's rescue of her bonnet when the wind took it some yards distant.

Georgiana noted that her brother's smile of contentment at this telling was in stronger proportion than the story warranted. She was glad that she had told him of the event. She did not wish to keep any thing from Fitz, even things of such inconsequence, ever since her misfortune with Mr Wickham the summer before. She wanted always to be able to speak of anything with her brother, to share everything she experienced; even if at times his naturally imposing reserve gave her anxiety over how to start. The few months past they had forged something of an intimacy whereby they shared converse as adults, as friends. She wished never to do anything to set that at risk. His positive reaction to her description of having met Nathaniel Hewitt on Castle Hill convinced her that she had done right to tell him—and so she had.

For Georgiana could not know that, during her walk round the castle ruins that afternoon, Darcy had tired of his book early on. Looking around him, he had decided to catch up with his sister and finish the inspection of the grounds with her after all. He had taken a similar path to hers and, in short order, had espied her cream skirts between crumbling walls. But on approach, he heard voices – hers and another, that one belonging to a man. Darcy had changed direction to come upon his sister from an angle that allowed him the sight of Georgiana and the new acquaintance with whom she conversed, without the young people's taking notice of him. He also heard their discourse... *and* saw the episode of her bonnet's flight. His sense of relief was palpable that she had not withheld this recounting from him, nor left out any portion of what had transpired.

Darcy looked at his sister as she met his gaze without guile. Perhaps Wentworth was right, he thought. Georgiana clearly adored her brother, but she could not be at his disposal forever, and to deny her a future with a worthy young man simply to delay his own loneliness would be unforgivable. He was not ready to concede that Hewitt was the right young man, not yet at any rate. But he would try to remain civil, for Georgiana's sake.

For the present, he arranged a lap robe about their knees, and they talked amiably of their day – or rather, Georgiana talked with Darcy making the odd comment here and there or laughing at appropriate moments at her enthusiasms. She even came to speak in a roundabout way concerning Nathaniel Hewitt and her attraction to the young gentleman. Darcy managed to smile even through the twinge in his heart. Unlike their journey earlier in the day, Georgiana was full of animation from her experiences and did not tire at all.

When they were but half an hour's ride from Pemberley, dusk moving in as the sun sank towards the horizon, Georgiana suddenly sat up straighter. "Fitz, I almost forgot!" She reached into her reticule, rooting around among the purchases it held, and pulled out a small item folded in paper. She held it out to him. "This is for you, dearest Fitz. Thank you for today. I loved our time together, brother."

Darcy took the parcel, felt something small and knobbly within the paper, and began to open it. An expression of hopeful anticipation stole over Georgiana's face as he looked at her, and she willed him to like his trinket. Revealed within the wrapping was a finely woven cord, perhaps four to five inches long. Threaded and knotted at intervals into the cord were three rounded beads of blue john. At one end was a larger rounded bead and at the other, a flat-worked oval piece about the size of a thumb to the first joint. On this flat piece, the natural striations of the stone gave one the impression of a landscape in violet, cream and blue hues, suggestive of an open area on the bottom, and hills behind at the top end of the stone.

Darcy looked up in wonder at Georgiana. "Is it not Pemberley?" she said excitedly, and he agreed; indeed, a painter could not have captured better the sense of where their home was situated. "It is a worry stone, Fitz. If you carry it with you, and stroke the beads with your fingers, you can leave all your concerns within it…" Darcy turned upon her a look of profound scepticism. "Oh, I know," she continued, "it will not truly. But I would like to think, Fitz, that it could give you some comfort when you have such weighty issues on your mind." She gave her brother a tentative smile.

Darcy took Gee's hand in his own, squeezed it warmly, and answered. "It has given me comfort already, my dear. I shall treasure it, and carry it with me always, right here." He indicated the small pocket of his waistcoat. He embraced Georgiana, and proffered a kiss on her brow, as the two in their carriage turned into Pemberley's gate. They were in complete harmony of feeling! But Georgiana noticed that her brother did not slip the worry bead cord into his waistcoat at once. He held it in his right hand, and unconsciously stroked it with his thumb as they came within view of the house.

Darcy Goes a-Courtin'

ぬぬぬ

All is well again in the Bennet household of Longbourn. Lydia has married Mr Wickham and moved to Newcastle, completing the restoration of the family's reputation; and Mr Bingley has returned to the country and proposed to Jane Bennet, restoring her good fortune and Mrs Bennet's faith in her beautiful eldest daughter. In this "What If" story that deviates a little from the book plot, there is to be a ball at Netherfield to celebrate the upcoming nuptials. Will fortune once again favour the Bennet family – particularly Miss Elizabeth?

ぬぬぬ

Bingley was delighted to hear his good friend Darcy announced as he finished a late breakfast. He immediately went to his friend and clapped him on the back in greeting, then ushered Darcy over to the table to join him. He called for a place setting for Darcy and, once his friend had been established with coffee (for Darcy would take no other refreshment) Bingley addressed himself to the gentleman.

"Darcy! Do you know I didn't expect you until tomorrow, my friend, but this is good fortune indeed. To what do we owe this early arrival?"

Darcy hedged a bit, unsure how much he wished to impart to Bingley. Charles Bingley was a good man, and certainly good for appealing to Darcy's lighter side; but the man had little reserve whatsoever, and anything said to Bingley would likely be repeated in all innocence to all and sundry—or worse, drawn from him without his even knowing it by his sister Caroline's arts. Darcy had suffered enough humiliation when Miss Elizabeth refused his offer in the spring; he was averse to saying anything that might bring his awkward plight then to public scrutiny now.

"Well," Darcy began, "I hope you will excuse the early intrusion, Charles. But I simply had to escape Town in all haste. Lady Phyllida Parkhurst got into her head to hold a grand masquerade on the betrothal of her niece Honoria; and you know her penchant for spectacle. She was insistently advocating that I *must* participate as Marc Antony to her Cleopatra. It was simply *not* to be considered, much less borne in the doing. I used you ill, my friend, in dissembling that you had need of me, but I hope you will not grudge me using you so."

Bingley laughed in his free and easy way, clearly savouring for a moment an image of his proper friend in toga and laurel leaves. He shook his head finally to offer forgiveness for being used. "Happy to have been of service, Darcy, both in the pretext and in providing you a safe haven. You know you are welcome in my home at any time whatever the reason."

Darcy nodded, feeling both relieved for the easy reception and somewhat guilty for deceiving his friend. Oh, the excuse as far as it went was true enough; but Darcy had not followed it all the way to a true explanation of why he particularly wished to escape to Netherfield Park.

Bingley continued, "I am uncertain how much respite you will enjoy here, though, Darcy, for you might know that we are holding a ball here tonight as well, to celebrate my engagement with Miss Bennet."

Darcy considered how to reply. "Yes, Charles, I am aware of it, I recall it from your recent letter. And if you desire it, I will attend your ball tonight to wish you both joy."

Bingley was astonished and conveyed such to Darcy, hastening to add that nothing would make him happier.

"It is only right I do so given your welcome this morning. And, at the least I will not have to subject myself to Roman garb." He joined Bingley in a chuckle. "I shall tolerate your ball as the lesser of discomforts; and I *am* truly pleased for you and Miss Bennet in your happiness. I would much rather celebrate that joyful event than take part in a bacchanal."

Once more, Darcy's comments, delivered in his usual stoic manner, brought an easy laugh to Charles. "Well, and I am certain your attendance tonight will be esteemed, Darcy; particularly as these things are always so heavily weighted with ladies. Another gentleman for a dancing partner is never amiss."

"Hmmm," replied Darcy. "Perhaps I have done myself no service. I should have been better escaping to Pemberley!" His friend looked at him to protest, but then noticed that Darcy smiled at his own remark.

How very odd, thought Bingley, *that Darcy appears so accepting of this obligation. Not the least reticence, and in remarkable good humour! Well, I will not think too long on it... it is enough that my friend is here and of fair disposition.*

Darcy had but one request further. "Bingley, I would ask only that you not mention my early arrival today to anyone. You know how I loathe balls and such; and though for you, I promise to attend and do my duty in filling the dance lists of otherwise slighted women. But you know how news flies about in this country, and I confess I will find it intolerable to reflect that my expected appearance has been speculated upon by all and sundry in the hours leading up to it."

Bingley could not quite tell if Darcy was jesting, but would not test his friend's present mood. He promised to tell no one of the early arrival. As it happened, Miss Bennet – his 'Jane', he blushed to think of her – had some dress fittings and other women's business in Meryton that day in expectation of their wedding trip, and Charles would not see her until the ball that evening. She would have been the greatest risk in his breaking his promise inadvertently.

His sister Caroline had condescended even to join Miss Bennet in her commissions, so the house at Netherfield would remain quiet. She would surely return only to repair directly to her chambers to ready herself for the evening.

As such, Bingley delighted that his friend's arrival gave him company to pass the day; and in Darcy's relief at how easily he had inserted himself into the night's events, he did indeed spend an amiable afternoon with his good-humoured friend.

ξ

As the hour for the ball drew near, Darcy stood in his dressing chamber with misgivings. Perhaps this had not been a wise notion after all. He did so want the opportunity to encounter Miss Elizabeth Bennet once again, but was he up to the challenge in so public a manner; and particularly here in Hertfordshire where Miss Elizabeth was in her natural element and he, most assuredly, was at disadvantage?

The day two months before that he had passed at Pemberley with the lady and her relations had signalled a marked improvement in his relationship with Miss Bennet. But his limited interaction with her since that day, particularly here in Hertfordshire less than a fortnight past, had been singularly lacking in any restoration of that intimacy they had begun to achieve; and he could not be certain that Elizabeth's good will toward him at Pemberley was not an aberration, rather than a change of heart.

Ah, well, he chastised himself. This is the consequence for acting rashly without consideration enough, something he customarily made a point to avoid. Now he was obliged to Bingley to attend his ball and make the best of it.

Darcy could hear guests arriving, the hall below filling with the general murmur of voices, the first strains of music as the orchestra readied for a busy night. His rooms were at the front of the house, overlooking the sweep of drive, and he looked out now at the front entry, saw the carriages and throngs of people milling around.

He experienced an instant of sudden panic when he recognized the Bennet family descending from their transport. There was Miss Elizabeth, arm in arm with Miss Bennet, beginning to ascend the steps. She looked particularly lovely in a silken gown of deep russet that mirrored the lustre of her hair in the torchlight.

Darcy noted that Miss Elizabeth's swept-up hair was threaded with pearls, and it took him back to a former occasion – an occasion the outcome of which Darcy would rather not dwell upon – when she had been similarly adorned. It had been a ball, in fact, in this very house the year before; and he recalled too well the utter dissatisfaction he had taken in the only dance he had shared with Miss Elizabeth. He determined that tonight would be different; *he* would be different.

His eye was drawn to Miss Elizabeth's hand resting lightly upon her sister's arm. He experienced a slight nervous tic to imagine it laying upon his own instead, to imagine taking her hand in his for a dance. From there it was a short step in his current distraction for his mind to wander, to imagine his hands lovingly clasping a pearl pendant around Miss Elizabeth's neck to rival those in her hair.

Shaking himself from this reverie, Darcy paced his room for a few moments. He must lose these flights of fancy, for it would take all his wits to negotiate this evening to any good end. Finally, he closed his eyes and drew in a breath, long and deep. Exhaling slowly, he stood tall, threw his shoulders back to stiffen his spine and his resolve, and made his way to the stairs to join the gathering revellers.

ξ

Upon his descent, Darcy first made to the receiving line, there to congratulate Bingley and bestow his wishes upon Miss Bennet for future happiness. That lady evinced clear surprise at Mr.

Darcy's presence, having lately been to understand that he would arrive the next day. But she recovered quickly and accepted his good wishes with quiet grace; adding her own delight that Mr Darcy was present at Netherfield to join in the joy she and Charles felt; and she wished him a pleasant evening. As he took his leave to walk through the crowd into the ballroom, Miss Bennet looked to Bingley with a quizzical expression, but he simply shrugged and laughed, then whispered something to her quickly before attending to the next guest.

Eventually Darcy came upon the dancing in the ballroom to see that Miss Elizabeth was engaged in the first of the evening with a young man he believed was clerk to her uncle Phillips. He stopped to watch as she glided effortlessly through the movements of the dance and laughed delightedly with her partner when the youth failed to negotiate the steps with the same grace. Once more, Darcy felt a physical sensation assail him at seeing Miss Elizabeth's natural liveliness and affability, a tremor that began in his head and made its way quickly downward until it reached his very toes, until he must force himself to concentrate on anything else.

How he could use some of her assured ease at this moment, for he was decidedly uneasy in his skin in this milieu, and most particularly in anticipation of her reception of him when he made his presence known to her! He glanced about the room idly until the dance ended, when he positioned himself so as to greet Miss Elizabeth as she turned away from her partner.

"Mr. Darcy!" escaped her, "What are you doing here?" Her surprise on seeing him was great. No word of his early arrival had reached as far as Longbourn, he was gratified to see.

"Miss Elizabeth," he replied, bowing to her. "I am a guest here." Realizing at once how stiff he sounded, he glanced at the floor, then back to her and smiled. "I arrived earlier today, against Bingley's expectation." He noted the parallel of this opening conversation with an earlier one at Pemberley in the summer when Miss Elizabeth, with her aunt and uncle travelling through Derbyshire, toured the estate while believing its owner to be away. The memory, the way Miss Bennet had appeared in every detail walking along the path in the park—his park; the awkwardness of both in reacquainting for the first time after his disastrous proposal at Rosings and his subsequent letter to her—all this was permanently stamped on his memory. But he had begun there to hope that a change in her esteem of him could be achieved. Now, he hoped this evening's interactions would yield an even better end than the friendly tenor they had established in Derbyshire before the unhappy news of her sister's elopement had undone them a few days later.

As such, he hastened to add, "I was particularly eager to offer my felicitations to the happy couple, and so moved forward my journey to Netherfield to arrive for the ball—Bingley had written to me of it, you see." He realized he was beginning to babble and, with another awkward smile, gave Miss Bennet the chance to speak.

ξ

Elizabeth Bennet, had Darcy but been able to see into her thoughts, did not know how to react to his statement. Indeed, she did not know how to feel at all in encountering Mr Darcy. It was not often that she found herself without her wit or at least a ready word, but the sudden appearance of this gentleman had rendered her speechless—just as on the similarly surprising occasion of his meeting her in Pemberley's park that he himself recalled. But she could not allow herself to linger on that memory, a time when they had started anew of sorts before Lydia's thoughtless antics put all thought of reconciliation out of bounds.

She quickly reflected that Jane had not forewarned her of the gentleman's residence at Netherfield now, and wondered what her sister could be playing at; but then as quickly realized that Jane could not have known of it, for she could not believe the information to have been withheld by design. While she struggled to find some remark for Mr Darcy, the gentleman spared her further embarrassed silence. "Miss Elizabeth," he said. "May I have the honour of the next dance?"

Elizabeth blushed slightly, and looked at her feet quickly before returning her gaze to Mr Darcy. "I am sorry to report, sir, that I was previously engaged for the next with Mr Wilkerson."

"Ah. Of course," replied the gentleman. "Of course," he repeated. "Well, perhaps another time."

"Indeed, sir, I would like that."

Darcy studied Miss Elizabeth for a few seconds to determine if her statement carried conviction. To his delight, he perceived that she actually seemed to regret her previous commitment, and was truthful in her remarks to him. He gathered his nerve to risk rejection yet again, and said, "Perhaps you will allow me, then, to reserve the honour of your partnership for the first of the second set?" His relief was palpable when the lady smiled amiably and assured him that these dances were now his to claim.

While Miss Elizabeth then allowed Mr Wilkerson's interruption to take her to the line for the next, Mr Darcy wandered aimlessly around the room. His eyes, however, kept coming back to the centre of the line, where Elizabeth moved fluidly through the music as occasion demanded, and stood in quiet contemplation (most decidedly against custom) when not so engaged.

Though she smiled at Mr Wilkerson and, to all outward observance, gave him her attention as she danced with him, her mind wandered to her just-ended encounter with Mr Darcy. Her heart leapt to think that he was here, and that he had asked her to dance with no outward inducement. She had felt bereft at having to deny his initial request; and was surprised but relieved that he followed the rejection with a further application. She felt strangely apprehensive at their pairing to come, yet exhilarated as well.

Darcy suddenly realized that he had been staring unabashedly at Elizabeth throughout the first of her pair with Mr Wilkerson. Whatever would she make of his mooning behaviour should she notice it? He must withdraw and content himself with passing the time until his own turn on the floor with her. He dragged himself away from the dancing floor, and walked through to the adjoining parlour which, as it neither had dancing nor cards but had been set aside for quiet conversation, held fewer people. Beholding a particular gentleman there in the corner, looking bored and distracted, Darcy approached the man.

"Mr. Bennet."

Mr. Bennet looked up to see who had called to him, and was surprised to see it was Mr Darcy. "Mr Darcy?"

"Allow me to offer my good wishes to your family on Miss Bennet's betrothal to my most worthy friend." Mr Bennet acknowledged the comment with a hesitant nod, as if wondering whether he was hearing correctly. Darcy added, "I am certain they will make a most harmonious marriage, given their similar temperaments. My friend is fortunate indeed in having earned your daughter's esteem."

"Yes, I daresay they will be happy" replied Mr Bennet, clearly in some discomfort to be in converse with Mr Darcy of whom, though they had met on several occasions in the year past, he knew little in truth, but few opinions to the good. What could be this gentleman's object in speaking with him now, he was at some pains to comprehend.

Rather than moving on once having performed this obligatory exchange, Darcy remained by Mr Bennet. After a few aborted attempts to engage the gentleman, he drew him at last into a conversation about books, which Mr Bennet found he enjoyed immensely, as did his partner by every indication. Mr Bennet began to wonder, with such informed opinions as the gentleman possessed, why it was that the community had taken against him when he first visited a year past with Mr Bingley.

It was in this attitude that Miss Elizabeth Bennet once more came upon Mr Darcy, for when her turn with Mr Wilkerson had ended, she had turned down fully three invitations to dance in order to come seek a few moments of quietude before the next, anticipated ones.

"Hello, Papa," she smiled. "Mr Darcy." She received nods from both gentlemen, and a benevolent smile from her father. "Mr Darcy and I have been discussing the merits of extensive libraries, Lizzy." At this comment, Mr Bennet gave his daughter a peculiar look outside the notice of Mr Darcy, a mixture of wonder and curiosity. She smiled, and wondered herself at Mr Darcy's amiability this evening. She would like to think that she played some part in it, however small, but could not justify the belief with fact.

The early strains of music began to filter in from the other room, reminding them all that the second set would soon begin. Mr Darcy claimed Elizabeth's attentions. "The orchestra calls, Miss Bennet. I believe you have promised me the next dance."

"Indeed you speak true, Mr Darcy." Darcy offered his arm to her, which she took lightly. As he covered her hand with his own to move into the ballroom, that same disquiet visited him as when he had imagined just such a touch in his rooms earlier in the evening. They each nodded to her father to take their leave, and wandered back to the dancing floor under the startled attention of Mr Bennet, who condescended even to follow behind in order to bear witness to the surprising spectacle.

ξ

As the dance began, Miss Elizabeth and Darcy were silent. They established as necessary the pattern of movement of the dance, a slow weaving of steps that brought them face to face with every few bars of music. At first, they did not speak at all, but their eyes met with attentive curiosity after each turn. Finally, Mr Darcy began to speak, unwilling to endure further the tense air growing about them. "I am gratified to see your sister, Miss Bennet, in such happy looks."

"Yes," replied Miss Elizabeth. "Jane is quite pleased with her Mr Bingley. Though she does not generally show her feelings with ease, she has been quite open in them since Mr Bingley affirmed his own to her."

"Mmm. I should imagine it *would* unlock reserves of emotion to have the object of our affections confirm that they are not misplaced." At this moment, the music demanded that the dancers separate again, and they were left to their own thoughts for a few turns, until their steps brought them to each other again. Independently, Elizabeth and Darcy wondered how their last exchange might apply beyond Jane and Charles. Their eyes met as the music brought them together again, and though they did not look away, their glance held questions that neither could answer. In awkward silence, they completed the dance, and turned to applaud the orchestra.

Elizabeth's mind was turning flips. She had so desired that Mr Darcy renew an acquaintance with her following their aborted meetings in Derbyshire; but their brief public encounters since that time had only confused her as to his opinion of her. The last time they had met, a fortnight before at Longbourn, Mr Darcy had been seated with Mrs Bennet for dinner—no chance there. But afterward, when the gentlemen joined the ladies in the parlour for tea, he had spoken almost not at all, and appeared uncomfortable in Elizabeth's presence. She had wondered then if he fully regretted ever having involved himself with her. His words tonight could be an overture to her, but could just as easily be polite acknowledgment of his friend's engagement... could simply be his (Darcy's) acknowledgment that he had consented to his friend's choice in Jane and, in so doing, made the night possible.

Meanwhile, Darcy wondered at Miss Elizabeth's understanding of their converse. She had said nothing, but her face had indicated a sweet pensiveness. Could she have realized that his remarks held an appeal in them, a desire for her to allow him to renew his attentions to her? She made no outward answer, yet had certainly displayed no distaste. He drew on his courage to resolve the discussion with her, to try to draw out if she would welcome his continued advances, when the orchestra began the next dance. Unfortunately, it was a lively and quick step, which allowed for no converse. For several minutes, Darcy went through the motions, awaiting an end to the dance so that he could again talk with Miss Bennet.

During the second dance, Elizabeth began to doubt Mr. Darcy's intentions. Though he had begun in an assiduous manner, and his latest converse was not only cordial but seemed to say so much below the surface, she noted that he now appeared to have lost his enthusiasm. He moved through their second dance together with perfunctory motions, as though he could not wait for it to end. The man was not aloof tonight as had been his custom in the past, and yet he was unaccountably quite discomposed. What Lizzy could not determine was whether she, and in what manner, contributed to his disquiet.

Oh, how she wished she could tell him then and there: that she knew, from her Aunt Gardiner's testimony, of what he had done for her family to resolve Lydia's shameful elopement with Mr Wickham; knew well the cost to him of saving her sister, and her family in the whole, by negotiating with a man he had good reason to despise. She wished to tell him that she had experienced so material a change in her opinion of him since, that she regretted her behaviour when she rejected him so unceremoniously in Kent last spring. But out of respect, she could not do this. She did not know if he would receive such compliments willingly; but she did know that he had devoutly wished his good deeds in the matter of Lydia's restitution to remain secret. And precisely out of her newfound concern for him, she could not put him in the untenable position of being obliged to renew sentiments he may no longer feel.

At last the dance ended. Darcy was keen to return to their conversation and, having duly recognized the orchestra, turned to her to see if he might escort her to the dining room for some refreshment – and discourse. He looked to Miss Elizabeth and saw a quizzical smile in her expression, as if pondering as well whether their time together might be extended. This encouraged him.

As he stepped forward, however, to beg her attentions to himself, Miss Elizabeth was suddenly surrounded by a sea of women. Mrs Bennet, pulling along her younger daughters Catherine and Mary, had come to claim Elizabeth to resolve a disagreement with Jane concerning her wedding arrangements. Mrs Bennet so concentrated on the issue at hand that she quite ignored Darcy, if indeed she noticed his presence at all, and any prior claim upon her second daughter was lost. The ladies' enthusiasm for their subject quite overtook all else, and they commandeered Elizabeth to find Miss Bennet and Bingley and join the debate. Darcy could only look on as the lady of his heart was spirited away from him. Her quick glance back at him seemed to hold an apology, and something else... regret?

Although Darcy was determined to renew his conversation with Elizabeth at first opportunity, he found himself sadly disappointed. Directly following her departure with her mother and sisters, Caroline Bingley found Darcy and planted herself at his side. She expressed over and again her raptures that Darcy had returned from town for the ball, as she could not imagine having to suffer through it without an intimate to rue the proceedings with her. If Miss Bingley noticed Darcy's distraction, she did not acknowledge it. (In truth, she *had* noticed, as well as his singular attention to Miss Elizabeth, and had purposefully accosted him to prevent his further encountering her country rival.) Darcy dutifully escorted Caroline through a set of dances, all the while searching the room surreptitiously for Miss Elizabeth, but without success.

Circumstance ensured that Mr Darcy and Miss Elizabeth found no opportunity for further discourse during the evening, and all too soon (or not soon enough for some) night eased into early morning. The crowd dispersed, the musicians secured their instruments, and all and sundry proclaimed the evening the best in their remembrance – even better than the last year's event at Netherfield – as they awaited their carriages to take them home to their beds.

Darcy, having extricated himself finally from Miss Bingley's singular attention, sat in his disappointment halfway up the stairs, looking down on guests as they bid farewell to Bingley and Miss Bennet. He was far enough away from the proceedings to escape the general notice of others, yet he would have cared not at all had any glanced up to see him sprawled ignominiously on the step. He had a good view of people as they departed. At length, the Bennet family, last of the guests as might be expected, came forward *en masse* with warm sentiments for Bingley and to reclaim Jane to themselves for only a few more weeks.

On seeing Miss Elizabeth among their group, Darcy rose and hurried down the stairs. As he neared the bottom, that lady happened to look up and see his approach. He noted that she blushed deeply, and looked away toward the door in apparent timidity. This reaction slowed his step. He approached her family, bowing formally while he pointedly wished them a good night. This task accomplished, he walked over to the object of his interest, attempting a casualness he could not feel.

"Miss Elizabeth."

"Mr Darcy." Each mirrored the discomfiture of the other in demeanour.

"I... er... You..." Darcy took a deep breath and began again. "May I tell you, Miss Elizabeth, that you looked lovely tonight." He coloured at the intimacy of his remark, and his tone became more formal. "Thank you for obliging me in a dance."

"My pleasure, Mr Darcy." At his nodded acknowledgment, Miss Elizabeth curtsied slightly to him. They stood looking at one another, unsure of how to move to the conversation each desired, unable apparently to recognize that their desires were the same. Elizabeth was just opening her mouth to speak when Miss Bingley swept up to the couple.

In feigned innocence – though in truth she had been watching the interchange between Miss Elizabeth and Mr Darcy closely with growing alarum – Miss Bingley began to talk to Miss Elizabeth of nothing in particular, monopolizing her attention. Mr Darcy, recognizing defeat in the wake of this intrusion, excused himself and retreated up the stairs toward his rooms. Near the top, at the last vantage from which he might still see the party standing below, he turned to glance back down. The Bennets were gathering their various coats and wraps from the footmen. Bingley stood smiling on all the proceedings as if never had there been a happier moment in his life. Miss Bingley stood off to one side, her eyes narrowed in some satisfaction and a smirk playing upon her lips as she watched

Miss Elizabeth. That lady now waited quietly at the front door for her family's imminent departure. She glanced up for one instant and tentatively smiled at Darcy, before lowering her eyes again. Darcy roused himself and completed his passage to the next floor, wondering at the meaning behind Miss Elizabeth's last glance as he walked to his room.

Darcy stood at his windows, watching until the last carriage could no longer be seen on the drive. Then, sensing that sleep would elude him for some time, he quietly left his rooms and made his way to the library, grateful to meet no one along the way. It was going to be a long night...

ξ

Charles Bingley was not the most observant of individuals in the normal course of things, but even he noted with alarum his friend Darcy's worn appearance at breakfast on the day following Bingley's engagement ball. "Good heavens, man! You look ghastly!"

Indeed, Darcy did not present his usual impeccable portrait. He looked as if he had dressed himself and in haste – his jacket uncharacteristically wrinkled, his cravat askew, his boots scuffed and in need of his man's attention, and his hair falling untidy onto his face. And he held himself in such a manner nearly sideways to Charles as to present himself in profile. Most odd, thought Bingley, in his usually forthright friend. Darcy shuffled over to the sideboard and selected a small plate of food and a coffee from the buffet there. Ignoring Bingley's remark, he sat himself again to Charles's right rather than in his customary seat on the left.

"Darcy, are you unwell?" Bingley asked with all concern.

Darcy winced at the volume of Bingley's voice. "No, Bingley, I am well, or will be tolerably so if you can but lower your voice. I have a touch of a clouded head from too much drink last night."

"Ah," said Charles, in a near whisper. "I understand."

"I had thought to find the breakfast room emptied by now and wished only some toast and coffee in solitude... why are you so late dining this morning?"

Darcy's implied insult, though in truth it was unintended, sailed over Bingley's head, and he replied in the joviality a whisper could muster, "Arose rather late today. I had trouble getting myself to sleep last night – or should I say this morning – after the excitement. Did not my Jane look beautiful at the ball, Darcy? I swear, it was hours after she left before her sylphic image faded from my sight. Who would willingly close their eyes to such a vision?"

"Yes, my friend, Miss Bennet looked well indeed." Darcy decided not to point out how like his future mother-in-law Charles was beginning to sound, so he settled for, "Her arm in yours certainly improved your looks, my friend." Bingley laughed, as was intended. "Where is your sister Caroline this morning? Has she breakfasted already?"

Bingley was taken aback. Now he truly suspected his friend to be ill, for Darcy to be searching out his sister, and in such a dishevelled form as he presented. "Shall I have Grenville fetch her for you?" he asked, trying to be solicitous.

"No!" Darcy stopped and put his hand to his head, the force of his denial having produced a stab of pain in his temple. "No, thank you, Charles," he repeated in quieter tones, "I merely wished to know if we might be spared her attendance."

Ah, thought Bingley, *perhaps he is himself after all, but for the effects of his drink.* To his friend, he said, "You are spared, then, for Caroline is dining in her room this morning. She is supervising Allen's packing of her trunk, for she will depart later to-day to visit our sister Louisa and Hurst for some days. Must shop in Town, you know, nothing hereabouts will suit for her. She will remain until they all make their way back for my marriage." Bingley knew his friend would be cheered by this news, and noted the show of relief which overspread Darcy's profile.

"Was she so very trying for you last night? I did notice that my sister scarcely left your person the entire night once she had found you."

"I was sorely tried last night, Charles, but cannot wholly blame Caroline for it. She was but one of many obstacles to my peace of mind."

Bingley thought again that Darcy really was out of sorts today, as he was not exercising his usual tact in talking to him concerning his sister. But he was not offended. He knew well Caroline's designs on Darcy, but also knew of (and even approved, if his opinion mattered) Darcy's lack of interest. A match between his good friend and his sister would be one certain to guarantee conditions of unhappiness and contempt after very little time—for them both and, by consequence, for Bingley as well. He was long resigned to the comprehension that he would never call Darcy 'brother.'

"I did see you dancing last night with Miss Elizabeth, though, before Caroline laid claim to you."

"Mmmm" was the only reply Bingley was to receive from this observation, so he tried again to rouse his friend to discourse. "Miss Elizabeth was quite fetching herself last night, was not she? I noted particularly how the colour of her gown complemented her hair and eyes. Did not you think it?"

Darcy sat still a moment, Miss Elizabeth's picture from last night as they had danced forming in his mind's eye. He smiled with sentiment at the memory, drawing a look of surprise from Bingley, whose concern over Darcy's state had now given him more acute discernment. "Why, Darcy, I believe you are smitten with my sister-to-be. Can it be true?" Darcy said nothing, but a blush of deepest hue crept up from his neck to fan out across his face, and darkened his eye. "You are!" cried Bingley in triumph, "You are smitten!"

Darcy winced again at the shout, then felt required to reply. "She is a fine young woman, Bingley, and most amiable." Bingley's smiled broadened. "But that is all; that is as far as my notice of her goes."

Knowing better than to tease outright in his friend's inebriated state, Bingley held his tongue on the matter; though he was certain that his friend dissembled, as far as Darcy's notice of the lady went. He decided to try a different tack.

"I plan to ride to Longbourn this noon, Darcy, to spend the day with my dear Jane and her family. Perhaps you would care to join me?"

"No." A pause. "No, I cannot."

"But, for pity's sake, why not? Oh, I know the Bennets when assembled are often loud and boisterous, but they mean well enough—and Miss Elizabeth in particular always behaves decorously even as she enlivens a room with her wit." He smiled encouragingly.

He received no answer, and tried one more appeal. "Please do come, Darcy. For we mean to walk into Meryton later in the morning to call upon Mrs Phillips. I am certain Miss Eliza plans to accompany us."

Darcy shook his head vigorously in the negative, then rested it in both hands, elbows on the table supporting him, eyes clenched shut, as if the quick movement had caused him great pain. Bingley spared his friend any additional urgings, but determined to try again after a while to cajole Darcy into accompanying him to Longbourn.

"Well," said Bingley. "I have done with my breakfast and can see you have some ailment to overcome. I will oblige you and leave you to the solitude you so pointedly crave." As he spoke, Bingley rose from his chair preparatory to leaving. When he had rounded the table, he turned back to look at his friend, and he all but forgot the comment on his lips as he was afforded the picture of Darcy full on.

"Good Lord!!!" Bingley exclaimed. "What has happened to you?" Darcy had failed to shift quickly enough when his friend had turned back; he had not managed to hide the right side of his face from Bingley; such that Bingley had a very clear sight of the sizable lump on Darcy's brow, and a bruise even now darkening to near-black over his right eye. "Darcy?"

Darcy winced again. "It is all right, Bingley, truly. I have only had a slight accident while riding this morning."

"An accident riding? Darcy, you are the best horseman I have ever encountered, indeed I have always envied your natural affinity with the beasts. Whatever could have happened? We must call a physician to have a look at you!"

For a moment, Darcy sat looking downcast. Finally, he resolved that he would not escape his friend's concern without a full accounting, and he glanced up at Bingley. "Oh, sit down again, Charles, will you, and I will confess it all to you." Bingley took his seat once again, studying his friend now with great anxiety.

"To begin, Bingley, I thank you for your concern but I do not need a physician." When Bingley looked to argue the point, Darcy glared him into silence. "This is but a slight bump on the head—we have both of us had worse in our lives—and I assure you that I will be fine when once the swelling recedes. Grayson will attend to me quite adequately when I go up. But for now, my only desire is for some coffee to clear my head, and then a quiet day within." He winced slightly. "I must confess I am relieved to hear of Miss Bingley's imminent departure. By tomorrow I will be my old self again."

To this, Bingley could not help but respond. "Darcy, my friend, you have not been your 'old self' for some time now. I have quite wondered at the changes in you in recent months."

"Indeed. I suppose I have undergone some alteration of late." He studied his friend a moment, grateful for Bingley's solicitous nature and grateful as well, if he could admit it, for an opportunity to speak of the weight he had been carrying these several months to someone who possessed intimate knowledge of the parties involved. Bingley wisely had held his own tongue during his friend's perusal, which discretion made up Darcy's mind at last.

"And yes, you were correct earlier as well in your surmise. I am smitten, Bingley, and more so. Miss Elizabeth Bennet captured my particular attention some time ago and, beyond that, she has captured my heart."

Bingley's countenance evidenced his delight; he gasped in pleasure, his merry eyes taking on additional brightness. "Darcy, how wonderful! A finer woman you could not have fixed on, always excepting of course my own dear Jane. How could you keep this knowledge from me?"

Darcy groaned. There would be nothing for it but to relay his entire history with the lady to his friend. Taking a deep breath first, he ventured shakily into the particulars. As Bingley's demeanour settled to hear the incredible events of past months, Darcy found it easier to continue. Soon he had related summarily the whole of his encounters with Miss Elizabeth Bennet in the year past, to include his disastrous proposal at Rosings in April; their new start at Pemberley in the summer which was so abruptly severed by Lydia Bennet's elopement; and his recent reintroduction to the lady, culminating in his aborted attempts to court her the night before.

Bingley sat in awe, unable to believe what he was hearing. Though he knew his friend to be an excellent man who exercised devotion on those for whom he cared or who depended on him, Bingley had never once to now suspected the depth of Darcy's feelings for Miss Elizabeth. He felt guilty that, in being so intent upon his own romantic entanglements, he had not been accessible to his friend.

"Darcy, I am gratified you have related this to me finally, you have all too clearly kept it to yourself too long. But I am more than a little curious still, as to how all this relates to your riding accident?"

"Hmm, yes. You see, last night after the ball, I knew I should never find sleep. I was too disturbed by the obstacles that had precluded my converse with Miss Elizabeth, too unsettled in general. So after you had retired, I retreated to the library. I am afraid I made rather too many forays to the claret bottle, while I searched for a clue to comprehend the lady's present state of affections. I am not certain at what time I drifted off to sleep in your chair, but it was near dawn, I am sure. Only a short time later I awoke, fuzzy in my head from wine and frustration."

Darcy looked so doleful that Bingley almost laughed, but caught himself as he knew to do so was the surest way to stopper his friend's tongue. Darcy continued, "So I roused myself with the intention of a good ride to clear away the muddle. I changed my attire quickly and went out to the stables early to avoid humanity. In hindsight, not my wisest course of action. I took your roan out, and it all began well enough. I felt better for the fresh air, if still a bit thick headed from drink and lost sleep. I rode for some while and found myself near the Bennet property. You are acquainted with that copse of trees just before the river path?"

Bingley nodded in recognition. He had grown to know the Bennet property well in the last several days through traversing it in Miss Bennet's company. Darcy went on. "Well, I looked to emerge from the copse when I espied Miss Elizabeth up ahead. I stopped near the edge of the trees to watch her progress. She was walking slowly along the river path, further engaged in reading a book. She was so lovely, Bingley, so totally absorbed in her reading that she was unmindful of anything else around her. She made her way to a tree then, that large oak that twists to overhang the river, and she sat herself in the crook of it, quite comfortably from all appearances. It must be a common enough practice, for it was accomplished with no detraction from her book, and she seemed almost to meld with the old oak, secure in its embrace like some sylvan nymph of old. I confess I felt jealous of that tree for an instant. The low early sun illuminated her most dramatically. Its rays lit her hair in a halo of chestnut, and lent an extra softness to her features. And now and again I saw her laugh at what she read. I was ... I was bewitched."

Bingley could not believe what he was hearing from this gentleman. Or rather, he could believe the images, could believe that Miss Eliza would catch Darcy's eye, for she was very pretty and her nature regularly engaging. What Bingley found unusual was the poetic tone of Darcy's converse, the rambling nature of his effusions.

Surely Bingley's friend was profoundly in love. He ventured to break Darcy's distracted musings to ask, "And did you speak with Elizabeth?"

"Oh no!" came the immediate reply. "The scene was so pure, so perfect, I confess it overawed me. After a few moments of observing her thus, though ogling her unawares was never my design, your *roan* spied a rabbit in the undergrowth of the wood, and gave voice to a desire to make chase. The nag's whinny drew Miss Bennet's attention, and she looked up in our direction. So intent was I to escape being found spying on the lady, I wheeled the roan around to make a hasty retreat. And between my haste and my dulled senses, I turned directly into a large branch which jutted into the path. It knocked me off the roan, and gave me the results you see here on my face."

Bingley gasped in surprise. This entire escapade was most unworthy of Darcy – he who always was so in control of his actions, and such a horseman. Miss Eliza certainly had overtaken his senses to make Darcy so muddled. "Did the lady see you?"

Darcy laughed, though there was little humour in the expression. "No, that was my only solace. I lay quietly on the ground for a moment, afraid to draw further notice, and when she made no move to rise from her perch in the tree, I finally picked myself up and retrieved the roan, which was nibbling at some leaves nearby. I rode back here directly, and made my way to the breakfast room, as you see me now."

"Darcy, you poor man." Bingley had difficulty keeping the amusement from his voice, as he could not help but find the situation farcical. But the surest way to alienate his friend was to laugh at his misfortune, and he wished to help him in any way he could do. "But you must relay your admiration to Miss Elizabeth, you must tell her of your feelings. You yourself gave me that counsel not long ago regarding Miss Bennet, and you were not wrong. You always advise me well – why can not you see that the same counsel pertains to you?"

"I *can* see it, Bingley. I do see it. But I find myself stricken in her company... too conscious by half of every stupid word or act. I believe I must be quite undone." He shook his head, the confession clarifying nothing but his continued bewilderment.

"Well, my friend, then I will take the lead for once. You must go and clean yourself up – for you truly do look abominable -- and take something more than coffee to clear the wine from your head at last – and then you will accompany me to Longbourn today. You must. I am determined that between myself and Jane, we will contrive to arrange some time for you to speak with Miss Elizabeth."

"Bingley, I can not call on the Bennets in such a condition! It would be a mortification!"

"And a well earned one, too! All this time suffering in silence when a perfectly... perfect... woman sits not three miles distant!" Bingley worked himself up into lecture worthy of Darcy himself once he started. The man obviously needed a push. "Would you wait some days in this anguish of heart while your bruises heal?" Darcy conceded that his friend had a point; to be so close to Longbourn and Miss Elizabeth without seeing her, without learning if their renewed friendship was something more, if she would condescend to a renewed appeal on his part – that would be unbearable to Darcy. Against his own misgivings, he allowed his friend to persuade him.

ξ

When Darcy came down some time later, he looked much improved. His eyes were clear, his grooming once again impeccable –all thanks to his man Grayson's talents, the man was a treasure – and the lump on Darcy's brow had subsided to a severity where it was nearly obscured by a judicious arrangement of his hair, also a remedy of Grayson's design. For the blackening skin around his right eye, however, there was no remedy. Darcy wondered still how to account for it to Miss Elizabeth and the Bennets, when Miss Bingley descended to take her leave of Netherfield.

"Mr Darcy! Whatever has happened to you?" she cried on spying his face. She began to fuss over him, but Darcy cut her off.

"A silly accident this morning only, Miss Bingley. I am unscathed, despite my appearance, I assure you. It is only my pride which has been hurt. Please do not trouble yourself over it."

It was some time, however, before Darcy could extricate himself from Miss Bingley's ministrations, and some little time longer before he and Bingley could actually get her into her carriage to wave her off on her journey. Both men experienced a sense of relief upon her eventual departure, but it was soon replaced with the anticipation of their upcoming meetings at Longbourn – with unabated joy occupying the sensibilities of one, and terror the other.

They claimed their horses from a groom, and rode to the Bennet manor; Bingley could not help but glance from time to time at Darcy, but his excellent horsemanship seemed to have been restored concurrent with his improved appearance.

On the gentlemen's arriving at Longbourn, much was made of Mr Bingley; Mrs Bennet in particular expounding on how lovely it was to see him again, as if she had not just seen him twelve hours before and for every day of the preceding weeks. Of Darcy, she pointedly took no notice, and if she wondered at his injury or even saw it, she called no attention to it. The younger Bennet girls, no doubt accustomed now to Bingley's daily visits, were nowhere in sight, having better things to attend to. Mr Bennet was secreted in his library and considered Mr Bingley's near familiar connection sufficient reason to preclude an interruption of his peace to greet him. So it was that only Miss Bennet and Miss Elizabeth could be cognizant of Mr. Darcy's appearance and discomfort. Miss Bennet was gently solicitous, expressing her quiet wish that the injury did not cause Mr. Darcy pain. He thanked her formally and assured her it was of little import.

Miss Elizabeth uncharacteristically said little to Darcy. She greeted Bingley with all the ceremony of a near sister, and then turned to extend a courteous welcome to Darcy. She stared pointedly at his blackened eye, but said nothing, though her glance kept darting back to it from time to time. After some while, Miss Elizabeth went to gather up her younger sisters for the walk to Meryton, and the group departed. Within minutes on the riverside path, Kitty and Mary had skipped on ahead, Kitty chattering about some new frock she planned to wear at the next assembly, and Mary countering with her desire to stop at Mr. Hartley's shop in order to rent that new piece of music she'd seen there the week past.

As the path narrowed to allow only two to pass together, Bingley hurried his step with Miss Bennet, ensuring that Darcy and Miss Elizabeth walked together behind them. Jane Bennet wondered at her gentleman's haste, until they were far enough ahead of the other couple for him to whisper his desire to allow them some moments to talk. Promising a fuller explanation, he allowed briefly that Darcy had confessed some liking for Miss Elizabeth, and Bingley wished to facilitate converse between them. Jane's initial surprise at Bingley's news soon led her to reflect that, perhaps there had been signs, indications of late, which she had not credited, of the truth of Mr Darcy's feelings for her sister. Wondering what her own Lizzy would make of them – for she too had appeared distracted, altered of late – Miss Bennet quickly fell in with Bingley to distance themselves even further from those behind.

Finding she was alone now on the path with the gentleman, Miss Elizabeth smiled at Darcy, a gesture he returned with more confidence than he could feel at that moment. Miss Elizabeth believed it incumbent to say something and, not wanting to search far for a topic, she seized upon the one which had commanded her curiosity since Mr Darcy's arrival at Longbourn. "I hope your injury does not cause you great discomfort, sir."

"No, indeed, Miss Elizabeth. I assure you that my pride was far more injured than my head in the acquiring of this bruise." He hesitated, smiled grimly, and then looked her in the eye boldly as he had often seen her look at him. "But then, there are those who would say my pride needs be taken down a bit."

Elizabeth laughed without thinking, then looked quickly to Mr. Darcy to see if she had overstepped herself. Perhaps his remark had not been intended lightly? But she noted he was smiling and did not appear to have suffered offense at her amused reaction. Indeed, there was a sparkle in his azure eyes that could not be accounted for by the cloud-strewn morning light. "May I ask, Mr Darcy, what is the nature of your injury? I mean, how you came by such a trophy?"

Darcy laughed at her phrasing, then stopped on the path, his smile fading as an earnest expression regarded her. "In truth, Miss Elizabeth?"

Though Elizabeth felt somewhat disconcerted by his solemn expression, she found herself nodding in answer, an even deeper curiosity roused by this tantalizing reply.

"In truth, Miss Elizabeth," he repeated, "*you* were the cause of this 'trophy' as you call it."

"*I*?" Elizabeth's expression was a jumble of incredulity and interest. "How on earth can I have been responsible for your disfigurement?"

As it happened, they had stopped very near to the gnarled oak tree which overhung the river, that same which Miss Elizabeth had sat under that morning as she read her book, and where Darcy had watched her from the copse of wood. Now, Darcy took a deep breath, sighed, and decided to confess all to her. He related for the second time that day the events of the morning, watching Miss Elizabeth's countenance closely as it moved from simple curiosity to amazement, and finally to carefully checked laughter. Darcy saw that she was holding back, and finally said, "You may well laugh at me, Miss Elizabeth. There really is no more appropriate response to my cowardice and its repercussions."

Of a sudden, however, Elizabeth found that the laughter caught in her throat. She looked at Mr Darcy and noted the soft expression in his eyes, a total lack of vanity associated with this encounter; and her inclination shifted from teasing to consideration. He stood before her in all candour, and she could not be unmoved by it. She shuffled her feet a bit and then, looking up at him with the same openness, said, "I own I did hear something in the wood this morning. I thought to investigate, but was too comfortable in my perch to give it up when, in the shadow beyond the trees, I could see nothing to excite my interest. Would that I had." With that, she reached up her hand and gently moved the hair on his brow to the side to see the full import of his injury; then she tenderly touched the bruise by his eye. "I am so sorry to have caused you pain, Mr Darcy," Elizabeth whispered, "I assure you it was unconsciously done."

Darcy recognized in her words a marked similarity to others she had uttered in their history, their converse during his disastrous proposal at Rosings some months past etched into his memory in every detail. But her light touch now and the concern her tone carried was nothing like that ill-fated night. The alteration was enough for Darcy. Without thinking, he reached up to take the hand which hovered near his face, drawing it down to clasp between his own. "Miss Elizabeth, you are too generous to trifle with me..."

ξ

Up ahead on the path, Bingley had revealed everything to Miss Bennet, and his lady willingly agreed to do everything in her power to further a match between her sister and Mr Darcy. As she reflected back, she could see that she had missed cues from Lizzy as well to suggest that her sister was more enamoured of Mr Darcy than Jane had credited.

Those two, she thought, *they are of a pair, are not they, in holding their affections so close?* Jane Bennet realized her own excited sensibilities of late had kept her from seeing what was right in front of her. Her own Lizzy was in love... with Mr Darcy! Little comments, glances, now came back to Jane to give her all the proof of it she required. She had been blind, as blind as Lizzy had been for some while. She wondered idly when her sister's opinion of Mr Darcy had undergone so material a change from her initial dislike of him.

Following their enlightening conversation, Bingley and Jane realised that they had gone so far ahead in their walk as to lose sight altogether of their friends; and they began to walk back as they had come in order to meet the pair and further the cause of love if they could. So it was that they came upon Elizabeth and the gentleman.

The two were standing underneath an old, gnarled oak tree with branches that trailed out over the river. The sun had come out from behind a cloud, and threw dappled light through the tree's foliage onto the couple. Elizabeth held one of the gentleman's hands between her own; with his other, Darcy caressed Elizabeth's cheek, as the two stood suspended in a kiss.

Bingley and Jane looked at each other for a moment with mischievous delight; it seemed their meddling would not be required on love's behalf. Then, after a moment or so to allow the lovers their pleasure, Bingley pointedly cleared his throat.

On being found in such a precarious attitude, Darcy and Elizabeth approached Jane and Bingley somewhat sheepishly. It was on Elizabeth's tongue to make some satirical remark—perhaps that being found compromised she had no recourse but to accept Mr Darcy. But on meeting her sister's delighted gaze, Elizabeth laughed ingenuously, and she and Jane embraced. Bingley clapped Darcy on the back, his face barely containing his knowing smile. The eldest Bennet daughter glanced briefly at Mr Darcy and thought that, black eye or no, he had never looked so handsome. She recognised the love and satisfaction in her sister's eyes as well, and felt a sense of gratitude to Mr Darcy for eliciting this joy in her beloved Lizzy.

"Jane," started Elizabeth -- after a second's hesitation to glance at Darcy, she turned back to her sister. "You will have to continue on to Meryton alone, and give my regrets to Mrs Phillips, if you please. Mr Darcy and I must return to Longbourn at once; for we have a matter of some import to discuss with Papa."

Jane nodded quite happily, and she and Bingley both made promise upon being petitioned, to say no word of this happy event to her aunt or sisters, until they would return home later to have the news confirmed with their father's consent. And so the two couples separated for the afternoon, each convinced that all was good and agreeable in the world.

Lizzy Gets a Lesson
["As She Was No Horse-Woman"]

ॐॐॐ

This episode falls outside the scope of Pride and Prejudice, as it occurs just after Lizzy and Darcy marry. But some time ago, one particular phrase jumped out at me, grabbing my particular notice for the first time in all my years of reading this novel, and it led to an idea. (I suspect that those of you who also reread this novel from time to time would concur that each time, you notice something – some line or scene – in a new or fresh way.) The line is this, from Volume I, Chapter VII, when Lizzy Bennet learns that Jane has taken ill at Netherfield: "Elizabeth, feeling really anxious, was determined to go to her, though the carriage was not to be had; and as she was no horse-woman, walking was her only alternative."

ॐॐॐ

A slow smile warm with satisfaction overspread Darcy's features as he emerged from a dream into wakefulness. Though he had reached that turning point whereby he was more awake than asleep—he knew he could not re-enter that blessed realm—he kept his eyelids closed, so loathe was he to relinquish the happy vision lingering behind them. He had dreamt that Elizabeth Bennet had accepted him at last and they had been married on the same day that his friend Charles Bingley wed the eldest Bennet daughter, Jane; that when he had introduced the question of a wedding trip, Elizabeth had expressed a desire to establish themselves at Pemberley forthwith, there to plan a journey together for the spring; that he had acquiesced with delight; and that even now he would awaken to find her sharing his chambers and his bed, 'at home' in all respects. Little wonder he should wish to retain those images for as long as he might.

Through this dreamy haze, a sound reached Darcy's ears; a sigh every bit as contented as his own attitude. It startled him into attentiveness; his eyes flew open as he recollected that it had *not*, in fact, all been a dream. He lay in his own bed at Pemberley with his newly-installed wife at his side; she nestled against him where her soft breath warmed his chest. Darcy smiled. No need to cling to his reverie; his life these weeks past had been his dream made perfect—culminating in his marriage only four days earlier.

Perhaps that dream had exacted a tax on his forbearance, in the shape of Elizabeth's family and friends in the weeks preceding that happy event; but he had recognized in Lizzy's doing all she could to shield him from the frequent notice of these, the extent of her care of him. She had been ever anxious to keep him to herself and to those of her family with whom he might converse without mortification; and though the uncomfortable feelings arising from this period took from the season of courtship certain of its pleasures, it added to the hope of the future—the start of which had now come to fruition.

When he had recovered sufficiently from this awakening discovery that life sometimes could rival dreams, he turned his head to look at Elizabeth – his Lizzy now – even in the dim room fancying he could note the chestnut highlights in her dark hair and the perfect smoothness of her complexion, as she slept. Even without those fine eyes being turned on him, she was the most beautiful creature! And she was, without a doubt, his. Yes, life was very good indeed.

He indulged in a silent perusal of his wife's attributes, certain he could never tire of looking at her. After some moments of this contemplation, the lady began to stir. Another sigh escaped her and she opened her eyes slowly as if to test her surroundings. She smiled at the bed canopy in general; then, turning her face to Darcy, she smiled again, much more broadly this time.

"Has morning come so soon?" she asked.

"Nearly. I believe dawn has only just broken." So saying, he rose from the bed and pulled aside the draperies at the windows. The coming day's soft-filtered light bathed the room in a hint of golden glow. He did not linger at the window, but quickly slid back into bed beside his lady, chuckling when she complained that his feet were cold. Tenderly, he stroked her cheek and then left a gentle kiss upon her lips. "Good morning, my love," he whispered to her.

"Mmmm." It seemed for a long moment that this was to be the only reply he would receive. Elizabeth's eyes had closed once more as if to drift off to sleep in the couple's cosy nest. But then she rallied. She raised an arm to stretch, but suspended the motion to reach instead and smooth away a stray lock of dark hair from Darcy's eyes, smiling again as she took them in.

Her husband – how strange that the word felt so comfortable after only a few days, her *husband* – possessed the most incredible eyes. Their shape was almost indefinable, nearly feline in nature, an attribute that lent them changeable qualities when encountered from different aspects, or when he was fuelled by particular emotions. In the year and more since she had met Fitzwilliam Darcy, and especially in recent months after they had admitted their mutual affection, Elizabeth had come to recognize and appreciate his myriad, varied expressions. But she loved none of them so much as that which she beheld now – his lids lowered slightly with sleep and ease, the startling blue shade of his irises picking up glints of gold from the window's early light, and a quiet contentment that spoke of his consummate love for her. Elizabeth smiled in satisfaction – gratified that no one but she would ever see those *particular* eyes of his.

She sighed to think how close she might have come never to feel the utter joy that was hers every time his gaze turned on her as it did now. She lifted her face up to his and placed a honeyed kiss just at one temple. As she moved to match it on his other temple, however, he intercepted her; and following, they became engaged in activities of a most pleasurable kind for both.

When sometime later the low winter sun fairly illumined their room, Darcy rose to dress. Elizabeth shifted into the space in the bed he had left, savouring the lingering warmth of him. She was half asleep once more when he returned from his dressing room, clothed for riding.

"Give Parsifal my regards, husband, and enjoy your ride," she said in a lazy drawl.

He came to perch on the bed near her. He stroked her hair back from her cheek, and then suddenly smiled with mischief. "You *could* join us, you know," he purred into her ear. The statement held a question, and Elizabeth could not determine at once if it was in earnest or a teazing one. Apparently, a serious one, as he then looked at her awaiting a serious answer in return.

Lizzy laughed—"Mr Darcy! You know I am no horsewoman." She regarded him incredulously as he again challenged her.

"I do know it, Mrs Darcy. But I am determined to cure you of the condition!" His smile lit his eyes in renewed invitation.

"I am serious, my love. Have not I told you, that if you required a wife who could ride, you should choose any other but me? I am less a horsewoman than I am accomplished at the pianoforte –

and you know how dreadful I play at that! I simply do not have the talent for a horse."

In all this speech, Darcy listened gravely with sincerity. But when she had done making her point, he chuckled. "Well, you know, my dear, you can only become proficient at something by the constant practicing of it." This perfect mimicry of his odious aunt earned a grudging smile from Elizabeth, but she glared at him with as much censure as her contented state could conjure.

He added, "I *can* teach you, though you say you have no talent for sitting a horse. I am something of a good rider, if I may be allowed to boast to my wife."

"You may! I well know what an excellent rider you are; I have had many opportunities to witness your talents there!"

Elizabeth Darcy, nee Bennet, had never been entirely comfortable on a horse; she overwhelmingly preferred walking when a carriage was not an option. Then again, riding was a pastime that Darcy had particularly loved since childhood. He maintained a stable worthy of note, knew the beasts intimately and mastered them effortlessly, had taught his sister to love them with a similar passion from an early age. And here was he now, offering to share that part of him with Elizabeth, even knowing that his own natural enjoyment must be diminished in doing so. The expression of this man's generosity of spirit continually amazed his new wife, the biggest wonder being that she had ever doubted he possessed such a heart, much less the lengths he would traverse to please her. This consideration alone led her to reconsider.

"Are you certain, my dear Darcy, that you have the patience for a student whose talents are so limited by nature?"

"All the patience in the world, for you. Whether the horses will oblige you in the same manner, however, I cannot speak to!"

His sudden laugh decided the issue for Elizabeth; she could deny him nothing when he smiled at her in that way. *I must never tell him of that particular power he possesses*, she thought.

"Very well, then. But on your head be it if any calamity follows." She smiled. "Shall we begin today, or would you prefer one last ride in peace?"

She willed him silently to accept a postponement of the onerous hour.

"There is no time like the present."

Suddenly, Elizabeth realised a welcome obstacle to the plan. "Oh! I cannot go with you today!"

He regarded her warily.

"My clothes," she said in a satisfied tone – "I haven't anything suitable for riding."

"Ah. Hmmm. That is indeed a concern."

"Indeed." She tried to remain serious; to stifle the smirk which threatened.

He studied her expression for a long moment before shrugging. *Good*, she thought; *I have dodged it for a week at the least – more if he does not press me to visit the dressmaker.*

"Lizzy," he began, and she smiled at his use of her intimate name. "Such a disappointment, is it not?"

"It is, my love. My disappointment cannot be counted."

"Are you certain this is the only reason you must retract your agreement, Lizzy?"

"It is, on my honour."

"Very well." As she sighed with relief, he added, "Then it is no impediment at all!"

"But—"

"I am certain we have riding clothes about the house somewhere that will suit you. I will ring for Mrs Reynolds and she will have you kitted out in no time."

Lizzy could not believe she had fallen so easily into this trap – it could only be the early hour that had made her so dull-witted. But she was well and truly caught and she knew it.

Darcy laughed heartily when she acquiesced, delighted despite its reluctant delivery. "Come; let us arrange some suitable attire for you."

While Elizabeth quickly donned a morning gown, Darcy duly rang for Mrs Reynolds and asked to locate any riding apparel in the house that might fit Mrs Darcy. The long-time housekeeper made a quick assessment of Elizabeth's form, but stood somewhat in the fidgets then, hesitant to speak.

"Mrs Reynolds?" Darcy addressed her. "Is there nothing, to your mind?"

"Goodness, dear me. It is only... well ... there is one set that might do nicely for Mrs Darcy." She glanced with a smile at Elizabeth before looking back to Darcy. "They were Lady Anne's riding clothes, Sir; if you are able to see them in use once more."

Darcy's surprise was evident. "Do you mean to say, my mother's clothes are still here? After all these years?"

"Yes, Sir," replied the housekeeper. "No one had heart to go through them immediately after your mother passed this life; and I had not the inclination to distribute or dispose of them. They have been maintained, in an unused room below-stairs."

"Well," said Darcy, shaking his head. "I think she would have approved of their use now for my wife, do not you?"

"Oh, yes, sir... I do believe it, most heartily!"

And so it was decided, almost before Elizabeth could agree to the scheme. Half an hour later, after sending two of his favourite ladies off, Darcy's wife was returned to him, kitted out perfectly, if it was not the latest fashion. He was astonished to see how well his mother's former clothes fitted his new wife. Perhaps it was faulty memory, but he would have guessed Elizabeth to be somewhat slighter than his mother had been. A curious sentiment stole over him, to see his wife in the garb he had so often seen his mother wear. But he could feel her benevolence in the air of the house, and in the peace of his soul. Yes, his mother would have approved this match for him.

"You look lovely, Lizzy."

Mrs Darcy laughed and replied, "Well, we found the best we could. Though they are elegant, excellently cut clothes, Mrs Reynolds had to ply her skills a bit with pins to fit them to me. You cannot see them, but I assure you if I turn the wrong way, you will hear how I feel them!"

"Ah. I did wonder at how your form matched so well with my mother's. Now the secret is out—it is all down to pins!" He laughed again. "Now, no more dawdling, let us be on our way. While you were occupied in pinning yourself securely, I sent word to the grooms to make a mount ready for your arrival."

Lizzy could see that Darcy enjoyed himself altogether too well at the prospect. Surely their entertainment this morning would be at her expense—but she could not grudge him this after all he had suffered in the last weeks of her family; after all he had given to *her*.

The couple left the house and walked, arm in arm, through the dewy park to the stables in the morning light. The sun, not high in the sky, formed a bright halo on the horizon. It looked to be a glorious day. Darcy could feel the tension in Elizabeth's grip on his arm as they walked along and he realised that, despite his brave wife having accepted his challenge to ride, she felt anxious yet over it. He looked at her countenance and saw a smile just a bit too fixed in place. He would need to introduce her to this ritual gently if ever she was to enjoy it.

When they reached the stables, he saw the two horses saddled and waiting – Parsifal and Scheherazade – as he had asked. But in view of his wife's apparent sensibility, he changed his mind. He spoke with Evan, indicating that the groom should restore Scheherazade to her stall, the mare would not be needed this morning after all.

Elizabeth looked at her husband with a glimmer of hope and no little amusement. "What is this, have you lost your nerve to teach me so soon, even before we start?" she teased. "I comprehend I am not confident of my skill, but I hope I am not as ill-equipped as all that!"

Darcy produced the hoped-for laugh, but then turned the table on his wife. "Not at all, Mrs Darcy. I simply decided that it will be best if your first lesson is with Parsifal."

Elizabeth's eyes grew wide with not a little apprehension. "Parsifal! Sir, I can see I was mistaken; for you do not underestimate my abilities, but rather the opposite! Parsifal is much too powerful and headstrong a beast for me!"

Her husband chuckled, opining to himself that he could think of no man (or woman or beast) that would be too formidable for his wife to meet head on – after all, she had held her own admirably on more than one occasion against Lady Catherine deBourgh; something many a strong man had been unable to do when faced with his aunt's wrath. But now he sought to alleviate Elizabeth's concern.

"You may set your mind at ease. We have not yet been married so long for me to contrive a convenient accident and rid myself of you!" The smile that lit his eyes confirmed his sport, and she clucked in reply though she could not help but follow with a smile of her own. "No," he clarified, "I am simply being selfish this morning. I cannot tolerate the prospect of any distance separating us, so we will ride Parsifal together today. He can bear us both easily, and it will facilitate my guiding your hand on the reins. Will that be acceptable to you for your first lesson?"

"Oh, yes! That is most acceptable," she replied. Darcy watched as his wife's answering smile released some of the tension in her expression. Darcy signalled to Evan, who brought a mounting box forward. He placed it near the stallion, and Darcy handed Elizabeth up to stand upon it. She watched as her husband then swung himself easily onto his mount, as if the act was as natural to him as breathing. They were of a pair, those two – man and beast – proud (not without justification), intelligent, and capable – and stubborn. Elizabeth hoped only that Parsifal also shared his master's heart and gentility under the arrogant exterior.

Darcy coaxed the animal next to the mounting box with no discernible effort, gave Lizzy a reassuring smile, and reached out his hand to her. She accepted it with her own. With his other arm, Darcy leaned down and encircled his wife's waist, lifting her handily to sit in front of him on Parsifal. After taking only an instant to shift their positions for comfort, too brief to allow Elizabeth's fear to manifest, he gave the slightest nudge on the reins, and Parsifal began to walk from the yard.

When she felt motion beneath her, Lizzy started. But though she could discern the powerful muscles of the horse flexing as it moved, yet she could also feel the solid wall of her husband's chest against her back, and arms that contained her protectively on either side. She relaxed into this cocoon, and determined to enjoy the ride.

They rode first at a walk through a wood behind the stables and, when they had cleared it and reached an open field to the west, Darcy took Elizabeth's hands and placed them on the reins, covering them lightly then with his own. He spoke to her, illustrating as he did the proper way to hold the reins, the grip neither too loose ('the horse will know it commands you') nor too tight ('you fear it') and how with the application of only small gestures, the horse would turn this way or that, increase its gait, or stop altogether.

In this way, Darcy guided Elizabeth through several commands to Parsifal. She noted the flick of the animal's ears from time to time as if it listened to her husband's instructions as well. She delighted when the slightest increase in pressure of her hold or a tug in one direction yielded a desired turn or decrease in walking speed by the horse. Darcy was delighted in turn with her spontaneous laughter after each small achievement. After some success with basic commands, Darcy had the stallion increase its speed incrementally. At last, they fairly flew across the field in a gallop that took the breath from Lizzy. How freeing it felt! She could well understand now that her husband took such pleasure from his rides – how much more than simple transport could it offer him. Of course, without his encompassing presence to hold her in her seat, she knew she would not trust her own ability to achieve a similar result.

For nearly an hour, they went through their paces thus. Lizzy grew confident enough with the reins that Darcy's concurrent hold on them gradually lightened and then, for a few triumphant moments, was removed altogether. Parsifal noted when Darcy gave over control fully to Lizzy, but the animal responded to her commands willingly enough. Finally, they turned again toward home, Darcy once more regulating the animal.

When they reached the wood and started to enter its path, Lizzy twisted in her seat to look at her husband, and he signalled to Parsifal to stop. "Thank you," she whispered, her face brightened by their recent exercise, flush with joy. "That was exhilarating." His smile was all the answer she needed to know that he was as gratified by her pleasure as she from the ride.

Once within the wood, protected from any onlooker's idle curiosity, Darcy released the reins and, taking Elizabeth's face tenderly in his hands, he kissed her forehead, then moved down to find her mouth. Thus they sat for some moments, lost in enjoyment of each other and their recent experience. Finally, Parsifal tired of standing about and began to paw at the ground. With great reluctance, Darcy took up the reins again and they made their way back towards the stable yard, Elizabeth nestled comfortably and completely at home against her husband's chest for as long as they remained in the blind and silent wood.

They arrived back to the stable, and Darcy handed Lizzy down onto the mounting box, and then he dismounted as well. He gave Parsifal over to Evan; but before the groom could lead the horse away, Darcy waylaid him. He reached into his coat and drew out a brown paper, unwrapped it to produce a carrot he had pocketed from the kitchen earlier. Lizzy laughed at first; until Darcy proffered the carrot to her and persuaded that she should tender it to Parsifal. She hesitated only a little before taking the morsel and then, exhibiting only slight bashfulness, Elizabeth approached the horse, her hand extended to offer the treat to him. The horse looked at her for a moment, and she whispered a heartfelt 'thank you' to it.

With a dip of its head and a soft nickering, the stallion acknowledged Elizabeth's gratitude and accepted the treat from her. It allowed her to smooth its forelock to the side before turning away with the groom; and Lizzy could not help but recognise that this gesture echoed one she had become so fond of employing on her husband in the mornings when his hair, tousled from sleep, fell into his eyes. This raised a pensive smile in her as they turned and walked towards the house.

"Darcy," she began, "may we do this again?" She took his arm and squeezed it with delight.

"Of course! You acquitted yourself so well this morning, my dear, you are quite ready for a mount of your own, I think."

"Oh, no!" He looked at her, but the expression she presented was not of fear, rather one far more persuasive to him. "No," she repeated, "I should much prefer it to be exactly the same – just the three of us."

Darcy covered her hand on his arm with his own. "Always, as you wish, my love... at any time of your choosing."

"Good." She glanced up slyly at him then. "But I should warn you, the time of *my* choosing will demand that the sun will have been risen for at least an hour before we set out."

He withdrew his arm from her grasp then and, instead, encircled her waist and drew her close in to his side. But he heard a quick intake of breath from his wife at his touch. He stopped and looked at her. "Whatever is the matter?"

Lizzy grinned. "Nothing, my love. It is only that you have managed to find one of Mrs Reynolds's pins!" They laughed together, and continued on their way.

Just before they reached the house again, Lizzy said, "Darcy, I would like to know something more of your mother. What she was like, her sensibilities? Would it be too painful for you to share your memories of her with me? For if nothing else, she must have been remarkable to produce two such children as Georgiana and you."

"No, not painful..." Darcy's eyes softened with gratitude, and he smiled as he contemplated again how much Lady Anne Darcy would have approved his choice of wife. "...my memories of all but her passing, indeed, are joyous ones. I will happily tell you stories of her. We have the rest of our lives for you to learn all my family's history." He looked gravely at his wife then. "Even the dark and dangerous secrets!"

Seeing by her countenance that Lizzy was indeed intrigued, he laughed. And together, laughing and talking, then went in to the house for a welcome breakfast and a history lesson.

ξ

*V*alentine

ᔕᔕᔕ

Although the common practice of delivering ornate cards of hearts and flourishes to lovers on Valentine's Day became prominent in the Victorian age, a little research showed that simpler expressions – cards, small gifts and the like – began long before. The British Library has a valentine poem written in 1415; associations of the day with romance go back to the Romans. Exchanges of simple love tokens were prevalent from the 1700's certainly. So the following little vignette is not outside the realm of possibility. It is my own little 'valentine' to a post-P&P, now married, Elizabeth and Fitzwilliam Darcy, my favourite couple.

ᔕᔕᔕ

Elizabeth Darcy sat at the ladies' desk in her sitting room going over household accounts. She had been married only a few months, and was still a bit self-conscious about her responsibilities as mistress of Pemberley. Though she was level-headed and practical, and growing up had been fairly well-schooled by her mother – and Hill – in the day-to-day management of a manor household, Longbourn could little compare to the vastness of Pemberley and its estate. The servant staff alone was eight times what she had known, and this did not fully account for other temporary and day labourers. As daunting initially as she found it, however, she would not wish for any other existence—not since she and Darcy had risen above their earlier difficulties, and now forged a life together in a union of mind, heart, body and soul.

Darcy continued to laud her efforts in having assumed the running of the household, from which she took great encouragement, if she would but admit of it. But then, she also knew his objectivity to be questionable; for undoubtedly he was enjoying still the first flush of wedded bliss wherein he could find no fault in his wife. She wondered laughingly how long she might depend on those sensibilities before his reason returned; and hoped her own innate confidence would have resurfaced in full before such time.

Certainly, the staff at Pemberley made the challenge less than burdensome – it was large and had been well-selected over the years; so, what was there, truly, for her to master except a relationship with the chief servants who, in their turn, managed all the others? This had been achieved with no effort at all – Lizzy could not imagine a more capable or congenial employee than Mrs Reynolds and, in truth, in only these few months found the housekeeper more guiding friend than servant; though that lady herself would never presume to allow those lines crossed.

All in all, this was an excellently-run home, and Lizzy had found no cause to change what worked so well. She had, however, assumed as her due the review and management of accounts, menu approvals, hiring and dismissal (thank providence the latter had not yet been necessary) of the domestic staff; and it was in review of some requests for household purchases that she now laboured. But she found her attention drifting, unable to maintain concentration on the ledgers for long.

Darcy had gone to Town four days ago, their first separation of any length since their marriage had taken place; indeed since they had become engaged. He had been obliged to appear there on matters of business. Although he had invited her to accompany him, she had declined. After a few months in residence, she was discovering still all the joys of Pemberley and the grace and natural beauty of its placement in the hills of Derbyshire; even in the deep winter of February, its appeal was inescapable. She had felt ill-inclined to leave it for London for even a week; and as she had visited Town for shopping just before her marriage at Christmastide, she had no outstanding commissions or requirements to want to see it again so soon.

She well understood her husband's strong attachment to this land in Derbyshire, its people, and his home – their home. The appreciation she had begun to feel for the varied landscapes and other natural wonders of the country upon her first visit the previous summer had only grown by leaps now that she resided here. She looked forward to the spring and summer when clement weather and road conditions would facilitate further exploration.

In addition to this reticence to leave her new home, Lizzy also had reasoned that it must be good for her and Darcy now and again to experience separations of short duration; to maintain some independence of their daily business. They should appreciate all the more their time together, then; they could not learn to despise one another—or worse, become bored—from too great familiarity, as she had seen so many do.

What Lizzy had not foreseen, however – could not properly credit – was that there is little of the rational in being utterly in love; and though her head had wisely made the choice to stay behind, her heart now took firm hold of her. She had misjudged the intensity of longing she would experience for her husband in the little things – his embrace when he came in from a morning ride smelling of fresh air and old leather; his captivating smile, held in reserve so often in public yet bestowed freely upon his wife at all moments of the day and with the smallest inducements; his deep, fluid voice, confident with authority, heard here and there throughout the day in all kinds of business; and heard again with such intimate, gentle inflection when they were alone. His fascinating eyes, so changeable in shape and colour with his moods and intentions—and especially that one look that he reserved for her alone, unconditional in conveying his love (and Lizzy could acknowledge that she had thrown out many 'conditions' to test that love before they had found their way to good understanding).

She missed his hands as well. Lizzy loved her husband's hands, for they were large as befits a tall man, but beautifully formed – and capable of such gentle application for their strength. She loved the touch of his fingers gently caressing her cheek; loved to run her own fingertips across his palm lightly until he would shiver and capture them in a warm clasp. She had found herself on several occasions in the last few days wandering into his dressing room just to conjure the semblance of his being in residence through the sight of his clothes or the touch of his personal effects, the lingering scent of him in the close room.

Oh, why had she not gone to London simply to be with him? His return was not expected for another four days at the least, as his last letter had indicated that his solicitors required such time to draw up papers for his signature. She had made a foolish decision – the next several days without Darcy must seem an eternity! She chuckled. It appeared he was not the only party still to shed the first flush of wedded bliss!

She roused herself from reverie with a will and tried yet again to focus on the accounts. She had got as far as the second line when she heard a muffled "ahem" from the half-opened door behind her followed by a knock.

"Beggin' pardon, Mrs Darcy," he said when she had called out to enter. It was Evan, one of Darcy's grooms. Curious to see him in the house, on this floor, she immediately grew concerned that something must be wrong. But she forced a smile for him and invited him into the room. He came a little way with reluctance, but his own expression took on concern in the surroundings; and Lizzy must admit he looked quite as out of place there in a lady's parlour, in his work clothes and boots, as he must feel.

"Sorry, ma'am, for disturbing you; but a letter's just come and I was asked specially to bring it to you straightaway. The maids was all involved with wash day, and the footmen and others with sommat else, so Mrs Reynolds said as I should bring it myself and directed me here."

This allayed her anxiety somewhat, if it was still unusual. Half her curiosity went to wondering what calamity had arisen to take the attention of all her household staff at once. But she decided to ignore it and presume they would resolve it sufficiently unless informed otherwise. Instead she came back to the groom, standing with a nervous smile, and the matter at hand. "A letter?"

"Yes, ma'am, one delivered express just now." With that, Evan took the necessary steps further into the room to the desk where Lizzy now stood, and held out a sealed missive to her.

"Thank you, Evan," she said. As she took it from him with a well regulated smile, trying not to display too clearly her elation at noting her husband's hand in the address, she offered, "Stop at the kitchen before you return to the stables, and have Molly give you some chocolate and biscuits." Evan and another groom, Bryce, were young men with a natural affinity for the horses they kept so well, but bright youths also; Darcy had arranged to educate them in reading and their figures and took a special interest in them both, often entrusting them with errands of sensitivity or import. Lizzy liked them well as much for their affability in general. In turn, the two grooms thought the world of their employer, and now his wife.

"Yes, ma'am, thank you, ma'am." Evan bowed deferentially and made a hasty retreat to collect on his good fortune. Though she had meant that good fortune to be formed of the refreshments to be had, Lizzy knew also that the young man held a *tendre* for the kitchen maid, and only hoped she was not inviting trouble now. She supposed her indulgent gesture was attributable to her own mood today.

She could hardly contain herself until the young man had left the room. Scarcely was he out the door than she turned back to her desk, opening the seal as she sat once more. Given the direction of her thoughts just before receiving it, she did not trust to read Darcy's letter standing, she felt weak in the knees just thinking of him. She glanced quickly at the salutation, "My Dearest Lizzy" before, as had become custom, flipping to the end of the letter to see her husband's signature. Strange, it was unsigned. Yet she knew the missive for his hand. Why would he send her an unsigned letter? Had he been interrupted in the writing of it, left it unfinished, then somehow posted it in that state? A bit disappointed not to see his name written in his neat, elegant scroll, she yet turned back to pore over the letter in earnest from its start.

My Dearest Lizzy,

Four days bereft of your company feels like forty. I could wish that you had chosen to travel to town with me, or that I had shown the sense to press you to reconsider. The house here feels cold, lifeless without you, and yet I cannot be induced to leave it for any purpose but my business. I have had a few invitations since being discovered in town, but have declined them all, having no patience for engagements if you are not here to carry me through them. I pass my time – when not in the company of my solicitors – in reading, or in the indulgence of writing letters to you, my dearest wife, pearl of my heart. I have half a mind to press my attorneys in future to come to me with business, so loathe am I again to part with you for any time. You have quite spoilt me for any form of solitary living–and from my incumbent return some days hence, you must bear the consequences of my constant presence at your side.

Lizzy smiled ruefully to herself at this. *I am not alone in suffering my decision to remain behind.* Her smile changed to a loving one as she noted his address of her. Darcy had taken to calling Lizzy the pearl of his heart on occasion, the endearment springing from two sources. The first was a remark made to him by Sir William Lucas on hearing of their engagement – that Darcy was carrying away the brightest jewel of the country; a remark upon which the lady made much whenever she wished to teaze.

The second originated from her preference (and now Darcy's) for having her hair adorned with pearls whenever she dressed formally. On the night they had first danced together at Netherfield Hall, she had thus been decorated; and Darcy harked back to that night often as the moment his fate was sealed, to love her for eternity. He had not been yet ready to accept the fact and fought himself over it, but now he would claim to have known it nonetheless, somewhere in his soul. Recalling this now made Lizzy ache all the more for her husband's solid presence.

I have seen few others than Messrs Gilchrist and Ransom since my arrival; but received a call this morning from Mrs Fenchurch, she having learnt I am in town and dragging behind her an apologetic Mr Fenchurch. The former Lady Honoria Parkhurst (surely you recall her from the dreadful masquerade she mounted upon her engagement to poor Fenchurch) expressed her disappointment at not finding you in residence with me here; and most vigorously she pressed that I send you her felicitations and her desire to host us at dinner when next we travel to London together—three courses at least! In all, their visit was tedium. I trouble myself to write of it now only because of the news (gossip as you might suppose) that Mrs Fenchurch came expressly to bring. I could not but think of the amusement with which you would have heard it. And I should dearly wish to believe I might bring a smile to you today. So I propose to recount the content of her monologue as well as I may, in as many particulars as can be recalled.

Lizzy did smile. She could imagine how much her husband would welcome receiving the Fenchurches, and could picture him offering all the forms of courtesy that society dictated – refreshment, conversation, weary attentiveness -- while conjecturing on how soon he could extricate himself from the lady's blathering and show them the door. Still smiling, and thinking that her husband had achieved his object without even recounting a word of Lady Honoria's gossip, Lizzy read on.

It appears there is a new recreation introduced into society just now, one which has been adopted with unprecedented zeal by the ton. In recognition of the saint's day tomorrow, Saint Valentine as it happens, which you know has been acknowledged some years now with quiet exchanges of love tokens among the general populace, there is a new fervour under way to outdo everybody else in magnitude of gift. Men of our acquaintance, who would otherwise maintain a stoical, dispassionate demeanour concerning the direction their affections take, have been pressed – or shamed – by their wives and lovers to outward displays of farcical proportions!

To whit, a ball was held last night at the home of Sir Oglesby Carr. Mrs Sutton, who was present, apparently flaunted a new bauble on her wrist composed of emeralds and diamonds, and revelled in the telling of how Mr Sutton presented it to her at breakfast wrapped in her morning newspaper with pink ribbons.

Mrs Larkin then produced her own wrist for inspection, similarly adorned in gems, but with an added entreaty that her admirers take in also her neck—where was revealed, just peeking out from its myriad folds, a necklace to match. This extravagance brought not only an apoplectic flush to Mrs Sutton, but resulted in her berating her husband violently for not having shown the foresight to provide her with sufficient jewels to compete.

Mrs Elliott then gave voice as to how her own Mr Elliott had presented her with a new chaise that morning, the interior lined in red velvet, and a note of undying affection engraved on a silver card on the seat; and promising a matched pair of greys to draw it as soon as her mother passed away and gave up Mrs Elliott's inheritance.

Lady Honoria, in the telling of it of course, professed to no interest in such matters, being above ostentatious display; but the penitent look decidedly fixed on Mr Fenchurch's face convinced me otherwise had I needed persuasion to doubt. He now intervened to relate that at this point in the evening's proceedings, several gentlemen received lethal glares from their wives on account that the trinkets they had received were not sufficient to join in the contest to determine "most beloved." One gentleman who was saved such disapprobation was Sir Oglesby Carr, by virtue of the simple fact of his having gone missing – his wife and every body else now wondering what had become of the man when a current of conversation determined he had not been seen in his own home for upwards of an hour.

But just as it appeared no one present could top Mr Elliott's gift of a carriage to his wife, the double doors at the south end were thrown open by two footmen and Sir Oglesby himself rode into the ball room on a white charger. Both man and beast were clad in the armour of their forebears, and the gentleman bore in addition a salver from which he strew rose petals as he made his way to his astounded wife. When he reached that lady, he began to dismount in gallant form, with a diamond tiara dangling tantalisingly from his glove. But he came down hard, lost his feet, and subsequently clanked to the floor, unceremoniously landing on his bottom.

The night ended shortly thereafter: for it took four men to turn Sir Oglesby upright again amidst his howls of pain, following which another four carried him upstairs to his rooms. Doctor Branford being in attendance immediately rushed off to treat his patient, eager to escape his own wife's unhappy attitude, no doubt. Word later came that Sir Oglesby had broken several ribs and his left hip – and had dented his armour most alarmingly. It had been the devil to extricate him from it.

But this was not the end of it. When Sir Oglesby fell, he lost hold of the diamond tiara, lofting it, spinning through the air towards a bowl of white soup; at which point his good wife Mrs Carr dived to intercept it. One can only imagine the ensuing panic brought on by the horse when the tiara entered the soup and, hearing his master's wife scream as she hurtled through the air towards it, the mount reared up and then ran straight through the crowd into the next room, upsetting no fewer than three tables of refreshments as he went.

Lady Honoria took some relish in describing these events to me, all the while clucking in admonishment of her friends for this ridiculous contest of superiority. She made certain as she did so to wave her hands about in the telling, in order to ensure my notice of the two (yes, two) new diamond and ruby rings adorning her fat fingers.

Lizzy, as she had begun to read this lengthy narrative, had dropped open her mouth in astonishment, both at the tale and that her own Darcy was recounting it to her and in such detail. It must have cost him greatly. Coming to the end of these paragraphs, she covered her mouth with her fingers, feeling (as she and her sisters were wont to say) that she could die of laughter! Indeed, so entertained was she by the recitation, she immediately went back to read the missive again. She could only imagine the agony Darcy must have suffered at hearing the full (and surely even more embellished) story in the braying tones of Lady Honoria Fenchurch.

When her mirth had subsided, Lizzy read further. She was, curiously, both anxious and unwilling to reach the end of her letter.

My dearest Lizzy, you may imagine, I am certain, the distaste with which I heard these ramblings, even as I strived for polite attention until they were brought to an end.
[Yes, indeed, thought Lizzy, I was right in my supposition of agony.]
It was with tremendous relief on my part that Mr Fenchurch finally succeeded in inserting a reminder about a second call they must make; and Lady Honoria Fenchurch,

anticipating another (and surely more receptive) audience for her gossip, exited in due haste, Robert Fenchurch taking up her rear with mumbled apologies for the whole of it.

"Oh, Darcy! my dearest love," Lizzy exclaimed aloud, as if he were there with her. "I must thank you for this! I know that you would not have recounted such detail but for my entertainment. I shall take care to show you, when you arrive home at last, that you achieved far more in the telling than just to coax a smile from me. How I do adore you for feeding my penchant to laugh!" Her smile softened then, grown gentler in sentiment. "For a brief moment, I nearly heard your voice; I could almost believe that you were here in the room with me. But I will not dwell on that—or I will return to the melancholy of missing you." Noting that there was one page only of Darcy's letter remaining to be read, Lizzy sighed, and continued with it.

I must tell you, however, that despite its painful tedium, the Fenchurch visit made one significant impression upon me. I realised that an expression of my love for you would not be remiss on this saint's day. Nothing of public spectacle, but yet a heartfelt declaration to you alone. I believe that you cannot wish the kind of extravagant gifts I have just been describing. But with you at my side, every day might be Valentine's Day; and I hope – no, I trust! – that you know well the boundless depth of my love. Yet despite such faith, perhaps I would like to honour Saint Valentine with an appropriate expression of gratitude to my wife for honouring me with her love.

But what gift could suffice to fill such purpose? Flowers you have in abundance, restored regularly as one bouquet begins to wither. Love notes are but pieces of paper, unable with even the wittiest remarks to measure fully my devotion. Though I know our love to be stout enough to withstand poetry, yet I have not the talent to write a verse which can do justice to you. And when I have wished to gift you with fine jewellery, you have protested that you are most satisfied with my mother's wedding ring handed down and need no other adornment. How can I argue with this last, when even the most radiant jewels must pale in my heart next to your face in early morning light.

You do make it most difficult, dearest wife, to offer a tolerable demonstration of my heart's fulfilment, even as I adore you effortlessly.

Lizzy's own heart changed as she read his words. The giddy laughter achieved on reading of London's latest follies gave way once more to longing. Oh, how she wished Darcy was here now, so that she could impress upon him that all she could need for happiness in the world was his presence; to be his wife, the *dearest pearl of his heart*, his partner in all things. And this she knew without need of reminders that she nonetheless possessed in abundance. With an ache in her heart—how quickly can laughter turn to tears—she looked to read his closing remarks, so engrossed now in seeking him among words on a page that she was unaware of every thing else.

There is indeed one token I have had it in my mind to give to you, my dearest wife, for some time now. I imagined once presenting it to you when I watched from an upper window as you arrived at Netherfield; this occurred long before I had any cause to believe you would ever be mine. Thus one conundrum is resolved, as to what to give to you; but it raises another. For the saint's day is but two days hence, and I am in town while you are at Pemberley. But I cannot bear to have my gift delivered to you by any other party. So, dearest Lizzy, if you please – put down this letter, and turn around...

For one moment, Lizzy was confused at these unfinished lines. She hesitated, then glanced about to see if another sheet had somehow fallen free; then, as possibility dawned on her, with disbelieving hope she turned her head around and looked toward the sitting room door. Framed perfectly in its opening, near full blocking it with his size, stood her own Darcy, smiling at her in that manner he reserved for her alone. Without conscious thought, as her husband stepped in and closed the door behind him, Lizzy flew across the room into his arms.

Some time later, Darcy ushered Lizzy across the room to stand in front of a mirror hung there. He stood behind her, and pulled a small parcel from inside his breast pocket. While Lizzy watched in wonder, he drew out a fine gold chain, unadorned but for a single, large, perfect teardrop pearl, and he proceeded to clasp the simple but elegant jewel about his wife's neck. Their eyes met in the reflection of the glass—a perfect union of mind, heart, body and soul. As she turned eagerly into his embrace, she whispered, "How ardently have I wished for you to come home."

Seasonal Disorder

১৯১৯১

Elizabeth and Fitzwilliam Darcy have been married for several months, for much of which Lizzy has been encouraging her husband to make peace with his aunt, Lady Catherine deBourgh. Now it appears that lady has thawed enough to bury the quarrel – but her timing could not be worse. This began life as the standalone short story contained herein, before it sparked my imagination – and led to a full novel-length plot with this in a modified form as its prologue.

১৯১৯১

[Pemberley, Derbyshire]

"Mr Darcy!"

Darcy's surprised attention swung immediately to his wife from the letter at which he had been glowering in resentment.

"My dear husband, I love my father with all the affections of a favoured daughter and even more for our common amusements..."

"Your father? What has your father to do with this?"

"... but I do not wish to be *married* to him," she finished, laughing.

"You... er, forgive me, I fail to understand."

"At the present, I require your *undivided* attention, Fitz. I have been speaking to you for some minutes and you have not heard a word." She laughed yet again as he took her point, and then continued. "I will take up only a moment of your time and then you may return to your wool-gathering and muttering like an old man, but I have something important to speak of and quite germane to the issue at hand."

Darcy met Lizzy's gaze and maintained it as he purposefully placed Lady Catherine's letter on the table next to his dish, resting his hand there after it. His smile was tentative, being unsure of what was to come. Seeing that his attentions were now firmly established with her, Lizzy launched into a communication she had not thought to make in quite this manner but for Lady Catherine who, even estranged from her nephew, somehow managed yet to direct matters to Lizzy's inconvenience.

"Let me begin by admitting I am *fully* aware that I have only just convinced you to accept your aunt's gesture of reconciliation, no matter how insultingly offered. You could not have expected any thing different, could you? I did not doubt her imperiousness or the condemnation of her tone and words, but still in all, I would have you reconciled with her. She is, after all, your relation – we may not choose our relations in the nature of things, but yet they are ours, and we should maintain them."

She realised she rambled about, must get to the point before her husband became exasperated. "*But*... having just now learnt from you the specifics of her proposal – that is her proposed *timing* for your visit – I must reverse myself and stand firm in this resolve. I will not travel to Kent; I cannot for an Easter observance nor, I should hope, will you go."

"Lizzy, this is nonsensical. You have just spent the last twenty minutes convincing me that family must be acknowledged; that my aunt's offenses to you and to me must be tolerated in the interest of maintaining relations – and that I should accept my aunt's summons in spite of her heinous manners, if only for the sake of my cousin. You convinced me! I have reversed my inclination on the basis of your arguments. And now you wish me to reverse them once more? What can the season of year have to do with it? I am not insensitive to the discomfort you will suffer at my aunt's hands, more so even than I should do, but..."

"My discomfort has nothing to do with my reticence, or at least no discomfort arising from subjection to your aunt's whims."

Absent further enlightenment from his wife, Darcy could only repeat himself. "It has been you encouraging me to mend relations with my Aunt for the year past. I have always considered my visits to her a trial; I would undertake this one with no less trepidation, and even more for the estrangement which has afflicted us this past year or more. But surely you know that I will not allow her to lay responsibility for my perceived transgressions upon you; she is to accept us both, together or not at all, and I stand unmoved in that." Darcy frowned in puzzlement. "I confess I would not have thought you so inconstant as to persuade me in this matter only to turn me back again once my resolve had been won, however grudgingly." His glance flickered again to the letter under his hand, the Darcy scowl momentarily reappearing with it.

"And I should not in different circumstances." Lizzy placed her hand atop her husband's and gave it an affectionate squeeze. "But circumstances being what it is, I *will not* travel to Kent for Easter." As Darcy took breath to speak Lizzy said, "Nor will I travel to

Longbourn, nor to Jane and Bingley, nor town nor anywhere. I will spend the Easter observance right here, at Pemberley... at home."

Darcy considered his wife, disconcerted by her vehemence. She certainly had his full attention now. "Mrs Darcy, if you wish to observe Easter at Pemberley, then by all means we will do so. I had no notion of it signifying so much to you."

Lizzy's laugh only further bemused Darcy. "It is not Easter which dictates my resolve. It is something far more important and constraining."

"And what is that?"

Lizzy did not speak immediately, but removed her hand from Darcy's and rose. She walked away from him slowly, eyes down and studying the carpet while she considered her words carefully. On gaining the far side of the room she turned, seemed to fix her mind, and marched resolutely back to her husband at the table. She looked at him, his curiosity arching his brows and giving him the air of a young boy. She sighed, then reversed herself and walked back across the room yet again. Darcy held his tongue admirably as she went through this ritual, though his frustration was writ large in his expression. After several turns in this manner, she was resolved. Once more reaching the table, she stepped up to her husband wearing an inscrutable face, and he looked up at her in anticipation finally of a reply.

She stood looking down at him. With his face upturned to meet her gaze, she noted again the feline slant to his eyes that sometimes suggested itself at such an angle; she smiled tenderly to see it now, for it was one of the things Lizzy loved most in her husband's myriad traits, those changeable eyes. She reflected upon them, upon the affection she read there; noting their pale blue shade tinged with glints of gold from the morning sun abundantly brightening the sitting room.

Finally, she looked down at the floor again, hesitant to meet those beloved eyes, as a quick blush rose in her cheeks. With her continued faltering, Darcy became quite concerned; he had seldom known Lizzy unable to speak her mind directly, and her current pantomime engendered an anxious wonder in him. Just as he made to coax intelligence from her and, if that would not work, he would resort to demanding it, Lizzy reached for Darcy's hand which rested still on the table though it had developed a nervous tic. She raised his wrist, uncurled his fingers to extend his hand, and placed his flattened palm upon her stomach. Then once more, she laid her own hand upon his, covering and caressing it there. The room was silent but for the ticking of the Boulle clock upon the mantel.

Dawning comprehension broke at last in Darcy; his jaw slackened and his pupils as they widened in enlightenment deepened the hue of his eyes. His tentative smile requested confirmation of his supposition, and she nodded vigorously, smiling herself in return. With one fluid motion, Darcy was on his feet, sweeping Lizzy into an embrace, and lifting her off her own feet to spin her around in euphoria.

Returning his wife to solid ground again – amidst her laughter – he asked once more for confirmation, this time in words so as to court no mistake. "Is it true? You are ... delicate?"

"I think it is you who are being delicate, my love, you may say it without reserve!" She laughed at him, even while raising her hand to lay it lovingly upon his cheek. "But yes, I expect a child. Or rather, we expect a child – to be born sometime early in May by all reckoning, perhaps even to share your own birth day. So you see it will be impossible for me to travel to Rosings for April except from direst need."

"Oh, hang Rosings!" cried Darcy. He started to spin Lizzy around again, but stopped suddenly, concern suffusing his expression. "Forgive me, madam, I should not abuse you so!" He swept around behind her to her chair and pulled it out, then gently ushered her into it while she laughed.

"It is all right, Fitz, you cannot hurt him... or her... by teaching too early the blissful merits of spinning about. I am quite well, I assure you."

"But..." His smile receded slightly, though the light in his eyes did not. "When did you know? Why did not you tell me before now? April is little more than..." He began to consider the months until Easter but his normally sharp mind was not of a condition to work coherently.

"Four and a half months, yes I know," his wife answered for him. "And the child will arrive scarcely six weeks after." She held her tongue until Darcy pulled his own chair around and sat down beside her, he being unwilling to relinquish the firm hold he had on her hand. "I thought to tell you a hundred times in the last few weeks, but I determined to be certain this babe was well and truly established before doing so."

Lizzy's words stopped short of recalling the loss they had suffered only a few months after they had been wed when an early miscarriage had cut short their joy. Though they had spoken little of it openly at the time, each had struggled with understandable fears that such a calamity might prefigure childlessness for the couple. That fear had only grown over the months when Lizzy had continued her courses.

"And are you? Certain?"

"Yes, I am certain now. And whilst I may have awaited a more ..." Lizzy glanced quickly around her private sitting room where they had been breaking their fast together, "auspicious moment for the telling, there is no harm in Lady Catherine forcing my hand. Indeed, I am grateful for it; I am not sanguine having secrets between us. And I would like to share our happy news with our family and friends over the next weeks when they arrive for Christmas."

Lizzy looked at Darcy now, his face suffused with joy, and she felt utter contentment with her life; until her eye upon the parchment on the table brought back the conversation which had spurred her announcement.

"Darcy, what are we to do regarding Lady Catherine?"

"I will decline her summons, of course! There is no question of any other reply!"

"I do so hate to see you to reject her outright. Even if she is detestably rude and has again rejected our invitation, still she has opened herself for the first time to reconciliation, if a very small and resentful step and upon her own terms." Lizzy stopped a moment and bit her lower lip with a mischievous grin. "Her stubbornness of disposition in general is not one with which I am unfamiliar."

Darcy narrowed his eyes and glowered at his wife before his lips turned up at the corners to give the lie to his dissatisfaction. "First you accuse me of your father's studied indifference, and now I am likened to my Aunt? It seems my deficiencies grow worse by the second in your opinion. I am stung by your appraisal of my character."

"Your character, Mr Darcy, is unassailable and you well know it. I adore you and all your deficiencies." Lizzy smiled and leaned in to kiss her husband's cheek. "Your Aunt, on the other hand, is not so quick to excuse them, such that even a small thaw in her exterior should not be treated lightly to cause further offence. I would like to see you reconciled with her especially now, for the sake of our growing family."

"Surely she must understand the reason –" Darcy stopped speaking, rolled his eyes heavenward and sighed, then looked back to Lizzy again with a wry smile. "No, of course she will not understand. She will find it a gross impertinence that we chose to disrupt her carefully balanced house party as a result of something we should have had the discretion better to plan."

The two shared a laugh at that, before Darcy went on. "But Lady Catherine is not my present concern. Her inconvenience is nothing to me against your welfare and, as her estrangement was of her own making, I am disinclined to give the matter any concession at all now in light of your news."

Lizzy countered with a suggestion. "We might invite her here again instead, to pass Easter in Derbyshire…"

"Here? With us, and you near confinement? Given the attitude of her letter, I think not."

"Why ever not? I cannot travel in an advanced condition, but I shall be perfectly capable of hosting family here. Anne must want for a change of scene now and again, and she has remained a friend to you even in the face of her mother's disprove." Lizzy's speech became rapid as she warmed to her argument. "And Fitzwilliam will come to fulfil his annual visit to your Aunt in what I know to be a more pleasing environment, so we should be favouring him in the bargain. You may be spared all the parading and obsequious civility of Mr Collins as well… although I shall miss a chance to reacquaint with Charlotte."

"What makes you believe that my aunt will even oblige such a request, having only now declined to travel for Christmas?"

"Why, our news, of course. She will not be able to resist."

"Indeed, that is my fear. Do you think she will sit quietly with your impending motherhood staring her in the face at every turn?"

Lizzy laughed. "Of course she will not. She will be beside herself to criticise every detail of bringing this child into the world and providing a proper home for the heir of Pemberley – and bewail the shades of Pemberley into the bargain. But if not that, then some other campaign would occupy her displeasure. Besides, Lady

Catherine's teeth may have less bite when she is removed from her own domain."

"Possibly, though you of all people have experience to the contrary and I should not believe it. I marvel, Lizzy, at your fortitude. Yet I am reticent at the thought of my Aunt coming here at such a time. At least in Kent when she becomes unbearable, I can find some business to call me away again. I doubt, however, I have the talent to conjure business that would draw *her* home when once she establishes herself at Pemberley."

"Oh, I am certain we can have no difficulty there. I feel assured that your Aunt will not overstay herself and will conjure her own reasons to suit; though I hazard you will not love the cure any better than the malady."

Darcy looked to his wife curiously, and she returned his gaze in challenge. She said, "Should Lady Catherine condescend to pass Easter at Pemberley, and think to remain long past it ..."

"... as she bestows her inestimable counsel, my dear, in every particular of child rearing... I have good reason to know of it from the past several years of Georgiana's custody." Darcy raised his eyebrows to emphasize his point.

"Yes, and to grace us with her extensive advice for our child," repeated Lizzy, then continued: "she will have to share our attentions with other family who will no doubt insist upon being present for the birth of the Darcy heir. Jane certainly, and I would wish that... as well as –" Lizzy's voice trailed off a moment, a sheepish grin forming as she regarded her husband.

Darcy closed his eyes and sighed in resignation as he completed the thought: "—your *mother!*"

"Indeed." She paused. Both sighed. "We cannot keep my mother away when it comes close to my confinement, but I venture to assure you that Mrs Bennet will succeed where we might not, in driving away Lady Catherine deBourgh!"

"Tell me, my clever wife, are you able to safely travel now? There would be no impediment to doing so?"

Now it was Lizzy's turn to be warily curious. She knew a journey at present to Kent would be out of the question with the arrival of their Christmas guests only a few weeks away. As such, she wondered what Darcy played at. "No, of course not; no impediment at all. What are you devising?"

"It is only that I have heard there are still vast estates for easy purchase in the Americas. I have lately been thinking... *very* lately been thinking... of establishing a new seat for the Darcy family. What would you say to taking ship, say in a week or two? Virginia, perhaps? I have heard the climate there to be fine and particularly conducive to child rearing."

His eyes took on a wicked glint as his wife giggled. "Or barring that, do you think our august Navy would accept my Aunt and your mother on conscription? I might be persuaded to wield the club myself to hasten their enlistment."

Lizzy laughed again at this, though Darcy noted a fleeting wistful expression cross his wife's face. He took Lizzy's hand to kiss it with great tenderness. His thumb slid to and fro across her fingers in caress as he said softly, "But I will not allow this news of yours to be overshadowed today. My happiness will not be tempered. Lady Catherine can wait until tomorrow, your mother can wait until tomorrow. For my cares, the whole world can wait until tomorrow! Today I will think only of you and our child to come."

His expression turned serious as his eyes slowly roamed his wife's countenance, taking in each feature individually with appreciation. He daily found reasons to bless his fortune that this woman had pledged her affection and her life to him; and now they would further entwine their lives with a child, a legacy of their love, and an heir to carry on the Darcy name. Nothing could touch the overwhelming joy that coursed through him as he wondered if the child would carry Lizzy's delicate ears, her pert nose, or her chestnut eyes: oh, please yes, her fine eyes.

Finally settling his gaze upon Lizzy's mouth, which had formed a broad smile during her husband's assessment, Darcy leaned forward as he threaded his fingers into her loosely-bound hair, and he lightly touched his lips to hers. He felt her smile slacken as his wife met his kiss, and for several moments they shared most pleasurably in the satisfactions of their news.

A knock sounded from outside the door and Darcy hastily stood and occupied himself in smoothing his cravat while Lizzy replaced a pin in her hair and called for their interloper to enter. Mrs Reynolds came into the room but checked herself on seeing the master still within.

"Oh! I am sorry, Sir, I can return later—" She blushed slightly and averted her glance to the windows.

"No, no, Mrs Reynolds. It is quite all right. Mr Darcy has some correspondence to attend to," Lizzy said as she lifted the letter from the table and held it out towards her husband with a mischievous smile.

"Hmmm," he said, ignoring the parchment in her outstretched hand. "I shall answer it tomorrow. But I do have business with Mr Gordon over the redesign of the glass houses in the west garden, so I will leave you ladies to your own affairs."

Before leaving, however, he bent to kiss his wife's cheek and lingered long enough to whisper that he would return to share a luncheon in her company if it met with her approval. She nodded her agreement immediately, and Darcy straightened and took his leave. He could neither contain nor conceal his smile of utter pride as he passed his housekeeper.

"He knows then, madam?" asked Mrs Reynolds after her master had gone.

"Yes, I was obliged to tell him after a letter arrived from Lady Catherine, summoning us to Rosings for Easter." She waved the paper. "I could hardly have him commit us to such a journey at that time."

"Well, and I am glad you did tell him, if I may say, Mrs Darcy. I was that afraid I would let something slip, so excited I am at the prospect of children at Pemberley again."

Lizzy smiled, and then returned her interest thoughtfully to the letter in her hand. "Mrs Reynolds, do you mind if we defer our appointment? I find I have little head for Christmas menus or accounts this morning."

"Of course! As you prefer." She smiled benevolently at the young woman. "The house will manage itself for another day." She curtseyed, a gesture which Lizzy acknowledged with a distracted nod, and then slipped from the room with no little satisfaction herself at this recent turn of events.

Lizzy fingered the letter in her hand a moment before smoothing out the folds in it and reading.

Nephew –

Notwithstanding your invitation to pass Christmas at Pemberley – the acceptance of which you must know to be impossible as my ministrations among the less fortunate are most critical at this season, and such prolonged removal from my tenants simply cannot be sustained – I am not above being moved by your continued pleas for clemency on my part.

I am not without mercy, though I find myself still grievously used by your betrayal of me, your dear mother, your cousin Anne and the promises which you found so easy to cast aside. I cannot but attribute it to an inability to recognise being imposed upon by a woman of lamentable family but irrefutable arts. You always have lacked discretion in your judgment, and now no doubt find to your cost that you would have been better served by allowing me more often to guide your path after your father's passing.

Your stubborn insistence on making your way without benefit of my vast experience and discrimination has now taught a lesson to which you must reconcile yourself for life; and with such continual daily reminders of your misjudgement as you no doubt suffer, far be it from me to add to your distress by reminding you of the permanence of your folly. What you have done cannot be undone.

I could more easily find compassion for the circumstance you have created for yourself, however, had you not broken faith with your innocent cousin, who even now frets over her prospects though she exhibits a brave front in accepting your breach of honour without claiming her due.

Indeed, it is only Anne's entreaties on your behalf which propel me to cast aside my better judgment and reinstate you to my company, though you shall have to prove your contrition through diligent attendance upon us both. I shall expect you as every year of late, in Kent for Easter's observance. I trust that sufficient humility on your part combined with my natural propensity for compassion shall reinstate some degree of cordiality and affection between us. After all, you are a Fitzwilliam as much as a Darcy, a connection I would suffer you to remember.

Lady Catherine DeBourgh

PostScript -- Since I suppose you must, it need not be mentioned directly that you may bring your wife. My unwavering service to the dictates of charity will of course impel me to treat her with more solicitude than she has done to my daughter or me.

Lizzy refolded the letter and placed it again upon the table. She shook her head in resigned amusement. It was going to be an interesting spring.

Anniversary Song

ﭼﭼﭼ

This one is somewhat of a fanciful indulgence –imagining Elizabeth and Mr Darcy a year after they have married. A warning: It is pure schmaltz!—with just a teaspoon of fantasy thrown in—because of course, we all need schmaltz now and again.

ﭼﭼﭼ

"Mrs Darcy?"

Elizabeth turned towards the door of her private sitting room on hearing herself addressed, and smiled at Lennox. The smile partly acknowledged the fine figure Lennox cut in his footman's uniform; a well tailored green and not a thread out of place in its embroidery around cuffs, neck and hem in the same deep shade of the Pemberley wood. Lennox had only joined the household staff a few months before and took obvious pride in his appearance, as did all their footmen. Why, for all he was tall when they took him on in late September, Elizabeth could swear he had grown a good inch or more just in donning his smart attire; and he had schooled his countenance always to reflect the deferential formality required of his position, though it could not belie the happy temperament that resided beneath.

The remainder of Elizabeth's benign attitude resulted from the pleasurable tingle she still felt on hearing herself addressed as *Mrs Darcy*. Even a year after she had accepted the name and, more importantly, the hand and life of the gentleman behind it, she now and again started a little at the title when any one used it. She wondered if she would ever become accustomed to hearing herself thus titled; but was certain that even with familiarity and comfort in it, she would never tire of the honour. The name always conjured an image of her husband (yet another title capable of conferring tingles) as he had looked at the front of the small family chapel on the day they wed.

Elizabeth laughed inwardly as she recalled as well the first morning that she had spent in this very room at Pemberley in her new role as its mistress, some days after her marriage. Ostensibly, she had sequestered herself to review household accounts supplied by Mrs Reynolds, with an eye to coming to understand the operation of the vast house. She had spent the first thirty minutes, however, with her glance darting about the delightful room in appreciation. Darcy had occasioned it to be repapered and decorated just for her arrival, and she had found no imperfection in his choices. They suited her.

The room had an eastern aspect and its cream-coloured walls with their simple repeating pattern of wildflowers took on morning sunshine as a robe, adding a glow of summer-out-of-doors to all it contained. Elizabeth had early on adopted the habit of breaking her fast in this room on the few occasions when Darcy was away, and now on the odd instance when they had no other residents or guests, the couple would share their morning repast together there as well in prelude to going about their day.

Even on wintry afternoons as today, the soft tones of its fruitwood furnishings combined with the fire in the hearth to produce a warmth of feeling that could not but welcome any occupant. Darcy had initially offered to make additional alterations to the room should Elizabeth desire them, as it was to serve as her private parlour; but she had rejected any such notion at once. Indeed, the only change she had ordered had been the addition of her own small writing desk from Longbourn, stationed beside a comfortable armchair.

That day so long ago now in her sitting room, Elizabeth had found herself in a struggle to concentrate on the accounts. After sufficiently appraising the room's details, she applied herself to the ledgers with a will. But after what seemed an eternity had passed, she had looked down at her quarto, meant for note-taking, and discovered that she had nearly filled the first sheet – not with menus, supplies or servants' wages as intended, but with the words *Mrs Darcy* repeated over and over again in varying confidences of hand. Well, to be precise, this was not *all* she had written—for occasionally she had added a *Mrs Fitzwilliam Darcy* or an *Elizabeth Darcy* to the page as well.

She had laughed initially when she discovered her idle scratchings, but then had turned scarlet with embarrassment even though she was alone, feeling the heat rise from her neck to her face. What if some one had entered and found the new mistress of Pemberley so engaged? They would question the master's sanity in his choice of wife, surely. She had hastened to destroy the evidence of her preoccupation, glad of the season's blazing fire in the grate.

Yet even as the parchment was placed atop the flames and had begun to burn, Elizabeth watched the letters on the page as they first curled, then were consumed. The words would remain forever written on her heart even as their ashes rose up through the flue to drift across Pemberley's park as a silent proclamation of her new revered status.

Today, nearly a year later, she had retired to her sitting room in late afternoon once again to review accounts. By now, however, it was habitual to maintain her concentration on the tasks at hand. And her task today was to finalise plans for the family's Christmas observance.

They would make a small party this year, in contrast to the last when Elizabeth's entire family had descended upon the estate, first for her marriage with Darcy, then to stay on for Christmas only a few days later. Elizabeth and Darcy had planned in the beginning to marry at Longbourn along with Jane and her Charles Bingley, but in the end had hit upon the idea of allowing that couple their day, and they themselves marrying only a few weeks later in Pemberley's own chapel. Dispensation had been obtained easily enough, and it had been done; with all the Bennet family and the Gardiners attending as well as Miss Darcy and Colonel Fitzwilliam on Darcy's side. Lady Catherine deBourgh, outraged by her nephew's choice, had refused to sanction the union by her presence.

They had all enjoyed a grand party then flowing into Christmastide and the new year, if it somewhat lacked in privacy for the young couple those first few weeks. But Elizabeth looked forward now to the next several days – her first *real* Christmas at Pemberley, as she thought of it – of quiet and intimate celebration.

Sweet Georgiana Darcy, of course, was to be in residence. She had arrived the day prior from town with Mrs Annesley, who herself would continue on to her own family in Shropshire on the morrow for a short visit. Expected to arrive even as Mrs Annesley would depart were Jane and Bingley, bringing with them Kitty who had passed the last month with the Bingleys; and dear Richard Fitzwilliam, more brother than cousin to Darcy and Georgiana, and a proven friend to Elizabeth during the tumult caused by Lady Catherine when it was confirmed to her that Darcy was to marry Elizabeth.

A final late addition to the group would be a Mrs Chaney, invited at the request of the Colonel. The invitation was happily proffered after Elizabeth had cajoled Fitzwilliam into divulging that the lady was a woman recently widowed when her husband, an officer in Fitzwilliam's regiment, had died in an accident. The Colonel had taken on as his obligation the welfare of the young widow as any good commanding officer would do; but Elizabeth suspected there was more to it than simple bereavement assistance. Behind the words of his letter she could sense that her good cousin held a special admiration for the lady. Of course, *he* would express nothing to the widow herself of any affection he felt for her, not during her year of mourning; but Elizabeth felt no compunctions against using Mrs Chaney's visit to subtly smooth the way for Fitzwilliam in the future. Since having experienced first-hand the various contentments of the married condition, she could wish it for all her friends where true affection existed.*

Darcy and Elizabeth had also this year invited Lady Catherine and Anne deBourgh, but his Aunt still had not forgiven the couple for their marriage and refused in a curtly worded reply. And Elizabeth had conferred a special invitation upon her friend Charlotte Collins to make up their party, having first secured Darcy's grudging acquiescence to tolerate Charlotte's sycophantic husband; but the vicar had determined that if Lady Catherine declined to attend, he should follow suit. No doubt he thought to further endear himself to that august lady by his steadfast refusal, but Elizabeth suffered compassion for the tedious manner in which Charlotte must surely look to pass Christmastide.

"Ummm, Mrs Darcy?"

Delight yet again rose from Elizabeth's toes to her fingertips at the sound of her name; until the footman's repetition of it drew her from her reverie.

"Yes, Lennox?"

"I have a message for you, madam, from Mr Darcy." He held out a silver tray upon which lay a folded parchment. Elizabeth noted the Darcy seal at its closure.

"How very odd." She took the letter, turning it over in her fingers while she regarded it curiously. Then she recalled that the footman still awaited release. "Thank you, Lennox."

"Yes, madam." The footman had barely shut the door behind him before Elizabeth opened her missive. It was quite short, only a few hastily scratched lines.

Soon we shall mark our Saviour's
lowly birth
Seek and ye shall find the path
to me there

This was quite curious indeed, thought Elizabeth. Whatever was the man playing at?

She had last seen her husband shortly after a shared luncheon. He had announced that he would spend an hour or so with Mr Gordon, the steward, before taking Parsifal out, as he had been obliged to miss his customary morning ride for an early snow squall which had swept through the dale. Elizabeth had kissed him on his way, then made her own to her sitting room and had been closeted there the better part of the morning. She presumed Darcy had returned and was about the house somewhere by now.

So what to make of this note? Undoubtedly, it was a riddle, though not in the standard form of one; and to what end? Was she to decipher it as such? It could not be poetry; it had not the metre of a poem, and Elizabeth knew from experience that Darcy wrote quite lovely lines when he was of a mind to do so. She would find little poems at odd times – stuck within the pages of a book she was reading; tucked into her work basket; or holding Darcy's place upon his pillow when she would awake to find her husband already about his day.

Besides, his poems were always signed "Your Stout Love," a throwback jest to their early acquaintance. The signature always made Elizabeth imagine her husband in thirty or forty years, Darcy a portly man elevating his legs to relieve his gout and running his hand over a bald pate in sad mimicry of his current habit of pushing recalcitrant dark locks out of his eyes. That image of age, so far from what future reality must surely hold – she could only hope – always made her laugh.

It must be a shortened riddle, then, the note. The first two lines were easy enough to decipher, they referenced Christmas; the third was scripture. The last, and all of it taken as a whole, was so simple as to be unlike Darcy's usual manner of thinking. Elizabeth giggled at the first interpretation which entered her head without bidding; but although she often teased Darcy about his legendary pride, even that could not extend to likening himself to God.

Once she discarded that nonsensical idea, feeling a modicum of guilt for her thoughts being uncharitable, she focused again on the simplicity of the message. Why not take its meaning simply as well? 'Our Saviour's lowly birth...' – a manger? A stable? Of course, it must be the stable. 'Seek and ye shall find the path to me there.' Apparently, Darcy wished his wife to meet him in the stable.

Still ignorant of his object, Elizabeth nonetheless decided to play along. This was most unlike her reserved husband; but whatever game he enacted, she trusted Darcy implicitly. Quickly she put away the accounts in her desk and secured them, then crossed through her adjacent bedroom into her dressing room. Though it was December, their weather had been unseasonably mild despite this morning's brief squall, and a fine woollen shawl over her Spencer should suffice for the short walk. As she wrapped herself in its soft expanse, she repeated the lines yet again and confirmed her impression that they must lead her to the stable. And a walk in the brisk air would offer a revival of good humour after long hours at her desk.

ξ

The air *was* brisk as Elizabeth walked up the slight hill to the stable block. Though the day had been mild, she had not considered that in this season the sun was early to set and, with the onset of darkness, winter's chill had set in again and quickly. She gave brief thought to returning to the house for a heavier pelisse, but shrugged off the cold and hastened her steps instead; she was nearly there.

She entered through the main door of the stable, looking about her but seeing no one at the first. She began to walk down the principal aisle, glancing at the horses in their stalls as she did so, and breathing in the distinctive smells of hay and leather and horseflesh. Rather overpowering at this moment, with all the mounts in their stalls for the night and the attendants just finishing up with feed and grooming, but she had grown to rather like the smell in diluted form—it reminded her of Darcy's riding coat. Elizabeth still was not fully comfortable with horses, but had grown significantly more so from the several riding lessons she had taken with Darcy. She was determined over time to become a confident rider, but as with all things (pianoforte came to mind) one must practice to become proficient.

About halfway down she found a groom in one of the stalls, cleaning mud from the hind foot of a roan. He looked unsurprised to see Elizabeth. "Evenin', ma'am."

"Good evening, Bryce." She wanted to ask him why he was smiling like an overfed cat when the groom asked, "Lookin' fer Mr Darcy, are you, ma'am?"

"Now why should you presume such a thing? Is it not possible I simply came down to visit the horses?"

The young man's smile broadened considerably as he took in her attire, unsuitable for equine pursuits. He nodded. "Sorry, ma'am."

If he could not manage to be contrite, at least he attempted to be helpful. "But if yer was lookin' fer Mr Darcy, he was with Parsifal last I saw him." He nodded again, in the direction of a stall at the end, an extra-sized compartment designated for the large stallion that was its master's pride.

With a quick word of acknowledgment, Elizabeth made her way to where Parsifal resided when he was not out roaming the Derbyshire hills with her husband. Generally taciturn in nature like his master and only responsive to Darcy's commands, the stallion had come nevertheless to accept Elizabeth's preeminent status at Pemberley through their lessons together, and he came now to the entrance of his pen to greet her. She spoke softly to the horse, asking if it knew what his master was playing at; then she grabbed a handful of oats from a bag nearby and fed the treat to Parsifal, being careful from experience to lay her hand out very flat to protect her fingers from inadvertent nips.

After Parsifal had enjoyed his treat, Elizabeth smoothed her fingers along his nose and forelock. The horse nickered softly. He looked on Elizabeth with what she could only believe was an *informed* eye and then, apparently when her quizzical countenance was not enlightened, he suddenly threw his head sideways. She found the gesture curious and smiled. Parsifal repeated it with vigour.

Elizabeth followed his direction then and saw what she had failed to notice on her approach: another note, this one secured to the far post of the stall and bearing her name on the front in Darcy's strong hand. Looking to Parsifal in surprise, she was further astonished when the stallion dipped his head as if nodding in approval. She began to wonder nonsensically if her husband and this beast were not somehow two halves of the same being, connected in thought and purpose.

Laughing at the notion, she took the few steps to retrieve the note and, with Parsifal looking on, she opened it to read near a fortuitously placed lantern.

In sunshine here bask the reds of Tuscany
As we drink in new beginnings
A bacchanal in paradise though
Clay gives way to slate

Elizabeth shook her head, finding the message completely obscure, then immediately read all of it a second time. She glanced up to Parsifal for enlightenment as the horse had appeared so well informed but a moment ago; but it seemed its commitment to assisting had concluded upon the note's being found. It simply looked at her now with an expression of natural superiority.

ξ

Not one to admit defeat at any gauntlet thrown in her path, even one figuratively issued by a horse—Elizabeth's courage always rose to the occasion when anyone tried to intimidate her—she read the note yet again, giving it fuller consideration. It named Tuscany, so far comprehensible: it was a region where Elizabeth and Darcy had spent a portion of their wedding trip in the spring following their marriage. It had indeed felt like paradise to them, though it had taken Elizabeth some while to accustom herself to Darcy conducting all their communication with the local inhabitants, she never having learnt to speak more than the odd phrase of Italian before their journey.

So, this clue must refer, quite specifically, to Tuscany. They had passed their leisure in the region at a delightful inn sitting near the top of a hill and surrounded by vineyards. Ah, of course! A *bacchanal*. Her husband must surely refer to the early evenings they had shared on their private veranda, drinking wine before dinner and enjoying the surprisingly strong sun which warmed their faces even as their hands warmed the deep red libations their glasses held.

This memory gave Elizabeth the insight she needed, as it was obviously meant to do. As they had enjoyed their late afternoon wines, they had looked out over the vineyards on the terraced hillsides... the Sangiovese grapes which would produce delightful 'reds' basking on their vines, growing plump and shining under the attentions of the sun.

Once she gained this understanding, the remaining line was simple translation to complete. Upon their return to Pemberley from their wedding trip, they had continued the habit, when at home alone together, to share a glass of wine before going up to dress for dinner. On those first clement days of summer, they would sit together on the south west terrace, discussing the events of their day or simply passing some quiet moments, while they looked out over their ornamental lake. *Clay gives way to slate* - a terrace of slate flagstone as opposed to the clay soil ones of Tuscany. Darcy was directing her once more, this time to their terrace.

Sighing, and granting a smug Parsifal with one last forelock caress, Elizabeth left the warmth of the stable, bidding a quick farewell to Bryce as she passed him. The groom nodded and wished the lady a pleasant evening.

ξ

Stepping lively both from the now-frigid evening air and a heightened curiosity as to the purpose of these conundrums she had been set, Elizabeth made her way back to the house; but she skirted the main door and entered instead through the gardens which led to the terrace. As she walked however briskly through it now, she smiled to herself to think not only of the intimate moments she and Darcy had shared there this year past, but of another day – a day of some import as it turned out – when she had toured these same gardens with her Aunt and Uncle Gardiner, believing the estate's owner to be away; and had then been shocked by his sudden appearance, to discover that Mr Darcy had returned home earlier than expected. That meeting had occurred nigh on a year and a half previous, and had been filled with revelations for Elizabeth—without it, she and Darcy might never have found their way to each other again.

Gaining the terrace, Elizabeth looked about at the low stone balustrade. No Darcy sat there, but unsurprising to her now, yet another note did, along with a glass half-filled with a deep and hearty Montecastelli, its aroma tinged with fresh black cherry and gentle tannins. She did not linger, but, giving in to a shiver, she took the wine and the note into the parlour, unsurprised to find the terrace door to the room unbolted and standing ajar for her. A fire was lit, as was a lamp next to a wing chair. Elizabeth dutifully sat and, placing her wine upon the small adjacent table, opened the third missive. Intrigue vied with a mounting if benevolent determination to take her husband to task when she might finally locate him. What was his motive, to send her off chasing proverbial butterflies on a chill winter's day?

ξ

Books abound yet no library

Business attended yet no clerk nor custom

Alone yet always with your smile upon me

Sanctuary

Could this be so simple? The room sprang to Elizabeth's imagination without any effort, her only hesitation in trusting she knew the answer being in the ease of it. In addition, the irony was not lost upon her that, should her surmise be correct, she was being directed to a place only a few doors away from her own sitting room which she had left only because Lennox delivered the first note – a circuitous path, to be certain.

Darcy's private study adjacent to his bedroom – their room rather, in truth – certainly fit the description she had been given. Not officially Pemberley's library – that was downstairs – yet its shelves held a myriad of volumes: books related to estate planning, or other business, as well as Darcy's own personal favourite books that he returned to time after time. And he did at times adjourn there to write letters of business when they required his utmost concentration; but it could not be called a place of business as such. It was, indeed, his sanctuary when he felt in need of solitary moments. Elizabeth could count on one hand the number of times she had ventured into the room since their marriage, though Darcy had always expressed to her a welcome to enter it as she chose.

That very expression was enough for her; she chose to leave it to him as his own.

But the last time she had joined him in the study had been some three months before, on the occasion of the installation of a portrait above the fireplace – a portrait of Elizabeth that Darcy had commissioned shortly after they returned from their wedding trip. She recalled how awkward it had felt sitting for it at the time, the whole process unnatural to her; more than once she had been chastised by the portraitist, a Mr Lovell, for bursting into laughter at the absurdity of it all. But despite a recalcitrant subject, he was able to produce more than a fair likeness in the end.

At first, Darcy and she had talked of hanging it in the hall with other family portraits; but in the end her husband wished to keep to himself alone the enigmatic smile she wore; and so she had acquiesced with pleasure to its placement in his study. An oft-repeated entreaty of Darcy's centred on his desire to know the temper that had produced such a smile, what thoughts had occupied his wife at the time. One day, perhaps, she would share that intelligence with him.

ξ

It seemed this day was destined to invoke memories! Rousing herself from this distracting one, Elizabeth stood up from the comfort of her chair to get on with her own commission and complete the task at hand. Warmed now from the parlour's fire, she removed her wrap, dangling it from her arm as she mounted the main staircase. When she gained the next floor she made her way towards the end of the corridor where Darcy's study was situated.

Elizabeth saw that this door, also, was ajar. It must be the right place. A quick glimpse in through the several inches of its opening revealed little, however. She knocked, hesitant to enter without direct invitation, but received no reply. For an instant she doubted her interpretation of the latest set of clues, so sensible was she of intruding into her husband's particular domain.

After waiting a moment, indecision warring with curiosity, Elizabeth made up her mind and pushed open the door to enter. Another fire welcomed and cast flickering light upon her portrait above it, giving an eerie semblance of life to the smiling woman there. Again, Elizabeth did not find Darcy in the room. But her eyes were drawn to the mullioned windows, below which a small table had been placed. It held candles that shone upon a bottle of wine and two glasses, as well as an assortment of fruits and cold delicacies. And propped up against one of the candlesticks was yet another folded parchment.

ξ

Elizabeth sighed at seeing this letter. She had been intrigued and engaged upon realising that Darcy was setting her on a quest of sorts; but when she had determined the most recent clue to be his study, she had hoped her curiosity was finally to be satisfied. Now it appeared she had still to arrive at the final stop.

And yet, the setting of the table certainly suggested an intention to abide here a while. Seeing *two* glasses next to the wine bottle only reinforced the impression. Elizabeth laughed to recall she had left her wine from the terrace in the parlour when she came upstairs; yet here was another just awaiting her.

Making her way to the table, Elizabeth lifted the parchment to find a single white hothouse rose lying beneath it. It drew a smile from her as she broke the seal on the letter and began to read.

My dearest wife –

Can you begin to know my joy in being able to write these words to you? Had I been told some twelvemonth past that my affection for you would become even stronger with time, I would have denounced the speaker as a liar, certain that no emotion could exceed the ardency of my love at the moment you accepted my hand. Yet the impossible becomes fact. Daily have I grown to love more deeply, view life more clearly, find reserves of peace I once believed impossible. And it is you have brought these to me. You inhabit my very soul.

Every thing comes alive with your touch – I came alive with your touch; and I have lived each day more fully for doing so with you at my side.

I would see us fill the rooms of Pemberley with children, every ringing peal of laughter a testament to our affections. I would see their children grow strong within its corridors, thriving in a house suffused with joy. I would see us grow old and grey together, yet blind to the changes of time; seeing always in each other the merits of our youth.

And when our time comes to pass our legacy to another generation, when God has called us to our last abode, still we shall not be separated. I would find you in heaven's estate. I would hold you in grateful arms to the end of time. I will know you by eyes that sparkle with wit, by the lilt of your laughter, and the spring in your step – by the manner in which you love me so well. You will know me for my stillness, and the beating of my heart for you. We will speak without words. We will have no need of them—for we will have eternity – to love.

My dearest Elizabeth; my own Lizzy; pearl of my heart.

My love.

Emotion welled in Elizabeth's eyes. She ran a finger lightly over Darcy's signature at the bottom of the page as a single tear escaped its bounds and slowly meandered down her cheek. Through blurred vision, she sensed rather than saw his approach from the shadows at the far end of the room, which had been sheltered in darkness. Even in the throes of deep emotion, Elizabeth must smile—Darcy had been there all along – in the room, and in her heart!

As he had since the moment they had met.

Her husband's progress was interrupted as he bent to pick some thing from the floor; but then she felt his strong hands come around her, enveloping her both in the shawl she had let fall as she read his letter, and in his arms. Without words they stood thus a moment, before Elizabeth turned in the embrace to face her husband.

"One year ago you married me. One year – a mere moment in time," said Darcy, his voice husky. And as he leaned down to meet her upturned lips at last in a kiss, he whispered, "we have eternity."

Worst Impressions

ⱭⱭⱭ

The only Pride and Prejudice-based story in this collection with a modern setting, this short story idea came from wondering idly one day how the social hierarchies of Regency England might translate into the rank structure of the military today. I have a rough outline to write a full-fledged novel adaptation some day; this stand-alone is one I wrote to test out the notion.

ⱭⱭⱭ

It is apparently little known among your optimist population that the last thing a recently distressed person—okay, woman—wants to hear to pull her from a funk is a chirpy platitude. It must be little known; or why would otherwise intelligent, albeit all *too* chirpy, well-meaning people keep trying my coping skills. Each new over-happy 'things will be much better in the morning' in lilting cadence (not a good kind, but that phony sing-song voice more often trotted out for toddlers) seizes my fingers up into tight fists at my side. Pick a platitude—any will do: 'cheer up, it's a beautiful day out there' has me swallowing bile, clamping my tongue firmly between teeth to prevent a reply that would astonish a sailor. The worst is 'smile, a frown only gives you wrinkles' or some variation on the theme: 'smile, it can't be that bad;' 'smile, tomorrow is another day;' 'smile, it takes fewer muscles than a frown.' Well, I think you get my point; aren't even you getting annoyed about now? – start with 'smile' and follow with any one of a hundred inane motivational poster slogans, and it probably rankles.

I'm not generally of dour disposition, which makes it all the more baffling to me that on the infrequent occasions that I plummet into a serious funk, I'm not given a little more slack. It's not as if I make a habit of teeth gnashing and wailing; I don't wear my heart on my sleeve as so many are wont to do. My private sorrows are generally just that. So when I do indulge, sympathetic murmurings might be nice. But if that can't be managed, at least leave me alone to wallow a bit until I am sufficiently able to resolve my own issues. It's a complex world we inhabit. *No one* can be happy *all* the time.

And besides, I am of the opinion that one cannot force happiness upon another! No one confronted with a wall of chirp says, *oh thank you! I'd totally forgotten to be happy until you brought it up – what was I thinking? How nonsensical of me!* In fact, the converse results—the attempt to cheer even the sporadic curmudgeon is more likely to backfire in spades than win a smile of gratitude. So, optimists—it's all their fault. Well, okay, chirpy optimists (there are some who aren't, somewhere. Aren't there? There must be.)

I was in one of those rare funks one morning about a year ago, in my office with the door closed to shut out the world as much as I could. (See? I do *try* not to inflict my lesser moods on others.) One of the finest, most accomplished chirpers in the world – Olympic calibre -- worked in a cubicle on the other side of the door and, frankly, I'd heard enough. One more sunny plea for a smile and I wouldn't be responsible for my actions. So I'd holed myself up, at least for the lunch hour, with a sticky note at eye level on the door daring my colleagues to enter at their own risk (underlined three times and followed by half a dozen very pronounced exclamation points indeed.)

Had I placed a moratorium on answering the phone as well, I might have had a chance to wait out the wallowing. But when it rang, I picked it up without thinking, without checking the caller ID; expecting, maybe hoping, that a work question would divert me from my growing self-pity.

Oh. My. God. It was he. The man I held responsible, the root cause of my funk. Destroyer of my last chance at happiness. The man who had exposed me to the derision of the world for disappointed hopes. Can you imagine the tailspin my control went into on hearing that voice? That arrogant son-of-a-something who had had the *colossal gall* to call me that day of all days? Well, let me tell you.

You know, as I think on it now, I'm giving you a bad first impression of me. (It's that damned mood I was in—unnatural enough that I don't handle it well even recalling it so long after.) This story has to start earlier to be told well—to be fully appreciated; several months earlier, in fact. I promise, you're not in for a misery-chick downer—really. So if you'll allow me, I'll begin again...

ξ

"How soon?"

I felt the tremor in my voice. Jack's words had floored me.

"End of academic year," he laughed, as if it was nothing to him. But I knew it wasn't. It couldn't be nothing. He had given eighteen years of himself and now was being categorically turned out – two years shy of retirement eligibility – because of a *stupid* rule. I told him so in a huff. *Move 'up or out,' indeed.*

It wasn't my nature to be petulant, but this rankled on several counts. I'd like to say the unfairness of it to Jack was paramount – of course, it *did* concern me – but if I'm honest, my own forthcoming loss fed my resentment.

You see, I work at a Military Academy. It stands in a picturesque location and, since I grew up here, it's comfortable; but there aren't many social options for singles who aren't into the local bar scene. Heck, for almost two years we didn't have a grocery store until one finally moved in a couple of months ago. No movie theatre, no mall. We do have two good restaurants in town, we're at least lucky there; and the university sponsors shows or events now and again worth seeing. But all in all, not a hive of activity. I left soon after college, returning several years later when my mother was ailing. When mom died, I stayed on in the old homestead. It was easier than starting over again elsewhere.

But if staying was comfortable, in the way of wearing a worn old sweatshirt, it wasn't especially satisfying. A small community, a thirty-something unmarried woman, an extra twenty pounds tending to stretch my description from 'curvy' to 'plump' at best – unattached for some time – and not the least bit outgoing; I'd drifted by default into being a stay-at-home, if barely avoiding shut-in status. I talked about getting out more, resolving to do so every December 31st. But I seldom followed through. When social occasions arose, I more often found excuses to decline than energy to get myself out my door. Nights and weekends were spent with favourite books, reruns of *Law and Order*, maybe a bit of sewing or knitting – oh, and I dabbled in writing novels, but kept giving up when my plots went nowhere. How could my lifestyle inspire anything read-worthy?

My socializing, as it turned out, was enjoyed through my job. I brought to my work the enthusiasm I couldn't seem to muster outside the office. My organization did research; studies for Pentagon brass. It was perfect!—compared to the highly introverted analysts that made up our staff, I was a social butterfly. I coordinated our various projects with other agencies or departments, mostly professors with recent advanced degrees and, as such, well versed in the latest academic theories and research in their fields. They in turn worked collaboratively with my guys when particular topics crossed their specialties. Since I managed all the resources for the organization—including personnel and money—and all the projects required some of each, I had my hand in at some level of every study we did.

I met all sorts of people in this capacity, and loved it. I worked long hours, I was good at what I did and everyone knew it. That helped with self-confidence, something I chronically lacked outside the office. I even managed to flirt on occasion, because somehow there were no expectations or consequences, nothing personal in it. I was generally respected for my competence, and liked for my affability. (Really – despite my opening lines.)

ξ

I hadn't dated anyone since mom died—a couple set-ups that went nowhere (did my married friends *really* think these guys a better alternative to being on the shelf?) and one former high school classmate (now unsurprisingly divorced) with very parochial views. To the last they were torture.

For all the gentlemen I met through work, very few were eligible, especially in my age bracket. Some army posts might be great sources for running into single men, but the mission of this one being to develop teenagers (at least at the start) into well-rounded Army officers and leaders for the nation, meant *this* post was more family-oriented in the personnel stationed here in order to serve as exemplars. And as I mentioned earlier, there was not a lot to do hereabouts to meet people if you weren't attached to one of those families. So it all contributed to a dearth of social life, eligible dates being slim on the ground.

Then Jack walked in—literally.

John Quincy Williams, Major, U.S. Army, stopped by one rainy afternoon to see our Director. It was a schmooze call to pass along a message from an old classmate. You know the thing: you travel somewhere, meet someone, they find out where you live and bring out a laundry-list of names, to see if you know them. And in this case, Jack did—or knew of him—so he had been charged with passing on regards from this new acquaintance. To my great fortune, Jack had decided to deliver them in person to my boss. It never hurt to have an excuse to make friends with a general around here—even only a one star.

The secretary being out, Major Williams had strolled office to office to find me—or rather, to find *someone* to ask about the boss's schedule, and I was the lucky someone working through lunch...yet again. His casual, unassuming manner attracted me immediately; and he wasn't half bad to look at, either, in his Class-As. There really *is* something about a man in uniform; I've been around them all my life and still catch my breath when I see a fine-looking officer. The handsome factor definitely ratchets up a notch when a toned and trim torso is encased in a well-tailored coat. And Jack was no slouch.

As I jotted down his message for my boss, Jack noticed a bumper sticker posted on my tack-board: *I'd Rather Be Reading Jane Austen*

"It is a truth universally acknowledged..." he purred. I nearly slipped off my chair.

That was the start. Minutes later he was leaning provocatively across my desk, as we debated whether television and film romanticized Austen more than she would have approved. Turned out Jack had chosen an English Lit major when he was a student here years before in order to meet girls—they only represented about ten percent of the student body at the time so every little advantage helped in upping his chances of finding a date—but he'd obviously paid attention in class, too. When he left my office some time later, we had a dinner date to debate it further. It took me half the afternoon to get back to the report I'd been drafting.

The thing about Jack is he's so... effortless. He finds enjoyment in everything; interacts with good humour and grace in any social situation. We began seeing each other a few times each week. Mostly dinner out and then back to my place for a video or, well, you know. Then every couple weekends we'd take the train into New York City, see a show or, if the weather was nice, just pick a neighbourhood at random to walk through and discover new little bistros and shops and taverns. Now and again we'd splurge on a boutique hotel for a night.

And we talked—about everything. Him. Me. Life. Films. Books. Jane Austen. He believed Fanny Price should have married Henry Crawford; and 'spiritless' Anne Elliot deserved no better than her cousin William Elliot, over which we disagreed vehemently. But we found common ground in the genius of the writing in general. I was appalled when I first learned that he actually preferred Charlotte Bronte (Jane Eyre superior to Jane Austen, *seriously?*) but then he smiled in that impishly attractive way he has and I forgave him even that.

ξ

So for him to tell me that he was getting out of the Army – virtually *forced* out because he'd been passed over twice in the promotion boards – well, that knocked the wind out of my parachute. He *could* stay until retirement at twenty years as a Major, but that wouldn't do for him. The withholding of a promotion yet again was too much a slap in the face, the last one he would tolerate. He'd decided to move back to Cincinnati instead; open up a bar with Dale Rousseau, a childhood buddy.

Nothing was mentioned of 'us' in the wake of this news. Of course, we'd never had any formal agreement to be exclusive. But I wasn't seeing anyone else. I didn't know if he was, didn't really want to know; though after a few months I'd grown to seeing him often enough that I'd have to wonder when he'd have had the time. And we had discussed *once* the big question of whether he should move in with me. In the end he only moved in a toothbrush and a few pair of skivvies and we called it good enough for the time being.

Our relationship was still sufficiently casual that I'd not *too* often considered a permanent future with him; but that was before this—before our options had dissolved. By May he'd be out—gone! I'd no great yearning to live in Cincinnati—and he hadn't asked besides! So that would be that.

He delivered this distressing news as we were sitting in 'our' booth at the Village Green in my little town. It's one of the two aforementioned good restaurants, in this case more a pub. It has a cosy atmosphere, is on the way home from the office, and I know all of the folks who work there. My mother grew up with the owner and half their clientele. But even without that connection, it was the most 'homey' place for miles, and possessed those other qualities to promote a local haunt: good food, good drink, fair prices and a really cosy, warm atmosphere. Oh, and several television screens for those games that just can't be missed! (football, basketball, baseball, curling. Even *Jeopardy!* and *Dancing with the Stars*.)

As I absorbed what Jack was telling me, I couldn't look at him, so I glanced towards the back dining room from where a few patrons were emerging. They were making their way toward the exit but the one in the rear stopped when he saw me. *Oh, great! Complete my bad day!*

"Good evening," he said, inclining his head, his comportment stiff.

"Colonel," I replied. He remained but said nothing else; only continued to regard me in a peculiar manner. It unnerved me. I gestured towards Jack. "Do you know...?"

He flicked a casual glance over to Jack before turning to stone. They eyed one another. Emotion rose quickly up Jack's face, suffusing it with ruddiness; even as the Colonel's drained in apparent contempt. Neither spoke. Finally, Jack recovered enough to sneer, *"Sir."*

The colonel barely managed a nod, remaining immobile until a waitress needed to get past. Then he turned to me abruptly, offered a hasty 'good night' and moved off; leaving me open-mouthed and bewildered.

"How the hell do you know *him*?" asked Jack. His eyes narrowed. "And how well?"

"Lieutenant Colonel Douglas? Only slightly, but as much as I ever want to. We've been thrown together to work Senior Conference this spring. He is superior, obnoxious and arrogant...has acted from the start like I couldn't possibly be competent to work alongside him."

Jack laughed. "Sweetie, don't you know your place? You're a mere civilian," he said, raising the age-old prejudice. "What could you possibly know to work that level of conference? Edward Douglas takes himself and everyone else seriously. He's the son and grandson of highly decorated generals. His dad was Storm Douglas – 'Raging Storm,' Class of '64." He puffed up his chest as he said the name, parodying the news anchormen who so often resurrected the man in their military reporting. "For Christ's sake, who do you think Douglas Auditorium here is named after?" Jack snickered.

"So? I'm the daughter of a decorated Colonel, Class of '72. And I've spent *my* career working for the Army. So far we're equal."

Jack snorted. "Not in his eyes. His family's a dynasty, Army royalty. It stands alone. It doesn't help that his mother's family –

she was English – goes back to the Norman Conquest, 1066 and all that." His pique softened and he took my hand, offered me his most beguiling grin. "Don't let it rattle you – no one's good enough for him."

"I feel sorry for his wife," I said, grumbling.

"Doesn't have one, not anymore. He married the daughter of some friend of his aunt or something, *from a good family in Rhode Island*; in other words, face like a horse." He laughed. "But he divorced her after a few years; she couldn't live up to his exacting standards."

He signalled the waitress and ordered more drinks. Curiosity got the better of me.

"So, obviously, there's something between *you* and Lieutenant Colonel Douglas, too. What is it?"

"It's an old grudge, of long standing. In fact, he's the real reason I was passed over twice. We were friends once, good ones. We met as plebes in our first year here in fact and roomed together last couple years. Then our careers brought us together again as Captains. At least, I *thought* we were friends; certainly it was there on my side – until he screwed me with our Battalion Commander. We were of the same year-group, both held company commands under 'Punch' Lewis."

"Stanley Lewis? The posthumous medal of honor winner?"

"Yeah, he was our Tac first when he was a Captain here; Ned Douglas and I were always at his house, became practically his sons. Then as a Lieutenant Colonel, he was battalion commander of 10th Group when we served with him. And we were in good with him. Lewis tagged us his rising stars, 'forces of nature.' Our companies, they consistently out-performed all others. We were on the fast track for promotion, both of us. Lewis couldn't say enough about how good we made him look."

"What happened?"

"The old man gave Charlie Company a mission—high visibility, it was a real chance to prove myself. Douglas was pissed he didn't get it, though he didn't have the guts to say so openly. Instead, he made underhanded comments about it being too big a job for me; after all, I was limited. I didn't have the grounding in military tactics that he had inherited, apparently. Wasn't a former star man or a Cadet Brigade staffer. Hell, my dad was a back woods lawyer. I only ended up at the academy because he couldn't afford to send me to civilian college."

"What happened with the mission, with Douglas's whining?"

"The old man didn't listen to him. Which rankled him even more. Lewis loved us both but he talked more to me—said he never knew quite what Douglas was thinking; but me, I'm an open book. But he could see Douglas's motive in his arguments—he was jealous."

"So you got the mission?"

"Yeah, I got it. And it failed. *I failed*; lost two soldiers in a stupid accident I had no way to anticipate. And Douglas was all over it. Bravo Company came riding in, saved the day, and then he was the first one at the after-action hearings to point fingers at me for the losses. He was so quick to jump on it all, almost as if he knew exactly what would happen. You'll never convince me he didn't sabotage that raid. I'd have been out on my keister then and there if Lewis hadn't still had some liking for me, he saved my bacon. Then Lewis was killed not long after. I had to rely on Douglas to set the record straight, it's certainly what Lewis wanted—we were both with him when he died. Only Douglas didn't, wouldn't. He threw me under the biggest damn bus you ever saw."

"That was the start of Douglas's meteoric rise, though; he made rank below the zones to both Major *and* L-T-C. The ultimate gentleman warrior! But my officer efficiency reports were dismal. Took me two Boards to pin on Major's leaves, and I've been battling uphill ever since. I turned around, for all it matters. No more dumb-ass mistakes. I'm a *good officer* but my record doesn't reflect it. Because of *him*." This last he spat out.

I squeezed his hand reassuringly. "Did you ever confront him over it?"

He shrugged it off. "Nah—sucked it up like a man. Lewis thought too well of both his Captains, and I respected *him* too much as my mentor to sully his memory by engaging in a public feud with Ned. I'll leave screwing people's careers to those who have the stomach for it. But thanks to Douglas's spite those years ago, I can't get a break. He's had them all."

Jack downed his drink and changed the subject then, suggesting it was water under the bridge; he was ready for a change of scene anyway. I couldn't get the image of Colonel Douglas out of my mind – standing there by the table, ramrod straight, a look of sheer loathing as he met Jack's eye. I could well believe all that Jack had told me and more of the colonel's ruthless ambition and spiteful conduct. Jack and I went to my place, but between my disappointment at Jack's leaving in only a few months, and the memories our encounter with LTC Douglas had dredged up, our mood had dampened considerably.

ξ

Isn't it funny how you don't recognize a book plot while you're living it?

ξ

It was the day after Jack left for good that I was in such a funk at the office. I was still fuming over the injustice of it all; especially as he had shown me during our last night together a photograph of the bar he and his friend had taken over. Dale Rousseau was standing in front of it proudly pointing to the sign above the door. Turns out Jack's high school 'buddy' was a voluptuous blond woman, all white teeth, short skirt, high hair and higher heels. And still Jack had made no suggestion that our own relationship might survive our separation. The best I'd gotten was a quick "I'll call you" as he slipped out my front door for the last time.

So when Colonel Douglas called me at work the following day, I was in no mood to entertain him. I was quite proud of myself; I held it together through the conversation even as I seethed inside. And the odd thing was, as I thought about it later, I had no clue why the man even called me. Most of it was silence, punctuated here and there with some inane platitudes. He may have mentioned the senior conference, but certainly there was nothing in it that required coordination. And there was no other reason on earth I could divine that we should be in contact. Was it possible the man had called just to chat? I could hardly believe *that* of him.

I ran into the colonel several times over the next weeks at official functions. He condescended to talk to me, but I didn't prolong conversation more than necessary. I stopped short of rudeness, it wasn't in my nature; but I couldn't forget what I knew of him. I was shocked, therefore, when one day about two months after Jack had gone, I stood to leave the Senior Conference opening reception and someone suddenly was holding my wrap for me. I turned to find LTC Douglas. He walked me to my car even; asked if I'd have dinner with him that Friday.

I'm not too proud to admit I lost it. This guy had driven Jack away. I told him just what I thought, accusing him of all the things Jack had been too gentlemanlike to say, and a few more besides. Growing paler by the word as I ran out of steam, he only apologized for taking my time when I'd done, and walked away, 'ramrod straight'.

The next morning, I shared this with a colleague, incensed at the man's nerve. At lunchtime, she came in and placed a folder on my desk. It was the official transcript of that botched mission that had derailed Jack's career. She had researched it for me; urged me to read it. I pushed it aside stubbornly, but at length curiosity got the better of me.

I'd been wrong, totally misled. Edward Douglas actually tried to mitigate his friend's accountability in the awful events that had occurred; likely had succeeded to some degree or Jack would have been decommissioned right then. Afterward he still supported Jack personally, even when subsequent hard evidence pointed to gross negligence in leadership by CPT Williams during the mission's execution. Furthermore, Douglas's quick remedial actions had *saved* the lives of several soldiers who might otherwise have perished due to the negligence. The report cited as well that this had not been the first incident involving CPT Williams's poor judgment; but it didn't elaborate further.

Paper-clipped to the report was a newspaper blurb dated less than a year later concerning Edward Douglas's divorce. It cited long-standing and flagrant infidelities on the part of Nancy Douglas with a fellow officer of her husband, one John Quincy Williams.

The reports mortified me. I thought of nothing else for three days, feeling completely foolish, losing sleep over my unwarranted behaviour towards Ned Douglas. Finally, mustering all the resolve I could, I picked up the phone. How I managed to apologize I can't say – memory fails trying to recall my exact words. But I remember his well enough, few as they were. They were long in coming – I began to wonder if he was still on the line – but when he finally spoke, he simply said "thank you."

And then he asked me out again.

During that first dinner, Ned admitted I was the only person he'd been truly interested in since his divorce. He'd dated little since; he'd never been good with women and his painful marriage experience had made him less secure. He knew he could come off as cold, but it was only that he never knew what to say precisely. From what he *had* said at that point, and his demeanour in doing so, I suspected his aloof temperament was also a defence mechanism against being hurt again.

He was much more confident in work situations, he said, where he trusted his capabilities. Talk about me feeling like a heel – but he wouldn't let me criticize myself. He was a true officer and gentleman.

On our next date, I learned he'd never read Jane Austen, but had seen the latest *Pride and Prejudice* film while sitting captive on a West Coast flight. He'd expected it to be similar to *Jane Eyre*, which he'd been forced to read in high school and detested for its melodrama. But he'd been pleasantly surprised to enjoy this film, despite his predisposition. He was willing to delve further, if I'd recommend a book to start.

I did, of course. I started him on *Pride and Prejudice*. And he's now read them all, and obliged me through all the films and mini-series, at least once.

But though we've *both* come to admire Jane Austen, the words of that *other* author are more applicable to close here... 'Reader, I married him.'

Pinker Heaven

ঔঔঔ

This little bonus offering is pure fantasy. It was borne of a weekend gathering at my place. We had met through an online forum, members collectively known as Pinkers (a contraction of the website name where we formed our close friendships) and we share a passion for Jane Austen. We had crammed all together into my little house for four days of revelry. We all shared also an appreciation of the 2005 film version of <u>Pride and Prejudice</u>. We had watched the film all together at my place the evening before. And since my bed for the duration was the living room couch and I tend to be a very early riser anyway, this little fantasy floated into my head the next morning as the rest of the house lay quiet.

Whether you praise or decry the merits of that particular film adaptation or fall somewhere in between, if you have ever held a soft spot in your heart for Mr Darcy – however you picture him – I suspect you may also find a smile or two within what follows. Although this one may physically resemble a particular actor in his features, this story celebrates the <u>singular</u> character of Mr Darcy we each love in some manner, as well as the power of an author and a book to unite people in friendship. (Note: Names have been changed to protect the innocent.)

ঔঔঔ

I opened my eyes and squinted at the clock on the DVD-player across the room – 6:10. A bit early given our revelling the night before, but I knew I wouldn't fall asleep again; may as well get up and clear the bed linens from the sofa, maybe work my online crossword puzzles before the others awoke for the day. I stretched my legs to get the stiffness out, sat up and rubbed my face. My cheeks and jaw held a bit of stiffness as well – still sore from laughing continually for the past two days.

Today promised more of the same, I was sure. All seven of us were getting along famously, had done since that first 'official' moment of my meeting Marilyn at the local airport, the first arrival. Though the fact of our collective rapport had not been unanticipated, still it was a satisfaction to know our expectations had not been disappointed. It had been quite funny: each new arrival on Thursday – and culminating on Friday when Josh delivered Sally – had been heralded by escalating shrieks of recognition followed closely on by unabridged laughter and chatter. We had introduced ourselves (such a nonsensical word given our long-held e-friendships), opened all our gifts, marvelled at the gorgeous dresses Robin had created for each of us and how well the accessories and accoutrements contributed by all complemented the gowns to form a complete Regency ensemble. We had celebrated Tammy's birthday, watched DVD's (both laughing and crying our way through *Cranford,*) and roared as we reached for "The Book" to record the latest Pinker witticism or double entendre.

Now, this afternoon, we would complete our physical transformation into Regency Ladies (there was little hope for our decorum as "ladies" to judge by a review of the entries in The Book) and gather to record our time travel on film for posterity. It was to be an activity ripe for more laughter, no question.

Contemplating the day to come with a smile, I stood finally and made my way to the loo. When I came out I noted the doors to the bedrooms still half-shut, the rooms still darkened by drawn shades, and a light snore emerging from some one, I couldn't tell exactly who or even which room – perhaps more than one of my friends engaged in the lullaby. I smiled and headed off to the kitchen, rinsing and refilling the coffee maker, then putting down some fresh food for the cat – wondering idly where Fergie had gotten to when he'd left my narrow sofa sometime in the night.

I padded back into the living room then and saw him, asleep on his afghan atop the corner of the desk under the front window, so I went to wish him a good morning. He stretched lazily as I smoothed the fur on his belly and he started to purr in that strange "snuffling" way of his; but he never opened his eyes – too early still to start the day, I supposed. I glanced at the clock again – 6:20.

I was just reconsidering my own decision to be up for the day when I glanced up from the cat and out the window. The sun was still low in the sky but offered promise of a good day. A light hazy fog hung low over the ground and the houses across the street, the mist meandering up from the river as the cold of the water met the warming air temperatures. I always call that low-hanging vapour "dragon's breath." Surely it would burn off as the morning progressed; but for the moment it held an ethereal, dreamy quality, a kind of peaceful interlude to ease me quietly into the day before the usual weekend business of the neighbourhood roared into life... dog-walking, lawn seeding, whatnot... not to mention several Pinkers still high on the experience of finally meeting face-to-face.

The cat chirruped as he curled his body in around the hand I'd left idly caressing his soft belly-fur, and I looked down at him as he opened one eye in acknowledgment of my affections and then shut it tightly again. When I glanced back out the window, then, I froze in place. The scene before me was the same it had been a moment before but for one addition. There appeared to be a man... a rather tall man... approaching through the mist from the direction of the river bank.

Despite the haze, I could tell it was neither of the neighbours who lived in the houses between which the man strode languidly – one of those being a swarthy Italian whose girth exceeded his length; and the other a gentleman in his late sixties, what little hair remaining to him decidedly silver. This man was neither of those things. He was, as I'd noted initially, quite tall, and very well apportioned – erect bearing, broad shoulders, a solid but shapely build, and a full head of dark hair curling slightly on his forehead and around the nape of his neck. He appeared, moreover, to be dressed in something other than 21st century attire – a loose open-necked linen shirt, breeches and boots, and a well-worn (and worn well) great coat. Yep, definitely a *great* coat!—that swayed seductively in rhythm to his gait.

Immediately, I laughed at my folly. I returned my attentions to the cat and said, "I think I drank one too many Cosmos last night, Fergs! I'm imagining things!" Fergie ignored me (excusable since, being deaf, he could not hear my exclamation.) I took my gaze back to the window to prove it a flight of fancy, and this time, blinked rapidly in succession. The hazy figure was still there! Although he took steps in the direction of my house, I realized he made no progress, never approaching closer but caught in some holographic form of suspended animation. I shook my head violently from side to side and chided myself. *This is impossible!*

I felt my head then, running my hands over my hair and my cheeks. I didn't *feel* any particular effects of my drinks the night before: no headache, nor ringing in my ears; no aches or pains beyond those customarily encountered on waking. So why was I hallucinating? Why was Mr Darcy – for I could surmise my apparition to be no one else given his general appearance – walking towards me without ever advancing?

I blamed Ellen's painting, sitting on its display easel just to the right of me. The scene outside so closely resembled it but for the houses on either side that I must have glanced at the watercolour when I walked over to the window and, given the misty morning outdoors, conjured up what I would instinctively have wished to see. I looked again at the small canvas, appreciating how the soft pink and blue of the background captured the early morning light of the piece and showcased by its contrast the shadowy figure of the gentleman walking through a field.

Ah, the power of art! I had heard of people in museums and such staring for so long at a painting that they experienced a feeling of entering into the scene depicted there – but I had never considered that I could in turn transport a scene to my own front yard! *Well, if that is indeed what has happened,* I determined, *then I'm going to enjoy this mirage for as long as it lasts...*

I reverted to the scene outside the windows, only to find that now that I had chosen to appreciate it while I could, the situation had altered once again. Instead of marching in place, Mr Darcy was now actually moving towards me, slowly emerging from the mist until he reached the edge of the road that separated us. There he stopped and, to my surprise, looked both ways before stepping onto the pavement to cross.

I found my own feet moving only seconds later, taking me out my front door into the yard, some part of me certain that by the time I arrived there, the mesmerizing scene would have disappeared. Once again, to my total delight, I was wrong. I stepped down off the porch as Mr Darcy entered the flagstone walk and an instant later, we met in the middle; oddly enough just at the location of one stone that Sally had pointed out the night before as resembling Darcy's profile in its shape. I confess I did not remove my gaze from my visitor to glance at the stone for verification of the resemblance. I was afraid the dream would vanish.

"Good morning, Mr Darcy," I said, part of me wondering where I had found the presence of mind to speak, indeed to even stand before him.

"Good morning, Miss --- er, forgive me. Undoubtedly you are acquainted with me, but I have not had the pleasure of prior introduction..."

"Teg," I answered softly, enthralled at the prospect of those rich deep tones pronouncing *my* name.

"Miss Teg," he finished, accented by a somewhat quizzical nod at the name, while my legs turned to jelly.

"No!" I replied. "Just 'Teg'. No 'Miss'... I mean..." I was flustered *now*, the enormity of this extraordinary meeting finally pressing upon me.

"Ah, yes! Teg, then. I had forgotten that society has 'progressed' to using given names and diminutives among even those of little or no acquaintance."

I nodded, mute and, I am certain, looking as dumbfounded as I felt.

"Well, then," he continued: "Tell me, Teg, to what year have you brought me?"

"...brought you?"

"I am grown quite accustomed to these occasional forays now. I believe my last summoning was in... hmmm, 1995? That one lasted a fortnight or more! No, there was one other not long after, though that was but a hazy glimpse that was reversed in an instant." He looked around him. "As the buildings and carriages... er, automobiles, you call them?... look little altered from the year 1995, may I presume not too great a period has transpired since then?"

"Ummm..." I could not proceed. This was all just *too* bizarre.

"Ah," said Mr Darcy yet again, nodding his head with sagacity. "This response is not unknown to me. I have encountered it before on occasion. I believe you experience some confusion as to my appearing here, do not you?"

I managed to nod, even as my knees started buckling beneath me. To my credit, as I felt myself falling, my gaze never wavered from the gentleman's face. Quickly, Mr Darcy moved to catch me, taking hold of my arm with one hand and, with the other, encircling my waist to help me stand once more. "Perhaps, ... Teg... a cup of tea is in order? A good strong brew sure to settle you? Have you any provisions for that libation?"

I nodded weakly.

"I shall be happy to explain my understanding of this phenomenon to you while you regain your equanimity with a restorative cup."

I rallied as best I could. "Yes, yes I do have tea. And I believe it might help me to sit down as well."

"Of course."

His arm still around my waist to guide me, we retraced my earlier steps and entered the house, whereupon (to my disappointment) he released me as I led the way into the kitchen. Mr Darcy had only taken a few steps through the front hall when a looking glass to one side caught his notice and he slowed to glance into it, then stopped completely and faced it to study his reflection.

"Ah, so that is my form now!"

"Your form? Do you mean, you don't know what you look like?"

"Well, you see, it seems to change somewhat every time! Quite disconcerting actually." I must have shown my disbelief at this, so he quickly said, "But come, we shall make tea first. Then I will explain everything to you, or at least as much as I comprehend."

He spared one last glance in the mirror as we moved on again, straightening and raising an eyebrow in what I took to be approval of his appearance, and into the kitchen we went.

"Mmm, the delightful aroma of coffee," he said, closing his eyes and inhaling deeply.

"Yes, it is only just made. Would you care for a cup?"

"I would indeed, I thank you. But first, a tea for the lady!" He looked about him as if he would perform the service for me in my weakened state, but could see no familiar objects for the proper brewing of the beverage.

I laughed (softly, of course, so as to provide no offence) and reached for the water kettle. Darcy watched with curiosity as I filled it, placed it on the electric heating element base, and flipped the 'on' switch, drawing another eyebrow raising from him. Then I grabbed my china teapot and two clean mugs from the dishwasher I had yet to empty from the night before. I placed loose tea in the pot, and poured coffee into one of the mugs. I had recovered myself enough to ask, "Do you take anything in your coffee, Sir? Cream? Sugar?"

"No, I do not. Just as it is will be perfectly adequate." He accepted the mug, raised it slightly in acknowledgment, and took a long sip. "Ah, far more than adequate, Teg; it is long since I have tasted coffee so finely brewed."

I blushed and covered my embarrassment by pouring water over my tea and getting out the cream and Splenda for it. As I moved about the kitchen, Darcy took another sip, then raised his mug to look at it.

"What shall I call you when I am *cross*?" he said; and I promptly dropped the container of cream on the floor.

"Wh...What?" I knelt to retrieve the carton which, thankfully, had been nearly empty and had not spilled, only splashed a trickle of drops around.

"Oh, forgive me, madam. I was simply reading the words on the beaker! I did not mean... surely you must know... that I am not the least bit *cross* with you?"

Sigh. That word again. Though the final scenes in the American version of the movie (which undoubtedly influenced this encounter) were not wholly to my liking, still I sighed every time I heard Mr Darcy pronounce that word for some reason in his silky, low voice. Shakily, I got back up from my knees now, though not before stealing a glimpse of Mr Darcy's calves clad in boots of rich, supple leather. I steadied myself against the kitchen counter a moment. "No, no. I am sorry. It is only... your voice... that phrase... oh, dear, I am afraid I could not explain it sufficiently to you without humiliating myself further. But it's fine, really it is."

Graciously, he asked nothing further. I turned around then, finished preparing my tea while my overly warm cheeks and colour faded a little. I started to pour tea into my mug only to wonder suddenly which one I had grabbed for myself. Glancing down at it, I was relieved to find I had not chosen 'Mrs Darcy' – that might be a hard one to explain! Instead, I began to giggle a bit when I realized I held 'Are you having a... pleasant trip?' and had I been more secure in my faculties, I might have asked him to read that one as well!

"Shall we..." "Are you..." We both spoke at once. Darcy nodded to defer to me, and I invited him to join me in the living room, hoping it had not been left in too dishevelled a condition the night before. I had this sudden wild urge to go running about the room, hiding stray litter in drawers and under cushions – but thankfully maintained enough sanity to realize that it would serve no good purpose as Mr Darcy was already there in the room with me. Fortunately, we had sort of picked it up the night before. As he made to take a place on the sofa, he looked quite naturally at the fireplace and did a double-take at the sizable canvas leaning against the wall on the mantle.

"Is that...?"

"Yes. It is you. Or rather, it is a photograph I took of a bust of an actor who portrayed you. You do resemble it very much in your face; but your build is different than his."

"My build?"

"Yes, your... form, your..." I realised I was starting to babble, and stopped again, discomposed. Paused. Felt the need to close this particular conversation. "It resides at Chatsworth in Derbyshire. My friends had it printed on canvas and gave it to me as a gift."

"How extraordinary! I am from Derbyshire myself, do you know? I am well acquainted with this fine estate, Chatsworth, it lies but six miles from my own." He studied the photograph a moment, then walked back to the mirror in the hallway and studied himself, returning again to the canvas. "A fair likeness, I would say."

"Very fair!" I replied, then blushed yet again at the multiple meanings.

Finally, Mr Darcy sat on the sofa, and I perched myself precariously on the red velvet armchair to his left.

"Mr Darcy," I began. "Can you explain to me, please, what is happening?"

"Yes, I can and will do so." He smiled at me with some empathy, and I tried to keep my concentration. I had never in my life swooned before today and here I was in danger of it for the second time in half an hour!

"I regret that I cannot explain the 'science' behind it, if you will, as I myself do not comprehend fully the laws of physical existence that can allow of this anomaly. The first several occasions I experienced took me very much by surprise – I will go so far as to say I was astounded and disoriented. But it seems every now and again I find myself pulled irresistibly from my own life amidst the pages of *Pride and Prejudice*, and plunketed down into a strange world of the future. Or at least what is the future to my thinking!"

"Every now and again? How often has this happened to you?"

"I cannot count perhaps more than three dozen or so incidents; and each of varying duration. One instant I am going about my day, and the next I feel myself being rather enveloped by a ... well, I can only describe it as a miasma, a 'shimmering' of warm air for such is what it feels... and thereafter as it fades, I find my surroundings have completely rearranged themselves. Gone are my familiar rooms and friends or relations, and in their place could stand a foreign room, a stable yard, a field, a pond..."

"How frightening!"

"Blasted terrifying the first few times, I confess!" He laughed now, though, quite in good spirits and showing no signs at all of discomfort. "The first time it lasted but a moment, and I was able to convince myself it had been a dream. I recall I was sitting with Bingley and his sisters. Miss Bingley had just made mention of some new fashion or the like she was reading of, I scarcely paid her any attention; when this odd tingling sensation – this shimmering as it were – was felt in my chest and grew within me until no part of me was untouched by it. I closed my eyes a moment to will away the sensation and, upon opening them again, found myself in a parlour of sorts, nothing like the drawing room at Netherfield I had occupied before closing them.

"As I struggled to understand what was transpiring, I heard someone exclaim 'It worked!' and I looked round to find five women standing all about, their attentions transfixed upon me. When my head stopped spinning enough to ask the meaning of it all, the shimmering overcame me once more, I blinked my eyes and an instant later was back sitting at Netherfield. Miss Bingley still droned on, and I simply surmised that I had dozed off in her company and had imagined the entire episode."

"But then it happened again?"

"Yes, shortly after that first instance, while sitting in my own library at Pemberley, the sensation came over me yet again. On this occasion I was transported to the stable of an estate in Hampshire, as I later discovered; where a young woman sat clutching a worn copy of *Pride and Prejudice* to her bosom and staring in quite reasonable alarum at my sudden appearance there. She very nearly experienced an hysterical fit.

"After some time – I am uncertain as yet how it was accomplished – we grew able to speak with one another, and I learnt that it was the year 1884. Some *eighty or more years* in the future! You might imagine my disbelief. I should have thought she sported with me but for her own alarumed condition when I appeared. The young lady could only explain that she had read Miss Austen's book from cover to cover several times in succession, had felt a strong passion to meet for herself such a man as I, and could explain no further how that eventuality came to pass.

She was able, however, over the three days I remained sequestered in the stable, to provide me with food and, more importantly, with news. I was astonished to find she had not prevaricated regarding the year – each newspaper she brought me showed the truth of it. And such news! I was astonished! Little could I know that in future even greater amazements awaited me than train travel, telegraphs, typewriting machines, phonographs and electric lighting. It was enough to wish myself back in my own time!"

I was enthralled by the story Mr Darcy was relating (not to mention mesmerized by the masculine, deep voice, the accent, his use of language, and those acetylene blue eyes trained upon me) but nonetheless to my embarrassment, a yawn escaped me. He quickly summarized.

"On the third day, as we sat discussing how I might try to enter society – as neither knew how to bring about my return and I could not remain in the stables forever – the shimmering began once more and moments later, I was home in my library. I hurried to find my sister –"

"Georgiana," I interjected.

"Indeed – certain to find her distressed over my disappearance, only to find I had been restored at exactly the moment I had departed. I spoke of this to no one. How could I have convinced them of the fact of my fanciful travel... indeed when I could not fully convince myself? Twice more in the next days I experienced such transposition. I once attempted to carry with me a relic of the future on a return, as much to convince myself I was not running mad. But on that occasion, the shimmering sensation escalated to nearly unbearable intensity without taking me any where; until in desperation I threw down the object and was immediately transported home."

"But how did you convince yourself they were not delusions?"

He laughed. "Miss..., er, Teg, I do not possess the abundance of imagination wanted, I think, to create the wonders I have witnessed! Could I conjure vehicles that fly a man to different continents in a matter of hours? Little boxes, or for that matter entire large walls with moving images such as that?" – he pointed to my television –

"Impossible! My thoughts, my feelings, for the most part, come from the pen of a lady who is deceased these five years... more to you, even... and certainly knew nothing of such things. And the alternative, that I have developed a madness – well, it is unthinkable, unacceptable to me. Ergo, these journeys must be real."

Sounded logical to me – well, as logical as the situation could allow.

"Over these months past, I have made the transformation some three dozen times. On each occasion, the years have advanced – the last, as I have made reference, being 1995 or thereabouts. But yet always I am returned to the same moment in my own life from which I departed. Most extraordinary! "

"And still you don't know *why* these leaps happen?"

"Indeed I do not. I have surmised, and believe I am correct, that conditions become supportive of this 'leap' as you call it, when my creator's novel goes through a period of unprecedented popularity, in combination with a concentrated emotional charge which generates then a cross-temporal magnetic pull. This much I have deduced with the knowledge gleaned from each successive episode I have experienced."

"But – is that really possible?"

"I would have said not, Miss Teg. And yet, I would also have asserted most violently in my own era that it is impossible for a man to travel to the moon!"

I noticed that he stretched his long legs out in front of him and flexed his foot.

"Would you like to remove your boots, Mr Darcy, and get comfortable?"

"Oh, no! It would be unseemly for me to do so, I could not."

"It is not unseemly at all in this age. You see, I have no covering on my feet. It is nothing now to slip one's shoes off when one enters the house; and since we don't know how long you may be here, you may as well be comfortable." Without his asking, I took his mug from him and went into the kitchen, returning a moment later with a fresh cup of coffee for which he thanked me.

Darcy hesitated, and then asked, "And what year did you say I was brought into?"

"2008."

"2008? Good heavens – a new millennia entirely!" He sat a moment pondering this information when I was surprised to see him smile and he chuckled. "Well, then, perhaps I might release my feet from their confinement for some little while – they have been encased in these boots some 200 years or more!"

He placed his coffee cup on the table and reached down to remove a boot, and I watched in fascination as he worked it very slowly down his leg, the fit being so perfectly moulded to the leg that it did not slide with ease. At the last instant that it cleared his foot, he smiled and sighed, his toes wiggling at their new-found freedom. Another moment and, without thinking, I had knelt down to pull off the remaining boot for him. He opened his mouth to protest, but I smiled complacently at him and he reconsidered, sitting back and allowing me to assume the customary role of his valet.

"Well, then. Two thousand and eight! May I presume that Miss Austen has reached a peculiar popularity of late?"

"Yes, very much so. *Pride and Prejudice* was released as a film a couple of years ago, and just of late her remaining novels have been produced for television. She is more popular now than ever."

"Mmm. Certainly that marries well with my hypothesis. I conclude from your own disconcerted greeting of me that this is your first such incident, is it not?"

I nodded vigorously. I still could not believe that Mr Darcy – Mr Fitz-chuffing-william Darcy himself – was sitting in my living room drinking coffee pretty as you please and discussing this aberration of the universe as though it was a common occurrence. About that time I also realized that I was still kneeling on the floor in front of him. If I looked directly straight ahead, I was met with the sight of his calves... deliciously long, shapely, well-muscled, masculine calves – no need of padding there – and I suddenly felt quite warm. I also felt quite self-conscious. I mean, here I was in my pyjama bottoms and oversized tee-shirt, my hair uncombed. I must look a fright to the poor man! But as he was taking it all in stride, I felt I should try to do the same.

Resisting with effort an urge to reach out and stroke a manly calf, I got up again, and took the chair next to him once more. But when just after, he flexed the newly emancipated leg it just seemed a natural thing to do; so I reached out to direct it onto my lap. I began to massage his muscles just behind the ankle.

"Miss...er, Teg... I..." he started with something of astonishment in his tone, a demurral on his lips. Then, "ah, well, I must accept that you have different notions of propriety in your century than those to which I am accustomed. I must place myself in your hands, so to speak, on matters of decorum." When I smiled and assured him we did nothing improper – he would not have to marry me for this infraction – he shrugged and deposited his other leg in my lap as well. "I must confess to a tightness in this one area," was all he said, pointing to his right calf, and so we settled in, he comfortably ensconced on the sofa, his legs resting across my lap and me happily tending to his calves while we continued our conversation.

"Do you know, I have always wondered if Miss Austen's other characters have experienced these 'leaps.' It is quite possible, I suppose, that they have done and, like me, are reluctant to discuss their experience for fear of being considered to have lost their minds."

"Somehow, Mr Darcy, I doubt it."

"Why is that? On what do you base such a conclusion?"

"Well, you see...," I began, unsure how confident I was of my information. But after all, this was probably just a crazy dream I was having that I myself would wake from at any moment, so why not play it out? "You do know that you *are* Miss Austen's favourite hero?"

"Am I indeed? A hero? I would not have thought myself anything of the like. And I was Miss Austen's favourite at that?"

"Oh, I don't know, though I venture to say you were when she wrote her book. After all, as a child, she did write her name in her father's parish registry with fictitious marriage banns to a gentleman called "Fitzwilliam" so I suspect she may have spent years perfecting your qualities in her mind before setting pen to paper."

"How extraordinary."

"But what I meant to say was that you seem to be a favourite with Miss Austen's *readers* and the ladies who see the films adapted from the novel. Many of them – many of *us* – recognize in you some sterling qualities and we come to... admire you... esteem you..." Oh, dear, I thought, in for a penny, in for a pound. "...love you."

"Surely not!"

"Well, at least love what you stand for in our hearts. A good man, handsome and desirable," (I noted he sat a little taller and squared his shoulders at this even as he blushed,) "and committed to caring for the people you love in turn. It is a heady combination, and so many ladies hold you up as an exemplar of a man, one whom they dream of having a relationship with..."

"I assure you, Teg, I am not without my faults! They have been most decidedly pointed out to me in recent months." Mr Darcy blushed deeply now, but was interested despite his discomfort.

"Oh, yes, I know." To this he started a bit. "But even those faults when they are under regulation may be understood as the natural human frailties of a good man. It makes you more real that you are not perfect. And, well, Miss Austen's other heroes just do not carry that same intensity, except possibly Captain Wentworth or Mr Knightley."

"Wentworth? Would that be Frederick Wentworth of Sussex? I have heard of the gentleman."

"It would, yes. I believe *Persuasion* to be Miss Austen's second favourite novel after yours, or rather her readers' second favourite, and Captain Wentworth has been known to cause hearts to flutter as well. But perhaps not to the degree, or rather in the numbers, that you seem to do. I do not believe the book is read quite as often as yours."

"I have not the talent to travel between novels to inquire of the good Captain if he has experienced these sojourns himself, nor the other gentleman you name. As such I will have to content myself with presuming I stand alone in them. But I thank you for your explanation. It offers a possible answer to a question that I have long pondered, of *why* I seem to be chosen for these incidents. I cannot claim superior knowledge of my worth in the opinions you express, but it pleases me to know I am spoken of well." I had to stifle a smile as he adopted a smug mien – just a little smugness, and it looked good on him.

All this while, I had been tending to Mr Darcy's calves and, once he got past his initial surprise and discomfort, he appeared to enjoy the exercise as much as I did. "I must tell you, Teg, you have a light, restorative touch – you have much relieved my fatigue, and I thank you."

"Well," I blurted out unthinking, "they don't call me 'Keeper of the Calves' for nothing!"

"I do not understand, 'Keeper of the... Calves'? Have you a farm here?"

I was mortified at my slip of the tongue. But I tried to laugh it off. "Oh, no, it is just a silly title of no real meaning, given to me by my friends. It would take too long to explain its derivation."

How could I begin to explain to him websites, and forums, and usernames and the like, when I barely understood enough to manoeuvre through them? But having mentioned my forum designator, I also suddenly recollected the six Pinkers who were at that moment sleeping in my home. I was about to mention them and tell Mr Darcy that I must wake them to share this experience with me, when the gentleman, who had been looking around at photographs of my family about the room, returned his gaze to the one of his bust on my mantle.

"May I ask you to confirm, perhaps, Teg, that my present countenance corresponds somewhat with that of the gentleman who portrayed me in this film you speak of, that it was he who sat for that bust?"

"Yes, it does correspond, at least your face and your voice somewhat. The actor's name is Matthew Macfadyen."

"And he is a handsome man by your account?"

"Very much so," I assured Mr Darcy, before asking that my own curiosity be satisfied. "So truly you find yourself looking different every time you make these leaps?"

"I presume so. I cannot speak for the earliest incidents, I was not privy to viewing my likeness then. But I have appeared in the guise of several gentlemen over time apparently. I first saw my image during one of these leaps in 1938, I believe it was. It was remarkably different from what I encounter in my own glass at home. And yet I felt no different. Then, in 1940, a different likeness altogether again, and I was shorter by several inches that time! It gave me to wonder if the ladies who conjured me were doing so in the form in which *they* perceived me."

"I am sure you are correct. Or more precisely, they perceived you in the form of the actor who portrayed you on the television or in the cinema in which you caught their attention. Or perhaps in the form they have carried in their imagination from their first reading of the novel."

"Precisely. I see we are in accord in this. I have often wondered if I would remain myself during these journeys had Miss Austen spared greater detail in describing her characters."

I laughed.

"And so, you envision me as this gentleman?" he asked as he pointed to the photo.

"I do sometimes now, yes."

He looked at me quizzically then, so I proceeded to tell him of a brief period in the eighties when I saw David Rintoul in the role, but that didn't last long, didn't quite feel 'right'; before I reverted to my own imaginative sketch of him. And then from the mid-nineties until 2005, whenever I read the book or thought of him – a fact, by the way, that he felt the need to detour and discuss, my penchant for rereading the book and thinking of him regularly – I had a somewhat different image in mind. A gentleman with curlier hair, and darker eyes, but still quite handsome if perhaps a bit older as well.

"Ah, I believe I know this man... or rather, have indeed donned his image at some point. Would that be my countenance in the year 1995 perchance?"

I laughed. "Yes, it would. Colin Firth was the actor in a miniseries that was televised that year. For a very long time, he was considered the quintessential Mr Darcy, and it was thought no one could ever again replace his image when ladies dwelt on you."

"Truly? And yet..."

"And yet, against my own expectations, Mr Macfadyen has succeeded in just that. It so happens that many of his features and attributes resemble closely the sketch I formed in my imagination when I first read the book. (I was only thirteen at the time.) I am sure this accounts for it in large part. For a huge number of ladies, I know, Mr Firth still reigns as the face of Darcy, so to speak. But this one suits for me quite well. And Mr Macfadyen's portrayal of you was well done, very sympathetic; putting forward to the audience additional sides of you we had heretofore not always seen enacted. I confess the gentleman won me over."

"Hmmm. Then it would seem I am beholden to the man for more than just the borrowing of his countenance!" We both laughed then.

"I must confess, Miss... er, Teg. I do apologize, the habit of formality is too well established, I fear, to allow of intimacies." I smiled, both to accept his declaration and to keep from laughing at the fact that this gentleman's unshod legs were at present laying across my lap! Intimacies, indeed. "In any event, Teg..."

"It's Tess, actually." I couldn't believe it; here I was giving him yet another name. The man was going to conclude I am a true lunatic. But the temptation to hear him say my own name... my *real* name... was just too great to pass up.

"Tess?" he said. I melted.

"Yes... Teg is a formation of my initials, but most people call me Tess, it is short for my full name as you might guess." I wouldn't even attempt to give him my myriad other nicknames, he'd think I suffered a multiple personality disorder.

"Ah, I see," he said, though possibly he didn't.

"Well, *Tess*..." I melted again. "I must avow your devotion to be formidable indeed. Other than that one occasion early on, I have never been transported to greet a single individual – it has always been a *group* of ladies among whose company I was admitted."

"Ack! I forgot them again!"

"You forget whom?"

"Mr Darcy, I assure you that your presence cannot be attributed to me alone, much as I would like to believe my devotion—and powers—that great. In fact, there are seven of us here, Pinkers! The others are still asleep as it is so early in the morning and we partied very late last night."

"Pinkers?"

"It is a nickname, a title rather, we use for our group. We all are members of a website... do you know what a website is?... well, anyway, we are members of a group that is devoted to Jane Austen and especially to her novel *Pride and Prejudice*. Including, of course, to you. And we have gathered here at my home for the weekend – the first time we have all met face to face after corresponding for over two years in some cases!"

I went on to describe for him how he himself held some responsibility for bringing us all together as friends, and more besides who had been unable to attend our weekend party. I told him of the impact the 2005 film had had on us all, our subsequent discovery individually of the film's official website and then becoming personally acquainted; and then, ultimately, our finding a second home as it were at our English friend's site. He plied me with questions, particularly interested in the idea that several of us were writers as well, and chose as our diversion of choice to more fully write of his own life and that of his acquaintances.

"And, do you write something at the moment, Tess?"

"Yes. I do, in fact... a WIP." I deviated a moment to describe for him the concept of a work in progress, posted chapter by chapter as I continued writing, then continued. "It centres on a romance for Colonel Fitzwilliam."*

"My cousin Richard?" he asked, as I sat gratified to know that I had guessed correctly the colonel's given name. "Oh, I am pleased. Fitzwilliam has been single far too long." He became pensive a moment then, and subsequently ventured, "So... er,... is it only my cousin who appears in this WIP of yours?" He had the sense to look a bit sheepish.

"Oh, no!" I assured him. "There are also storylines for Georgiana, and Kitty Bennet, and Lady Catherine, and Anne deBourgh..."

Mr Darcy drew his brows together, looking the slightest bit disappointed. He looked such the deprived little boy that I could tease him no longer.

"And, *of course*," I added, "it all takes place at Pemberley over Christmastide where they are your guests, so naturally you and Mrs Darcy appear prominently as well!"

He brightened at that; then my words seemed to register. "Mrs Darcy?"

"Yes, of course."

"But..." He stopped, sighed a few times in succession, then said: "I have no doubt, Tess, of your having provided a suitable wife from your imagination, but I confess I myself doubt of ever marrying if Miss Elizabeth Bennet cannot change her opinion of me. I do love her so well, that I cannot entertain any thought of accepting another into my heart."

"Mr Darcy, please, let me assure you that..." I hesitated now, realising that I had no idea how this time/space/fiction travel thing worked and whether Mr Darcy could (or *should*) know the outcome of his own story at the hands of Jane Austen. Would it somehow change fictional history if he were to know his own ending in advance? Had he never yet gotten through the entire plot of *Pride and Prejudice*? Or if he relived it over and over as people read it, would his knowledge at any one point in the book lack what he would have understood in a later part of the book from a former iteration? It boggled my mind even to try to unravel it. But I certainly would not wish to be architect of the destruction of that story for future readers.

While I determined what to say, Mr Darcy sighed. "I suppose at some point I will do so, marry that is, it will be required to gain an heir." He looked so sad that I was tempted to end his angst then and there. "But..."

"Mr Darcy, may I ask you at this point in your life, what is your circumstance with relation to Liz, er... Miss Elizabeth Bennet?"

"As to that I cannot say with certainty, I hardly know. You comprehend my particulars?" I nodded, smiled. "I visited Longbourn with Bingley within the last fortnight, in hope that Miss Bennet and I might reconcile our acquaintance. But I came away as confounded as when I had arrived. I do not believe she despises me still, but I cannot be at all assured she is willing to entertain a renewal of my suit. I am, Tess, at a complete loss as to how to proceed. I have lately received a visit from my Aunt – a most troubling visit – and it has precipitated my immediate return to Hertfordshire. Indeed, I was walking in the garden at Netherfield in the early morning after a sleepless night, trying to determine how to proceed, when I felt the onset of my transport to you! That is why you find me clad in such a state of undress. I should never willingly appear in public in this disarray!"

I rather thought his 'disarray' was very becoming, but refrained from saying so. I also registered that this was pretty much exactly where my bookmark now rested near the end of my own copy of the novel. Interesting!

"Bingley has now entered into an engagement with Miss Jane Bennet, and so I cannot believe but I shall be thrown into Miss Elizabeth's company from time to time. I do not know how to endure it if she spurns me again."

"Mr Darcy, I do not believe it my place to tell you how your life carries forward..."

"No, indeed, I have regulated myself most determinedly, and resisted all opportunities to hear particulars. I would not ask it of you, though I must confess my curiosity runs high."

"But I can assure you, Mr Darcy, that I feel justified in my own interpretation within the stories I write, and I believe I can share with you that you do not end unhappily in them. I believe you become quite content."

"That will have to suffice, then, will it not?"

I smiled. "And now, Mr Darcy, may I wake the others? They will, of course, be so anxious to meet you."

"Certainly. I shall be honoured. I should like very much to make the acquaintance of this extraordinary company of friends."

He removed his legs from my lap and sat up straight; and I rose and began to leave the room. I had barely reached the doorway, however, when I heard him exclaim, and turned around to find him looking doubtful, a hand across his chest.

"I believe, Tess, there will not be sufficient time!"

"You are leaving?" I asked. "So soon?"

"I believe so. I should be happy to oblige you were this within my regulation, but I fear that is beyond my power."

I returned to him as he stood. "It has been a singular pleasure, Tess. I regret that I do not have the wherewithal to influence this process or I might forestall my departure."

We stood looking at one another. "May I ask," he said, "What is the current custom for farewells among... friends?"

I smiled and must have blushed, as I felt warm all the way down to my toes at his choice of word. Then, fearing he would vanish suddenly and my chance would be lost, I rose up on my toasty toes, and kissed him on his cheek. (I dared not do more.)

"A very agreeable custom," he offered. "And you are a most obliging lady."

We walked then, to the door and down the front steps, my hand tucked under his arm. I could actually feel a slight tingling sensation from under his shirt sleeve, but couldn't for the life of me determine if that was his 'shimmering' or – well, or mine. Halfway down the walk, I released his arm and with a bow, he turned to walk away; until an exclamation from me stopped him.

"Mr Darcy, wait!" I cried, and went running back into the house.

"The shimmering sensation is quite strong, I fear, I do not believe I can wait long," I heard as I came out again a moment later carrying his boots.

"You may need these!"

He laughed, and took the boots from me, gazing down at his stocking-clad feet. When he looked up again, a suggestion of affection lit his eyes as he wordlessly leaned forward and placed a lingering kiss on my cheek. And then he started walking back across the road. Though some of the mist had lifted, there was still a fair amount to be seen.

"Oh, and Mr Darcy?"

He turned and looked at me. "Please do not give up on Miss Bennet."

"My dear friend, Tess, I cannot do so, whatever her wishes may be." Then he smiled, a dazzling smile that carried to his eyes, to his entire being. I watched, with tears forming, his straight back and broad shoulders and proud carriage as he gained the neighbour's lawn; and just noted that as he reached the river bank still carrying his boots, he stretched and flexed his free hand, and simply... dissolved into the haze.

ξ

I stood there, watching nothing, for several minutes before rousing myself. I walked back into the house, sad yet exhilarated, some part of me wondering if, now he was gone, I would wake up from this dream; and when I did, hoping the feeling of euphoria would remain. And it did! Against all the laws of physics I could understand, Mr Darcy really *had* appeared in my living room that morning.

As I sat on the sofa, grinning at the warmth it still retained from Mr Darcy's occupation, Marilyn shuffled out of the bedroom and sat in the club chair, immediately logging in to the laptop. I went to take my tea mug into the kitchen, and Sammi was coming up the stairs from her basement guest room. Not long after, Bonnie and Robin joined us, and Tammy emerged just a moment later. We sat in the living room with our various teas and coffees and bagels and cereal. The day had begun.

When Sally arrived not long after, we decided to watch *Death at a Funeral*, as a couple of our party had never seen it and the others were happy to oblige in a repeat viewing. When the opening scene came on the screen, I looked at Matthew Macfadyen's face in close-up, and I smiled. No, he wasn't Mr Darcy. And yet, a somewhat altered image of him, and animated uniquely with quite a different personality, would *always* be Mr Darcy to me now. For I had met him.

You may wonder if I have any proof that these events really happened. Sadly, I do not, any more than Mr Darcy himself could take proof of his journeys back with him to his world. (Oh *why* did I return his boots to him???) I had only the echo of his voice in my ears, the residual feel of his kiss on my cheek and of his calves under my kneading fingers.

I contemplated telling the others of my morning excitement, but in the end, what could I say that they would believe? And if they did believe, would they *ever* forgive me for leaving them asleep and oblivious to it all?

So no, I have no proof. But to my dying day... that's my story and I'm sticking to it!

* *A Fitzwilliam Legacy*, a novel available soon.

PREVIEW

Principles of Pride
A Novel of the Darcy Family of Pemberley
(working title)

By Tess Quinn

♌♌♌

Principles of Pride *is partly a retelling of the principal storyline in* Pride and Prejudice, *that of the interactions and obstacles between Elizabeth Bennet and Fitzwilliam Darcy while they journey towards personal and mutual understanding. But my novel encompasses more as well. Told by Georgiana Darcy after a passage of years – in her own words, using details of her family history and extensive use of letters and journals – the perspectives in this narrative so well known to many of us are those of the Darcys. And interwoven with these familiar events, we are privy also to another theme: the unfolding of a loving relationship between brother and sister as it matures from dependence into friendship, even as Georgiana grows into a woman.*

You may well recognize words or phrases – indeed entire scenes and paragraphs now and again – as having been borrowed directly from Pride and Prejudice, *sometimes in their original context, sometimes altered in use. This novel is a blend of Miss Austen's content and about three-fourths original composition. You will find several new characters integrated with familiar ones, the development of some that played only small supporting roles in canon, as well as entirely new dialogue and scenes.*

The chapter excerpted here takes place in the spring, as Darcy prepares for his annual Eastertide visit to his aunt, Lady Catherine deBourgh, at Rosings Park in Kent.

♌♌♌

Volume IV: Spring – Chapter 1

Excerpt. Letter from Lady Catherine deBourgh

Friday, 17 March
Rosings, Kent

Nephew.

Whatever do you mean by purposing not to attend us for Easter? What matter is it that Fitzwilliam is still at large? I shall tell you: it is none at all. You have long passed Easter at Rosings. Do not you possess the means of independent travel and an equally independent mind? If your cousin returns while you are here, he will make his own way to us. But you have a duty to another cousin. My daughter has not seen you these eight months or more – and moreover, Anne depends on the plan with the greatest pleasure and certainty. You may do as you like to me; but you cannot upset her hopes again. It will not be borne—do not disappoint. Georgiana is safely away to Derbyshire. You can have nothing to keep you in town. I shall expect you as always.

Company is thin, I confess, with Lady Simsbury attending her daughter's lying in, and the Russells gone off to Scotland – imagine, at this time of year; Augusta has always wanted sense – but this is no impediment to you. We shall make do with what I have at my disposal. Indeed, I depend upon you to add to our society. I have for too long been obliged to summoning the Hunsford rector and his wife of an evening. Mrs Collins is well enough, I suppose, a respectable woman—a sufficient match for a vicar— rather plain and dull. But she has enough sense to seek my counsel in all manner of things. These recent days their calls have been somewhat varied from having by them some relations– Mrs Collins's father and sister from Hertfordshire; and a cousin to Mr Collins. Sir William's chief quality being that he understands his daughter's excellent fortune in being placed at Hunsford—and he reveals his hands in his expression at the card table, to _my_ excellent fortune. He will have gone before you arrive, but the ladies remain behind. The sister is silly and ignorant; but some interest is provided in the person of Miss Bennet, however. A genteel, pretty kind of girl—not yet one and twenty—she gives her opinion very decidedly for so young a person—possesses a tendency for impertinence which should have been corrected long ago—one cannot wonder at it, I suppose, with so little education as *she was afforded. Such neglect is inexcusable in her mother. Miss Bennet wants instruction in preserving the distinction of rank—but she can, at least, entertain when she is reasonable.*

Where has Fitzwilliam gone off to for so long, at any rate, to everyone's inconvenience—

ξ

With no greater events than are customary during a winter in town, and otherwise broken only by a brief journey to Pemberley to see to its business, did January and February pass away. February brought snow and early March rains the like of which had not been seen in some time; and resulting both in enforced refuge at home for those still in Town and in caterwauling over their interrupted diversions. Darcy complained of neither, though the inclemency of the season made for messes of slush and mud without.

Georgiana and Mrs Annesley had travelled with Darcy to Derbyshire in January and remained there upon his return, such that he had not even the distraction of his sister's company to speed the passage of short days and long evenings in Berkeley Square. Bingley had only just succumbed to travel with his sisters to Norfolk to escape the mess in town; Richard still away on the Duke's business; and Winstead was absorbed in plans for his marriage which had at last been formally negotiated. Altogether had Darcy not the comforts of his club of an evening, the occasional exercise afforded at Angelo's, and letters of business to see to, he would have had no cause to divert his thoughts from Hertfordshire and a young woman who resided there.

As it was, she continued to call upon his imagination too often. He should have foreseen that his foray into society in search of a suitable candidate for a wife would prove utter folly. He might have had his pick from amongst any number of ladies before he could drop to one knee but none were tolerable enough to tempt him; none would do for him, nor as a fit example to Georgiana.

All manner of girl had been paraded before him: silly things with no thought unrelated to fashion and gossip (those forming the majority); others ready to anticipate or accede to his every opinion without question in far too simpering a manner; dour, withdrawn specimens frightened as a mouse when spoken to or looked at; or worse, those robust, loud types flitting about every where – most on the shelf from long having been passed over by other men. No more than half a dozen ladies of his acquaintance merited credit for some understanding of note; and these, all too often, had long grown dull from marriage to indiscriminate gentlemen possessed of no appreciation for what fortune had bestowed upon them. Darcy could have had dalliances with more than one of those as well, had he chosen to do so. But though commonplace enough, such things held no merit with him.

He had discarded the entire experiment when he rode for Derbyshire, and vowed not to renew the torment even when the little season would take up with new entries in the hunt. He did not avoid all society – by his custom accepting invitations when it suited and repaying in kind as warranted; an occasional sponsored evening at the theatre or a concert, where conversation was not principally the order of the day. But even in these, he took care to give no encouragement where he was unwilling to suffer in consequence.

Yet despite its being now some months since he had encountered Miss Elizabeth Bennet, her redoubtable obstinacy endured: steadfastly she refused to vacate his mind. Indeed, her calls upon his thoughts became all the more frequent for his having found no one of interest to supplant them.

If he walked through Hyde Park of a morning, he would swear he heard a perceptive lilting laugh from behind him but, turning, would find nothing but a breeze stirring new-budding branches. At the club he would start upon hearing the porter announce the arrival of Mr Jenney; recalling with some chagrin that Miss Bennet— that being *Jane* Bennet, the eldest of that family's daughters—indeed might yet reside with her relations in Cheapside. On those not infrequent occasions when his friend Bingley must form comparisons between their company of an evening and his lost Miss Bennet, Darcy saw her sister's shade and commiserated in stoical silence. He had never spoken to Bingley regarding Miss Bennet's being in town; still he could wonder if her sister next in age might join her there, if they all might meet one day on the street in some mutual surprise.

Riding to Angelo's or at the theatre of an evening, were he to catch a glimpse of a light and pleasing figure as it moved round a corner, his inclination was to follow and cross paths once more with a peculiar intelligent countenance, dominated by fine chestnut-hued eyes and framed with soft curls of hair nearly the same shade. One day in particular – a rare sunny day in mid-March as it happened, when he had chosen to walk home from his tailor's – he could have sworn he had seen Miss Elizabeth through a shop window as he passed. By the time his wits turned back his step to look again, the lady had gone. But for days afterwards, the fleeting image occupied him: a pretty, laughing girl, her arm linked with that of a woman some years her senior as they completed a commission.

So pronounced became all these distractions that on occasion Darcy very nearly decided to mount his horse and ride into Hertfordshire, intent on finding a cure for his preoccupation by confronting the author of his disordered mind. He felt utterly bewitched by this woman who, even absent the scene, made her presence felt in his head without his leave and despite his best efforts to expel her.

Darcy rebuked himself regularly for making too much of his memories of the lady. *You are a fool*, he admonished the weak indulgences of his wits. *Miss Bennet has no supernatural claim upon you. She is but a woman.* But a woman unlike any other of his acquaintance; one who could excite his senses as easily as his intellect, even from afar.

He was an eminently rational man and shook his head to clear it. *Were I to return to Hertfordshire I would see that the fancy I have built in my imagination is only that – a puckish sprite which would prove to bear little resemblance to the flesh and bone that lent it her name.* He did not, however, act upon the notion of revisiting the scene of his bewitchment – perhaps as much for the disturbing pleasures provided him by her continued intrusions upon his soul as from any fear that he would not, indeed, change his opinion of the lady.

ξ

Eastertide was to take Darcy to Rosings to his aunt's. He had made this seasonal visit with regularity since before his father's passing, to honour his mother's affections for her elder sister. He had not thought seriously, however, of going thither this Easter until it was nearly upon him. Indeed he had used Richard's extended absence as just cause for delaying – but for a letter received of his Aunt in rebuttal to his own. It seemed fate was to take a hand in his cure! Miss Elizabeth Bennet herself had travelled to Hunsford to stay with her friend, the former Miss Lucas! Miss Bennet had been in

Kent several weeks already; was at that moment there, perhaps even sitting in his aunt's drawing room!

Of course, he had no proof to suppose the woman his aunt depicted was, in fact, his own *Elizabeth* Bennet. Any one of the sisters might have been invited to travel with Sir William Lucas and his young daughter; as likely perhaps one closer in age to the Lucas girl. But Darcy again took up the letter and read the description afforded by his aunt: *"...not yet one and twenty...gives her opinion very decidedly for so young a person...tendency for impertinence... a genteel, pretty kind of girl... wants instruction in preserving the distinction of rank ...entertain when she is reasonable."* Surely such particulars taken together could be attributed to none of the Bennet daughters so well as Miss Elizabeth; and acknowledging the intimate friendship existing between Mrs Collins and Miss Elizabeth from their youth, it could be only she. Darcy was convinced of it.

This, then, was his opportunity to dispel once and forever the lady's claims upon his rational mind. In the rarefied setting of Rosings, the inferiority of Miss Elizabeth's qualifications would show itself; an ill fit for society despite her natural country charms. Her family and station, education and limited experience of the world—all the deficiencies which had, over time, softened in consequence in his memory—would now reclaim their place to counter her attractions. Indeed, he came quickly to feel that this obligatory call upon his aunt would serve him quite well.

He had taken up pen and paper and confirmed his change of mind, writing nothing of his reason for doing so. If Lady Catherine wished to believe it down to her own talents of persuasion, it was nothing to him.

ξ

"Good heavens, Darcy—you are quite complacent. One might suppose you to look with *favour* on the prospect of calling in Kent for some days."

Darcy scowled.

"Ah, now I am comforted; for there is the face to match the occasion. I thought for an instant you had arrived at a happy anticipation of Rosings and its residents; perhaps even think to reside there yourself before long?"

"You are absurd, Fitzwilliam—" but Darcy laughed nonetheless "—and well you know it! Could I ever have resolved to marry Anne deBourgh, I would have done the objectionable deed before now."

"And yet if her recent letter to me is not misread, you have not dissuaded our Aunt of the notion..."

"It is not for lack of endeavour, as you also well know! She hears not my repeated objections. But I will not be browbeaten into marriage, I am neither so malleable nor inconstant; if she clings stubbornly to her resolve, so do I to my own."

Colonel Fitzwilliam snorted. "I should not make a wager against *that* battle of wills," he said, a gleam in his eye.

Darcy paid no heed to his sport. "Anne no more wishes the match than I..."

"Yes, but should you succumb to Aunt 'Dragon's' will, Anne has not enough of it to withstand her mother—"

"I have no intention to 'succumb'." Darcy's acerbic tone now suggested the matter was concluded. But Fitzwilliam was not silenced. He had been thrown into his cousin's company since he and Darcy were children—knew him intimately and was immune to every tactic the man naturally employed to intimidate.

"Why do not you agree to it, Darcy? You will expand your estates by half again, and I imagine Anne to be no demanding sort of wife, sickly as she is. Take her companion along with her and you can go on much as you do now. Lady Catherine cannot live forever. And I dare say there is no one else who *has* met your approval." He added under his breath, "How I should like to meet the woman who can!"

Darcy disregarded that last muttering as well. "If it is such an attractive proposition, *you* may offer to our cousin. You have my leave and my good wishes for felicity."

"Not while *Fitzwilliam Darcy* takes breath," said Richard with a chuckle. "Do not you know you were destined for one another from your infancy? By your own mother *and* hers?"

Darcy winced at the oft-conjured argument. "You know as well as I the notion never entered my mother's thoughts but with her sister's insistence; and even then she gave no promise, nor encouragement. My aunt simply believed as she wished to do...then *as* now." Darcy diverted his attention out the carriage window. "Now if you have done with your sport..."

Fitzwilliam acquiesced and they rode in companionable silence nearly until they made the stop along their journey, when Darcy asked his cousin about the business he had recently concluded. The Colonel, though he had assured Georgiana he would not, had travelled to Spain at the Duke's bidding. He had addressed his mission in little over a month; however, the inclement winter and a scarcity of ships prepared to make the crossing kept the gentleman three times as long.

He arrived back finally to find Georgiana gone to Derbyshire and Darcy preparing to attend their aunt for his usual Easter visit, despite his having formerly determined against going. Fitzwilliam himself declined to accompany Darcy, being so lately arrived in Town. But then he realised that to stay behind would oblige him to a later visit without his cousin—his lifelong friend, his brother sufferer—to offset their aunt's attentions. They may as well endure her together and have it done another year. He had some leisure owing, and *she* had an excellent cook. So he had written her hastily to expect him, and charged his man to pack for Kent.

Over their breakfast stop, Darcy caught his cousin up on doings about Town while Fitzwilliam posited on the concerns of war. Then, once again on their way through Kent, Fitzwilliam reverted to his favourite diversion: teazing his taciturn cousin.

"Lady on your mind?"

Darcy's head swung to the Colonel. "Whatever do you mean?"

"Only that the scene without is well known to you and hardly picturesque. So I presume the distracted gaze and smile you wear must find their inducement in a different sort of beauty. Tell me, who is she?"

"Richard, you are an old woman at times with your tittering, do you know?" Darcy tucked the image of Miss Bennet safely into a corner of his imagination and presented his usual countenance. "Perhaps it is *you* should take a wife, to provide you with adequate sources of gossip and nattering. I have no predilection for it at present."

"It is hardly gossip and nattering!" the Colonel protested. "We must speak of something." He received no reply. "Tell me then, what news of your friend Bingley?"

"He has gone into Norfolk with his brother."

"Then he does not plan to return to Hertfordshire? What of the house he took there?"

"Hmmm." Darcy regarded his cousin a moment. "He has not spoken of it, but I should not imagine he will keep it. It did not suit in the end."

"Pity. You have never spoken much of the time you all passed there. Was it intolerable? I always thought the country quite handsome. The shooting I know to be adequate. My adjutant hails from thereabouts and can hardly restrain himself praising the fowl to be had."

Darcy agreed there was nothing objectionable about the country in general; in fact some excellent riding was to be found, the sport sufficient. And then said no more, though his countenance was unsettled.

After a moment, Fitzwilliam started again. "I noted the banns Sunday last for your friend Winstead. So he intends in the end to acquire his adjoining properties, does he?"

"Mmm."

"I recollect the match is a good one; and his acquaintance with the girl – Miss Graham is it? – is of long standing. I do hope he likes her at the least."

"What?" Darcy emerged from his reverie. "Oh! Yes. To his credit, he does. In point of fact, he loves the girl. He feels quite assured of his satisfaction with her."

"Well done, Winstead!—rich *and* contented!"

"Indeed. Such happy fortune is rare enough, I suppose."

"My finical cousin!" laughed the Colonel, "though I cannot but agree in the main. My mother lectures me always it is as easy to love a rich woman as one without means; but I have yet to find it so—or at the least one with a fortune who will have *me*."

Darcy grunted what might have passed for acquiescence, or indifference.

"What do you think, Fitz?" pressed his cousin. "If I were to run mad with love of an unsuitable woman, would you advise me to throw prudence into the wind and follow my heart?"

"Certainly not."

"Why?"

"*Why?* Because it is universally accepted that 'mad' love rarely outlives the first night of a marriage bed, following which one is left without happiness *or* means."

"You are right, of course. No," he said, drawing as he did so a small roll of linen from within his coat – Darcy recognized at once the neat embroidery stitches of his sister adorning its face – "this is the only housewife I require for the present." He sighed and, when that went ignored, sighed again pointedly. "The privilege of choosing for love alone lies with those only—like yourself—who have the means to overlook more practical deficiencies."

"I suggested nothing of the sort. I should advise anyone of my acquaintance, regardless of station, the same as regards the matrimonial state. One must weigh all the conditions of an alliance in determining a likelihood of lasting satisfaction."

Fitzwilliam did not contain himself. "You make me laugh, Darcy; but is it possible always to be so rational? Is it sound? Can you be so certain you would never act in this way yourself if you met a woman who suited for affection?" He received no reply, sighed, and said, "Well, you have not to persuade *me* of it."

They passed some moments while Darcy exampled a friend he had, in fact, advised in this manner not long past. This friend had managed to find himself in an awkward circumstance concerning a young lady from a manor near to his own; and Darcy had taken it in his part, in concert with the gentleman's family, to extricate him from what only could have proved a most unfortunate alliance.

"A bit harsh, I should think, Darcy; if he truly loved this girl. Do not you consider, if this gentleman's present competence proves sufficient, that he could allow of greater significance for his own preference?"

"Perhaps—were not the lady's preference for his competence; and were not he to face censure from the very society whose graces his father gained him over great time and trouble. When one's generation stands just within an acceptable circle, one cannot be too prudent in maintaining place."

"I suppose," sighed Fitzwilliam; "though it pains me somewhat to acknowledge we are all so unrepentantly callous." He smiled. "The man remains fortunate in his friends at least, Darcy, if Aphrodite withholds her favours from him."

As Darcy spoke of Bingley's near escape from Miss Bennet (for such were the parties he exampled, though of course he did not name either out of delicacy and propriety) he could not but return to his own experience of her sister. *It is good*, he thought, *to talk of this*—it only confirmed his anticipation of relinquishing any wild notions of Miss Elizabeth once for all. By recitation of those reasonable objections he had made to Bingley's courting the eldest daughter, Darcy saw them again in the light of day, as it were. The result of this discourse was his being persuaded of the success he should achieve in *his* present purpose.

As they left the high road for the lane to Hunsford, Richard ventured one final turn on the subject. "Tell me, Fitz," he asked, "in truth, have you ever yet met a woman who gave you pause?"

Darcy regarded him warily, but his cousin's expression evinced only benign interest. It was on his tongue to reply firmly in the negative—and so he was as surprised as Fitzwilliam to hear, "Yes—once." But despite having ignited Richard's curiosity, he would say no more than that he had recovered his senses before allowing irrevocable feelings to grow.

Conversation waned awkwardly until they reached the lodges where the turning would take them to their aunt's house. The colonel then gave his attention to a rather gangly gentleman at some short distance. The man was pacing back and forth with an expectant air, muttering to himself. Darcy glanced out the window as his cousin wondered aloud who the man was.

"The vicar of Hunsford," Darcy answered with a sigh, "acquired some months past..."

The pacing gentleman had now recognized the approaching carriage, stopped to face its occupants, and offered a deep bow, his hat in his hand sweeping dust up from the road as he did so.

"...a man, I forget his name," continued Darcy as they made their turn into the Park, "who has not one agreeable quality, who has neither manner nor sense to recommend him..."

"You have met the man, then?"

"I have had that misfortune, yes; in Hertfordshire, as it happened. He has relations there, some cousins, whose manor is entailed to him."

"What then did our aunt see in him to offer the benefice?" Fitzwilliam chuckled as the vicar now turned and hurried back up the lane towards the parsonage.

"Need you ask?" Darcy's brow went up minutely. "A clear and profound reverence for Lady Catherine deBourgh!" They shared a last laugh as the house came into view.

ξ

"At last you are here! I expected you an hour gone—" Lady Catherine said as she stretched her neck to present first one cheek and then the other to her nephews in their turn. Despite being a tall woman—a handsome one in her day—both her nephews bested her by several inches; their hasty kisses of greeting accomplished, the two gentlemen glanced to one another over her head. Colonel Fitzwilliam's eyes rolled heavenward and he grinned. But Lady Catherine took no note. Her large frame had turned already and was leading the way into the private parlour, as she called back to them: "Come and see Anne. She has been waiting for you."

Her daughter was seated near the hearth, some work lying idle in her lap and she looking no more expecting of any one than a teapot could do. The companion was in service adjusting the fire-screen—despite clement spring air, Anne deBourgh often felt a chill. She was thin and small; pale and sickly with insignificant features and little animation. In every season fires blazed from the hearths of Rosings to provide for her comfort. The effect often was stifling for visitors. Darcy and Fitzwilliam had grown to expect this, however; they greeted their cousin with courtesy, stopping some moments and then moving away to the cooler, outer part of the room when civility allowed.

Thus began, in the same manner it had done for several years past, the gentlemen's annual visit to Rosings Park and its inmates. None of them could have surmised, with so customary a beginning, the astonishing end to be set in motion some weeks later.

ξ

*Completed novel to be published in late 2013 or early 2014.

Acknowledgments

Heartfelt thanks to all my friends who continue to share and encourage my love of writing Austen-based fiction – both those who critique for me, and those who read strictly for enjoyment. Although I love to write – and especially in this genre – the joy in it would be diminished, and the torture inherent in the writing process much greater, without an audience of enthusiastic, generous, forgiving (on those occasions required) readers. You know who you are – and I hope you know how much I value your opinions and your friendship.

27643785R00167

Made in the USA
Lexington, KY
17 November 2013